ALSO BY CAROLYN HAINES

Rock-a-Bye Bones

CAROLYN HAINES

St. Martin's Paperbacks

For Michelle and Bryan Ladner,

and the new and wonderful addition to your family

This is a work of fiction. All of the characters, organizations, and events portrayed in this novel are either products of the author's imagination or are used fictitiously.

ROCK-A-BYE BONES

Copyright © 2016 by Carolyn Haines.
Excerpt from *Sticks and Bones* copyright © 2017 by Carolyn Haines.

For information address St. Martin's Press, 175 Fifth Avenue, New York, N.Y. 10010.

ISBN: 978-1-250-08517-7

Our books may be purchased in bulk for promotional, educational, or business use. Please contact your local bookseller or the Macmillan Corporate and Premium Sales Department at 1-800-221-7945, ext. 5442, or by e-mail at MacmillanSpecialMarkets@macmillan.com.

Printed in the United States of America

Minotaur hardcover edition / May 2016
St. Martin's Paperbacks edition / April 2017

St. Martin's Paperbacks are published by St. Martin's Press, 175 Fifth Avenue, New York, NY 10010.

10 9 8 7 6 5 4 3 2 1

Acknowledgments

A book is a wild blend of facts, imagination, snippets of the past, conversations, dreams, and nearly forgotten moments in time. Many thanks to my friends who have been a part of this strange process. And to the professionals who play such an important role. Kelley Ragland, Elizabeth Lacks, Marian Young. Thank you.

1

Thanksgiving is no time to leave a desperate woman alone in a haunted house with a knife and a giant squash. Pumpkin spatter covers every horizontal and vertical surface in the spacious kitchen. I heft the five-inch blade and advance on the nine-pound vegetable that defies me. I intend to magically turn the gourd into homemade pumpkin pie, but so far, things are not working out the way I envisioned.

"I'm a lot better with jack-o-lanterns than pies," I say to my red tick hound, Sweetie Pie Delaney, who wisely sleeps *under* the kitchen table, an area still free of pumpkin guts. She lifts her bloodshot eyes to send a sympathetic stare, and then dozes off. She knows that if I make a mess of the pies, she'll have a treat. Sweetie is not a finicky hound, but it happens that pumpkin pie is one of her favorites. And she doesn't care if it's baked into a flakey homemade crust or tumbled out of a bowl.

A shutter bangs against the side of the house, reminding me to call a repairman to make a few necessary improvements before Old Man Winter comes to Zinnia, Mississippi, for an extended visit. Outside Dahlia House, my family plantation in the heart of Sunflower County, the wind is sweeping across the barren cotton fields. The harvest is in, and winter is coming. But in the warm, cinnamon-smelling kitchen, I am looking forward to a festive Thanksgiving dinner with my best friends in the world. I am playing host—a new role for me.

I turn to the recipe and study it harder. Always the overachiever, I have *two* large pumpkins. Part of one is baking in the oven, but I have another big one on my cutting board. I have been assured by Millie Roberts, owner of Zinnia's most popular café, that pumpkin puree from scratch is far superior to canned. I'm beginning to have second thoughts. What sounded so easy coming from Millie's mouth has turned into an orange orgy in my kitchen.

Putting the knife down, I decide on a break. Cinnamon and maple-flavored coffee in hand, I step out on the front porch. Sweetie and my black cat, Pluto, are at my side. White wicker rockers offer a comfortable seat, but I settle on the steps. Here I can look straight down the driveway. The sycamore trees that line the shell drive are leafless. The white skinlike bark, peeling in places, always makes me sad. November, like the gloaming, can be a melancholy time. Endings. I'm not good with endings.

Soon, though, the barren fields that stretch to the horizon will sprout new growth. Spring will return. Another cycle. This year, I have determined to make the holidays joyful.

I've invited all of my Zinnia friends to have Thanksgiving dinner at Dahlia House. Normally I enjoy the holidays at Tinkie's or Harold's—the two designated party givers in the Delta. This year, I want my home to be the party location. November marks the anniversary of my return to Sunflower County. When I'd come home two years ago, tail between my legs, I was destitute. Dahlia House was on the tax assessor's list to be auctioned off for back taxes. Since my return, I'd opened a successful private eye business, Delaney Detective Agency, hooked up with the best partner on the planet, Tinkie Bellcase Richmond, and acquired three horses, a dog, a feline ruler of the universe, and one very badass haint named Jitty. All in all, a very busy time.

The first months I'd been home, Dahlia House had felt cold and empty. My parents had died in a car accident when I was only twelve. My aunt Loulane, my father's sister, had raised me until I went to college. Not so long ago, she passed away, too. While I was adjusting to the failure of my acting career in New York, my first breakup with Graf Milieu, and the return home in bitter Broadway theatrical defeat, I'd also found Jitty, my resident ghost.

Jitty is part comforting parent, a big dollop of Hell Hound, and an equal measure of butt-kicker and provoker. She links me to the long history of Dahlia House, the Delaney family, and a system of morals and values instilled in me at an early age. From my father, I learned about justice and fair play. From my mother, I was gifted with a firm resolve to never be a victim, never accept defeat, and never, ever betray a friend.

When my parents were alive, Dahlia House was a holiday destination. My mother loved parties and she loved to dance. She had luncheons, coffees, drink gatherings, formal dinners, game get-togethers—whatever sounded fun.

My favorite memories, though, centered around Thanksgiving and the preparation of the traditional foods that define the holiday. My mother was an exceptional cook, though never a slave to the kitchen. Roasted turkey, dressing, fresh green beans, Brussels sprouts and chestnuts, ambrosia, and pumpkin pies were always on the menu. Even as a little girl, I was allowed to help with the food preparation. I can still remember my mother watching closely as I chopped celery for the dressing.

"Chop it fine, Sarah Booth. No big chunks." And she would lean over me, her hair tickling my face and filled with the scent of Opium, so light and yet enticing. No matter how I try, I'll never be able to duplicate those holidays when I was wrapped so tightly in the protection and love of my parents. This Thanksgiving I want to bring Dahlia House to life the way my mother did.

Only one small problem. My mother was a born chef and party giver. I, on the other hand, am a much better guest at someone else's table. Thinking of tables and guests, I slipped back inside the house. I had to get back in the kitchen and accomplish something other than mayhem. When I returned to the scene of my defeat, I inhaled deeply. At least my kitchen smelled like Thanksgiving.

"Good lard almighty!" A whiff of gardenias came with the outraged voice. Jitty has arrived. I close my eyes and bite my lip. Though I wouldn't trade her for anything, she is a bane. If she says one word about dying ovaries, I am going to chase her around the kitchen with my knife. Of course she's dead already so it's an empty threat, but it would still give me great satisfaction.

"What have you done to the kitchen?" Jitty asked. She sashayed into the room in the most outrageous outfit I've yet to see her wear—a black and white nun's habit.

"I'm making dessert, and while the kitchen may be a mess, it isn't nearly as bad as that getup you're wearing. You are officially cut off from any more Whoopi Goldberg movies." My threats were empty and we both knew it. "Get out of the house right this minute. If you draw a lightning strike down on you by pretending to be a nun, I don't want any part of it." I edged away from her. "What order do you belong to, the Holy Tormenters, or maybe Our Lady of the Aggravators? No religious leader in her right mind would let you into a convent."

"I'm not just any nun, I'm Mother Superior, and you'd best be listenin' to my advice, Missy." She pointed at the chunks of pumpkin and the blob of guts and seeds. "That's supposed to turn out to be a pie?"

"Pumpkin pies." I am a bit hesitant to admit that a pie was my goal. What I have is a pan full of rubbery and disgusting baked pumpkin chunks. The slimy guts are spilling off the table and half out the garbage can. Add to that the flour dusting the floor and the eggs I meant to whip but accidentally dropped, and I have to admit, I've made a remarkable mess.

"You did all of this to make a pumpkin pie?" She honestly can't take it all in. "Let me know if you ever decide to make cream puffs and I'll take out extra insurance on Dahlia House."

"That's so funny I forgot to laugh." I should be used to Jitty's acerbic commentary, but she can still get me riled, which is great fun for her.

"Have you ever heard of canned pumpkin?" Jitty is appalled. "Seriously, Sarah Booth, this looks like the jolly orange pumpkin exploded in here. How about 911, call Millie's Café and beg her to come to the rescue."

"What's with the nun getup?" I've learned to keep the focus on Jitty and off me.

"I'm doing my part to get that difficult Delaney womb filled up with an heir to Dahlia House."

"And you intend to accomplish that by dressing as a nun?" Not even I could follow that logic.

"I'm the ultimate mother," she said. "Now listen up. I'm about to lay some wisdom on you."

I had to think fast to avoid another lecture on how my biological clock was ticking and how my ovaries were turning black and shriveling with each passing second, not to mention the Delaney penchant for tilted wombs and bad judgment in the romance department. To Jitty, an heir was the only thing that mattered. Since I'd recently broken off my engagement, she was doubling down on dire fallopian predictions. "It would be a lot more helpful if you would roll out the pie crust. So far, I haven't had a lot of luck with that."

She took a look in the bowl where I'd mixed flour, butter, a little salt, and some cold water—just as the recipe called for. Instead of workable dough that could be rolled thin and placed in the bottom of a pie pan, I'd achieved a glutinous mass of . . . paste. And it kept making noises, as if it were alive, possibly suffering from a bad case of gas.

"Baby girl, that lump of glue is beyond my help. Divine intervention can't save that mess. Fact is, I'd burn it before it turns into a golem. I think it may have a heartbeat." She backed away from it.

"Oh, for heaven's sake!" I picked up the bowl of lumpy, wet dough and realized, for once, Jitty was not exaggerating. A little bubble of air escaped the goop, followed by a burp. That was enough for me. I used the big wooden spoon and scraped it into the trash. If it came to life, it could do so at the end of the driveway, not in the kitchen.

"Maybe I should call a priest to give it the last rites." Jitty was so pleased with her wit she could hardly contain her glee.

"Do that. It'll be worth watching, since you can't use a phone." My illusions of being the master chef were taking a serious drubbing. Thank god for Millie. She could bake a pie with a snap of her fingers. I could call her if I got desperate.

"Is this a bad time to discuss what I've come to talk about?" Jitty asked.

"Depends on what you want to discuss." The fact that she *asked* didn't bode well. "If it's about sperm or ovaries, this is definitely not a good time."

"Which man you gone put at the head of that holiday table, Sarah Booth? Being the hostess, seems to me like you've got yourself in a pickle. You'll be at the foot of the table by the kitchen door, but who's gonna sit at the head, which implies a whole lot. The man you put there is the one leading the pack for your affections."

She had a point, and I had a solution. "Harold will sit at the head of the table." I hadn't given it a lot of thought, but this was the perfect seating arrangement. Harold Erkwell had once asked for my hand—and put a four-carat diamond on my ring finger. At the time, I didn't know him well, and his tactics seemed a bit ham-fisted. Since I'd been home, though, Harold and I had developed an abiding friendship. And he was, hands down, the best party giver in six states. "Harold is always the host. Coleman and Scott can each sit on a side." I was very pleased with my resolution.

"You can't keep all those men dangling like meat in a processing plant. They keep hangin', there's gonna be an awful stink."

"Jitty! That is a truly awful visual. I may have to scour my brain with Comet to clean it out."

Her soft, low chuckle told me how pleased she was. When I looked at her again, she'd removed the wimple and was shaking out her dark Afro. "That headgear gets hot."

"Not as hot as the pit of hell, which is where you're destined for impersonating a nun."

She only laughed. "Thanksgiving is hot on our heels. You should throw out all that mess you made and order everything from Millie's."

She had a point, but I wasn't defeated yet. "I'll give it one more try. Most girls learn to cook from their mothers, but I never really had that chance."

Jitty instantly softened. "Aunt Loulane tried, Sarah Booth, but you didn't want to learn from her. You missed your mother, and Loulane was wise enough to know she could never fill those shoes."

"Yes, she was very wise, and to this day I remember most of her adages. As she used to say, 'Time heals all wounds and brings wisdom to those who seek.'" Aunt Loulane had a saying for every occasion. While I'd hated hearing them when I was a teenager, now I used them with relish.

"Why don't you give me a hand with the cooking?" I asked Jitty. "Surely during the time when you were alive with great-great-great-grandma Alice you were a good cook."

"I'm drawin' a blank—"

"Jitty, give me some tips on pie crust."

"Can't do it, Sarah Booth. It's time for vespers." And with that she was gone. And I'd learned something new about the ghost who shared my home. She didn't like to cook. She was, for all of her one hundred and fifty years, a thoroughly modern ghost.

My failure with the pie undeniable, I sacked up the sad remains and took them out to the road for trash collection early the next morning. I stamped down the driveway, my breath fogging in the crisp air. Above me, the stars kept the black night company. The acres of land belonging to Dahlia House spread on either side of the long drive, and I stopped when a startled herd of deer broke in front of me and leaped the pasture fence. In a moment they were absorbed by the darkness.

When I'd left the trash, I jogged back toward the house and my warm bed. Before I made a second assault on pie production, I needed a trip to the Pig, as we called the local Piggly Wiggly grocery, to buy more flour and butter and two cans of pumpkin already processed to perfect pie consistency. And perhaps I would call Millie in the morning and see if she could give me some tips.

I washed the dishes, prepared the coffeemaker to turn itself on at six a.m., and went to bed. I had plenty of time to master the art of pie baking. Even if I didn't, my friends would step up. I had many blessings to count, and as I walked through the dining room, I started on my list.

I caught a glimpse of a terrifying specter in the mirror above the sideboard and let out a squawk of fright before I realized it was only me. The new growth of my hair, which gave me the appearance of Woodstock, the bird in the Snoopy cartoons, was standing straight on end and coated in flour. Even though Tinkie had taken me to "her girl" at the most expensive salon in the Delta, my hair was still a terrible mess. I'd caught it on fire in the last case we'd worked, and I was very lucky that it was only hair that burned. It could have been so much worse.

Still chuckling at my fright, I went to my room and promptly keeled over in bed. I'd entered a dreamless state of deep slumber when I heard the doorbell ring. I looked at my phone on the bedside table—three o'clock in the morning. It had to be a dream. Though I heard the chime again, and even Sweetie set up a bark, my attempts at baking had exhausted me. I rolled over, pulled the pillow over my head, and refused to get up.

The creak of a squeaky wheel finally drove me to wakefulness. When I found out who was interrupting my sleep, I was going to have a hissy fit all over them.

Creak, creak, creak! I opened one eye to catch a glimpse of a woman in a black minidress pushing one of the huge old baby prams with the folding leather top.

The only thing I could think was *Rosemary's Baby* and I leaped from the bed to land on the far side of the room. "Get out!" I hissed. I'd watched the movie with my mother and a group of my friends when I was in sixth grade, and the image of that black perambulator sent a primal chill through me. "Get out!"

"It's just a baby." The woman pushed the carriage slowly toward me. "Just an innocent baby."

A shaft of moonlight came through the window and I saw Mia Farrow's shorn head—that looked too much like my own. "You have to get out of here." I gauged the distance to the doorway and wondered if I could leap over the bed and make it to the door before she got me—I had no doubt her intention was to do terrible things to me.

"Remember, Sarah Booth, it's only a baby."

At last the Mia image faded to reveal Jitty. I didn't always like her antics, but she'd never before awakened me in the dead of night while impersonating an actress who played the role of a woman who gave birth to the Antichrist.

"You have taken this one step too far," I said through gritted teeth. "Not only did you wake me out of a dead sleep, you scared me into next year. I've missed Thanksgiving and Christmas and all I have to show for it is my stubbed and bleeding toe." I had smashed my toe on the bed frame, which didn't help my mood.

"Answer the damn doorbell, Sarah Booth. I wouldn't have to resort to extraordinary measures if you didn't sleep like you'd fallen into a forever coma."

"What doorbell?"

"The one that rang about two minutes ago. And rang again. And—"

Before she could finish, the bell rang nine times in rapid succession. "What the hell?" I found a pair of jeans, pulled them on, then trotted barefoot down the stairs to the front door. Before I opened it, I turned on the light and stared into the empty night. There was no one on the porch.

"Screw that," I said, flipping off the light.

"At least open the door," Jitty said. She was suddenly right behind me.

"There's no one—"

"Sarah Booth, please open the door. Right this red-hot minute."

Jitty seldom said please so I opened the door fast. I was in the process of slamming it closed again when what I'd seen registered on me. A white wicker bassinet had been pushed close against the front door. A pale pink blanket covered the basket, hiding whatever was hidden inside. More ominous was the pool of blood that seeped from the basket and slowly crossed the bitter cold boards of the porch.

Before I could do anything, a vehicle's engine fired and a dark-colored Ford pickup, older model, sped away from Dahlia House at breakneck speed.

2

"Call 911!" I commanded Jitty as I pushed back the blanket to reveal the still face of an infant. The newborn had been wiped clean, but the blood of birth still smudged its features. I couldn't tell if the child was bleeding, or even if it was breathing. My bare feet seemed to have frozen to the gray porch boards, but I managed to pick up the bassinet and haul it inside. I ran to the kitchen, where the oven I'd heated earlier still warmed the room. Hands shaking, I lifted the blankets and examined the infant, who began to squirm and cry.

"She's okay," I said aloud, as if to reassure myself. "Jitty, she's okay."

Still wearing the black guise of Rosemary, Jitty leaned against the wall. "See why I had to wake you up? The doorbell rang several times, but you just hid under your pillow."

I had a vague recollection of the doorbell, but I didn't have time to argue. I picked up the phone and called the Sunflower County sheriff's office. While the baby wasn't bleeding, someone surely was, and the pool of blood on the front porch told me that whoever had delivered the baby to my doorstep was badly injured. I wondered if the mother of the infant was bleeding out.

When the dispatcher said she'd call Coleman and send him to Dahlia House, I called Doc Sawyer and then my partner in Delaney Detective Agency. Until help arrived, I bundled the infant in a blanket I warmed by the oven and pulled her into my arms and held her close. The small sounds of fretfulness stopped, and the baby was instantly asleep.

"She likes you," Jitty said, as if it were a miracle.

"I saved her from freezing. Why shouldn't she like me?"

"That maternal instinct is kickin' in." Jitty tugged at her black mini-dress. "Time for a wardrobe change, and company is at the door." In a little sprinkle of black confetti that disappeared before it hit the ground, she was gone.

Before I could turn around, I heard Coleman Peters, the sheriff of Sunflower County and a man I had unresolved feelings for, call to me from the front door. "Sarah Booth, what's all the blood at the door? Are you okay?"

"In the kitchen," I answered.

He strode toward me, his footsteps loud on the hardwood floors. When he pushed open the swinging door into the kitchen, he stopped dead in his tracks. "Where'd you get a baby?"

The tone of the question was wrong. "As if I couldn't

have one myself? There's nothing wrong with my reproductive organs."

"Hard to do without having sex, and that hasn't happened for a while," he said drolly. "I know. I'm keeping score, as best I can."

I wanted to smack him, but I was holding the infant. "She was left on the front porch. Someone took off in a dark pickup, like maybe a 1990 model Ford, single cab, long wheel base." I'd come to know my pickups because I'd been shopping for a used truck. A 1990 model was a little too used, but I liked the design.

"Someone just abandoned her?"

"I'd tell you in sign language, but I'm holding a baby." I was aggravated and didn't try to hide it.

"I didn't realize just holding an infant could send a body into hormonal fluctuation, but you're sounding a might testy, Sarah Booth."

"Indeed she is." Tinkie pushed through the swinging door and stopped beside Coleman. Instead of saying anything else, she merely held out her arms to the infant. "Give her to me."

"How do you know it's a her?" I asked.

"The blanket is pink. Don't you know anything about babies?" Tinkie advanced and I put the baby in her arms. "Oh, my word, look at that hair! She's got enough hair for a dozen babies."

"Is she okay?" Coleman asked. "There was a lot of blood on the porch."

"She's fine, and Doc Sawyer is on the way. But someone is seriously hurt. We need to find the person in the truck before she dies." I paced the kitchen. Who else would leave a newborn but the mother?

"Good point. I'll call the SO and put out an APB on

the truck." He kept staring at the baby as if he'd never seen one before. She was exceptionally pretty with that mop of red hair and pale complexion.

"Who would leave a baby at *your* door?" Tinkie asked.

"Is that some slur against my maternal abilities?"

Tinkie's laughter was like a delicate chime. "You are so sensitive! Of course not, but Dahlia House isn't exactly on the beaten path. Why would a person drive all the way down your long driveway to leave a baby on the front porch? There are plenty of houses closer to the road."

She made a certain kind of logic. "Maybe they didn't want to be seen."

"Or maybe this baby was left here especially for you," Coleman said. "Sarah Booth, you haven't been buying babies on the black market, have you?"

"Have plenty of fun at my expense," I said, pretending to still be aggravated. "What we need to focus on is finding the bleeding person. What if the mother is really hurt?"

All humor was gone from Coleman's voice as he put an arm around me. "We'll find the mother, Sarah Booth. Now I'll call child services and we'll get this young lady into a foster home until—"

"No!" Tinkie and I said together.

"You can't do that." Tinkie had instinctively turned to shield the baby. "Sarah Booth and I will take care of her until we find the mother. It shouldn't take long. She simply can't go into the system."

Coleman frowned. "I can't just let you take her. I have to turn her over to child services."

"If you do that, it could take months for the mother to get her back. These first few days are so important for the bonding process," I said. I didn't have a lot of experience, but I'd read articles. And I could lay a line of bullshit when necessary. "Failure to bond can be a very serious psychological issue. It could damage her permanently."

"That's right." Tinkie followed my lead perfectly. "If a child develops an attachment disorder it can ruin her life. Sociopaths and psychopaths start with attachment disorders. This baby needs love, security, the chance to bond."

"And you and Sarah Booth can give her that?" Coleman sounded more than a little skeptical.

I looked at Tinkie and the way she held the baby cuddled to her chest. She'd always wanted a child. Fate had decreed she would never have one. "Tinkie and Oscar would be the best home," I said. "She'll have everything a baby needs to thrive. And it's just until we find the mother."

"What if the mother doesn't want her?" Coleman asked, and deep in his blue eyes I saw real concern. "What if she dumped the kid and took off? Or what if she wants the baby back but has issues of her own? Tinkie, you know you'll have to give her up. I don't think this is a smart move."

Tinkie inhaled slowly. "I know it's emotionally dangerous, but I promise you, Coleman, I won't fight the natural mother. That wouldn't be right. I just want to give the little girl a good start."

The debate halted as Doc Sawyer, a "retired" general practitioner who still ran the emergency room at the county hospital, entered the kitchen.

"Well, well," he said, eyeing the baby and all of us standing around the kitchen. "Looks like the stork came by and left a bundle of joy. Where's the mother? Why am I here?"

"Long story," I said, "Tinkie will fill you in."

As Doc picked up the baby, I followed Coleman to the front door.

"I don't like this. There are a million ways this could go south and Tinkie is already too attached." He opened his forensic kit to begin working the blood at the front door. "If this turns bad, Tinkie is going to be hurt."

He spoke with wisdom, but there were also dangers to the child. "The mother can't be far away. The baby hasn't even been properly cleaned. And you know as well as I do that once that baby is in the system, it could be devastating to her."

"I don't disagree. Child services does the best job they can, but they have no budget and they have more cases than they can work."

"This fostering is temporary. I promise. Just for a day or two?"

He nodded. "You've got forty-eight hours. After that, I'll have to follow the law."

"Thanks, Coleman. Now let me throw on some boots and a jacket. Dawn will be here soon and I need to get to work on finding the woman who had that baby."

"There's a lot of blood here, Sarah Booth. I'm no expert on childbirth, but this doesn't look right to me, even if she delivered on your front porch."

He was right about that.

"That baby could have frozen to death out here. How'd you know to look out the door at three in the morning?" Coleman took blood samples and photographs as he talked.

"The person who left her rang the doorbell. Repeatedly. She waited in the driveway until I went out on the porch and picked the baby up. She made sure the infant was safe before she left." And she had been bleeding heavily. It tore at my heart. "I think whoever left the baby was trying hard to make sure she was taken care of."

Coleman pushed his hat back on his head as he stood up. "The more I hear, the less I like it. It sounds like the person was desperate."

"And the question to ask is why? Why didn't they just wait for me to help them once I'd taken the baby inside?"

"Because they have something to hide." Coleman's frown said a lot. If it was the mother who'd left the baby and who was bleeding so profusely, she was in serious trouble. A woman who abandoned her child—but made sure it was safe and then ran away—had to be in a world of hurt.

"You think she's a criminal?" I somehow couldn't put the mother of that beautiful child in the category of felon.

"I don't know, but she's running from something or someone. The bigger question is why you, Sarah Booth? Why Dahlia House? You weren't picked at random. The baby was brought here, specifically, to you."

"Because the mother wants someone to find her. That's what I do. I find people and things."

"And you're damn good at it." He gathered his evidence and came to stand only inches from me. "I'll let you know what I find out."

"Thanks, Coleman." He'd helped me more than he knew. I hurried back inside before my feet froze to the porch.

3

"She's one hundred percent healthy, with one tiny glitch," Doc said after he'd examined the infant. "Born maybe three hours ago. Someone cut the umbilical cord and clamped it off. I've cleaned her up, but she needs some warm clothes."

"Shopping!" Tinkie almost squealed with pleasure. "I can't wait. They have the most adorable, girlie dresses at that boutique on the corner. There is this pale pink and green frock that reminds me of sweet peas. Remember those vines that grew behind the football stadium, Sarah Booth? In the spring they smelled like heaven. Well, the dress has a pattern almost like those sweet peas, and—"

"Hold on there, Betty Halbreich," Doc said.

"Betty who?" Tinkie and I asked in unison. We did

that sometimes when we were channeling each other's thoughts.

"The world's most famous personal shopper," Doc said, proud that he'd gotten one over on Tinkie. "You're the fashion queen of Zinnia and you don't know Betty Halbreich?" He pretended dismay. "She's dressed everyone from Lauren Bacall to Jackie Kennedy."

"How do you know this?" Tinkie's eyes narrowed.

"I was at the dentist office yesterday and had a long wait. I read a lot of magazines."

"Whew!" I dramatically wiped my brow. "I thought you'd gone rogue fashionista on us, Doc."

"Well, before y'all rush off to turn this darling infant into a prop for your clothes fetish, let's talk some basic nutrition."

I felt the blood flush my neck and cheeks. I hadn't even thought of food. I wondered if the baby had even had a chance to nurse. "I'll go to the store. What should I buy?"

"Too bad the whole business of wet nursing is gone," Doc said. "Nothing like a mother's milk to build a healthy immune system and give a child a jump-start."

"Don't look at me," I mumbled. "Just give me a list."

"We'll start with this formula and see how she takes to it," Doc said, writing down a mile-long list of things to get. "And when she's settled and strong, we'll talk about vaccinations."

"Hopefully, we'll find her mother," I said, aware that Tinkie was unnaturally quiet. She was kissing the baby's fingers.

"There is one more thing. She'll need some surgery."

"What?" My heart thudded into my stomach. "Is she sick? She looks fine to me. She's maybe a little hungry, but—"

"As I was trying to tell you, the little girl is polydactyl."

"But you said she was one hundred percent healthy." Tinkie's face had gone ashen.

"And she is." Doc picked up her right foot. "See that extra toe? It isn't anything but a vestigial digit. Best to have it removed when she's a little older, but nothing to worry about right now. I believe the best clinic for this is in Massachusetts. Boston Children's Hospital. This kind of surgery is a specialty of theirs."

"She'll have to have surgery?" Tinkie was appalled. "She's just a tiny baby. That's too much!"

"Hold on, Tinkie. It isn't brain surgery. And, Sarah Booth, a lot of people might have overlooked it. But the good news is that it may help you find the mother. This is an inherited trait. Doesn't mean the mother would have to be polydactyl, but she might be."

"What are the odds?" I asked.

"I'll have to conduct a bit of research. I don't recall seeing another case of this in Sunflower County, but there are plenty of children I never see these days. Some go to Memphis or Jackson and some never see a doctor. Or her family might not be from around here at all."

"Is there an obstetrics clinic or facility near?" I asked.

"This baby was born without benefit of a hospital," Doc said. "But if the mother was bleeding as severely as was indicated, she'd have to get medical attention. I'll call the local hospital. You might ask DeWayne to call the Memphis and Jackson hospitals. They won't give any information to you because of privacy laws. They'll be a lot more inclined to talk to Coleman or Deputy DeWayne."

"What about a midwife?" I asked. Doc knew a couple of old granny midwives and often worked with them to be sure of a healthy baby and mother.

"I'll make some calls, but I can tell you none of the midwives I work with would have let a new mother leave the premises bleeding that way."

"Anything could have happened," Tinkie said. The baby was snuggled against Tinkie's chest, dainty fists clutching empty air.

"She needs food," I said. I recognized those fist gestures. Puppies and kittens did the same to bring the milk down.

"I'll be at the hospital," Doc said.

"I'll make a run to the Pig." I grabbed my coat and purse and a pair of boots from the mudroom and headed out with Doc. I wanted a word in private.

He'd parked behind my mother's old roadster, which I now drove. "Watch over Tinkie. She's tough as nails, but this is her Achilles' heel," he said.

"I know. But maybe if she and Oscar keep the infant for a little while, it will soften Oscar to the idea of adopting. Tinkie wants a child. I think Oscar does, too, but he has some kind of issue with adopting."

"It isn't that." Doc patted his wild white hair that reminded me of Albert Einstein. I couldn't remember him with dark hair, though I'd known him all my life. "Oscar has his reasons. That's all I can say. If Tinkie gets too engrossed in that baby, it could be calamitous. When she learned she couldn't have children, she came very close to a breakdown."

I didn't know the details of Tinkie's past. She'd told me a few things—very private things. I knew she'd suffered, but I wasn't aware of the true emotional toll. "Should I keep the baby? I let her do it because I was trying to help."

"You can't take the baby back now, Sarah Booth. We

have to let this play out. Just keep telling her that the mother will return and the baby will have to go home."

"Will do." I put on a smile though my gut was writhing with anxiety. In trying to do a good deed, I may have put my partner on the line for emotional pain.

Doc patted my shoulder. "Maybe this will work out as you anticipated. Oscar and Tinkie could give a child a wonderful, loving home. Maybe Oscar will reconsider once he's exposed to the infant. Your intentions were noble, Sarah Booth."

"Road to hell and all of that," I said.

"Well, you'll have plenty of company along the road, including me."

I blew him a kiss and watched as he drove away from Dahlia House. What would Sunflower County ever do if Doc really retired? What would I do?

I pushed that thought away and jumped in the car. I had a hungry baby to care for. We'd need diapers and everything else on the long list Doc had written.

While Tinkie prepared the formula for the baby, I searched the attic for the nursing rocker. It had been used for generations of Delaneys. Once I found the antique chair, I took it to the private detective offices. Tinkie could feed the infant *and* work. Multitasking might mitigate the bonding. "You can see how the other half lives, working moms and all."

Tinkie was a natural. She had a dishcloth on her shoulder and the baby sucking a bottle in her arms as she settled into the chair and slowly tipped to and fro.

"You look like you know what you're doing." I was

shocked. Tinkie was no sloucher in the child-care department. The baby had also been diapered.

"I'm not a total nitwit. I've fed and clothed infants before."

"When?" I realized that in my thirty-four years it was
possible I'd never cared for an infant longer than two or
three minutes.

"Sarah Booth, a bunch of the girls we went to college
with were married and pregnant before we graduated.
Baby showers, parties, lunches. Most of those children
are in grammar school, if not high school."

I tried to wipe the blank look from my face, but I was
too late.

"You've *never* taken care of a baby?" she asked.

I could only pray Jitty wasn't listening in on this conversation. I'd never hear the end of it. "Maybe I just don't
remember."

"The feel of a child in your arms is something you'd
never forget."

I'd held the infant, and my life wasn't significantly
changed. Sure, she was adorable, and she had tugged
at my heart because she was so alone, with her mother
missing. But that was where my thoughts went. To the
missing mother. "I'm sure I'll get a taste of caring for the
baby once the newness wears off for you."

"Keep it up with the old-time colloquialisms—you're
sounding more and more like your Aunt Loulane, who
died a spinster."

"Below the belt, Tinkie. She gave up a potential husband to take care of me."

She laughed, and I was reminded of silvery chimes.
She had the purest, lightest laughter when she was truly

happy. Holding and feeding that infant had put her in hog heaven, to yet again quote an Aunt Loulane turn of phrase.

"Taking care of you was more important than any man," Tinkie said. She pierced me with her serious, blue gaze.

"You know the baby is going home to her mother. You can't fall in love with her, Tinkie. It will break your heart."

"Oh, posh, Sarah Booth. I'll have her for two days at the most. We both know if her mother isn't found by then, Coleman will have to put her into the system. Sure, I'll be attached, but it isn't like I've taken her to raise. She has a mother. I know that."

I sent a laser blast of truth-seeking her way and read only guileless innocence in her eyes. "Don't get hurt."

"I wouldn't dream of it." She winked.

"Then let's get on the stick looking for the baby's mother. I hope to goodness she's okay. That was a lot of blood."

"It sure was." Tinkie lifted the baby to her shoulder and burped her. "I think just until the real mother is found we should call her Libby, after your mother, Sarah Booth."

Shock rippled over me. Tinkie read my reaction and grinned. "We can't keep calling her baby or infant or *it*. She needs a name, and I'd like it to be Libby."

"Sure," I said, more pleased than I wanted to admit. "We can call her that until her real mother tells us her name. Now I'm going to run out to Betty McGowin's house and talk to her."

Betty was the best-known midwife in the area. Some said she had more expertise than the ob-gyns that came to Zinnia three days a week from Memphis. "Coleman is checking the hospitals."

"Sure thing." Tinkie slipped the baby into a papoose-type carrier where she had both hands free. "On your way back, would you pick up something sweet from Millie's Café? I have a craving."

"Sure thing." Now I was really worried. Tinkie never ate dessert. She had the figure of a sixteen-year-old because she didn't eat sweets or junk food. "I'll bring a surprise."

I was out the door before Tinkie could change her mind. I left them sitting in the rocker, the early morning sun creating a golden aura around them like a Madonna and child.

It was a half hour drive to Betty McGowin's house and on the way I had plenty of time to rationalize how okay it was for Tinkie to take charge of baby Libby.

A baying hound crept out from under the front porch of Betty's house. I recognized the same determination to defend her owner that my hound displayed. No one was likely to sneak up on Betty McGowin, that was for sure.

"Hush that up, Blanche Dubois," Betty said as she came out on the front porch, drying her hands on an apron. I hadn't seen an apron like that since the last time I'd seen Aunt Bee on *The Andy Griffith Show*. Betty was a tall, angular woman without an ounce of fat on her bones. She stood at least five-eleven, maybe six feet tall, and she was midnight black and spoke with the diction of the lower Delta.

"Can I help you?" she asked, coming down two of the three porch steps to stand beside the blue tick hound that could have been a kissing cousin to my wonderful Sweetie Pie.

"Sarah Booth Delaney." I held out a hand. "Would you mind if I asked you a few questions?"

"Libby Delaney's girl?" she asked.

"Yes, ma'am."

"I can see her in you, and your daddy, too. I heard you were a private investigator." Her face gave away no secrets. "You're here working on a case?"

"Yes, ma'am. I'm looking for a woman who gave birth last night."

"And what wrong thing has this woman done?" Betty was in complete control of the conversation.

"She hasn't done anything wrong. Someone left a baby on my front porch. The baby is fine, but there was a lot of blood by the bassinet. I need to find the mother. She may be seriously hurt."

Betty's expression didn't change, but she waved me up the steps and into her house. The first thing I noticed was a copy of Da Vinci's painting of the Last Supper. I'd seen the same print several times in homes across Sunflower County, and it reminded me of Mrs. Horne, one of my beloved grammar school teachers. I used to stop by her house in the afternoons and she attempted, unsuccessfully, to teach me to knit. "This picture reminds me of one of my favorite teachers. She had one just like it."

"Mrs. Lucy Horne left me that painting when she died," Betty said. "She set a great store by it, and she knew I did, too."

"Mrs. Horne died while I was in New York."

"Yes, when she was ailing, I would stop by her place for a cup of coffee and a talk. She often spoke about you and your parents. She never believed the wreck that took your folks was an accident, Sarah Booth."

Her statement startled me. "Did she say why she didn't believe it was an accident?"

"She wasn't well, and I didn't press her, though in hindsight I wish I had."

I wished for one ten-minute conversation with Mrs. Horne, who was not the kind of person to see conspiracies behind every camellia bush. Why had she said such a thing to Betty McGowin? This was a subject I needed to probe, but not right now. I had to find the baby's mother or little Libby would end up in the welfare system. And it was possible the mother would face charges for abandoning her child.

"I want to talk about this later, but right now, I need to find the mother of this baby. The sheriff has given me forty-eight hours before he calls child protective services. Can you help me?"

Betty waved me into a kitchen chair and put two coffee cups on the table. From an old-fashioned Dripolater she poured dark, aromatic coffee. "I may be able to help. Tell me about the baby."

I gratefully sipped the coffee. "She has red hair and possibly light eyes. Too early to tell. She's healthy and Doc said the mother hadn't been abusing alcohol or drugs. She's a healthy infant who needs her mama."

Betty listened, her intent gaze searching my face for whatever clues she could find. "Anything unusual about the baby?"

I debated how much to say, but it seemed pointless to ask for help and then withhold useful information. "The child is polydactyl."

"I see."

I knew then she knew the mother. The question was, would she tell me? As a PI, I had no authority to make her talk. Coleman did, but I didn't want to threaten Betty with the law. It seemed wrong. "Please help me find the mother. I swear I'll do whatever I can to make sure she receives medical treatment and is reunited with her daughter. If this drags on too long, it will be worse for her."

"I don't know the mother."

I read her face. "But you know the family."

"I may have delivered the mother. It's not a Sunflower County family. If the baby is related to the family I'm thinking about, they live in Bolivar County."

This wasn't good. Coleman's jurisdiction was Sunflower County—and no further. "What's the name?"

Betty shook her head. "They gave me a false name, and it was years ago. The only thing I really remember is that the baby girl had six toes on her right foot, and the mother didn't seem surprised."

"That baby must be this baby's mother. Are you sure you can't remember?" This was more than frustrating, but I didn't doubt Betty's sincerity. She had no reason to fabricate such a story.

"You might check with the health department. This family, as I remember, didn't have reliable transportation. They came to the Sunflower County Health Department because it was closer than either Rosedale or Cleveland. Bolivar is a big county and hard for those without a good means of travel."

"I'm not the most popular person at the local health department. The nurse, Mrs. Skinner, thinks I should be in prison." When I'd first become a PI, Tinkie and I had broken into the local health department for some much needed records. The head nurse there had a long memory.

"And you think I might be?" Betty laughed. "Times have changed a lot and the best doctors in Memphis and Jackson work with me and other trained midwives. But there are still those who view me as little more than a witch doctor, and that nurse you're referring to is one of them. When I get a pregnant mother with complications, I send them to the clinic where a doctor can help them. These young girls, some of them are hooked on bad things." She shook her head. "Drugs are takin' a toll on our young people, Sarah Booth. And their babies."

"Yes, ma'am. Coleman talks about the drug problem and how it's taken over rural America. Thank you for this information. I'll try with the health department." I finished my coffee and stood. "Doc Sawyer says many nice things about you. He values what you do."

"Doc knows I serve wealthy families and those who can't afford the hospital. If it weren't for me, things could be a lot worse for some young mothers and their children. I urge them to see a doctor, and the ones who can afford it do. The others rely on me and my herbs."

"If you should be visited by a mother who just delivered, would you let me know?"

"I will," she said. "You have my word. A baby should have its mother. And while a girl will sometimes give up a child because she wants to do the right thing for the infant, she should do it in the light of day, not in the darkness of night. For her own sake as well as the child's."

"Thanks, Betty. I'll let you know what I find out."

"It was June when I delivered the little girl with six toes. If my memory serves me, she'd be close to graduating from high school."

"That's a good place to start."

I gave the hound a pat on my way to the car, and when I turned around, Betty was on the porch. She gave a wave and then went back in her house. Funny how we were linked by Mrs. Horne and a print of a famous painting. Betty was someone I could count on if the chips were down.

Driving to the local health department brought back many anxiety-producing memories of school vaccinations and encounters with the head nurse, who always seemed to have it in for me. To my delight, the nurse was on vacation, and the young woman at the front desk had no memory of me or my past.

When it came to giving me access to health records, though, she was as intractable as her boss. I left with nothing—except an idea. I dialed the source of all knowledge in Sunflower County, Cece Dee Falcon, society editor at *The Zinnia Dispatch*. Several months ago I'd read a story in the paper about the health department receiving a grant to put all of their medical records on computers. Those computers would link with the mecca of Mississippi medicine in Jackson.

Cece, who in high school had been Cecil, was one of my closest friends. Her bravery in claiming her life on her terms made me humble. And her keen ability to sniff out information *and* her slender hips made me envious.

"Hello, dar-link," she said, sounding more like a Gabor than the real deal.

"Cece, I need some information from the health department. I have to find a family with polydactyl propensities."

"And why should I help you?" she asked archly. "Seems like the stork made a delivery to Dahlia House early this morning and no one bothered to call me."

Uh-oh. "That's why I'm calling now."

"Day late and dollar short, Sarah Booth."

All I could do was offer an apology. "I have forty-eight hours to find the real mother before the baby has to go to child services. I've been a little busy. I knew Tinkie would fill you in." It was a guess, but not a wild one. Tinkie probably stopped by the newspaper to visit Cece while on her way to Zinnia to buy little Libby the latest fashions.

"Tinkie did stop by." Cece's frosty tone melted. "She is adorable, Sarah Booth. Right down to her six little toes!"

Nothing like a baby to bring a person to her knees. "So can you help me with the health department records?"

"What do you need?"

"Some information on a client from about seventeen years ago."

The silence told me my request was complicated. At last Cece spoke. "Harold knows someone who might be able to help. I'll give him a call."

Harold, because of his work at the bank, was well connected in the world of international finance—a world where computers ruled. He'd come to the aid of Delaney Detective Agency more than once with "unusual" ways to obtain information.

"You're the best, Cece."

"This comes with a price tag, you know."

I could easily visualize her wicked grin. "Whatever it is, I'll pay it."

"I've been itching to do a story on Betty McGowin, the midwife. A feature. Will you talk with her about it?"

"Sure. I'm not certain I have any influence, but I'll try."

"Your mother helped get Betty established as a midwife here," Cece said. "Libby Delaney went to bat, with help from your father and Doc, against the medical establishment when they tried to shut Betty down."

Far back in my memory, a slim bell rang. I'd been a child, but I had a vague memory. "Betty does a lot of good for people."

"She does. And I want to tell her story. Several Nashville celebrities have hired Betty to move in with them while waiting on the birth of a child. She sure can zip her lip, though. I can't even get her to talk to me."

"I'll ask," I promised. "Now let's find the baby's birth mother and then I'll focus on your story."

"Stay by the phone." There was a click and Cece was on the case.

4

I was on the way to Hilltop, Tinkie's home, when the phone rang. Harold went on a ten-minute rant about little Libby's personality and beauty before I could get a word in edgewise.

"Can you get the health department records?" I finally inserted my question.

"All but done," he said. "I should have an answer for you soon."

I was curious about one point. "Does it ever worry you when I ask for something like this?" Harold was one of the most ethical people I knew. He kept the bank's information close and never divulged personal financial information. He wasn't the kind of man who meddled in the business of others. Yet he never failed me if he could help with information that cracked a case. He'd hired a hacker to get medical information without even a hint of hesitation.

"Sarah Booth, you've never asked me for anything meant to harm another person. Justice rides a slow horse, and sometimes that horse needs a little help going uphill. I see you as the one-woman embodiment of the Justice League. In fact, I've ordered you a Wonder Woman costume. You'll indulge me by trying it on, won't you?"

Harold's trust in me was never to be taken lightly. "Thank you, and I would be honored to play Wonder Woman."

"I can visualize you in that delightfully skimpy costume with your golden lariat of truth. You could, maybe, lasso me and tie me up."

Harold was taking this way over the top. "Uh, we'll see."

"It's a small request, Sarah Booth." He sounded slightly hurt.

"I'm not really into role-playing like that, but maybe for next Halloween."

"I'll hold you to that promise. And just so you know, I called Coleman, who got a warrant for the records." His baritone laugh rang through the phone. He'd snared me, hook, line, and sinker.

"Well played," I said. "And just so *you* know, when I see you, I'm going to hurt you."

To my surprise, Oscar was at Hilltop. His new silver Infiniti was parked at the steps, and when I let myself in the front door, I heard him in the kitchen with Tinkie.

"What does little Libby want? Tell Uncle Oscar."

I stopped in my tracks. Oscar was speaking in baby tongues.

"Isn't she a doll? Tinkie asked. "Oh, Oscar, having her here is like a gift from God. I can't imagine life without her."

I called out as I entered. "I'm in the house!"

"Come on in," they chorused.

To my amusement, I found Oscar with a towel on his shoulder and the baby in his arms. From a naked newborn, little Libby had turned into a seven-pound fashion plate. She wore a perfectly coordinated pink polka-dot onesie and a headband sporting a huge peony and little pink glitter booties. The outfit was a bit saggy because it was too big, but Libby made it work.

Oscar, on the other hand, was festooned with a huge splotch of baby upchuck on the front of his very expensive suit. A clot of something I didn't want to identify was in his hair. "Looks like the baby has won you over," I said.

"Look at that red hair," Oscar said. "She's a ginger. My grandmother was red-haired."

Both of them were baby gob-smacked. "She's cute," I agreed. I'd hoped to get Tinkie to go with me to run down the possible address of the baby's mother when Coleman called it in to me, but I could see Tinkie wasn't going to part with the child. I'd have to work this lead on my own.

"Any news on the mother?" Tinkie's tone was carefully cool.

"Maybe a lead. Waiting to hear from Coleman. Want to go with me when I do?"

"I'd better stay with Libby. Oscar is wonderful with her, but she needs a mother's touch."

If Oscar heard any alarm bells, he didn't show it. He was as smitten as his wife. "Just remember, you two, this baby has to be returned to the birth mother. Don't get too attached."

"Of course not," Oscar said. "This is temporary. But while she's here . . ." He grabbed a fresh bottle. "We're going to take care of her."

My cell phone rang and Coleman was on the line with an address for the young woman born with an extra digit. The location was on Fodder Gin Road just across the county line in Bolivar County. "I have no jurisdiction there," he said, the warning to behave and stay out of trouble implicit.

"Got it." I wanted to talk to him about Tinkie and Oscar, but if I did, he might send child services for the baby immediately. It was best to find the baby's mother as quickly as possible. "I'll call you when I've run down the lead."

"You'd better," Coleman said. "And Sarah Booth, I hate to have to tell you this, but you should know."

Immediately I felt my gut clench. "Know what?"

"Gertrude Strom, or a woman matching her description, was seen on Highway 1 north of Vicksburg headed this way."

Gertrude, the former owner of The Gardens B&B, had been charged with murder and was awaiting trial when a numbskull judge had lowered her bail. She'd jumped and run. For reasons I couldn't fathom, Gertrude hated my guts. She'd shot my fiancé in the leg and almost crippled him—ultimately resulting in the breakup of our relationship. I couldn't figure why she hated me, but I had plenty of reason to hate her. And I was afraid of her. *Irrational* didn't begin to describe her.

"So the authorities are on the alert, right?"

"They are, but you're headed over to Bolivar County, and Highway 1 goes through it. Just be aware and stay safe. If you see her, don't try to confront her."

The highway ran along the Mississippi River. The idea of running into Gertrude made my jaw tighten. She wouldn't get a second chance to hurt me. "Thanks for the heads up."

"Caution, Sarah Booth. If you see her, call the authorities. The highway patrol is putting up roadblocks. They should run her to ground. You let them take care of this."

They should have put up roadblocks days ago. Mississippi law enforcement ran at a total budgetary deficit. There was never money for personnel or equipment. "I'll be careful." And I would also stop by Dahlia House and pick up my gun. Gertrude looked like an older woman who might be featured in a British comedy, but she was no laughing matter. While I didn't intend to push a confrontation, I would be ready to take action if she forced the issue.

Fodder Gin Road was a rutted dirt track off Highway 12 that took me west toward the Mississippi River. There was little chance of running into Gertrude Strom on the pig-trail that served as access to a trailer community right out of the 1960s.

The mobile homes were parked on a treeless plot that wasn't so bad in November, but in the summer sun, they would be broiling. Litter blew across the road, and in the distance I saw several children playing on a lone swing set. As I drew closer, a little boy waved a stick at me, but his expression was friendly, not aggressive. When the car stopped, children surrounded me. Candy might not be good for children, but I wished I'd had the foresight to buy some chocolate treats.

A young girl with dark auburn hair sat on a broken bench strumming a guitar. When the children quieted, I could hear the stirring ballad she sang about lost love. It wasn't a song from the radio that I'd ever heard, but it was powerful.

"I'm looking for—" How could I explain my mission to children too young to be in school?

"Give her some room," the guitarist said as she came over, holding the twelve-string with her right hand. On the outside of the hand was a tiny little extra digit.

"I'm looking for Pleasant Smith," I said to her.

"So am I," she said bluntly. "I'm her sister, Faith. What do you want with her?"

I didn't want to go into the whole baby situation, so I took another tack. "I'm concerned for her. Do you have any idea where she might be?"

"You'd best talk to Mama," Faith said. "We've been looking for Pleasant for better than a month. Can't find hide nor hair of her. The only consolation is we haven't found a body, either."

Her total lack of emotion made me wonder if she was serious or playing me. "You think she's dead?"

"You'd better talk to Mama. I shouldn't be speaking out of school." She pointed to one of the trailers. "She's in there. I gotta watch these young'uns. It's my day and if I don't keep an eye on them no telling what trouble they'll get into."

The kids had scattered, and for urchins on twenty-four-inch legs, they were quick to disperse.

"One more thing. That song, I've never heard it before, but it was lovely."

"Pleasant wrote it. She was gonna be a big singer-songwriter in Nashville before she went missing."

Her eyes were dry, but I could see she was hurting. "I'm trying to find your sister. I want to help her."

"I hope you do. Like I said, talk to Mama. She'll tell you what she can."

"Is the sheriff looking for your sister?"

Faith snorted. "Right. We called and told them when she didn't come home, and they said she was just another kid sick of rural Mississippi who took off for greener pastures."

Bolivar County wasn't Coleman's terrain and anger heated my cheeks at the blasé attitude toward a missing girl who was obviously pregnant when she'd disappeared. Faith had her hands full supervising the kids, so I went in the direction she'd indicated and climbed the metal steps to the trailer door.

My knock was answered immediately by a thin woman in a sea-blue top that matched her eyes. Though a little faded, her red hair told me I was likely in the right place. "I'm trying to find Pleasant Smith," I said.

"Who are you and why are you looking for Pleasant?" she asked.

"I'm a . . . friend. I want to help."

Her response was an instant outburst of tears. "Have you heard something from her? I'm out of my mind with worry. Pleasant's been missing for more than four weeks. She went to the store to get some milk, and she never came back. Her abandoned car was found on the side of the road, broken down." She wiped the tears from her face.

From a room behind her the squall of an unhappy child came to us.

"I have to see about my sister's baby girl. I'm keeping her so Fidelity can work," she said, motioning me to follow. "I'll put on a pot of coffee and you can tell me why you're hunting Pleasant."

I followed, mentally trying to figure out the best way to tell this woman that her daughter might be in serious trouble. It wasn't going to be an easy conversation.

When the coffee was brewed and the toddler was quieted, Charity Smith sat down at the Formica table with me and two cups of hot coffee.

I wanted to tell her the complete truth of why I was there. She deserved to know that her granddaughter was alive and well—but first I had to be certain Libby was her grandchild. Charity seemed torn up by Pleasant's disappearance, but I didn't know her role in the events that had ended with a baby and a pool of blood on my front porch. "Mrs. Smith, I'm a private investigator." I showed her my badge. "I've been hired to find Pleasant."

"Why?" she asked.

"Let me just say that finding your daughter would benefit my client."

The toddler sat in the middle of the floor beating an assortment of plastic containers together and squealing with delight at the noise. She looked up at me with blue eyes as clear as her aunt's. I wondered if little Libby would have the same startling eye color. "She's a beautiful baby. What's her name?"

Her eyes filled again, but she checked her emotions back. "That's baby Sapphire, my younger sister's girl. Pleasant was pregnant when she disappeared." She said the last with some bitterness as she rubbed her forehead. "Pleasant had everything in the world going for her. She was going to escape. Then she showed up pregnant and refused to tell anyone who the father was. She should have had the baby by now. If she's alive." A lump moved down her throat, but she clung to her stoicism. "That young man that stopped by here yesterday looking for her was worried about her and the baby, too."

"What young man?"

She shook her head. "Some musician. Said he was friends with Pleasant. She was supposed to perform with him, he said."

"But you didn't know him?" The danger seemed obvious to me, but Charity didn't see it.

"Pleasant had a lot of friends, and this boy was so solicitous about the baby. He was worried when I told him Pleasant had been missing for four weeks."

"Did you get his name?" I asked.

She frowned. "He said his name, but I didn't write it down. Nice young man in a black pickup. He really seemed worried about my girl." Her face brightened. "I didn't write his name down but he said he gave Pleasant a ride down to Delta State University when she applied for her scholarships. Her car wouldn't run, so it was a godsend when she was able to catch a ride." She went to a kitchen drawer and began riffling papers. "Here it is. She left a note. 'Mom, Luther is giving me a ride to DSU. Back by five.'"

"Do you know this young man?"

"He played drums in a little band. He was very concerned about Pleasant."

Charity was a trusting person. She'd allowed me into

her home without question. When a young man came asking about her daughter, she assumed it was out of concern.

"If he comes back, you need to call me right away." I held up my hand to stop her protestations that he was a good boy. "He may know something to help. If I'm going to find her, I need some leads."

"What can I do?"

"Do you have a photograph of Pleasant?" This would go a long way.

She went to a shelf in the den and brought back a high school photo. She took it out of the frame and handed it to me.

"I'll give this to the sheriff's department." But first I snapped a picture with my phone. I'd prepared a list of questions, and I didn't hesitate. "If Pleasant ran away, where would she go?"

"She didn't run away. She had everything ahead of her. She was a top contender for a scholarship to Delta State University in the music department, there was interest about her songs in Nashville, she made good grades at the high school even though she has to miss a lot of days. Faith, Pleasant, and a few older teenage girls take turns watching the children around here so their mothers can work."

That was a lot of responsibility for high school girls to shoulder.

Before I could frame another question, Charity continued. "I take in ironing and some catering, when the work is offered. I've done the best I can with no education and no husband. Mine walked off and never came back." She laughed. "Talk about a jerk. He said he was goin' for cigarettes. He couldn't even be original."

"Do you have any idea who the father of Pleasant's baby is? She might be with him."

"I couldn't get a peep out of her. Not a single word. If she had a beau, she was all secretive. I got worried the father was some big shot from Nashville who was filling her head with dreams and was just gonna steal her songs and leave her stranded. I've heard lots of stories how such a thing can happen to a talented young girl."

"Do you think she's with someone in the music business?" At least it was a place to start, though half of Nashville was comprised of those with a big dream about making it in music. If Pleasant was using an alias, I'd be no closer to finding her.

"No, I really don't. If she was runnin' off to Nashville, she would have said so. And if she was makin' any money, she'd be sending something home for Faith. Those two girls were close as peas in a pod. Pleasant loves her family. She loves me and her cousin here. Growing up in the trailer park and getting mocked by all the kids in school, teased about where she lives and who she is, I can see why she'd want to bolt and run. I also know she wouldn't do it." She looked me square in the eyes. "Someone took my oldest daughter. They snatched her up and took her, and no one will do a damn thing to help me find her."

5

An hour later, I was pumped up on caffeine and fueled with righteous anger. The sheriff of Bolivar County, one Hoss Kincaid, hadn't lifted a finger to find Pleasant. He'd assumed, because of her family conditions or her pregnancy or her age or all of the above, that she'd run off. So he hadn't even tried to look. Not really. Sure, runaways happened all the time, but Coleman wouldn't have been so blasé about a missing, pregnant girl. Especially when her broken-down car was abandoned on the side of the road, as I'd learned from Charity Smith.

I hated driving to Rosedale, but my options were limited. Hoss Kincaid might have useful information. The second troubling aspect of Rosedale was that it sat on Highway 1, the road Gertrude Strom was suspected of traveling on toward a possible return to Zinnia. Gertrude was more than half a bubble off. To return to the area where every law officer in uniform knew who she was, what she looked like, and what she had done was downright insane. She'd also jumped a big bond, leaving a bondsman stuck. I knew Junior Wells, and he wasn't the kind of man to take kindly to such a loss. He'd be gunning for her, too, and that was literal. Junior loved his weapons and he knew how to use them. In my black little heart of hearts, I wouldn't be upset if someone ended Gertrude Strom. I blamed her for my breakup with Graf and for a lot of other things, too.

Rosedale is a small town not half a mile from the Mississippi River. I'd loved coming here and driving up to Levee Road to sit with Cece, who was Cecil at the time, and Tammy Odom, now known as Madame Tomeeka, the best psychic in the Southeast, Coleman, and several others in our high school gang. We'd play guitars and sing, and even though I had zero talent, no one told me at the time.

Pleasant Smith was talented. The song she'd written still haunted me, and I thought about the tough choices in life she'd woven into her song. No matter how old or young, those choices were still hard to make and accept.

Main Street was empty, but I parked behind the sheriff's office just to be on the safe side. I didn't want to come out and discover that Gertrude had set up an ambush. She meant to kill me. I had no doubt. As much as I blamed her for some of my problems, she blamed me for everything bad that had ever happened to her. Me and my dead mother, which was ridiculous.

My anger toward Gertrude seeped into my aggravation with Hoss Kincaid and his total lack of action. When I pushed into the sheriff's office, I was loaded for bear. He stood in front of the counter, and I recognized the sheriff from the billboard on the county line declaring Hoss Kincaid was a "work-hoss" against crime. Right.

"What's the status of the missing person report on Pleasant Smith?" I asked, rushing my jumps in a way I knew was stupid. I couldn't help myself. Hoss sported a handlebar mustache, à la Sam Elliot, and his baritone was nearly as deep. He might be crap for a law officer, but he could make a million in voice-over work.

"Miss Sarah Booth Delaney, you come busting in here demanding information. That doesn't work well for me, little lady."

He knew my name, and I wondered why. I'd never been in trouble in Bolivar County, and I didn't think Coleman and Hoss were especially close lawman friends. "Have you done anything to find Pleasant Smith?" I slapped her high school photo on the countertop.

Hoss eyeballed me long and hard. "I heard you were uppity, but I also heard you were smart. You're not acting very smart. I don't have to cooperate with you, and I'm not inclined to put up with your attitude right now."

His words sobered me up immediately. He'd hit the nail on the head. I was asking for his help, and he was under no obligation to give it to me. A private investigator had no more rights than a citizen when it came to cooperation from law enforcement. He didn't *have* to tell me a damn thing.

"Could you tell me what progress you've made on finding Pleasant Smith?" I restated my inquiry. When he arched his eyebrows, I added, "Please."

"The problem here is that Miss Smith disappeared with a set of facts that doesn't support abduction. Her car appeared to be abandoned because it had stopped working. There wasn't a single indication that foul play was involved. Looked to me like she'd decided to strike out for a better life."

"She was eight months pregnant. Hardly a time for a kid without any money or support to decide to begin a new life." I kept my tone level and professional.

"No one saw a thing," Hoss said, twisting the right side of his mustache like Oilcan Harry. "She took off to buy milk. She picked up a gallon at a little grocery and that was the last anyone saw of her."

"And you figured she took her gallon of milk and hitched her way to a new life?" I did try not to sound like a smart-ass. I was about seventy percent successful.

"No, I didn't figure that at all. See, she left the milk in the car. I figured she started a new life sans milk."

I deserved that remark, so I swallowed my pride and nodded. "Where does the investigation stand now?"

"We have a missing person bulletin out. Her photograph has been sent to major Mississippi towns, New Orleans, and Memphis. We never got a single hit. If she went to those areas, she stayed under the radar." He calculated. "She'll be harder to find now since she's likely had the baby."

"The baby is safe. Someone left her on my front porch. She's received medical care and Sheriff Peters is involved." Where Libby was concerned, my trust factor was sorely lacking with Hoss Kincaid. He'd done nothing to earn my confidence.

"You have the baby but not the mother?" He had the decency to look concerned.

"Yes. I believe Pleasant was abducted and is being held somewhere." I gave him the rest of the details about

Libby but skipped over the fact that the baby was in the Richmonds' care. He could get those details from Coleman. I felt my jean's pocket for my car keys. It was time to move on. I wasn't gaining any ground here. "Thanks for your help, Sheriff. If you get any leads would you let me know?"

"I might," he said, deliberately provoking me.

"Thanks again." I headed out the door before I lost my temper and said something I would truly regret.

By the time I got back to Dahlia house, I was longing to see little Libby and get a dose of baby love. I would never admit it to Jitty, but in the short few moments she'd been completely mine, I'd felt a strange stirring in my chest.

I called Tinkie for an update and filled her in on what I knew.

"If something has happened to the mother, do you think Oscar and I can keep little Libby?"

"Tinkie, the optimum outcome is to find Pleasant Smith, the mother. Imagine how she's feeling."

Tinkie's sigh was audible. "I know. It's just that Oscar loves her as much as I do. I never thought he'd come around to adoption, but he's talking about it. Seriously. And not just to placate me. Libby has him wrapped around her little finger. She is a Daddy's Girl in the cradle."

If anyone could school a one-day-old infant in the art of man manipulation it was my partner. Tinkie could hand out Ph.D.s in DG training if she chose to. I'd never seen a more successful model of "make a man do what you want and love doing it."

I entered the foyer and closed the front door behind me, still listening to Tinkie rave about the baby. "Tinkie, don't set yourself up for heartbreak. Love little Libby, but know it's temporary."

"I know, Sarah Booth. I'm indulging in a bit of fantasy, but she isn't my baby."

That sounded rational, but baby fever wasn't something one could will away. "Why don't you drop the baby with Madame Tomeeka and come help me with the case."

"Tammy's out of town. She's in Memphis visiting her daughter."

I tried to think of other friends who might take care of little Libby—to give Tinkie a break from the bonding that was going on. Cece was at the newspaper and wouldn't change a diaper for a lottery win, and Millie had her hands full at the café. Harold was great with dogs and kids, but he was at the bank working.

"Okay, I'll give you a call if I find anything."

"You do that." I heard the baby coo and my own heart melted. Those baby sounds spoke right to a woman's inner core.

I hung up and turned to the kitchen when I yelped from fright. A woman in a floor-length shirtwaist dress with her hair pulled into a bun stood in the parlor door. She had a baby in one arm and two clinging to her skirt.

"Motherhood is the most blessed of all conditions," she said in a light, pleasant voice. "I have been blessed with a passel of children, all smart, all eager to journey into the world."

I knew it was Jitty, but I had no clue who Jitty thought she was. Her habit of jumping around in time and space made me crazy. At least this was better than Rosemary with the spawn of Satan. "Give me a clue, please."

She loved to make me guess.

"My brood calls me Marmee, and my girls grew up to be literary heroines."

"Margaret March." I had her pegged. "The perfect mother who raised a family of perfect girls."

"The mantle of motherhood rested lightly on my shoulders. I had the talent for it."

"And modest, too. I somehow don't think Louisa May Alcott is writing your lines."

"I have no need of a speechwriter. I'm my own woman and I raised my darlings to be the same. They are perfect models of womanhood, but they are not vapid. They think, they do, they live, and, by god, they love."

"Lucky they reside in a book. Otherwise, they might have been burned for witches with their progressive views." I had a mind to devil Jitty a bit now that she was assuming the mother of all mother disguises. I knew what was coming next.

"Even Jo did her duty and produced an heir. Several, in fact, and they were the joy of her life." Jitty dropped her beatific expression, and her plump white cheeks thinned, the skin shifting to the light mocha shade that was my haint. "When you gonna jump in the sack with one of those men sniffin' after you and get yourself with child?"

"It might be nice if I loved the father of my child."

Jitty waved the phantom children from her skirts and they evaporated, as did her skirt. She had on skinny jeans and my favorite pair of boots. "Love comes and goes, Sarah Booth. Every relationship has its ups and downs. True love isn't guaranteed, but the love of a child is something you need to experience."

I didn't doubt her evaluation, but I did question her timing. I'd just ended my engagement. I wasn't ready to jump in the sack and get pregnant just because Jitty thought I was behind schedule on producing an heir.

"You're going to pressure my ovaries into an early death." The look on her face was priceless. I plied my advantage. "You know stress can kill healthy ovaries. Think of all those eggs shriveling away, defeated by cortisol and other stress hormones." I had no clue what I was talking about, but lack of facts had never stopped Jitty. What was good for the goose was good for the gander, as my Aunt Loulane, fount of Proper Lady Wisdom, would say.

"You are lyin', Sarah Booth Delaney."

I suppressed my grin and gave her my most serious expression. "I'm not."

"You are too."

"Not."

"Are too."

"Not!" I grabbed my abdomen. "I can almost feel them dying right now." I went into a high-pitched, pathetic voice, " 'Make it stop. Make it stop. Stress is killing me.' Now that's the sound of some cracked eggs shriveling into dust because of pressure."

Jitty waved her hand at me in disgust. "You think you're smart, but you are just a smart aleck."

"Jitty, I'm doing my best."

She sniffed. "Keep that little Libby for a day or two and I'll bet your eggs get a whole lot better."

"Or it could be I discover I don't like minding babies."

"Your mama is rollin' in her grave."

I had to laugh then, because the one thing I knew about my mother, Libby Delaney, was that whatever path I chose to follow, she'd support me one hundred percent.

"Give me some time, Jitty. There are a lot of fish in the sea." For once, I was going to get the last word with my know-it-all haint.

" 'You don't need scores of suitors. You need only one . . . if he's the right one,' " Jitty replied, stealing a line from the Alcott book. And she was gone before I could think of a retort.

I put my pistol in the trunk of the car, called up Sweetie Pie and Pluto, and waved them into the front seat. I loved to ride with the top down, but it was securely in place due to the cold weather. I was headed to Bolivar County once again. I wanted to talk to the clerk at the convenience store where Pleasant Smith was last seen. Sheriff Hoss Kincaid hadn't mentioned questioning the clerk, and if his attitude was any indication, I doubted he'd made the effort. He'd written Pleasant off as a runaway. End of story.

Gertrude Strom was on my mind as I drove. She'd abducted my fiancé and shot him in the leg, all to punish me for some breach of trust by my mother. The whole thing was a fabrication, a story made up in the coils of her fevered brain. She'd demonstrated crazy again and again, and returning to the area around Sunflower County was just one more example of how nuts she was. Coming back here after jumping bail was stupid, and one thing about Gertrude, she wasn't dumb.

Was she so crazed and vengeful that she'd risk prison just to hurt me again?

I wished I could think the answer was no, but I knew it was possible. Probable. She would risk her freedom to hurt me. That was not a comforting thought.

On the way to the store, I called Madame Tomeeka, a woman with such talents that she drew customers from

Memphis and New Orleans. I had tremendous respect for Tammy, but I was also wary. Tammy's dreams had foretold danger for me and Tinkie more than once. While some believed that forewarned was forearmed, I accepted that her dreams made me anxious.

Still, anxious was better than poleaxed.

"Tammy, I need your help. When you get back from Memphis, I want to have a séance."

"I'm not in Memphis."

I was stunned that Tinkie had out and out lied to me. Maybe she'd been mistaken about where Tammy was. I chatted with my psychic friend, and ten minutes later, I'd arranged for a gathering at Dahlia House to allow Tammy to attempt to figure out where baby Libby's natural mother might be. Tinkie, Millie, and Cece were all on the guest list. And when I called Millie, she offered to bring a homemade chicken potpie and bread pudding. Plans set, my focus returned to the job at hand.

In the distance I saw the lonely convenience store with two gas pumps and an awning that looked like a tornado had had its way with it. It wasn't a place that inspired a desire to stop, but it was the only place to buy a few groceries, gasoline, and maybe a soft drink within a twenty-mile radius. Nothing but the two-lane highway and barren cotton fields could be seen in any direction. Desolate would be an accurate description.

I pulled around to the north and left Sweetie and Pluto in the car while I entered. I prowled the interior, assessing the clerk behind the counter. He was a young man, probably just out of high school. Tall and thin, he looked to be more the artistic type than a jock. High school had probably been an unhappy experience for him.

He stood at the cash register, reading a copy of *Madame*

Bovary. Definitely a bookworm. When I put a soda on the counter, he looked up with a lazy smile. "Will that be all?"

I paid for the drink and opened it, taking a sip. "I've been hired to find Pleasant Smith."

He went deathly pale, not exactly what I'd expected. "I haven't seen her in a month," he almost whispered.

"Were you working here when she came in for some milk?"

He nodded, his hands shaking a little as he put the novel down on the counter.

"Can you tell me what happened while she was in the store? Maybe she said something that would indicate where she was headed."

"She was going home. She'd come to buy milk for her cousin, the baby her mama keeps."

"So she purchased the milk. Anything else?"

He thought for a minute. "No, she didn't buy anything else. She picked up some guitar strings I'd ordered for her."

"You'd ordered?"

He blushed a deep red. "She broke her D string, so I ordered a new set for her. As a present. She could really play that guitar. You should hear some of the songs she wrote. She's gonna be a star."

He lost all self-consciousness when he spoke of Pleasant's talent. The boy clearly cared for her, whether she knew it or not. "Did she get the strings?"

"Yeah." Glumness settled over his features. "She didn't get to use them, though. She disappeared. Her guitar is still at her mama's trailer."

"Where was her car found?"

"Abandoned on Highway 12. I told her not to trust

that old beater. She was a pretty good mechanic, when it came right down to it. She kept the piece of crap running, but it broke down all the time. She should've had a better car."

"How far from here?"

He pointed toward the farm road that disappeared into the distant vista of brown fields. "That's Highway 12, the quickest way back to Fodder Gin Road, so that's the way she went. Her cousin was hungry, and there wasn't any milk in the house. She barely had enough change to pay for the milk."

A young pregnant girl who'd spent her last change on a gallon of milk didn't register with me as a likely candidate to run away. "Tell me about Pleasant. You knew her."

"I did. She's a good girl. Somebody took her and they're still hanging on to her." His face pinched up in frustration. "She'd never have taken off like that. Not expecting a baby and all. She'd talked all her plans out with her mama and they'd figured out how Pleasant could catch up on her studies next semester. She had a great chance at getting a scholarship from Delta State. She wanted to study the music business. She would never have run out on her dream of being a songwriter and performer."

"Did you go to high school with her?"

He nodded slowly. "I did. She kept to herself. The other girls were jealous because she was so pretty and she had talent. She got the lead in the school plays when she tried out. The band director used some of her songs. She'd met this Nashville agent who was gonna make it happen for her." When he looked up at me, he was angry. "She wouldn't run out on all of that. She wouldn't run out on—" He broke it off and didn't continue.

"What's your name?" I asked.

"Frankie Graham."

I made a note and then asked. "The store here. It's called the Three Bs. Why?"

"Booze, bacon, and barbecue. The owners think those are the three necessities of life."

"Frankie, were you more than friends with Pleasant?" I'd be willing to bet he was in love with her.

His head dipped low. "I tried to take care of her. I helped her with the car and gave her my cell phone when she needed to make calls about her songs." He looked up. "I wanted to be more than that, but Pleasant had a ticket out of the poverty and the desperation all around her. She didn't need me hanging on and dragging her down."

The doors of the store burst open and two large men, red-faced with alcohol and bluster, pushed in.

"Well if it isn't Candyass Frankie." A tall blond boy with rippling muscles reached across me and picked up Frankie's book. "So you're reading about a madam. The whorehouse kind? That's the only piece of ass you'll ever get around here, Stringbean."

The other boy reached into the cooler and pulled out a six-pack of beer. He came to the counter. "Come have a beer with us, Frankie. We'll show you how to grow a pair." They looked at each other and laughed.

"Don't make the little wussy cry," the blond said.

Frankie rang up the beer without comment.

The bell on the door signaled another customer— this was a flurry of activity for a store stuck in the middle of nowhere. A pretty young girl sashayed past the two young men and put a twenty on the counter.

"Pump one," she said.

"Oh, baby, I'd like to give you my number one pump,"

the blond boy said. The other slapped his back, almost choking on laughter.

"Word around the high school is that your nozzle is so small I wouldn't feel it," the girl said with complete aplomb.

Bada-bing! If I'd had her self-assurance in high school, it would have been a less miserable experience. She prissed out the door, her perfect sun-streaked blond curls bouncing behind her.

The two boys went to the door to look out. In the moment of privacy, I asked Frankie, "Cheerleader?"

He nodded. "Her boyfriend will beat the snot out of these guys, and it wouldn't be a bad idea. They were tormenting Pleasant the last time she was in the store. She gave it right back to them."

I snapped a photo of each guy while they were busy guffawing and man-patting each other's backs for the bawdy comments. Frankie might not have been the last person to see Pleasant before she vanished.

"Hey, pencil dick," the beefy brunette said as he flicked a finger under Frankie's nose, "I don't have the money to pay for the beer. I'll bring it back. Later."

Frankie picked up the six-pack and put it under the counter. "That's against store rules."

"And you're gonna take my beer?" the young man asked.

"Yes." Frankie was scared but determined.

"You sure you want to try that?" The beefy boy reached into his pocket and brought out a switchblade. "I might gut you or I might slice your car tires."

"You can't have the beer. I'd have to pay for it and I don't have any money." Frankie wasn't brave, but he was fiscally responsible. He wasn't going into debt for beer.

"Weasel face, you'd better—"

I dialed 911 and when DeWayne answered, I spoke loudly. "Deputy Dattilo, there's a robbery in progress at Three Bs Grocery on Highway 12. Could you send several patrol cars, please? One suspect is brandishing a knife."

That was all it took. The two young men hit the door, leaving the beer. Tires smoked as they churned out of the lot.

"Sarah Booth! Sarah Booth!" DeWayne squawked at me. "I don't have jurisdiction in Bolivar County."

"I know," I said. "It was a scare tactic, and it worked. But those boys are headed east on Highway 12. They may dip into Sunflower County and they need to be picked up. They were in the store the day Pleasant went missing, and they're real macho assholes. I'd like for you or Coleman to question them. You know, as in really *question* them."

Neither Coleman nor DeWayne would slap a prisoner around, but if given the chance, I'd do it to those two.

"I'll be on the lookout, and I'll call Hoss."

"Good luck with that," I said. Hoss had not impressed me as a man of action.

"Coleman asked me to deliver a message, Sarah Booth."

"What's shakin'?"

"There was a triple homicide at Gokee Plantation."

That news was like a gut kick. "Not Hector and MaryBeth?" The Gokees had been friends of my parents. They were salt of the earth.

"No, no, the Gokees are just fine. Three unidentified males. They were shot execution-style in one of the farm sheds."

This wasn't good news. I'd only recently learned that

the private airstrips found on a lot of plantations had become part of drug and gun trafficking. The landowners were often ignorant of any activity. Isolated equipment and farm sheds tucked away in agricultural land that seldom saw traffic had become the perfect place for thugs to hide drugs and guns as they made their way to various distribution points.

"Those people are very dangerous. Is Coleman okay?"

"He's working with the Mississippi Bureau of Investigation, the feds, and Memphis officers who have a lead on Tennessee gang involvement. He's okay, Sarah Booth, just buried in work. We need more officers."

DeWayne wasn't kidding. Crime was hopping in Sunflower County, and Coleman was short staffed in the best of times. "I'll call him later."

"I'm headed your way. If I see those two clowns, I'll bring them in and soften them up for you."

"Thanks, DeWayne." He made me smile.

When I hung up, I found Frankie staring out the window at the empty landscape. "I keep believing her old junker of a car will pull up and she'll get out. I'll bet she's had the baby by now."

"What happened to her car?" I asked.

"I found it on the side of the road, fixed it, and drove it to her trailer. I'm sure it's still there. Charity can't make it run, and no one has the money to really get it fixed."

"Was there anything in the car that might indicate what happened to Pleasant?"

He shook his head. "The milk was still in the front seat. That's what was so strange. Like she got out of the car and started walking, leaving behind the very thing she'd come to buy."

"She wasn't walking." I had a clear picture of what

happened. "Someone picked her up. Someone who meant to keep her."

But who would abduct an eight-month pregnant teenager? And what had they done with her if they'd left the baby at Dahlia House?

"Frankie, do you know a man named Luther? He was asking about Pleasant yesterday."

"Pleasant knew a lot of guys. She was so pretty, and boys were always tagging along behind her. I don't recall that name."

"He gave Pleasant a ride to Delta State."

His eyebrows rose. "She wouldn't tell me who she was riding with. She let on like it was another girl."

"If you hear from Pleasant, call me." I gave Frankie a card. "Or if you think of anything else."

"I will." He didn't look hopeful. "You know, I should have closed the store and followed her home. I had a bad feeling. I did."

"Hindsight's twenty-twenty, Frankie. You can't think like that. If someone meant to grab her up, they would have gotten her on the way to school or somewhere else. Do you happen to know the name of her agent in the music business?"

"She told me, but it didn't register. I should have paid more attention." He began to tidy the counter in an effort to keep his hands busy.

"Who's the father of the baby? That could save me a lot of time, Frankie."

He looked totally miserable. "I don't know. I never asked. I didn't want to know."

"Sometimes the father of an unwanted child just wants to make it go away."

It was an ugly, dark thought to leave him with, but if

he knew anything, I had to force it out of him. "You said she used your phone to make some calls? May I see?"

He handed the phone over. "There's nothing there. She deleted all traces. I've already looked."

He spoke the truth. There were no Nashville numbers in the call log. Coleman could maybe send the phone off to a tech lab, if he found it necessary. I gave him the phone back. "Call me if you think of anything." And I was out the door. I'd head home along Highway 12, which ran straight through the cotton fields.

It was on a road much like this one that my parents died in a single-car accident. No one had been able to explain how it happened or why, and the brief conversation with Betty McGowin tugged at me. What had happened that long ago night?

I'd been orphaned at twelve, and my father's sister, Aunt Loulane, had moved to Dahlia House to raise me. She'd given up her life for six years—without complaint—to stay with me until I went to college. Who would do that for little Libby?

As the miles spun beneath my wheels, I felt a twinge of guilt that I hadn't mentioned the baby to Charity, who was her grandmother. But Charity Smith had her hands full with a teenage daughter and a niece to raise. And Libby was safe at Hilltop with Tinkie and Oscar and by now probably a postnatal care unit.

Libby was where she needed to be until we had facts instead of speculation.

Sweetie Pie and Pluto had been exceptionally well-behaved while I was in the store, and on the ride back Sweetie had been content to stick her head out the window and let the wind flap her ears. Pluto snuggled against my thigh. He didn't care for the cold wind.

"Home at last, Children of the Corn," I told the critters as I pulled into the driveway. I often referred to them as the demented children who killed all adults in the Stephen King classic. They seemed to like the reference.

My phone rang and I answered Doc Sawyer's call.

"Sarah Booth, you'd better come to the hospital."

"What's wrong?" I hated the way my heart leaped into my throat and my head filled with tragic thoughts. Was Coleman hurt? Had Libby contracted a virus? Was Tinkie okay? The worst images jumped into my head.

"DeWayne found a male in a 1998 black Ford pickup about two miles from the hospital. DeWayne was on the prowl for those two offensive young men you called him about, and he noticed that someone had run over the mailbox at the old Bickerman place. He checked it out and found the driver had parked behind the barn. He bled out sitting in his truck."

"What?" I wasn't certain why this involved me, but the idea that someone had bled to death was awful.

"I matched the victim's blood to the blood on your porch. It's Rudy Uxall."

"Who?" I asked. I'd never heard the name.

"Rudy Uxall. He'd been stabbed. That's why he was bleeding all over your front porch." Doc's voice held grief. "I could have saved him if he'd come to the hospital. It was a simple knife wound. I could have patched the artery and stitched him up."

"Why would he leave the baby with me, then drive to an abandoned farm and hide while he was bleeding to death? Why didn't he drive to the hospital? He was only a few miles away."

"The only thing I can think is that he didn't want people to know about the baby. Or he abducted Pleasant and this was his way of making amends. Either way, he won't be telling us anything now."

"Do you know anything about Rudy Uxall?"

"No, I don't. He's from Bolivar County, and his family doesn't seem to have much use for doctors. He's about twenty-four, and whoever stabbed him is responsible for his death. He was murdered."

A lot of things crossed my mind. Had Libby's mother stabbed Rudy? Was she even alive? There had been some kind of altercation, and Rudy was dead. Whoever was responsible, even if it was Pleasant Smith, could go to prison. And what would become of Libby?

The whole thing was a damn mess.

"Thanks, Doc. What does Coleman say?"

"He's out at the Gokee plantation with three dead gangbangers from Memphis. DeWayne's running the investigation on Rudy Uxall. The body is en route here for an autopsy." He paused briefly. "I'm worried about that baby, Sarah Booth."

"I'm worried about Tinkie."

Doc sighed. "You and me both. She's called me a dozen times today, wanting information." He hesitated. "Sarah Booth, she was asking if I thought she could produce milk for the child."

That took the wind out of my sails. It was one thing to care for the infant, and quite another to assume the maternal role of Guernsey Mama. Tinkie would never, in a million years, leak milk on her expensive wardrobe. This was serious.

"I'm not liking the sound of this, Doc."

"Sarah Booth, the baby is perfectly safe. Tinkie and Oscar, I'm not so sure. They're in love with that child."

And Doc didn't know the half of it. "I'll be in touch."

"You should go with DeWayne to check out the crime scene where Rudy bled out. You might learn something useful."

Doc wasn't a private investigator, but he had a good sense of what warranted investigation. "I'm on it."

The Bickerman farm was sad. There was no other way to describe it. The farmhouse, which had once been white clapboard, was a weathered gray with thick paint peels determinedly clinging to the wood. The front porch sagged, and the roof was on its last legs. Another good storm and it would cave in on the house.

I found DeWayne behind the old weathered barn beside a black Ford pickup. When I walked to the side of the truck, I could smell the blood. It was pooled in the seat and spilled onto the floorboard, leaking out the driver's door. Rudy Uxall had bled a lot. And why? Why hadn't he gone for help?

"I sent the body for an autopsy." DeWayne was photographing the scene.

"Doc told me."

"Just doesn't make any sense why someone would hide out here and bleed to death."

"Unless someone was chasing him." A completely new scenario played out in my mind. Somehow, Rudy had taken the baby and delivered her to me, but someone had tried to stop him. Who?

"Could be," DeWayne said. "I'll keep you posted on what I find."

"Has Coleman made any progress on the three murders at the Gokee place?"

"He'll fill you in, I'm sure."

DeWayne wasn't withholding information, he knew Coleman would be in touch when he had something to tell. I shared what I'd found about Pleasant and shot him a message with her photo. I had a call to make, and I needed to ask some friends for help. "I'll be at Dahlia House if you need me."

6

Rick Ralston was one of the best private investigators I knew, and Nashville's music scene was his home base. I made a call to Rick and hired him to check around the Music City on the hope that Pleasant was alive and well and plying her musical trade. That would be the best outcome, though I felt it was a long shot. After meeting Charity and Faith, I didn't view Pleasant as the kind of young woman who would have a baby, dump it, and take off to find fame and fortune.

Rick was a musician himself, and he had contacts in the underground world of those trying to break into the Nashville scene. He'd worked as a bouncer at the Bluebird Café, one of the premier locations for singer-songwriters to perform. If Pleasant's music was as good as her family and Frankie seemed to think, it was possible she'd been at the club.

When that was done, I called Tinkie to check on Libby. "How's the baby?"

"She's perfect. Oscar and I have figured out how to change diapers and get the formula at just the right temperature. You should see him when he holds her."

"I'll bet that's something to see." Oscar had refused to consider adopting. He'd also given Tinkie grief about Chablis, saying the dog was nothing more than a barking rodent. It sounded like his tune might be changing about a baby, just like it had about the pup.

"We have an appointment with the top surgeon for polydactyl removal at Boston Children's Hospital. The foot is such a fragile thing, Sarah Booth. If the surgery isn't done properly, it can result in trouble down the road."

"Tinkie, you may not have the baby tomorrow."

The long pause told me Tinkie's iron will had engaged. "Even if she isn't ours, Oscar and I have decided we want to provide the surgery for her."

They were two of the most generous people walking the planet. And they were going to get their hearts ripped out and crushed. I had to take action. Fast. "I'm calling Madame Tomeeka to host a séance tonight." I waited but Tinkie didn't respond. "We have to find the mother, Tinkie. Coleman can't let you keep the baby. He'll have to take her tomorrow. It's best if she goes home with her mother. Or her grandmother." I told her about Charity.

"I know you're right."

"Come over about six."

"Okay." She hesitated. "I'll bring the baby."

"Good. I'm sure Madame Tomeeka would love to meet her. How many outfits did you buy her?"

"I love shopping for her," she said in a forlorn tone. "At least she'll return home as a fashion icon."

"I expected no less." Tinkie, with her petite figure and big blue eyes, could make a flour sack look like Dior. She had presence and class, and she could definitely accessorize.

"I'll be there at six. I could bring some canapés?" she offered.

"Not to be rude, but who made them?"

"Cook." She laughed and it did my heart good.

"Then bring them. I still suffer nightmares when I think about those doggy treats you made. Holy cow. You had to apply for a toxic waste permit to dispose of them." Talk about a cooking disaster. They made Harold's impish little dog's eyes water, and Roscoe could eat anything and digest it.

"Six it is. And Sarah Booth, I will survive giving her back."

"I know." I didn't believe it for a minute, but she was trying. "I'll invite Harold tonight, too."

"What about Coleman?"

"He's got a triple homicide to contend with. Which is the only reason he hasn't been by to take Libby to Child Services."

"Then don't invite him. How about Scott? Maybe he could sing some lullabies to Libby. He should write a song for her."

"She's newborn. She shouldn't experience the blues until she's at least four months."

"You and your rules. See you soon."

I hesitated about Scott, but in the end I called. He couldn't stay long, but he'd work with us for a while before he had to get back to his blues club, Playin' the Bones.

I'd barely hung up the phone when I heard the *rat-a-tat-tat* of a machine gun coming from the kitchen. Panic made me duck behind my desk. Gertrude Strom had found me, and she was heavily armed. My gun was still in the trunk of my car. I duckwalked to the window and looked out. I might make it out to the car and retrieve the pistol, but a handgun wasn't really adequate for a shootout with a machine gun.

And where had Gertrude gotten a machine gun?

That's when I noticed Sweetie Pie snoozing against the wall. Pluto had piled into Tinkie's chair, no doubt with the intention of leaving black hair everywhere so Tinkie could throw a fit when she stood up sporting a hairy butt.

If the critters were calm with bullets blasting everywhere, something was amiss. Like Jitty. I threw caution to the wind and sailed toward the kitchen. When I pushed the door open I found a stout woman with the blackest eyebrows and a very unattractive haircut. She wielded a machine gun, spraying bullets over the room. Thank goodness ghostly bullets didn't break all my dishes.

"Jitty, dammit, stop that right now. What is wrong with you?"

"I set an example for my boys and they lived up to it. Never underestimate the power a good mother has."

"Put that damn gun down! Now!"

"Nobody talks to Ma Barker like that. Herman, Doc, take her out!" She waved at the window and fool that I was, I ran toward it to check the backyard, thinking additional gunmen were on the way.

"There's no one there."

She lowered her machine gun and blew on the end of it. "Just goes to show when you raise your boys to be outlaws, you can't expect 'em to come when you call."

I knew her then, the notorious Arizona Donnie Clark, aka Ma "Kate" Barker. She'd died a bloody death in Ocklawaha, Florida, with her young son Fred at her side. This after a violent crime spree that netted more than three million dollars in ill-gotten gains. And yet it wasn't enough. In 1930s money, that would have been tens of millions. Once the Barkers gave themselves over to crime, they couldn't stop.

"And that is my point exactly." The ferocious expression faded and the matronly figure slimmed to my ever-slender haint. "Without a proper mama, Libby could grow up to be a criminal. I think you and Tinkie should file for joint custody."

"Libby has a mother and a grandmother. Just because they're poor doesn't mean they aren't loving and wonderful guardians."

"Poor ain't nothin'." Jitty was indignant. "Miss Alice raised her brood, with my help, when we ate turnip greens and cornmeal mush three meals a day for weeks at a time. Lord, if we saw a potato we thought we were the luckiest folks in the area. We were poor, but that didn't mean Alice let her young'uns get away with anything."

I'd heard the stories of how my many-greats-grandmother, Alice Delaney, had survived widowhood, the death of a child, and so much more during the horrors of the Civil War and Reconstruction. The truth was, I never tired of hearing them. Jitty brought the past to life.

"What would Grandma Alice do about Libby?" I primed the pump.

"She'd take that baby and run with her, if that's what it took to keep her safe."

"Charity Smith's isn't an unsafe home." I had to make

that point clear. Charity seemed to love her children and niece as much as any mother could. Her circumstances were harsh, but I'd been raised believing that money wasn't the first thing a child needed—love was. "She's going to love that baby, Jitty. We can't steal her."

"Yes, you can." She morphed back into her Ma Barker persona.

Jitty had prodded me to do some outlandish—and criminal—things. But stealing a baby wasn't her normal mode of operation. Unless she knew something I didn't know.

"Is Pleasant dead?" I hated to even ask.

"You know I can't give away the secrets of the Great Beyond."

I watched her closely. She was hedging her answer— because she knew the mother was alive. "She's alive. If you know where she is, you'd better spill it. She deserves to know her baby is safe."

"What if she doesn't care?"

"I don't think that's the case, Jitty. I think Rudy Uxall stole Libby. Now why he did such a thing, only to leave the baby on my doorstep, I can't answer. But I'm going to find out. That's one thing I promise you. And if Pleasant doesn't want her child, maybe she will let Tinkie and Oscar adopt her."

"What about you? You found her."

Jitty had baby fever worse than Tinkie. "She's a baby, not a cookie. It isn't finders keepers. Tinkie and Oscar can give the baby things I can't. They've made an appointment for her at Boston Children's Hospital. That's way out of my reach."

"Who are you trying to convince, me or yourself?"

Jitty was wise beyond her years—and she was old. "I'm a single person with a job that requires long absences. Tinkie and Oscar can afford a private nanny or whatever Libby needs."

"And what about love? Who can give that the best?"

The question stopped me, because it was one that needed an answer. "I don't think Tinkie can love her better than I can. Love can't be quantified that way. I think Tinkie will choose to make the time to love her." I squared my shoulders. "I don't know that I'm ready to make that sacrifice yet. Libby deserves someone who is ready."

I almost cringed, expecting the barrage of recriminations Jitty was sure to fire off. From the first day I'd come home to Dahlia House, she'd been all over my ass to get pregnant and have an heir. Libby wasn't my flesh and blood, but if she was adopted, she'd be the legal heir. There would be Delaneys to reside in Dahlia House for the future.

"Your mama said the same thing when she got pregnant, Sarah Booth." Jitty had grown pensive, and the Ma Barker persona was again replaced with the mocha-tinted beauty of my haint. "I remember when she told your daddy she was pregnant. She worried that she wouldn't have the focus to be a good mother. She wanted to accomplish things, to fight for justice, to organize literacy groups, and if she were alive right now, she'd be fighting against the corporate chemical companies that spray poison over the cotton. But when push came to shove, she chose you."

I'd never doubted the love my parents had shown me. One of the bitterest realities of life was summed up in one of Aunt Loulane's old adages—you can't miss what you've never had. And I had had that rarest of things, complete and unconditional love. And, boy, did I miss it.

"Why didn't they have another child?"

"I don't know. It would have been easier for you— their death—if you'd had a brother or sister to share the sorrow. Loulane was a godsend and a remarkable woman, but she was an older generation. Young grief is the most intense and the most damaging. As we age we learn to handle loss with more ease, because we've accepted the process. We are born to die. But to a young person, that kind of death is like being skinned alive."

Jitty was far wiser than even I'd suspected. "I wish I'd had a sister."

"Aunt Loulane would have been institutionalized." The pity party was over. Jitty was back on track, reminding me that I could be a pain in the butt. "Two children as headstrong as you, it would have put her in the hospital."

"Maybe I would have been the evil one and the other would be the good sister."

"Not a chance. Your mama encouraged you to be independent and to get things done. That combination always leads to a willful, determined child. A sibling would have been no different. But just know that you were chosen. You were wanted from the moment of conception. Libby and James Franklin could have done things differently, but they didn't. You were their heart the moment you entered the world."

"I want that for little Libby, too. I don't know that I'm ready to give it. Maybe I'm afraid to love with all of my heart again."

"You won't have a choice, Sarah Booth. When the time is right, you'll fall in love again. Whether it's a man or a child, it will be out of your control, and it will happen."

Jitty didn't predict the future, but I didn't doubt her words. "Thank you."

"Even if Tinkie keeps that baby, it'll get your maternal juices working. I say by New Year's, you'll be searching for a mate. The only thing you'll have in mind is flinging him down on that big four poster and riding him like a wild monkey in the circus."

"Jitty!" The image she gave me was shocking—coming from her. But it shouldn't have been. In her day, I'll bet Jitty sashayed around the men and drove them nuts until she settled on Coker, the man who stole her heart and lost his life with my great-great-great-grandfather on a blood-soaked battlefield.

"Don't you Jitty me! I'm privy to some of your thoughts, Missy. The things you do with that lawman and his cuffs! And Scott Hampton, I get goose bumps thinking about those fantasies. You'd like that man to run your frets!"

"Stop it!" It was extremely unfair that Jitty could read my mind and invade my personal fantasies. "This is too much, Jitty. You've crossed a line. You cannot bore into my head like a Japanese beetle into a pine."

"I always knew you were a blockhead." She was way too pleased with that jab.

"I mean it, Jitty. I can't do this. If you're able to read my most private thoughts, that leaves me nowhere to go." I was truly upset. "I don't mind you poking and prodding me to get laid or procreate or snatch up some lusty sperm before my eggs decay. I can take that. I can even put up with your constant sexual advice. But you cannot get into my fantasies."

At last her grin slipped away. "You're really mad, aren't you?"

"I am. I have to have some privacy. Even from you."

"What if I told you I couldn't read your thoughts?"

"Then how did you know about Coleman and Scott?"

The grin returned, lighting up her entire face. "What if I told you I was a mighty good guesser and that any woman who wasn't dead below the waist would be thinking exactly those same thoughts."

I had her. Joy of joys, at last. "So that's what *you* would like to do with Coleman and Scott?"

"And what if it is?" She was almost aglow with mischief. "Maybe when the moment comes I'll whisper a little inspiration in your ear."

"You stay out of my bed *and* my head! I can manage very well on my own."

"The proof of that is in the puddin', as your aunt Loulane would say."

It was time to end this conversation. When Jitty was quoting Aunt Loulane to me, my wisest course of action was to cut and run.

"Madame Tomeeka is coming over here to have a séance tonight. Maybe she can find Pleasant Smith. I want you to stay clear. No funny business, no knocking or clapping or fluttering of curtains. Tammy already suspects you're here."

"Would it be such a terrible thing if she knew?"

"I don't know. What if you disappear if others know about you?"

She eyed me with calculation. "You care. You don't want me to leave."

"Sad as it is, you are my family, Jitty. I don't know what I'd do if you disappeared, too."

She nodded and slowly began to fade. "I'll be back," she whispered in a thick Schwarzenegger-style accent. And she was gone.

7

Millie arrived first with trays of hot chicken potpies from the café. She was the best cook in ten states. Since I'd returned home, she made a point of dropping by with delicious dishes, and she always brought enough for Sweetie.

I'd made my famous pimento cheese spread and put it on celery stalks and crackers. I also had wine ready for the after-séance social. First, though, I wanted to see if Madame Tomeeka could get a line on Pleasant. She was going to ask the spirits for help locating the teen. We were also scrying for the missing girl with a crystal and a map. Cece was bringing a large map of the area, including Nashville and New Orleans, another hot music scene. If we were lucky, the crystal, when suspended over the map on a silver chain, would be drawn to Pleasant's location.

My guests arrived, and Libby, dressed in a leopard print onesie with matching booties, was the object of adoration. She wore a black bow in the sheaf of red hair that crowned her little head. I'd never seen a baby with such a head of hair, but as Jitty would quickly point out, I didn't have a lot of experience with infants. Much oohing and aahing ensued as everyone held the baby. I had to admit that Libby handled the strangers and attention with joy. She cooed and grinned, and each little sound or movement brought her adult audience to our knees. One seven-pound baby had slain a room full of very tough adults.

By six o'clock, we were seated around the tiger oak table in the music room. My mother had used it for cards and board games when I was a child, and it was perfect for the gathering with Cece, Millie, Harold, Tinkie, and Scott. Oscar had opted to keep the baby in the den so he could watch a football game.

Tammy went over the rules of the séance. We were to hold hands, not break contact no matter what happened, and to remain silent at all times. "Our only goal is to find Pleasant Smith," she said. "If the spirits will help us in this endeavor, we'll be forever grateful."

I half expected Jitty to pop up and make life difficult for me, but she didn't. I didn't hear so much as the jangle of her silver bracelets or the ruffle of the curtains at the window.

I watched the faces of my closest friends as they concentrated to help me find a missing girl. How many people could say they had such loyal supporters. I felt someone's gaze and discovered Harold staring at me. He gave a long wink. Someone's foot nudged mine under the table. Scott cut me a look. I nudged him back and then moved my leg. Playing footsie with the sexy blues guitarist might be a lot of fun, but our goal was to find Pleasant Smith and I couldn't allow a distraction.

I'd lit a series of candles in a circle in the center of the table, and as Tammy asked for spirit guidance, the candles guttered, as if a sudden wind had disturbed their flame.

"Sarah Booth, who is in this house with you?"

For a moment I was speechless. "Uh, no one. Who would be here? Just the critters."

Tammy opened her eyes and captured me in a steady examination. "You have a spirit here, someone who is watching over you. You're protected. Your mother has seen to that."

"If dead folks can watch over someone, then I'm sure Mama and Daddy are looking out for me." I hated lying to Tammy and all of my friends, but Jitty was someone I couldn't share. What if once I exposed her, she disappeared? Then I would be all alone.

Tammy only chuckled. "One day, you'll tell me who is here. She's so strong, I know you're aware of her. Until then, let's find that baby's mama."

Every person around the table watched the scene with curiosity. How many of my friends had sensed Jitty? Tinkie, for sure. Cece, probably. But now wasn't the time. "Absolutely, let's dive in. Libby's mother is our first priority."

Tammy closed her eyes and inhaled. For several long moments, there was only the sound of our breathing. The sense that someone else had joined us came over me, and I knew it wasn't Jitty.

"Rochelle," Tammy said. "Thank you for coming to assist us. We're seeking a young mother. She may be in serious trouble."

Tammy nodded as if she were agreeing with something. I looked around the table to see everyone spellbound, perfectly still.

"Rochelle is a spirit I work with often," Tammy said. Her eyes were closed and her voice had little inflection. Had I not known that she'd entered a trance state, I would have called Doc Sawyer on the spot. "She heard my request. She doesn't know anything about Pleasant, or how to find her, but she will see if there is help for us on the other side."

I wondered—if Tammy could contact a spirit like Rochelle, could she also contact Jitty, if she chose? Did Rochelle have to make herself available?

"Help me, please." The voice that came from Tammy's body was that of a terrified girl.

Every hair on my body stood on end.

"My baby. My baby. Help me. He's going to kill me." The young woman sobbed as she spoke.

Tammy started forward and gulped down air. "Thank you, Rochelle." She inhaled deeply again.

"Is the baby's mother dead?" Tinkie asked. "You can only call spirits at a séance. So is she dead?"

Tammy shook her head. "The vision was a gift from Rochelle. She is a protector of young women and children. I can only tell you what I saw. The young woman looked out a very dirty window. She put her hands to the glass and left bloody prints. I could feel her emotions. She's terrified. She is all alone, but she is very much alive. She has the sense that time is running out for her, though."

"Where is she?" Scott and Harold asked.

Tammy only shook her head. "Woods all around. It could be anywhere in the area, or it could be a million other places. She was bundled up, so she is cold. Let me try to connect with anyone who can give more specific information."

She went through the ritual of quieting herself again. When her posture shifted and her head dropped back, I knew she'd connected.

"I have a young man here," Tammy said, and her voice and posture changed, though she never left the chair. "He's confused and lost. He hasn't accepted that Death has taken him."

The hairs on my arms began to tingle.

"He doesn't remember his name, but he has a message. He's saying 'baby' something. 'Baby girl.' He's showing me a symbol. Milk. It's a gallon of milk."

My body tensed, I couldn't help it.

"He's fading in and out, and I can't understand him because he's so disoriented, but he has something urgent he needs to share." Tammy struggled, her brow furrowed. "I see water. Still water. Cypress knees. Green, green, green." She ducked her head as if to escape something. "So much green. Help her."

She snapped out of the trance. "I'm sorry, he's gone." She tilted, almost falling out of the chair, but Scott caught her and steadied her. "Could I have some water?"

Tinkie, choking back a sob, jumped up and went to the kitchen. Tammy reached over and touched my hand. "I'm sorry I couldn't be more specific."

"It's okay, I think I understood some of it." We were all acutely aware of Tinkie's distress. "Pleasant had gone to buy a gallon of milk when she disappeared. I think she's alive, maybe living somewhere tropical. Somewhere with lots of green plants and leaves."

Tammy gave me a nod of approval. "Those are the images I got. A place lush and isolated."

"She not only abandoned a baby, she left a budding music career," I said, telling them about Pleasant's song-writing and acquisition of a Nashville agent to represent her work. "If she's alive and surrounded by woods and green, I don't think she's there voluntarily." The case had suddenly taken on a much more dangerous hue.

"I agree," Scott said. "Do you think the young man trying to communicate with us was Rudy Uxall, the young man who bled to death? He did leave the baby on the porch. Maybe he was trying to save her."

"From what?" Tinkie put a glass of ice water in front of Tammy.

"There was danger," Tammy said. "The young man couldn't explain it. He simply was too confused. He's not even certain he's dead. His perception of everything is skewed, but Scott could be right. There was a sense of urgency in his agitation that had nothing to do with his situation."

Rudy Uxall was a good lead, and one I would follow up on in the morning. I hadn't gotten a definitive answer, but I'd been prodded in a direction. That was the best any private investigator could ask for.

"Let's adjourn and get some food," I suggested. The scrying session would have to wait until another time. Tammy's unsteadiness concerned me. The session had drained her of energy.

Tinkie shot up out of the room and rushed to find Oscar and the baby as if she were afraid they'd vanish into thin air.

Scott, who'd remained unusually silent during the evening, came up behind me and rubbed my shoulders with strong fingers. I sighed in relief.

"You've got more knots than a sailors' rope-tying class," he said, digging deep into the muscle. "If I had half a day, I could work them out."

My shoulders had just begun to relax when Cece sidled over to us. "That's not the thing about Sarah Booth that needs working out. In my expert opinion, she is desperate for a good man to jerk the kinks out of her."

"Cece! Just because you're happy with Jaytee doesn't mean you can diagnose what I need."

"Oh, baby girl, everyone in town has diagnosed what you need." She laughed, and Scott joined in.

"I'd be happy to volunteer, Sarah Booth. My contribution to your . . . health."

"Don't gang up on me," I warned them.

Cece ran a perfectly manicured hand through my short, short hair. "I prefer your long curls, but this isn't so bad. Tinkie's hairdresser did an amazing job with that burned-up thatch you had on your head."

"Yes, she did."

Scott rumpled my hair, too. "It'll grow back. And I still owe you, Sarah Booth. You risked your life and saved the club from burning to the ground."

"Yes, she's brave about everything except love," Cece said. "Tammy, any predictions for when Miss Delaney might take a trip to the wedding chapel?"

"I don't have any insight into that," Tammy said.

"You leave Sarah Booth alone." At least Millie came

to my defense. "It takes time to heal a heart. Give her a chance to get her balance back."

"Sarah Booth isn't a girl, she's a grown woman. She'll find her way," Harold said. "She knows we all have her best interest at heart."

"I'm not talking about a career move," Cece said, hands on hips. "I just think she ought to get laid. Makes life so much more enjoyable!"

"Enough!" I held up both hands. "Please. I feel like a pot roast at a table of starving people."

"Sarah Booth is right." Millie patted Scott's arm and winked at Harold. "I know it's hard to wait, but pushing a woman into a relationship never works." She looked around to be sure my partner wasn't in the room. "It's Tinkie I'm really worried about."

"Dah-link, I'm thinking the same thing." Cece faced me. "You have a problem on your hands."

I couldn't even pretend I didn't know what she was talking about. "I don't know what to do. That baby, overnight, is her and Oscar's world."

All merriment fled Cece's face. "When you find that baby mama, there's going to be hell to pay."

"I know."

"I'll give Coleman a call," Cece offered. "Maybe it would be best if he took the infant to Child Services sooner rather than later."

"No!" I didn't mean to sound so emphatic. "Tinkie has her because that's what's best for the baby. Pulling her away now won't keep Tinkie and Oscar from getting hurt, but putting Libby into the system might be damaging. We're in this. We'll just have to keep on course to the bitter end."

8

I wasn't the type to suffer prophetic dreams, but the conversation with Cece must have lodged deep in my subconscious because I spent the night chasing after little Libby, who had suddenly grown into a baby with Olympic track abilities. She crawled faster than I could run. I chased her over the river and through the woods, while she scooted about like a nymph from Greek mythology.

In the background of the dream, Tinkie searched for the baby, calling to her in a plaintive voice. She sounded like a lost soul.

I woke up at daybreak, exhausted. I had to find Pleasant Smith—for Libby's sake and for my partner. And I had to find out who'd stabbed Rudy Uxall. He was my best lead.

First on my agenda was Rudy. I called DeWayne, who filled me in on his investigation into the young man's death. Uxall had been stabbed in the thigh. The blade had nicked the femoral artery, and medical care could have saved his life.

"An inch to the left and it would have been a muscle injury and Uxall would be alive," DeWayne said. "If he'd gone to the hospital, he'd be alive. I found out something else, too. Rudy got into a fight with a muscular blond man about a month ago at the Waystation Bar on the Bolivar County line. The fight was about a pregnant woman who'd been playing and singing in the bar."

"How'd you find this out?"

"I tracked down Rudy's family. Hoss Kincaid had to break the bad news to them about Rudy's death. He said one of the Uxall brothers told him Rudy had been in a fight with an ex-con."

"Name?"

"He didn't know. But the brother, Alfred Uxall, said the fight was about a pregnant singer. It has to be Pleasant. Alfred denied knowing anything about Pleasant or how Rudy was involved with her."

"Thanks, DeWayne."

"How's Coleman's case going?" I missed Coleman. I'd become spoiled by having him as a sounding board.

"He hopped a private plane to Memphis this morning at six. Should be back by two. He's with the three bodies, waiting for the autopsy. He's worried, Sarah Booth. This kind of element in Sunflower County is more than we can manage. Even with help from the state investigators and the highway patrol, we can't cover the land area we need to patrol."

"Watch Coleman's back," I requested.

"Will do."

DeWayne gave me Rudy's address, which turned out to be not too far from the road where Charity Smith lived. Although it was in Bolivar County, I went anyway. Hoss Kincaid would just have to get over himself.

When I pulled up in the yard, I knew I'd made a mistake. Rudy's kin had gathered to wake his death. They were a burly group of four large men and the fiercely unhappy glare they sent my way should have warned me off. I couldn't let it.

A big man, at least six-foot-six, came toward the car. "We're not interested in talking with anyone," he said. "You can leave the same way you came in."

I introduced myself and got a long glare for my troubles.

"Maybe you didn't hear me," he said. "Get back in your car and leave."

"I've been hired to find a young woman who recently gave birth to a child. Rudy has been linked to the baby. You can either talk to me or talk to the sheriff in Rosedale." I hated to be blunt to a grieving family, but sometimes kindness wasn't the ticket. I was working against a ticking clock, in more ways than one. "What's your name?"

"It's none of your business, but my name is Alfred. Rudy didn't have nothin' to do with a baby, and even if he did, he's dead now and can't pay child support."

I inhaled slowly to keep my temper in check. "I didn't say he was the father."

"You said linked. What else could that mean?"

"I don't know what his relationship with the mother of the child might be, but I need to find her. Now. It's urgent."

Maybe he realized I wasn't going away and it would be simpler to answer my questions than to fight about it. "What is it you want?" He waved the other men to the front porch of the house where they gathered in a clump to watch me as if I might turn into a dragon.

"Do you know this woman?" I showed him the photo of Pleasant on my phone.

"She lives around here, but she disappeared, like four weeks ago."

At least he didn't deny knowing her. "Have you seen her?"

"Last I saw her she was broke down on the side of the road on Highway 12. I was headed to the tire shop over near Clarksdale."

"She was alone on the side of the road?" I wanted to add, *and you just drove by,* but I didn't. Once upon a time a man would never leave a woman—especially a pregnant woman—stranded on the roadside. He'd stop and fix the car or see to it that she was driven to safety.

"She was sittin' on the hood of her car. I would've stopped, but I had to get a tire for my boss and have it ready. If the tire shop closed before I got there, I'd have lost my job."

"How well did Rudy know this young woman?"

He considered. "They were friends. I've seen 'em talkin'. Not sweethearts. Nothin' like that. Rudy said she was nice to him." He shrugged. "End of story."

"Not quite. Rudy had Pleasant's newborn infant daughter."

The big man tilted his head back. "Rudy had her baby? What for?"

I wanted to knock his brain into gear with the flat of my hand. "That's what I need to find out. Why would

Rudy have Pleasant's newborn daughter? Why would he drop her off at someone's house, and then drive to an abandoned farm instead of going to the hospital? He was wounded and he knew it."

"You're asking me to explain Rudy. No one here can do that. I told that deputy who came asking that Rudy got into a fight over a month ago with some character. All I know is Rudy tied up with the guy and it was over Pleasant. I don't know the particulars." He pointed to a woman who came out the screen door of the house and stood staring at us. She wore a navy dress with white dots in a fashion that made me think of another era. "That's Rudy's ma, and she couldn't' tell you why he did half the things he did."

"Pleasant Smith may be in trouble. Serious trouble. Her life could very well be in danger." More likely she was dead, but I didn't say that. "Rudy may have been the last person to see her alive. Do you know where he was Tuesday night?"

"Rudy don't live here most of the time, but you can ask Ma if you're bold enough to do it."

I only rolled my eyes and walked past him to where Mrs. Uxall stood at the edge of the porch. She was a tall, stout woman dressed in her Sunday best to attend to the funeral details of her son. I wasn't oblivious to the situation.

"Mrs. Uxall, I'm sorry for your loss." I started to introduce myself.

"Get off our land," she said. "You got no call snoopin' here. Rudy was a good boy, and today I got to make arrangements to put him in the ground. I don't need nothin' you're wantin' to say unless it's to tell me who murdered my boy."

"I don't know who stabbed Rudy, but I'm looking into it. He's very much a part of my case, which involves a young woman whose life hangs in the balance." I explained the situation to her.

She shook her head. "Rudy wasn't always smart, but he was never mean. He couldn't hurt anything. He couldn't chop off a chicken's head if he was starvin' to death, so don't go tryin' to say he hurt a girl and took her baby."

Mrs. Uxall wouldn't be the first mother who had blind spots for the criminal inclinations of her son. "I'm not saying anything about Rudy. Don't forget your son was stabbed, and maybe by the same people who took Pleasant. I'd think you'd want justice."

"You think that missing girl was the reason someone killed my boy?"

"It's possible. He may have been trying to help her. Look, I need to find Pleasant. If she just had the baby, she may need medical attention. Time is critical. Don't you think she should be reunited with her child?"

She thought a minute, and her face softened. "If Rudy took that baby, he had a good reason to do it. He didn't confide in me, but he set a store by that girl. He was a friend to Pleasant, and he told me she could sing like an angel. He said she was gonna be famous, and when she was, she'd hire him to be her security. If he was fighting about Pleasant, it was because he thought someone meant her harm."

"Back when she disappeared, do you remember anything Rudy might have said? Maybe he was trying to help her. Maybe he said something that would help us locate her."

The others had slowly drawn closer to us as we talked. They were big people—tall and broad shouldered. If

Rudy took after them, he would have been a good body-guard for Pleasant. If he had been trying to help her, then he had been stabbed for his efforts.

"I didn't see Rudy much after Pleasant disappeared." Mrs. Uxall pondered that statement for a moment. "He said he was movin' in with friends, but he didn't give no details."

"Your other son," I indicated the man I'd talked with, "saw her broken down on the road."

She whirled on Alfred with a speed that astounded me. The next thing I knew she was beating him on the head with her purse. "You passed a pregnant girl on the road and didn't help her. What did I teach you?"

He ran through his excuses about picking up a tire, but she was having none of that. "I'll deal with you when we get back from the funeral home." She faced me again. "That's all I know. If I think of anything, I'll call. Rudy wouldn't hurt Pleasant or her baby. If he had the infant, it was because she gave her to him. That much you can take to the bank. Now I gotta go." She brushed past me and went to the car, her other sons following.

While I was in the area, I decided to stop by Cotton Gin High School. I wanted to talk to the band director and some of Pleasant's friends. If she'd run away, surely a classmate would know. If she hadn't gone of her own free will, maybe some of her friends could tell me who had shown an interest in her in the last few months.

Built in the 1960s, the high school followed the archi-tectural design of a chicken hatchery—a long, low, flat building with windows that could be pushed out at an angle. The school had been built in the days before central air, and window units hung off the building like ticks on a dog. Everything reeked of poverty. Cotton Gin High School had been erected and then left to slowly decay from lack of funding. It was a sad place, with an open field parking lot for the students and a faculty lot, with one visitor parking spot, near the front door.

When I stepped inside, the deteriorating conditions were forgotten as the sounds and smell of high school assaulted me. Young girls clustered at lockers to giggle and stare after the boys who paraded down the hall like peacocks.

The different cliques, almost identical to the ones in existence during my high school years, were easily distinguished. The cool girls—those without acne and with glossy hair and slender thighs—giggled and practiced cheers halfway down the hall. The geek kids were buried in lockers, sorting through a mountain of books. The jocks squeaked down the hallway in athletic shoes. Twenty years had passed, but nothing had really changed. Except I felt terribly old. The fresh-faced students, many self-conscious and the rare few who exuded security and determination, were my past. How had so much time slipped by me?

"You lost?" a very tall young man asked.

"I need to speak with the principal."

"Down the hall, to the right." He rearranged his backpack and continued to his next class.

I followed him, stopping at the door of a large glass office where several women worked at desks. The principal's office. Oh, I'd been here before, and always because I was in trouble. Funny how guilt oozed from me just because of the proximity. I pushed the past away and stepped into the reception area.

"Can I help you?" a pretty brunette asked.

"I need to see Mr. Bryant." I gave my name but didn't show my PI badge. A minute later I was seated across the desk from the principal.

R. B. Bryant had twenty years heading one of the poorest schools in the nation under his belt. He wasn't a man who wielded his authority with a swagger. He was soft spoken and friendly. When I explained what I wanted, he offered his full cooperation.

"Pleasant Smith was an extraordinary young lady," he said. He leaned back in his chair, the springs squeaking. "The whole school was buzzing about her music, and I have to say she seemed to write songs with a great maturity. She had a shot to escape the poverty here, and I had hopes she'd bring resources back to Bolivar County."

"She was a good student?"

"Exceptional. We have some very bright students here at Cotton Gin High, but sometimes brains aren't enough to escape the quicksand of environment."

His words struck a chord with me. "Pleasant could have made it, couldn't she?"

"She could have. It was almost a done deal, from what I know. Scholarships for the plucking, interest from an agent in Nashville. Someone with Pleasant's talents, getting a degree from Delta State University right here in Cleveland, and then rocketing to fame—it would put us on the map. And it would give the kids here an example, show them it could be done. Unless you've seen success firsthand, it's hard to conceive. So many of my students come from generations of dire poverty. They can't imagine a different life."

"What do you think happened to Pleasant?"

He leaned back in his chair and stared out the window.

"I've thought about this every day since she disappeared. She took the pregnancy in stride, and to my knowledge, she never revealed the name of the baby's father. That takes a lot of grit for a young girl to pick up a burden like that and carry through by herself. She had responsibilities taking care of children at home, but other than those days, she didn't miss school, until she disappeared. Someone had to take her. I just hope she's still alive. That baby should be due any day."

It was clear Principal Bryant cared about the students in his charge. Law and order took a second place to compassion. "Did Pleasant ever talk about the future?"

"She planned to make it in Nashville and come back here to open a music studio. She wanted to record the next generation of Mississippi blues players. She said she wanted to talk to that new club owner over in Zinnia when he got his club going."

Scott. She had meant to talk to Scott. It didn't sound as if Pleasant had abandoned all of her dreams voluntarily. "Pleasant had an appointment with a music agent, do you happen to know who it was?"

"Tally McNair, the band director, could probably answer that. She and Pleasant were close."

"I realize Pleasant never said, but do you have any idea who the father of her child might be?"

Bryant leaned forward, the chair squeaking again. "It's a puzzle. She never showed any interest in the boys at school. As far as I know, she never had a date. She was totally focused on her music and getting a scholarship to DSU. Of course, she's a young woman, and no number of rules and restrictions can counteract youthful impulse. But Pleasant thought things through." He frowned and looked down at his hands for a moment. "I wondered if she'd been raped. Her family situation isn't the best. That trailer park has some rough customers."

"I'll check that possibility out." If Pleasant had carried her rapist's child, it wasn't inconceivable that the man had decided to shut her up before she could sue him for support, or worse, send him to jail. The bad thing about this case was that almost anything was possible, based on the evidence I'd gathered to date. Which wasn't much. And time was running out. Coleman couldn't wait much longer to take official action. He had to uphold the law, and he'd already cut me as wide a margin as possible.

The principal telephoned the secretary in the outer office, instructing band director Tally McNair to come to the main office. "There's a teacher's lounge next door. You can talk in there."

"Thank you."

"I hope you find Pleasant and her baby and they're both okay. She worked hard to make some opportunities for herself. My gut tells me something terrible has happened to her, but I hope I'm wrong."

"Me, too," I said before I shut the door and waited in the hallway for the band director to arrive. When she turned the corner and came toward me, I was surprised to see a young woman who might have passed for one of the high school students. Tall and slender, Tally wore her dark hair pulled back in a ponytail that swung with her animated walk.

I introduced myself and we stepped into the empty teacher's lounge. "I can't be away from my class for long," she said. "What can I do for you?"

I explained who I was and what I wanted, and her eyes filled with tears. "Oh, god, can you find her?" She gripped my hand. "You have to find her."

"I'm doing my best. Who was the agent Pleasant was planning on meeting?"

Tally's face fell. "She never told me. She was so secretive about that whole Nashville agent thing because she didn't want the deal to fall through and then to face the ridicule from the students. They were hard on Pleasant. Some of them were downright cruel."

"Because of her finger?"

Tally's laughter was deep and easy. "The finger was the tip of the iceberg, though it was a real showstopper when she played the guitar. She'd learned to use it, believe it or not."

I could only imagine how an extra digit might come in handy. "So what was it?"

"Where she lived, the extreme poverty. Mean girls sense a person's weakness, and that was Pleasant's weak spot. She was defensive about her economic circumstances, and she wore it on her sleeve. A certain clique of girls realized that and tormented her. I told Pleasant they were merely jealous of her talent, but words don't salve a wound to the heart."

"True. What's strange to me is that Pleasant simply disappeared, and no one in authority pushed Sheriff Kincaid to look for her."

"I did, for the first two weeks. Then it was so hopeless." Tally brushed a tear from her cheek. "A lot of girls simply stop coming to school. It's too hard. They have responsibilities at home. Pleasant was pregnant. Maybe I wanted to believe that she'd gone to Nashville to pursue her dream."

"Who did Pleasant hang out with?"

"She was a loner, mostly."

"I need some names. The girls who were her friends and her tormenters." I held the pen poised at my pad.

"I'm not sure I should give names." Tally rubbed the tips of her thumbnails against her forefingers in an unconscious gesture of nervousness. "Things are so regulated in school now. I don't mind telling you, but it could get me fired."

I understood her predicament. If I were a law officer, she'd have no choice but to tell. But she owed nothing to a PI, so her allegiance was to job. Understandable. "Can you give me the name of a student who would know their names and might help me?"

Tally fidgeted more.

"You want to help Pleasant, right?"

She nodded.

"If you won't tell me the names of the mean girls, tell me someone who will."

"Marcia Colburn, but please don't say I gave you her name."

"I won't. Now, before I go, tell me about Pleasant's songs. What were they like?" I'd heard the one ballad that Faith had been playing in the trailer park. It was a haunting melody with lyrics that seemed too mature for a high schooler to have written, but as I got to know more about Pleasant, I realized she'd packed a lot of life into her seventeen years.

"Pleasant was able to blend folk and blues in a unique way. She wrote about things people of all ages feel. Love, loss, the desire for revenge, hopelessness, though she wasn't one of those so-serious people who wallow in depression." Tally laughed self-consciously. "Her music just spoke to people."

"I'm surprised she didn't share information about her Nashville agent with you. Aren't you something of a mentor?"

"Pleasant didn't trust. If you've spoken with her family, you understand why."

I took exception to that. The Smiths were poor, but Charity appeared to love her children. "Her mom tries."

"No, no, I didn't mean that. The place she lives is on the thin edge of desperation. I always had the sense that someone in the trailer park raped Pleasant. I don't have any proof, but that was my thought."

"Did she ever mention a fellow named Rudy Uxall?"

Tally frowned. "No. Not to my knowledge. But Pleasant was close-mouthed, as I said. She didn't share a lot of information. She kept things to herself. The good and the bad."

"What about Frankie Graham?"

"Oh, Frankie. He was in the band before he graduated. A sweet kid, but no talent at all. More of a bookworm. I know they were friends, and before he graduated, Frankie seemed to look out for Pleasant."

"Could they have been romantically involved?"

"Anything is possible, but I never saw that. He was more like a big brother. But ask Marcia. If anyone knows, it'll be her. She and Pleasant were close."

"Where is Marcia?"

"As luck would have it, she's in the band hall. Follow me."

9

Marcia Colburn was a slender girl who came out of the band hall carrying a flute case. She wasn't unattractive, but she was a girl who would never stand out in a crowd. She glanced over at me, then lowered her gaze. "Miss McNair said I should talk to you."

"If you don't mind," I said, trying to put her at ease. "I'm trying to find your friend, Pleasant. Maybe you can help."

"Is she alive?" she asked, suddenly eager.

"I believe she is."

"What made her run off like that?"

"I wish I knew. Maybe she'll tell us when we find her."

A shadow crossed Marcia's face.

"Do you know something that might indicate where

she went? Someone she was meeting? Anything like that?"

Marcia looked down the hall, which was empty since the students were in class. She motioned for me to follow her to a big oak tree behind the band hall. When we were out of sight of the main building, she brought a pack of cigarettes from her purse and lit up. "Pleasant wasn't who you think she is," she said.

"What do you mean?"

"Everyone thinks Pleasant is this quiet, smart girl who is going to break out of Cotton Gin High and go on to stardom. But she's not the saint everyone paints her as. My best advice to you is to let it go. Pleasant is fine. She always comes out on top."

"Tell me about her." Marcia was angry and bitter, possibly at being left behind. While I couldn't trust what she said one hundred percent, I would sure get to see the flip side of my missing girl.

"Pleasant sings like an angel, and she can write a song that will wring your heart out. But she's not Miss Goody Two-Shoes. She likes to smoke and drink and cuss. Smoke a J when she can. She's normal, like the rest of us."

"Except she was pregnant." I made the point as calmly as I could.

"She didn't want that baby. She hated the idea of it."

Marcia's description of her friend was the polar opposite of what I'd come to believe about Pleasant. Teenage girls could be deceptive, but we seemed to be speaking of two different young women. "She could have had an abortion," I said.

"With what money?" Marcia looked at me like I was dumber than a rock. "Where would she get five hundred dollars? And how would she get to Jackson and back?

That old beater of a car couldn't be trusted to go ten miles."

"Perhaps the father would have paid for it."

Again she shot me a look that said 'what world do you live in?' "If Pleasant had known who the father was, she might have asked him."

I couldn't hide my shock.

"She wasn't some little virgin who got caught." Marcia tossed her hair. "Pleasant knew what she was doing."

"If she knew so much about sex, how did she get pregnant? A smart girl would have taken care of that possibility with pills or an effective form of birth control."

Marcia shrugged. "Birth control pills cost a lot of money. Nobody has ninety dollars a month for pills. Condoms break sometimes." Her face fell into an expression of boredom. "I don't know. Pleasant kept the details of her sex life to herself. All I know is she liked the bad boys. She was drawn to trouble in tight jeans. Maybe she was high and got carried away."

This picture of Pleasant didn't jibe with anything else I'd been told. "What kind of drugs was she into?"

"She never met a high she didn't like."

"If she didn't have money, how did she buy . . ." It was a stupid question. "But she wasn't sweet on any particular guy?" Young people weren't sentimental about love and romance. They were a different breed of cat.

"If she was, she didn't say so. I gotta go. I have to meet someone."

"Surely she must have told her best friend who she was in love with."

Marcia gave me a look. "Maybe back in the old days when *you* were dating, things worked like that. A girl fell in love and had sex, and they got married and lived happily ever after. Things aren't like that now. Especially not here. A smart girl can trap a guy, but look at what she's got when it's over. Nothing worth having."

If Marcia exemplified the average teen's beliefs, we were in a lot of trouble. I felt sorry for her.

"Two people can care about each other and be stronger together." I sounded like some proselytizer for true love—something I wasn't certain I believed in.

"Nobody falls in love now. There's no point. There's no house with a picket fence or a Prince Charming or a happily ever after. We'll get old and fat and have kids we didn't want who'll do the same thing we did, exactly like our parents. Don't you get it? There's no hope here."

She started to walk away but I caught her arm. "That's only the reality if you accept it. There are ways out of here."

"For you maybe. Maybe for Pleasant, if she took off. Not for me. In ten years, I'll look just like my mama. Old and sucked dry." She snatched her arm away from me. "I gotta go."

"Marcia, who were the girls who were mean to Pleasant?"

"I'm not a ratfink."

"Be a friend. Tell me."

"Ask Brook Blevins and Lucinda Musgrove."

She marched away from me, never turning back. If this was Pleasant's best friend, I couldn't help but wonder about her enemies. This was a situation I would have run away from, too.

Time was running away from me. Lucinda Musgrove was out of school for the day. She had a meeting with a scholarship committee at Delta State University. Not for academics, but for her theatrical, dance, and music abilities. Lucinda and Pleasant had been the two top contenders for the scholarship. Though I couldn't put my hands on the high-schooler, I knew Lucinda's mother, and I knew where to find her. I focused on Brook Blevins.

Principal Bryant arranged to call Brook to the office—on the condition that she was willing to talk to me. The minute she walked in the door, I knew she was a mean girl. Privileged, arrogant, narcissistic. She assessed me with a sneer. "You're too old to be a student, so what are you doing here and what do you want with me?"

"I'm a private investigator, and I've been hired to find Pleasant Smith."

"Check the landfill. Trash follows trash."

I clenched my hand to keep from slapping her sullen face. Most teenagers didn't get under my skin, but this young woman was a bully. And she had every advantage that most of her peers never had. Her Escada floral lace-print jeans cost more than her high school teachers made in a week. The lace-up sneakers she wore priced out at well over two hundred dollars. Every item of her wardrobe was expensive. Add to that the fact she was a beautiful girl, and it made me even angrier.

"Tell me what you know about Pleasant." I forced a smile.

"She was a freak. She had six fingers, which is what happens when siblings breed."

"Polydactylism is actually an inherited trait. It has nothing to do with incest."

"Oh, so you're the incest police?" She laughed. "Call it whatever you want. She was a trailer trash freak."

"I heard she was talented."

Brook pushed her silky blond hair behind her ear. "She could sing and make up songs. So what?"

"Who were her friends?"

"Freaks don't have friends."

My restraint was about to slip. I wondered what Hoss Kincaid would do to me for assaulting a minor. I was pretty sure it would be worth it. "Who did she hang out with?"

"Her trailer trash friends, I guess. Look, she came to class. She went home and did whatever freaks do." Her eyebrows rose. "There was that one boy, Frankie something. Another geek. I saw them talking some before he graduated."

"What about Marcia Colburn?"

"What about her?"

"Was she one of Pleasant's friends?"

She laughed. "Marcia is another loser. Maybe they were friends, but no one ever invited them to parties or anything like that."

"Was Pleasant a good student?"

"How would I know? I didn't have to sign her report card or anything." Brook held out her hand, inspecting her manicure. "I really have to go."

And not a moment too soon. It was all I could do not to kick her in the butt when she walked away. Life would take some of the starch out of her, but I suspected Brook Blevins would lead a life filled with a few elite friends and the rest of the world would never measure up to her high standards.

I pulled up in front of the Three Bs quick stop. I hadn't passed a single car on the drive over from the high school.

Fallow cotton fields stretched in all directions, and as far as the eye could see there wasn't an indication of life. A tin sign advertising Fanta drinks wobbled in the wind that cut across the fields.

The bell over the door jangled as I stepped inside. Frankie Graham was behind the counter, reading another literary novel. He looked up and grinned with pleasure when he recognized me.

"Did you find Pleasant?"

His eagerness made it harder to give him the negative reply. "We haven't given up."

"She's been gone a month. Why are you looking for her now?" Frankie asked.

If he was romantically involved, he was sure a good actor. "We have reason to believe she's alive. Or at least was alive two days ago."

"Did someone see her?" He came out from behind the counter and put a hand on my arm. "Please, tell me."

I needed a DNA sample, because I felt it was highly possible Frankie might be the father of the child. It was time to tell him the truth. "Someone left a baby on the front porch of my home. We believe it's Pleasant's baby because it has six toes on one foot."

"Polydactyl! She told me all about it, how it runs in her family. Not everyone has it, but most of her family members do." A wide smile spread over his features. "She's alive. If she had the baby, she's alive. Where is she?"

"We don't know. But we *believe* she's alive."

"Is the baby okay? Is it a girl? Pleasant really wanted a girl."

"The baby is a perfectly fine little girl. She's being well taken care of."

"We have to find Pleasant. We have to." He gripped the counter as if he might fly up to the ceiling.

"We're doing our best. But we know Pleasant was alive when the baby was born." I filled him in on all the details of Libby's arrival on my front porch, and on the death of Rudy Uxall. "We can't be sure, but it looks to me as if Rudy was trying to help the baby."

"Why would he bring the baby to you?"

If only I had that answer. "It doesn't make sense, but that's what happened."

"This Rudy." He bit his lip. "I wish I had a picture."

I whipped out my phone and pulled up the photo I'd taken of Rudy's older brother, Alfred. "He looks something like this."

Frankie wasn't very good at concealing his emotions. "I know him. He was in here the day Pleasant disappeared."

"Are you sure?"

He nodded. "Those two asshats who were here the other day, he was with them. He stayed in the truck. When they started messing with Pleasant, he got out and started to come inside, but he didn't." He considered. "He looked upset."

"From what some of the students at Cotton Gin High told me about Pleasant, she may have invited some of that rude attention."

Frankie bristled. "What do you mean by that remark?"

"Her best friend said she liked bad boys and drugs."

Frankie's arm jerked and sent a container of mints crashing to the floor. "That's just a . . . a . . . a damn lie." Heat jumped into his cheeks. "Pleasant wasn't like that at all. She was a good girl."

"Good girls don't get pregnant."

The red drained from his face, leaving it white. "Everyone makes mistakes. Every single one of us. You can't say Pleasant was a bad girl because she made one mistake."

"And who did she make a mistake with?" I asked.

"She can tell you when you find her."

Frankie was a loyal friend. I had to give him that. He wouldn't blow her cover no matter how mad he got.

He picked up the peppermints and came around the counter. Tall and skinny, he stood his ground. "Pleasant was focused on her studies and her music. She made straight As. Who told you otherwise?"

I had no allegiance to Marcia Colburn, so I told him.

"She clung to Pleasant like a fat gray dog tick. She was never her friend, just someone who saw a possible ticket out of Hicksville." He pushed his hair back. "Pleasant was a loner. She didn't make a lot of friends, and Marcia pushed herself. Pleasant wasn't the kind to be mean, so she let Marcia hang around and be part of the music. And this is the thanks she gets. That little bitch."

Somehow, he'd made me feel sorry for Marcia. Brook Blevins was another kettle of fish. "What about Brook?"

"High maintenance." He shrugged. "She's beautiful and vicious. She got it in for Pleasant and really made school hell. I never could understand why Brook, Lucinda, and that crowd hated Pleasant so. They went out of their way to pull pranks to humiliate her. Brook had a leather glove with an extra finger made. She would pick her nose with the little pinkie. It was gross. And she would do it right in front of Pleasant."

Brook was a bitch with a capital B. Frankie was right about that.

"I have two very different pictures of Pleasant. One is a good girl who shouldered responsibilities, and the other is this wild child."

"I'm telling the truth. Nothing was more important to Pleasant than her music. Ask her mother or her sister. Ask the band director. She was all about her music, and that baby wouldn't have been in her way. I would've asked—" He halted.

"Asked what?" I thought I knew the answer, but I needed him to say it.

"She needed a clean break from here. No ties. She would have been rolling in money once she sold some of her songs."

"So she wasn't wild, sleeping around?"

"Hell, no." He was angry.

"Frankie, if she was hanging out with tough guys and in a situation with drugs, you need to tell me. That would at least give us a place to start looking for her."

Frankie reached behind the counter and came back with a plastic drugstore sack. "Here." He pushed it at me.

Inside the sack was a prenatal vitamin and a receipt.

"When she could, she worked at the Riverview Motel as a janitor. She gave me twenty-five dollars to buy these vitamins because she wanted her baby to be healthy. That was the last money she had. She'd spent the rest on taking her cousin to the doctor when she got sick. That was money she'd been saving to go to Nashville when her agent made a deal."

"Why would Marcia and Brook paint Pleasant as a bad girl?"

"Brook is jealous, and I'm sure Marcia's just mad. Pleasant escaped without her."

"Okay. Tell me about the Riverside Motel."

Frankie put the vitamins back under the counter. "I know she's had the baby, but she can still take them. Maybe they can help." He cleared his throat. "That car of hers wasn't reliable, but when it would run, she'd drive over to the motel and clean rooms, make beds, do laundry, that kind of stuff. She was going to Nashville over the Thanksgiving break. She said her agent had shown her songs around and had some interest. She was beside herself."

"Someone has to know who her agent was."

"Tally McNair would be the best person. She encouraged Pleasant. She has to know."

He was dead right. Pleasant had no one else to talk with. Tally had stonewalled me. And she'd sent me to Marcia as Pleasant's best friend. But why?

"Thanks, Frankie. Would you mind giving a DNA sample?"

"Why?"

"Because I think you're the baby's father. And I'm curious why you won't just say so."

"You can't say that! You can't. I won't be a chain for her."

He was in love with Pleasant. If the baby was his, he'd surely claim her, but there was no point pressing this issue now. "Since I've found Pleasant's mother, I need to tell her about the baby. The infant is in good hands, but I'm sure Mrs. Smith will want to take custody of her. Do me a favor, don't mention anything about the baby until I have a chance to tell Charity in person. The infant is being well taken care of, I promise."

Frankie looked unsure. "Mrs. Smith has her hands full. Pleasant was so worried if her music career didn't take off that she and her baby would be one more burden on her mom. I won't say anything. But tell her soon. She has to know her grandchild was born safely."

My heart leaped at the possibility Tinkie would be allowed to keep Libby—at least until Pleasant was found. Frankie wasn't going to press his rights, at least at the moment. No matter what Charity Smith decided, I had to tell her about the baby. Or Coleman would—as soon as I told him what I'd learned.

Nothing had changed at the trailer park, except the younger children were under the charge of a different teenager. The families in the park were chipping in to help each other so that the mothers could work. The hardship was carried by the teens, who offered daily child care—and missed school. Pleasant had managed to miss classes and keep her grades up. It would cost some of them greatly, though.

Charity held a fussing baby Sapphire when she came to the door and invited me in. This was going to be tough, and I should have done it as soon as I realized she was the grandmother. Though she offered coffee, I declined. Once I confessed, she might not be so hospitable.

"A baby was left on my porch. I think it's your grandchild."

Shock and then hope washed over her. "The baby is healthy? Where is Pleasant?"

"The baby is healthy and is being well cared for. I'm searching for Pleasant, and I won't quit until she's found."

The one emotion Charity Smith didn't register was anger. "How did you find the baby?"

I told her the whole story. "My partner, Tinkie Richmond, and her husband, Oscar, are caring for the baby. They call her Libby."

"Libby?" She looked blank, as if the name were the most important information I'd revealed.

"That was my mother's name. Since she was left on my front porch, Tinkie thought . . ." What did it matter what we'd thought? "I had to be sure you were the family before I told you about the child. I'm certain she's your grandbaby. I can take you to her or bring her to you."

Charity looked around her trailer. Though it was neat, everything in it was dated and decrepit. "I want to see her."

"Absolutely. I can take you right now. And bring you back with her."

"Your partner, is she able to care for the child?"

"Yes. The Richmonds have already made plans to take Libby to Boston Children's Hospital for examination of the extra digit on her foot."

"They would do that for a child who isn't their own?"

"They *will* provide health care for the child and Pleasant. And Oscar is setting up a college fund for Libby."

"Why?" Charity asked. "Why would they do such a generous thing for a child who isn't blood?"

"Because that's who they are. They love Libby. I can assure you, Libby and Pleasant have two champions now."

Sapphire, who'd finally settled into sleep, began to cry and Charity picked her up. She offered a bottle, which the baby drank greedily. I held my breath. Charity seemed to be in a fog. She wasn't angry, which surprised me.

"Take me to see my grandchild," she said, at last. "I'll make arrangements for someone to care for Sapphire if you can give me a few minutes."

"I need to go by the Riverview Motel. Maybe someone there can give me a lead to find Pleasant. I'll pick you up on my way back and take you to the baby."

"Pleasant was a good girl. She cleaned rooms at that motel. And played her music sometimes. Nothing else. She did get pregnant and I don't know who the father is, but she wasn't a girl who slept around."

I put a hand on her arm. "Maybe someone noticed undue interest in her. I'm not suggesting . . ." But then I did have to suggest that Pleasant might not be the good girl her mother thought her to be. "I have to ask. Was Pleasant doing drugs?"

"No. And if you think you can take my grandchild from me by tarring Pleasant with gossip, it won't happen."

At last the grandmother in her came out. "That isn't my intention. I promise. I want to find Pleasant. Some of the high school kids said Pleasant was involved with drugs."

"Marcia Colburn, right? I told Pleasant not to feel sorry for that girl and let her hang around. Trouble. Marcia is describing her own life, not Pleasant's." She got up and went to a small table holding a Christmas cactus and a blooming peace lily. From a drawer she brought out a stack of papers. "Here's her report cards. All A's. Comments from teachers talking about her maturity and intelligence. She kept the kids around here one day a week and still made straight A's. Does that sound like a druggie to you?"

"No."

She calmed down. "I know you're just doing your job, but those girls were so jealous of my daughter. Now, when she's missing, they try to slander her. It's just wrong."

"Teenagers can be malicious and often heartless."

"Yes, they can."

"I'll pick you up on my way back to Zinnia, after I stop by the motel. I hope I find a lead."

"I'll be ready." Her fire had dampened beneath her grief. "It's not right. Pleasant should be with her baby."

"I couldn't agree more, and I haven't given up on finding her. I'll be back as soon as I can." This would give me time to alert Tinkie. She would at least have a chance to adjust to the fact that Libby's grandmother had been found.

10

When I was parked by the office of the Riverview Motel, I called Tinkie. The short drive had given me an opportunity to carefully plan how I would tell her that Charity wanted to see Libby. Lucky for me, Oscar answered the phone.

"This has to be done," I told him after I'd brought him up to speed.

"I know." He sounded totally defeated.

"She's a very nice woman. She was impressed that you and Tinkie had scheduled an appointment for Libby at the children's hospital."

"I hope she lets us take her. The foot is delicate. A botched removal could plague Libby for years to come."

"Look, Charity is a sensible woman. Let's see what she says."

"Do you want to relay this information to Tinkie?"

That question let me know how much Oscar dreaded telling his wife that Libby's grandmother had been found and was coming to call. "No." I was his equal in cowardice. "I can't tell her. I can't."

"It's okay. It's my place." He sounded like a man walking to his death. "I'll pack up her things and have them ready. The one thing we don't want to do is upset Mrs. Smith. Maybe she'll let us visit with Libby."

"She seems like that kind of person." I tried to keep emotion out of my voice. This was hard enough for Oscar. Me playing the role of Weeping Wanda wouldn't help. "I should be there in an hour, maybe ninety minutes."

I hung up and composed myself as I went to the hotel's office. The young woman behind the counter looked bored, until I asked about Pleasant.

"Where is that girl?" She pushed her dyed black bangs out of her eyes and snapped her gum. "She missed a gig four weeks ago and I haven't heard from her since. I thought she was responsible."

"A gig?"

"Have you heard her play her guitar and sing? She had a following. Some young folks came down from Memphis and up from Vicksburg just to hear her. She had the motel full on the Friday nights she sang."

"Where?" The Riverside Motel didn't have a lounge or a lobby.

"Parking lot," the woman said. Folks would sit in their cars, like the old drive-in theaters. It was something. Each weekend, it was a bigger crowd." She snapped her gum. "I told the owner he should pay her, but he's such a cheapskate."

"She was performing for free?"

The young woman wasn't much older than Pleasant, but she'd seen a lot of life. "Bastard took advantage of her. In the long run, it's gonna cost him 'cause now she's gone."

"Actually, she's missing, which is why I'm here."

She snapped her gum three times. "Missing? As in . . . taken?"

"That's what I'm trying to find out. I'm a private investigator and I've been hired to find Pleasant. Was there anyone here in the motel who showed an interest in her or her music?"

She leaned on the counter that separated us and frowned. "There were boys, of course. Pleasant was a beautiful girl. Couple of kids from Vicksburg." Her face brightened. "They called yesterday, asking when she'd be back singing. Left a number for me to call."

She retrieved the number before I even asked.

"Anyone else show an interest?"

"Kids loved her music, and a lot of the older folks, too, but I don't remember seeing anything upsetting. Pleasant handled herself like a pro. She never mentioned trouble."

"Did you ever see anyone who looked like this hanging around?" I showed her the picture of Alfred Uxall on my phone. He looked enough like Rudy for an ID.

"Nope. That's a big fella. I would have remembered someone like him."

"Thanks for your help."

"Let me know when you find her. She's due to have that baby any minute."

"Will do." Now it was time to pick up Charity and face Tinkie.

When I turned down the drive to Hilltop, Charity sat forward. "This is some place," she said.

"Yes, the Richmonds are lucky people."

Her unease grew when I stopped and got out. She followed suit, but her steps were slow as we went to the front door. Oscar answered as soon as I knocked. The first thing I noticed was Tinkie standing behind him, Libby in her arms. Beside her were five pieces of pink luggage and a Pack'n Play, all ready to go.

"We took the liberty of buying a car seat for her," Oscar said.

Tinkie blinked back tears. "She's a wonderful baby."

Charity stepped past me and went straight to Tinkie, who yielded the baby and then turned away to wipe the tears from her cheeks.

"She is a beautiful girl," Charity said, awed by the baby. "I wonder if Pleasant ever saw her."

Her statement almost opened my floodgates, but Oscar and I both maintained. If we started wailing, Tinkie would lose it completely.

"We've booked an appointment for Libby . . ." He looked at me as he hesitated. "For the baby in Boston tomorrow. Just a preliminary examination. We'd like to pay for the surgery, if that's what you decide."

"You want to take my grandchild to Boston to the doctor for possible surgery?" Charity smoothed the baby's red hair as she talked.

"Yes, we do." Oscar held his ground. "She needs this. It will make a difference in her life."

"And if I don't want to do that, I'll just walk out with her?" Charity, too, had taken in the luggage. "With all of these things you've bought her?"

"Of course," Oscar said. "They're Lib . . . hers."

"You can call her Libby. I like that name. That's who she can be, until Pleasant gets back to name her."

Tinkie finally met Charity's gaze. "Thank you. We've grown so attached to Libby. We hoped all along that her birth family would be found. She is such a special baby."

"She puts me in mind of Pleasant, when she was born. She had a sweet disposition just like this baby."

To my utter astonishment, Charity held the baby out to Tinkie. "My daughter is still missing. I've got my niece, Sapphire, at the house, and she's more than I can keep up with. I think Libby would be better here—but just until Pleasant is found."

Tinkie reached for the child and cradled Libby against her chest. "Thank you. Thank you."

Charity held up a trembling hand. "This is temporary. I can see you've fallen in love, and you know it can't be permanent. But for the time being, it would be good for the baby to be here. You took her in when she had no one else. I can see it's hurtin' you to give her up, but you're willing to do it."

"We would never try to take your grandchild," Tinkie said. "May we still take her to Boston?"

Charity nodded. "That would be a wonderful thing for her. My mama had an extra toe, and later in life, it gave her a lot of pain." She stepped back toward the door. "Now I have to get home to my niece. A neighbor was kind enough to look after her for me, but babies require a lot of attention and work." She smiled. "You'll find that out."

"And we thank you for that opportunity," Oscar said. He put his arm around Tinkie and pulled her and the baby close. "We'll call with the results from the doctor's visit."

"That would be good." Charity edged toward the door. I was still gob-smacked at the turn of events. "Ms. Delaney, if you could take me home."

"Sure. Sure thing." I walked out of the house into the sunshine. When I looked back, Tinkie and Oscar were framed in the doorway holding Libby and each other. They were the perfect family—who'd just escaped a tragic parting.

On the drive back to Fodder Gin Road, I wanted to thank Charity for her generosity. It was awkward, though, thanking her for leaving her grandchild in the hands of strangers.

"They'll give her back when Pleasant comes home, won't they?" she asked. Doubt was evident in her grip on the car door.

"They will. You have my word."

"They already love her."

I couldn't deny it. "Tinkie has wanted to adopt for a long time, but her husband has been reluctant. Maybe this experience will bring Oscar around, and maybe they'll offer a home to a baby who really needs one."

"Thank you for finding a place for Libby. Why do you think Rudy Uxall left the baby at your house? Why didn't he bring her to me? He knew me. Knew where I lived."

I'd given this some thought. "All I have is suppositions. Maybe he wanted to go to the hospital, and Dahlia

House was on the way from wherever he came from. I don't know."

"Maybe my daughter told him about you. Everyone knows you solve mysteries. Maybe she knew you'd look for her."

More than anything I wanted to offer Charity hope that her daughter would return to her. But I couldn't lie. How would a seventeen-year-old girl in Bolivar County know anything about me? We could have lived on two different planets and not been more alien. "I don't know."

"Pleasant is smart. She had that baby and put some thought into where to send her. I think she and Rudy acted to save Libby's life. Whoever killed Rudy Uxall has my baby girl."

If that were true, then Pleasant might now be in serious danger. "Charity, would you mind stopping by the sheriff's office and talking to Coleman Peters? I know you live in Bolivar County, but the baby was brought here, so Coleman is involved. He's a friend. He's trying to help us." It would also clear things up about Libby and child services. So far, Charity had the best claim to the baby, and she'd approved Tinkie. Coleman would also insist on a DNA test and we'd have scientific proof that Libby was a Smith.

"I'll take help anywhere I can get it. I want my daughter home."

Ten minutes later, I pushed open the door of the sheriff's office and ushered Charity in. Coleman, looking like he hadn't slept in two days, offered us both a cup of coffee.

"What can I do for you?" he asked when we held our cups.

"Coleman, this is Libby's grandmother, Charity Smith."

"I see." He didn't waste any time getting to the DNA

test. "Would you mind if I did a cheek swab and had that verified?"

Thank goodness Coleman wasn't swayed by emotions. I'd taken Charity to be Libby's grandmother because of the polydactyl genetics, the physical likenesses, and my desire to find Libby's family. A DNA test would confirm the relationship without a doubt—legally.

"Swab away," Charity said. "Sarah Booth said you'd help us find my daughter, Pleasant."

"Yes, ma'am." He motioned the dispatcher, Francine, a woman who adored my mother and also showered kind acts on me. "Get a DNA swab, please."

While we waited on Francine to bring the kit, I filled Coleman in on all I'd learned in my talks at the high school and the Riverview Motel. Though I'd uncovered some leads, I had nothing that indicated where Pleasant might be.

"Good work, Sarah Booth. Now I need a word alone." He gripped my upper arm and directed me to his private office. When he closed the door, I felt a ripple of excitement combined with fear. Coleman wasn't one to act impulsively and the look in his eyes was all business—and not the kind involving monkeys.

"What have I done now?" I thought back on my many potential sins.

"Not a thing. It's Tinkie I'm worried about."

"Charity is allowing Tinkie and Oscar to keep the baby until Pleasant is found. They're taking Libby to Boston for a doctor's appointment."

"The grandmother is okay with this?"

"I took Charity to Hilltop. She saw Libby and Tinkie and Oscar. She was satisfied the baby is in good hands. Coleman, she's barely keeping her head above water.

Pleasant was her hope, the one truly good and amazing thing in her life. She loves Libby enough to want a better future for her. If Pleasant doesn't come home, she may allow our friends to be a big part of Libby's life."

"I hate to think that young woman is dead, but if she is, allowing Oscar and Tinkie to be a part of the baby's life would be a good thing."

"I never thought of Tinkie as a particularly maternal person. I know she loved the idea of having a child. You know, the dressing and primping and all of that. But I always felt that when it came to dirty diapers and up-chuck and feeding at all hours of the day and night, Tinkie would quickly get her fill." I swallowed a lump in my throat. "You should see her and Oscar. She had formula in her hair, and Oscar had baby powder all down the front of his suit. And I've never seen them happier."

"Scary." Coleman patted my shoulder. "I thought it was a bad idea to let the Richmonds care for Libby. Maybe you've proven me wrong."

"And maybe not."

"Sarah Booth, love without risk is not worth having." He stepped closer. "I made a mistake with you. And with myself. While I chose a path I thought was honorable, I didn't honor my own heart. Will you ever be able to move past that?"

My own damaged heart wasn't ready for this conversation. Not by a long stretch. I put a hand on his starched shirt, and beneath my palm I could feel the strong beat of his heart. "I forgave you long ago. In fact, there was never anything to forgive. You did what you thought was right, and I respect that. I did then and I do now. I'm just not ready. Can you give me a bit more time?"

His hand moved from my shoulder to my cheek, which

he cupped with gentleness. Something felt trapped in my chest. "Time I can give you. I know Scott came back to Zinnia, hoping to win your heart. You have feelings for him. I can see the shared emotion between you. And Harold, who plays his feelings for you off as a social convenience. More than any of us, he loves and respects your courage."

"I—"

His thumb touched my lips to silence me. "I don't know that I'm the best man for you, but I want my chance. Just promise me that."

The only thing I could do was nod.

"And just to be sure you don't forget . . ." He tipped my face up and kissed me with such a searing promise that I put my arms around his neck to keep from falling over.

His arms tightened around me, and with that one kiss he took me on a journey through time. The April sun warmed my body as my friends sang Pete Seeger songs while Cecil played the guitar, and we sat around a bonfire lit more to honor the spring than for warmth.

Coleman's arms cradled me as we rode Mr. Gruber's farm horse on a perfect fall afternoon. We galloped along the sides of cotton fields sprouting the white bolls that smelled of dirt and the future. From there I traveled to Harold's front porch and a party where Coleman kissed me and I learned that I had fallen in love with him—had perhaps loved him for a very long time.

When he ended the kiss, his strong arms continued to support me. "Did you learn anything?" he asked with that teasing note I loved so much.

"I did. You own a great deal of my past, Coleman. More than I knew."

"I don't want the past, Sarah Booth. I want the future. And the present. I'm a greedy man."

My body demanded that I answer yes. That I turn the lock on his office door, to hell with Charity Smith and Francine and DeWayne, should he return to the office. I needed Coleman, and if I let this moment slip away, I might never have the courage to act again.

He kissed me again, and I stopped thinking. The world collapsed into a kiss that spoke far better than words.

A tap at the door brought us both to awareness of our surroundings. "Don't stop."

"This isn't the place." His breathing was rapid, and his desire was evident.

"I don't care. I want this dance between us ended."

He put his hands on my face. "And I want you to choose me because you love me, not because you need . . . a release."

I stepped back. "You are a devil." I tugged my shirt into place and tried to calm the pounding of blood in all the wrong places. Not a drop of it had gone to my brain.

"Just remember, Sarah Booth, there's plenty more where that came from." He walked past me and opened the door, speaking to Francine, cool as a cucumber. Oh, he would pay.

11

On the way back from taking Charity home, I stopped by Hilltop. I was worried about Tinkie. In all the years I'd known her, I'd never seen her disheveled. When she came to the doorway, she wore a necklace of pacifiers. Gone were the Cartier pearls that were her normal style. Tinkie had been stripped of her vanity, and I didn't see that as a good thing.

Oscar was sound asleep. He hadn't gone back to the bank, but had remained at Hilltop with Tinkie and the baby. No longer was he driven by the excitement of making money. No, he was smitten by a seven-pound drool and poop maker.

I had to stay objective. If Libby bewitched all of us, no one would find her mother.

"Did you ask Charity Smith to leave the baby with us?" Tinkie asked as she led me to the kitchen.

"No. I didn't. Tinkie, I have some leads to find Pleasant. Do you think you could get a sitter for the baby so we can do some work?"

She ignored my question and asked one of her own. "Charity came to that decision on her own?"

"She did, Tinkie." I put a hand on her shoulder to get her full attention. "We have to find Pleasant. I fear the girl is in serious trouble. And Rudy Uxall has been murdered, probably trying to help Pleasant."

"Maybe she's fine. Just doesn't want the responsibility of an infant."

"Tinkie." I grabbed her shoulder and spun her to face me. "Look at me. We have to find this girl."

She slumped into a chair at the kitchen bar and her eyes filled with tears. "I know I'm behaving like a crazy woman, but I can't help it. This baby is the most perfect being in the world. You have no idea, Sarah Booth. I know she isn't mine, but it doesn't matter. I would do whatever is necessary to protect her. Anything."

"I understand." I reached for the baby, but Tinkie turned away, blocking me with her shoulder. "She's settled now. I don't want her to cry."

"Okay." But it wasn't. Tinkie had taken possession of Libby, and in her mind and heart, that baby belonged with her. "But I need your help."

"I can't. My time with Libby may be short, and I want to spend every second with her." She brightened. "Can I bring her along?"

"No." Pleasant's disappearance might involve violence. Not the place for a child.

"Why are you so mean about it?" she asked.

"Tinkie!" I wanted to snap her out of it.

She pushed a greasy strand of hair back. "I'm sorry. I know that wasn't fair. You let me take Libby in the first place. You could have kept her for yourself."

"I'm not in a place to be a mother," I said.

"But I am. I'm ready. Oscar is, too. It didn't take Libby an hour to win him over. He would adopt her in a second."

I went to my friend and drew her against me. "She has a mother, Tinkie. She does. And her mother probably loves her, too."

She faced me. "I know. I'll do what's right—when I have to."

"You promise you understand this isn't permanent."

"If it were, I'd be the happiest woman alive."

"Say it."

"This is a temporary arrangement. Libby will go home with her mother when Pleasant is found." Her eyebrows drew together. "Are you positive Pleasant is the mother?"

"Coleman ran DNA. He'll have results soon enough. And we have no clue where to look for the father, though Frankie Graham would be my guess." A subject change was in order. "Why don't you help me make some calls?"

When I'd first come home to Zinnia, solving mysteries had been the thing that saved me. When Libby went home, Tinkie would need a lifeline to grasp. The detective agency would fit that bill. It had saved me, and it would save her when the time came.

I gave her one of the numbers I'd gotten from the Riverside Motel. "This is a man who showed interest in Pleasant's music. Call him. I'll call the other."

With great reluctance, Tinkie put Libby in her bassinet and picked up her phone. She dialed and so did I. The man I spoke with was Randy Hunter.

Randy was a graduate of Delta State University and a musician who'd given up the dream to manage a home improvement store in Vicksburg. He was open and willing to talk about Pleasant—and express his fear that something bad had happened to her. "She was like lightning when she played and sang," he said. "Folks were drawn to her. Jealousy was aroused."

He spoke with the precision of a songwriter, and I was curious. "You're a store manager? Do you still play?"

"Yeah, I'm the man who can tell you how to repair almost everything in a home. I let the dream of playing music go." Regret edged his voice. "I had to. The year I graduated from DSU, I married. My girl was pregnant and I loved her. We both wanted the baby. My music was a side effort, and with Babette and Julie in my life, I had to make a living to give us all a decent life. Besides, I was never as good as Pleasant. Nowhere close."

He didn't sound jealous. "So who do you think would want to harm her?"

"A group of girls showed up the last time she played. They hung on the fringe of the audience. When I went by them to go to the bathroom, I heard one girl say that Pleasant was trailer trash and didn't deserve the breaks she was getting. High school girls are meaner than a roll of barbed wire."

"Could you describe the girls?"

"There were three of them. Pretty, well-dressed. They came in a silver BMW roadster."

"License plate?"

"I'm sorry, I didn't even think to look. They parked way in the back of the lot and stood in the darkness. They were young and slender. Perfect, like those girls always are. They have everything, and they're jealous of a kid who has talent. Some people never have enough, you know?"

Oh, how well I knew. "Did they interact with Pleasant?"

He thought. "Seems to me they knew each other. Just the way those rich girls acted. At least they knew who Pleasant was. Maybe they go to high school together."

Which was exactly what I was thinking. "Did you notice anyone else who seemed out of place?"

"Not that I can think of. The people who gathered really loved Pleasant's music. She touched us with her melodies and lyrics. Just a simple guitar and a girl with talent."

"Expect a call from Hoss Kincaid, the sheriff of Bolivar County."

"Now hold on a minute—"

"I have to turn my information over to him. Pleasant is missing. You might think of another detail that will help us find her. This isn't a problem for you, Randy. I promise."

"Okay, I'm happy to help. I've been worried about Pleasant, but I was just a fan. I thought maybe she'd moved or gone to college or something good. Damn. Sure, I'll help find her anyway I can. You think she's okay? And the baby. My god."

He sounded distressed. "The baby is fine. Pleasant is still missing."

There was a brief silence. "Now I'm really worried for her. Tell the sheriff to call. I'll try to think of more details."

I thanked him and hung up.

Tinkie's report was much briefer. Paul Owens ran a chain of bars and had his eye on Pleasant for a performer.

"He said she was that good," Tinkie said. For the first time in a while I saw a glimmer of interest in finding Libby's mom. A twinkle of compassion for Pleasant. "He said she was a fine young woman with a big future ahead of her."

I told her about the mean girls. "Tomorrow, I'm going back to the high school. Surely the students have to register their vehicles. I'll find out who the BMW belongs to, and I'll get a copy of some of Pleasant's songs. My PI friend, Rick Ralston in Nashville, is working with us, but he needs something solid to go on."

"Good idea," Tinkie said. Her attention was already on the baby, who slept peacefully.

"Let Oscar tend Libby and you come help me."

She shook her head. "My time with her is short. I won't lose a minute of it."

"Don't get your heart broken. And give Chablis some attention. She was your baby long before Libby arrived." But my advice fell on deaf ears as I let myself out of the house.

Dahlia House stood like a sentinel in the November dusk. The beauty of the house, the stark trees along the drive, and the pinks, purples, and corals of the sunset made me stop the car and simply stare. We live amid such beauty, and so often ignore it. Dahlia House, a single light aglow in the front parlor, made my heart ache. This was my home, and the largest part of my life had been lived in the protection of those walls.

I rolled on down the drive, my melancholic mood destroyed by the pounding of horse hooves as my herd came out of the back pasture and raced along the fence line, welcoming me home. Reveler led the pack, his beautiful gray head bowing and stretching on his long neck. He had such power. Behind him Miss Scrapiron was a delicate combination of speed, grace, heart, and intelligence. Bringing up the rear was a black shadow. Lucifer was a stout horse with feet the size of large saucers and a flowing mane and tail. Zorro rode such a horse, and Zorro had always been one of my heroes.

The horses sped past me to the barn. Their internal clocks knew it was feeding time. I parked and opened the door to let Sweetie and Pluto out so they could join me. They loved to go to the barn.

"You have some 'splaining to do!"

I knew the line from *I Love Lucy*, but this was a sharp female voice, not Ricky Ricardo. I peeped in the front doorway as Sweetie and Pluto fled for their lives. A tall, red-haired Lucille Ball stood in the foyer, hands on hips. She shook a finger at me. "Ethel is not going to be happy with you. You left the baby at Hilltop."

"Jitty?" The figure was so real, I had to wonder if Lucille had come to visit from the Great Beyond. I walked up to tug her red hair, but my hand went right through her.

"Ouch!"

"Jitty, that didn't hurt. Ghosts can't feel."

"That's what you know, Missy. I got feelin's just like you."

"Nope. If you don't get fat or age, you can't have feelings. Emotions are the things that eventually wreck our bodies. Twilight makes me crave Jack Daniel's. Sunrise makes me desperate for French toast or a Bloody Mary. You never crave anything. Your body can't be wrecked, hence you have no feelings." I was proud of my logic, circular though it was.

"I have plenty of feelings, though Ricky Ricardo forgets that sometimes. On the show and in real life." She leaned forward, squinting her eyes. "You look pale. You need some Vitameatavegamin. For health!" She produced a brown glass bottle and a spoon. "This'll put some hop right into your rabbit."

That skit from the television show was one of my all-time favorites. I watched as Lucy poured a big spoonful and she touted the health benefits of the concoction. The spoon slid into her mouth, and then her expression made me laugh out loud. No matter that I knew the comedic routine by heart. Jitty was perfect as Lucy, from her black-checked dress to the little pillbox hat that sat atop her red curls.

"Jitty, you are too much. Can I film you? I mean, will you show up on film?" I wasn't sure about the rules of ghost photography.

"You should be payin' attention to what I'm sayin', not calculatin' ways to get rich."

"You're a hoot, but I don't think I need any Vitameatavegamin. I'm healthy as a horse. Even doc says so."

"Tinkie needs it! She's the one losin' sleep and tendin' to a baby night and day. She's plumb tuckered out."

"I don't think Lucille Ball would use the words *plumb* or *tuckered*. She wasn't Southern, though, if she had been, it might have been quite charming." I tried to imagine Lucy's wacky routines in a Southern drawl. She'd mastered the Cuban accent when she mocked her husband.

The pretty redhead slowly faded and in her place was my haint. She still wore the elegant checked dress and the cute little totally useless pillbox hat. "When I'm playin' Lucille, she talks like I want her to."

"Your point is well taken. As much as I appreciate

a chance to see you perform that classic comedy skit, I can't help but wonder why you're here in the guise of a comedian."

"Not comedian. Mother. Lucille Ball broke ground when she had a baby in real life and incorporated the baby into her television show. She was a working mother who played a stay-at-home mother. The brilliance of such a thing has never been fully appreciated."

"And your point is?"

"A baby doesn't have to be the end of anyone's career."

I couldn't tell if her message was directed at me or Tinkie. "Meaning?"

"You know what I mean, Sarah Booth. Mothers come in all shapes, sizes, temperaments, and talents. You had a mama who could do it all with one hand tied behind her back. She could love and fight and mediate and never blink an eye."

I'd been on the verge of melancholy when I drove up to Dahlia House at the time of day my mother used to call "the blue hour." She, too, had been struck by sadness at the close of day. Now, Jitty made me miss my mother more than ever. "Thanks."

"Missin' Libby isn't a bad thing. Because you can see the love you miss in her is exactly what you'll have to give your own child."

In one more moment, Jitty would be talking about dying ovaries and blackened, shriveling eggs. "Enough." I held up a hand. "I see where you're headed."

"Call your partner. Buy one of those papoose sling things that mamas carry young'uns in. Make her put that baby in it and get back to work."

"So you weren't about to tell me my eggs were dying, tick-tock and all."

"Me?" Jitty looked hurt. "I'm not sayin' a word. I *won't* say a word. Not even when your fallopian tubes dry up and fall out on the ground."

And of course she had to have the last word by disappearing on the fading scent of roses.

12

The buzzing of my cell phone in the pocket of my jeans woke me the next morning. I chose to ignore it. I was exhausted and starving. Eventually the sensation of my stomach digesting my backbone would push me out of bed. At the moment, a bit more shut-eye was important.

But it was not to be. The phone buzzed—and then rang—relentlessly. I rolled out of bed and stumbled to my jeans. When I found the phone, I was highly tempted to hurl it out the window, but I checked to see Betty Mc-Gowin was calling. I came wide-awake with a much different attitude, eager to talk to the midwife.

"Mrs. McGowin, are you okay?"

"Yes, ma'am, I'm fine. I thought you'd want to know a

young man was here early this morning asking for medicine to ease a woman's cramps after childbirth."

My heart rate jumped. "Did you get his name?"

"I did, but it won't do you any good. He made it up."

"What was he driving?"

"Dark blue pickup. Couldn't see the plates, and I couldn't go out and check or I'd have made him suspicious. I want him to come back if the mother doesn't get better."

"Smart."

"He wasn't a nice man."

"How do you know?" I didn't doubt her, I just wondered what evidence she'd seen.

"He was dirty, and he stank of liquor. His eyes were red and runny, like he's been doin' a lot more than drinking. Just one of those shiftless boys given over to drugs and laying around in front of a television. Pasty skin. He hasn't seen the sunshine in a long time."

"Any distinguishing scars or anything?"

"Let's see. He had light hair. I couldn't tell if it was blond or red because it was shaved so close to his head. Blue eyes. He was at least fifty pounds overweight. Five foot ten or eleven." She paused. "There was something at the corner of his right eye. Maybe a scar, maybe a birthmark. The skin was whiter there. About the size of a quarter."

"Would you work with a sketch artist?" I didn't know if DeWayne would be mad at me for butting in, but I had to try. Betty lived in Sunflower County, so the local sheriff's office could get involved.

"I'd be happy to come into town and help. I'll get dressed and be at the courthouse at eight o'clock."

"Thank you, Mrs. McGowin."

"Have you found any trace of that baby's mama?"

It was hard to say. "No, ma'am. We're following leads today."

"Would you ask Mrs. Richmond to bring that baby by? I'd like to take a look at her."

"I'll have her stop by your house. She and Oscar are taking the child to Boston for a specialist to examine the extra digit. They want to pay for the surgery."

"Bless them," Betty said. "Childhood is a place of great cruelty to anyone who is the slightest bit different. Tell Sheriff Peters and Deputy DeWayne to expect me."

"I'll make sure."

I put the phone on the charger and jumped into the shower. Fifteen minutes later, my hair still wet, I was dressed and ready for the day. While the coffee brewed, I called DeWayne and alerted him to the impending arrival of Betty McGowin. He rightly pointed out that a young man asking for medicine wasn't illegal, nor did it prove that the man was involved in Pleasant's abduction. He also agreed to work with Betty to come up with a composite—just in case.

Sipping the black coffee, I went over my notes and decided another trip to Cotton Gin High was in order. I had to find the driver of the silver BMW Randy Hunter had seen the mean girls driving at the Riverview Motel, and I needed to check more facts with Tally McNair.

Sweetie Pie whined at the door of the car and Pluto stood on the porch with his back to me. My emotions warred. I loved taking them with me, but if I ended up engrossed at the school, they'd be trapped in the car.

Sweetie hit a low E minor with her sad howl and I opened the car door. "Come on, but if you're bored, you'd better not damage the car." Not so long ago, I'd left them in the car while I went sleuthing and they'd chewed and clawed their way out of the ragtop. And a good thing, too. They'd saved my life.

The day was sunny and brisk, and Sweetie hung her head out the passenger window and Pluto curled along my thigh, kneading his sharp little claws through my jeans and into my tender skin. I couldn't tell if he was messing with me or truly content, so I let him be.

On the drive, I called Tinkie. Jitty's visit as Lucille Ball had inspired me. I would never tell her, but she was correct. Tinkie had to learn to live her life, with or without Libby. She and Oscar couldn't stop working and living simply because they had a baby to care for. Life continued. Tinkie's only lifeline might be this work.

"What time is your flight to Boston?"

She yawned. "Not until four this afternoon. We'll arrive late and we have the first appointment in the morning. We'll be home shortly after lunch tomorrow. Is Mrs. Smith worried about us taking Libby?"

"No. She's fine. I'm worried."

"Stop it." She yawned again. "I'm too exhausted to argue this morning. Libby wasn't interested in a session with the Sandman last night."

"Get your clothes on, put the baby in a papoose carrier, and meet me at Cotton Gin High. This isn't a request."

"You can't boss me, we're partners." She yawned in the middle of her declaration.

"I'll send Coleman to roust you. Tinkie, if he thinks you're going to be hurt when that baby goes home, he'll take her now. Get up and get out of that house. We have a case to solve."

I easily imagined her mulish expression. People said I was hardheaded. And it was true. But when Tinkie planted her feet, she made me look wishy-washy. "Tinkie, I'm counting on you."

"Sarah Booth, you are impossible."

"I've heard that before. Too bad." I pushed ahead. "Good thing Oscar bought a car seat. I'll be in the band hall. When you go in, could you stop at the office and check for any student who drives a BMW?"

"A high schooler at Cotton Gin High drives a Beamer?"

"Times have changed."

"So it seems."

I hung up and pressed the gas harder.

Driving around the student parking lot, I found the Beamer with no problem. It was a beautiful car, carelessly parked so that it angled in the path of a compact. The conclusions I drew about the driver were not pretty.

Tinkie would find the owner, and I had some questions for Tally McNair. Skirting the office, I went directly to the band hall. I could hear the students practicing "Here Comes Santa Claus." I'd almost forgotten the importance of marching in the Christmas parade for the local high school band. For a split second, I time traveled to my high school years. I'd played the flute, briefly. Only once did I march, when I was in seventh grade, but it had been such a big moment. Aunt Loulane had walked the entire parade route—at a discreet distance. She wasn't worried that anything bad would happen, but she knew it would be a moment when I felt very alone.

"Ms. Delaney, what are you doing here?" While I'd been wool-gathering, Tally had seen me. She didn't add "standing outside the band hall door like a stalker." She didn't have to. Her expression said it all.

"Do you have any of Pleasant's songs?" I hadn't meant to be so blunt, but I'd been caught off guard. "Her mother said you would have them." Why not throw in a half-truth?

"Her mother said I had her songs?"

Her gaze slid away from mine. Red alert! "Yes. Pleasant told her mother she'd entrusted her music to you for safekeeping. I need to see it."

"Of course." She motioned me into the band hall. Ignoring the drums and squawking of woodwinds and tinny brass, she led me to her office. When she closed the door, I sighed in relief at the quiet.

She went to a filing cabinet bursting at the seams with papers. "Pleasant showed me a couple of songs, but I thought I gave them back to her." She pulled out several files, flipped through them, and at last turned to face me, nodding. "I was mistaken. Here they are."

I took the sheet music, which had been written by hand. "Pleasant knows musical notation? She's only seventeen." I could barely write English at seventeen.

"She's a serious musician. I told her if she intended to pursue a career, then she'd have to be able to put her songs on the page, get copyrights, learn how to arrange and produce. That scholarship to Delta State would have put her in a position to step into a career."

I snapped photos of the sheet music and gave them back to Tally. "This is all you have?"

"Yes."

"I'm going to text a composite drawing of a young man to you later this afternoon. Would you show it around to your students, ask if anyone saw this man hanging around Pleasant?"

"Sure."

"Who drives the silver BMW in the parking lot?"

She hesitated.

"You've lied to me once. Maybe you'd better rethink your position here." I knew when to press an advantage.

"I want to help, really. I'll tell you what I know. The Beamer belongs to Amber Tallaniche."

"From the furniture store?"

"Yes." She tidied the files. "Amber's part of the clique of girls who were mean to Pleasant."

"I know all about them," I told her. "They're next on my list for some hard questions. Do you think those girls are capable of hurting a pregnant teenager?"

"Maybe."

That wasn't the answer I'd anticipated. "You think they could kidnap or otherwise harm Pleasant?"

"Those girls are used to getting what they want. They believe it's their due. Lucinda lives in Sunflower County, but her mother pulled strings to get her into Cotton Gin High because her odds at getting scholarships were higher. This is a very poor school. Lucinda, Amber, Brook, those girls have had many privileges, and they're going to school here to scoop up every good thing offered. They expected to walk away with all the offered scholarships and awards. Pleasant upset their plans. She's a top contender for the Delta State scholarship. Or she was."

"A girl who drives a BMW to high school doesn't need scholarships."

"The title of valedictorian helps with college acceptance. Amber will go east to school. Both of her parents are Princeton graduates, and while that's a plus, it isn't a guarantee."

"So it's Brook and Lucinda."

"Be careful. Those girls are treacherous." Tally was

oblivious to the students throwing erasers at each other. One boy jumped a row of chairs, tripped, and hit his chin on the floor. I rose, horrified that he might have snapped his neck. Instead, he jumped up, blood streaming, and began chasing a girl, who danced out of his reach. The chaos in the band hall finally dawned on her.

"Every year the school board tries to cut the band program. They view it as unnecessary. Any little incident can push the board over the top. But these are high-spirited kids and they have so little. They need band and music. Right now, I'd better call them to order or some-one will be injured."

We stepped back into the din. "What does Lucinda play?" I yelled.

"Clarinet. She's very good."

"And Brook?"

"Clarinet also."

"Thanks." I escaped before my eardrums were perma-nently damaged.

13

Tinkie, with Libby resting comfortably in a designer black-and-white sling, was sitting in the principal's office beside a pretty young girl, who obviously smelled something obnoxious, judging from her expression.

"Sarah Booth, this is Amber. She drives the nice car."

"Since when is it a crime to have nice things?" Amber asked. She looked me up and down. "My mom is taking a load of clothes to the Goodwill. Maybe you should take them."

Tinkie stood up, sending Amber into screeches of pain. She writhed about in her chair with great drama. I didn't understand what had happened until I noticed Tinkie's stiletto squarely on Amber's big toe. Tinkie stood with her full weight on it.

"Oh, dear," Tinkie said, looking down and not moving an inch. "I am so sorry. Could you please shut up, you're disturbing the baby."

"Get off my foot." Amber gripped the edge of her seat. "Get off me now."

"Oh, dear." Tinkie started to move and then stepped back with force.

Amber threw herself over in the chair Tinkie had vacated. "You're going to break my foot."

Tinkie leaned down close to her ear. "Yes, I am, you simpering little brat. Now straighten up or I'll pierce your toe."

"Yes, ma'am."

Tinkie stepped away and Amber pulled her foot into her lap. Tears streamed down her face. Her lip curled and she started to say something, but when she looked at Tinkie's grim expression, her mouth shut with an audible snap.

"You have some questions for Amber?" Tinkie asked me.

"The Riverview Motel. You were there four weeks ago."

"So what?"

"So I think you and your buddies are involved in Pleasant Smith's disappearance. When I prove it, you can kiss Princeton and all the rest of the goodies life holds for you good-bye."

"I didn't do anything to Pleasant. Why should I care about her? In seven months, I'll leave this dust pit behind. It was my mother's brilliant idea for me to come here because I could excel. No competition." She flipped her hair. "Pleasant Smith is nothing to do with me. She's my past."

The big-fish-in-a-little-pond syndrome. "What about Brook and Lucinda?"

"Maybe you should ask them."

"Oh, I intend to. You're involved in this, Amber. I advise you to cooperate and help us, or I promise you, the future you think you deserve won't bear any resemblance to life in juvy hall and a future with a criminal record. By the way, you're old enough to be tried as an adult."

So maybe I was stretching the truth, but it had the desired effect. Amber glanced out the window and then back at us. I realized she was taking cues from Brook, who'd ducked in behind some lockers. I opened the door and started toward her, but she shot down the hall. I turned back to Amber. "Your friends can't help you now."

"You can't hurt me."

"Right, you're the Gingerbread girl." Tinkie edged her heel closer to Amber's toes. "Are you so sure about that? Recall what happened to the Gingerbread boy?" She got in Amber's face. "He was eaten."

Libby woke up with a giant squall and then upchucked all over Amber's dress. The clotted and pungent formula spewed across the black silk blouse and several chunks flew in Amber's glossy hair.

"Oh. My. God," Amber squalled. "Look what you did. My mother bought this blouse in Paris. It's ruined."

"Oh, I believe it is. Libby has excellent aim." I was unable to hold back the laughter any longer. Tinkie, too, was giggling.

"Amber, dear, vomit is so caustic. I hope it doesn't wreck your dye job. There are . . . clumps of clabber in your hair."

Amber rose and started toward the door.

"Not so fast," Tinkie said as she comforted Libby,

who was none the worse for wear after the projectile vomit explosion. "We have questions for you."

"I can't answer questions. I stink!" She clenched her teeth and shuddered.

"Too bad. Sit." Tinkie pointed at the chair.

Amber hesitated, but she obeyed. Tinkie had won the war. Amber was a girl who didn't yield, but she was afraid of Tinkie. Or maybe it was Libby, our own little secret weapon.

"What have you done with Pleasant Smith?" Tinkie was so direct, I eased into the background. She had the floor and she knew what to do with it. It could have been my imagination, but Libby watched every move Tinkie made.

"I don't have that girl." Amber touched her hair, found the upchuck, and dissolved into gagging sounds.

"You want to clean that vomit off, then you'd better tell the truth."

"I don't know what happened to her!" Amber edged toward breaking.

"I don't believe you. And you'll sit here until that vomit molds and turns green."

Tinkie's threat was bolstered by class change. Students passed by the window of the office and saw Amber. Laughter and finger-pointing ensued. Amber, probably for the first time in her life, was mocked and ridiculed by students outside her grasp. She'd been knocked from her pedestal by seven pounds of charm.

"Lucinda had a plan to torment Pleasant, but no one intended to hurt her," Amber said. "I wasn't involved. I didn't participate at all. My mother would kill me if I got in trouble and lost my chance at Princeton."

"But you knew about the plan and did nothing." Tinkie handed Libby to me. She was ready to get tough. "If something has happened to that girl, you are as guilty as the others. Do you hear me? I'll personally see to it that you spend the best part of your youth in prison, and trust me, little girl, Oscar and I have donated far more money to judicial elections than you or your parents will ever think about."

Later, I would ask if that were true. Now, though, I sat down, cuddled Libby in my arms, crossed my legs, and enjoyed.

"The others were going to play a joke on her the next time she sang at the Riverview Motel."

"What kind of prank?"

"Lucinda had some friends in Nashville in the music business. She had one coming to pretend to be an agent. You know, make Pleasant think she was on the way to the big time, and then pull the rug out from under her."

The cruelty of these girls was breathtaking.

"Why would you do that?" Free of the baby's weight, Tinkie paced in front of the girl. Any minute now, the principal or someone might enter the office and the spell would be broken. It was time for Tinkie to take it on home.

Amber was near tears. Tinkie had put the fear of justice into her. "Pleasant and Lucinda were competing for a full scholarship to DSU. In music. The top scholarship included room, board, some expense money. The second-place scholarship covered tuition, not room and board. Lucinda needed the top scholarship. We all knew Pleasant had the best chance, and there was only the interview portion of the application to go."

"Embarrassing Pleasant wouldn't ruin her scholarship chance." I didn't see the logic.

"It would if she missed her appointment to be interviewed." Tinkie drove her point home. She'd figured out the girls' motive. "You were going to do something to make her miss that interview." Amber had the good graces to drop her gaze to the floor.

"You would steal her chance? A girl with nothing to fall back on?" Tinkie's voice quavered with outrage. "You are a little monster."

Libby gave a crow of approval. Well, it was more like a gurgle, but I knew she was proud of Tinkie for getting to the bottom of the issue.

Tinkie was far from done. "And you drove the girls over to the Riverview Motel to check it out so you could plot against Pleasant." It wasn't a question.

"Yes, ma'am." Amber had been humbled—or was possibly smarter than she looked.

"You're an accomplice. You'd better hope Pleasant is found safe and sound and that whatever mischief you girls intended didn't play a part in her disappearance."

"No, ma'am. I swear it. There was nothing said, in front of me, about abducting Pleasant for any length of time. Just long enough so she missed her appointment." She squirmed in her chair. "Don't tell the other girls I ratted them out. They'll kill me. I mean, they'll ostracize me and I'd just as soon be dead. Lucinda rules the school."

"Is Carrie Ann Musgrove her mother?" I asked.

"Yes."

Tinkie shot me a look of warning, so I shut up.

"You and your friends need to pray Pleasant isn't harmed." Tinkie went to the door and opened it. When Amber jumped up and ran for it, Tinkie stepped in front of her. "Send Lucinda in here right now."

"I can't! She'll know I blabbed. I have to get this . . . vomit off me."

Tinkie's eyebrow arched.

"Okay, okay. She's in history this period. I'll get her."

"Before you go, do you know anyone who looks like this?" I showed the photo of Alfred Uxall on my phone.

"Yeah, Rudy."

"And how do you know him?"

"He went to school here but dropped out a few years back. He'd been held back so many times I guess he was ashamed to keep showing up for class." She laughed and the cruel girl showed through.

"Did you ever see him around Pleasant?"

"She was a freaking geek magnet. Rudy and that worm Frankie. Losers. They were drawn to her like flies to a turd." And she was out the door like a shot.

"Why don't we pay a visit to Carrie Ann before we question Lucinda?" My partner was flushed and breathing hard. "By the way, you were amazing!"

She reached for the baby, and I released Libby into her arms. "Let's get out of here. Lucinda will come here and wonder what Amber is babbling about. Good plan. We'll use psychological warfare on them."

"Brilliant." And we were hoofing it out the front door of the school in ten seconds flat.

Carrie Ann Musgrove, née Binder, was the queen of Sunflower County High School when I attended. In the female hierarchy of public schools at that time, the majorettes were top of the heap, followed by the cheerleaders, then the friendly girls, then the female athletes, and finally, the brainiacs.

Above all of those categories, Carrie Ann Binder had reigned supreme. She was the girl with talent, with opportunity, with drive. Carrie Ann Binder had been on America's Olympic gymnastics team. She had been the best in America on the balance beam. Her picture had graced the ever-popular breakfast cereal, Wheaties.

And when she was just eighteen, Carrie Ann traded it all in for pregnancy and a shotgun wedding to Charles Musgrove, a local contractor. Perhaps she'd made the best choice, but based on what I knew about her daughter Lucinda, things didn't look all that peachy.

Tinkie got directions to Carrie Ann's house from the Internet, and when we turned down a rutted dirt road, I slowed the car. "This can't be right. Charles Musgrove is one of the foremost contractors working in the state. This area is seedy."

"Carrie Ann and Charles divorced five years ago, Sarah Booth. You are so-o-o-o behind on the gossip. She moved to June Bug, which is a community on the line between Bolivar and Sunflower Counties." She pointed at an abandoned trailer and a barn whose roof had collapsed. "But I didn't expect it to be this dismal. Charles caught her cheating. Photos, the whole thing. I guess the judge ruled against alimony for her."

"Talk about the wages of sin." We bumped along. Sweetie was hanging over the backseat licking Libby and making her laugh. "Surely Charles would have provided for his own daughter, though."

"Lucinda sounds exactly like Carrie Ann. Maybe he'd had enough of both of them."

But a real man doesn't walk away from his responsibilities. No matter what. I didn't know Charles Musgrove so I kept my comments to myself.

"Carrie Ann tricked Charles." Tinkie continued the story without prompting. "She went after him, bragging to several classmates that she would be his wife before the year was out. And that's what happened. She got pregnant and insisted that he divorce his wife and marry her."

"It takes two to tango. She was a teenager. He was what? Twenty-five? I'm not defending her, but he could have kept it in his pants."

"True. She was smart and he was stupid. But can you imagine living with Carrie Ann for any length of time? She was awful to us when she was a big deal. Remember? She told everyone in school your parents were drunk and deserved to die."

Oh, I remembered. Vividly. "Yeah, she's awful. Still doesn't excuse his part in it, and Lucinda is his child . . ." I looked at Tinkie. "Rut-roh."

"Oh, my." Tinkie caught the same wavelength. "Maybe Lucinda *isn't* his child. Charles wrecked his marriage and married a human spider, all because he thought he was going to be a father. What if he isn't and never was? No wonder he doesn't provide for Lucinda."

Call me a sucker, but I felt a glimmer of pity for Lucinda. Ultimately, maybe she was nobody's child.

We pulled up at a small brick house. The yard looked like a tornado had just blown through. My pity for Lucinda notched up. She hung with the wealthy girls in high school, but she could never really belong. Coming from this home would be a hard road. I could only imagine the manipulation it took to keep her friends from dropping by for a visit.

"You're feeling sorry for Lucinda," Tinkie said. "I know you. Always the champion of the underdog. The girl is healthy. Why can't she push a lawn mower or pick up trash? She's not afflicted with anything except a huge ego and a lack of morals. Don't feel sorry for her. She's lazy."

Motherhood had brought out the mama bear in Tinkie. "You're not thinking of a move to Alaska, are you?" I asked.

"Have you lost your mind?" She marched through the weeds to the front door. "I knew better than to put on my good shoes, but here we are at God's little acre." She banged her fist on the door. She was acting more and more like me than . . . me. "Carrie Ann, open this door and do it right now."

When the door opened, I did a double take. Carrie Ann Musgrove looked nothing like the petite contortionist who'd been the most popular girl in high school. It had been rumored of Carrie Ann that once she locked her thighs on a man, he had to call the Jaws of Life to get free. Now, she was dowdy, overweight, tired looking, and not all that clean.

"Tinkie Bellcase Richmond, what are you doing here?" She caught sight of me. "And you, the professional snoop. What brings you here?"

That was all it took. Sweetie Pie and Chablis leaped out the car window and rushed to Tinkie's side. Sweetie's hackles rose, but she didn't make a sound. Chablis moved in closer and growled.

"My, my, look at you," Carrie Ann said. Her small eyes held malice. She drank in the sight of Libby papoosed on Tinkie's chest, and then zeroed in on me. "Unless you managed a two-week pregnancy, Tinkie Richmond, you got someone else's baby. The question is whose?"

"We'll ask the questions," I said.

"Those dogs need to learn their place." Carrie Ann

propped herself against the front porch column—which happened to be a four-by-four someone had nailed up a bit crookedly. "You'd better round them critters up and put them back in the car before I show you my shotgun. I could blast that little one into pieces so tiny you wouldn't have anything to bury."

"Give it a try," Tinkie said.

"State your business and get gone."

"Your daughter is implicated in a kidnapping." Tinkie pointed to Libby. "The mother of this child is missing, and Lucinda has something to do with it."

"Prove it." Carrie Ann might have lost her looks, but she still had her signature attitude.

"Don't worry. We will."

"If you had anything on my daughter, the law would be here instead of you. Get off my property. And take that little bastard with you."

"We'll find Pleasant. Alive or dead. And when we do, the law will be here." Tinkie started to leave but spun back to face Carrie Ann. "What happened to you? Twenty years ago, you had the world by the tail."

"Life happened. You've always been pampered and protected by your daddy's money. I never had that. I practiced gymnastics seven days a week all through high school for that one shining moment at the Olympics. My entire life peaked then. After that, it was all downhill for me. The male athletes get jobs as spokesmen or coaches or whatever. What's left for a woman? I came home from the Olympics and realized it was all over. I couldn't go back to the Olympics in four years. I would be too old, over the hill. So I took a shot at the good life I deserved."

"You trapped a man into marriage *after* you broke up

his first marriage. And the child isn't even his. Who is Lucinda's father?" I was goading her for a reaction, and I got one.

"Get off my land." She rushed off the porch and grabbed an old rake with only four tines. It had been left in the weather and rusted away, a perfect metaphor for Carrie Ann's life. She raised the rake as if she meant to hit Tinkie with it. I started forward, but there was no need. Sweetie and Chablis were on the job. Cujo had nothing on them. At last, Pluto slipped around the corner of the house, waiting in case the cavalry was needed. Typical cat, he refused to expend energy until it was absolutely necessary.

"Hit me," Tinkie said to Carrie Ann. She motioned for me to take Libby, which I did as fast as I could. "Hit me. I dare you. I will kick your ass into the middle of next week."

"Tinkie!" I stepped in front of her. She was acting like a moron. She was only five-two and weighed less than a hundred pounds. I was always amazed that she could balance on five-inch stilettos and not topple over. If Carrie Ann tripped and fell on my partner, there was no doubt Tinkie would be crushed to a grease spot on the grass. "Don't be ridiculous. You aren't going to duke it out in the front yard." My partner was way, way over the top emotionally. Baby love clouded her judgment.

"She's responsible." Tinkie was almost breathing fire. I'd never seen her so out of control.

"If she is, she'll pay. Let's talk about this." I leaned down. "You have a plane to catch. Pull yourself together and let's get back to Zinnia. You're lucky Bellow has a private jet." I wasn't a big fan of Yancy Bellow, but he owned the plane that would whisk Tinkie, Oscar, and

Libby into Boston for the doctor's appointment and home within a matter of hours. The trip via private plane would be much easier on the little family.

I broke up the staring match by grasping Tinkie's arm and turning her away. "Libby and I are leaving. You can stay and fight or drink tea or do whatever. I can't drag you and I'm not going to watch this descend into grounds for a lawsuit." I started to the car.

"I hear you got left at the altar, Sarah Booth Delaney," Carrie Ann called out. "Better snare a guy quick. The bloom is off the rose."

I stopped in my tracks. "Kill her, Tinkie. You have my permission." I didn't turn around, but I heard Tinkie cursing as she waded through the weeds back to the car.

Carrie Ann stood in her blighted front yard, an empty Cheetos bag fluttering past her in a gust of wind. "Don't come back here or I'll greet you with some double aught."

We ignored her, but the minute the animals were safely in the car and the door closed, Tinkie rounded on me. "Carrie Ann is involved. The stink is all over her."

"Possibly it's just poor hygiene. She looked rather unkempt."

"She's guilty. She and that girl of hers. When I get back from Boston, I'm going to prove it."

"Good plan." On the one hand, I was relieved that Tinkie had taken an interest in work. On the other hand, she was something of a loose cannon. "I'll drop you at your car and then I'm—"

My pontificating was interrupted by the ringing of my phone.

Rick Ralston, the PI in Nashville, was calling.

14

I put the phone on speaker as I drove. Tinkie fed Libby, who was chugging down the formula. She had the appetite of a laborer. I eyed her with wariness now that I knew she could shoot vomit ten feet and hit a moving target.

"What have you found?" I asked Rick.

"Some very interesting facts."

"Tinkie and I are all ears," I said. "Be quick, Tinkie has to leave shortly."

"Those songs you sent to me, I got a friend to play them and sing. I realized they sounded familiar. I made a tape and took it around to some of the agents I know. I had some real luck and hit on Benny Hester, one of the biggest agents in Nashville. He knew the music. In fact, he's representing the woman who claims she wrote the music."

"Pleasant? Is she in Nashville?" I shot a sidelong glance at Tinkie, who had stopped breathing.

"No, that's not the woman who claims to be the songwriter." Rick's voice was thin and tinny on the speaker.

Tinkie and I both were on the edge of our seats. "Who?" We said simultaneously.

"Tally McNair. She's a high school band director in Mississippi."

"Are you sure? Young woman with black hair. Personable." I didn't want to believe Pleasant had been sold out by her music mentor, the one person she should have been able to trust.

"I didn't think to get a description, but I will. She's a band director, though. I'm sure of that. Can you run her down?"

"I'll see her in about five minutes."

"She's in big trouble. She said they were her songs when she signed on with Benny. He got a rising young star, Laney Best, to cut a recording. They've made a high-budget video and have planned a big release of the song. There's a lot of money in this. I heard Laney sing it at the Bluebird Café a few weeks ago. It's a damn fine song and brought the house down."

"Thanks, Rick. Look, Tinkie will be home from Boston tomorrow. I think we'll drive up to Nashville with a photograph of Tally McNair. I want to be certain we're after the right woman." I could easily send a photo of Tally, but I wanted some alone time with Tinkie.

"Sounds like a plan. I'll make an appointment with Benny. We'll get this sorted, and hopefully you can find the young woman who is missing."

Tinkie looked out the window, away from me.

"That's our hope." I hung up. My friend was in pain, and I didn't know what to say. I kept to the topic of work. "Head on to Boston. We'll deal with Tally when you get back tomorrow." Thank goodness we'd arrived at the school. Tinkie was about to break my heart.

"I'll call when I get back," Tinkie said, but she averted her gaze.

After I'd waved Tinkie, Libby, and Chablis out of the parking lot, I walked to the band hall. Tally had the kids playing another Christmas tune, and they sounded great. I'd loved singing "Frosty the Snowman" with my dad, who could sing. How had two talented parents produced a child whose singing voice was like an icepick in someone's ear?

I didn't want to alert Tally that we were onto her. No, I had a better plan. I snapped a photo of her through the window and headed back to Zinnia and the sheriff's office.

When I walked into the office, my entire body flushed at the sight of Coleman. Our searing kiss came back to haunt me with as much power as Jitty. And with a lot more pleasure. Sweetie Pie bounded forward and gave Coleman a good licking. Pluto decided to play the Egyptian card and hopped to the counter, where he struck a sphinx pose. Solid black with golden green eyes, he looked like he might rule the universe.

For my part, I avoided Coleman's provocative look. He had me in retreat, and he knew it. I'd shown my hand when I reacted so strongly to his kiss.

"Sarah Booth," Coleman said lazily. "DeWayne's got a composite for you. Thanks for sending that midwife, Betty McGowin, in to talk to him."

"I thought you were in Memphis."

"Got home late last night. I'm hoping my part in the triple murder investigation is done. This ring of criminals is bigger than DeWayne and I can manage, and it's spread all across Mississippi and Arkansas, wherever there are large tracts of isolated farmland. I can cut the tail off the snake here in Sunflower County, but they need a regional or national initiative if they want to chop off the head. These criminals are entrenched and smart."

I was glad twice over that he wasn't investigating gangs that dealt in drugs and guns. Those were violent people with no regard for life. "So you're home."

"I am." He grinned and gave me a wicked wink. "Your powers of observation amaze me."

"Keep it up. I've had to deal with Macho Kick-Butt Tinkie and a spewing baby this morning, and besides . . ." I let it hang there. "I've solved the case."

"Do tell." Coleman was really feeling his oats. He hadn't been so filled with mischief in a long time.

"It's Tally McNair. She did something to Pleasant so she could steal her music. I'm going to Nashville tomorrow evening to talk with a music agent, Benny Hester. He signed Tally to a contract to license her songs. Only they aren't Tally's; they're Pleasant's songs."

"That's motive. And I can see where McNair would have opportunity and means. So where is Pleasant?"

"That's what I need you to help me with."

"Go on."

"You don't have jurisdiction in Bolivar County, and I don't trust Hoss Kincaid to do anything, much less the right thing. So I'm going to lure Tally over here, and then you can arrest her."

"On what charge?"

"Theft, fraud, identity theft. What do I care? Just arrest her, put her in the box, and let's sweat her. Maybe I can give her a tune-up."

"Stop watching *NYPD Blue* reruns, Sarah Booth. We don't give tune-ups in Sunflower County."

"This case may be the exception." If Tally McNair didn't come forth with helpful information, I'd work her over. The idea of a grown woman stealing from a teenager—to say nothing about putting a very pregnant young girl in danger—made me want physical retribution. In the corner, DeWayne was laughing and not doing a lot to hide it. He apparently enjoyed the repartee between his boss and me.

I decided to enlist him on my side. "DeWayne, find a stocking and I'll put an orange in it. I hear that's the thing to use when a criminal won't talk."

Coleman was laughing now. "Okay, I'll arrest her. But you aren't going in the cell with her, and just so you know, we don't have a 'box' here to sweat anyone in." He laughed again. "The things you get in your head."

I made the call to Tally and told her I had a lead on Pleasant. "Deputy DeWayne Dattilo here in the Sunflower County sheriff's office has put together a composite sketch of a man who may have been involved in the abduction." I wasn't lying. DeWayne had the composite of the young man who'd been by Betty McGowin's house asking for medicine for cramps for a woman who'd just delivered a baby.

"Really?" Tally sounded suspicious.

"Please stop by and see if you can identify him."

"I have no clue who took Pleasant. How can I identify anyone?"

She was getting on my last nerve. "We need to know if

you've ever seen this man. Maybe hanging at the school or watching the band. You know, suspicious behavior."

"Oh. Okay." She hesitated. She was smarter than I'd assumed.

"Now, Tally. It's urgent. If this man has Pleasant and we can find him, we may be able to save her."

"I have a hair appointment."

"Okay. Hold on." I half muffled the phone with my hand. "Sheriff Peters, she can't help us. She has a hair appointment."

"Does she know she may be condemning Pleasant Smith to injury or death?"

"She's not an idiot. She has to know." I gave it a beat. "I guess she doesn't care."

"Up to her," Coleman added. "I hope she's aware of potential legal repercussions."

I spoke into the phone. "Okay, Tally, if you won't help."

"Wait a minute. What repercussions?"

"Depends on what happens to Pleasant, I guess. You'd have to talk to the sheriff about that. I'm not a law officer, you know. I'll put the sheriff on the phone."

"No! No! Don't do that. I'll come look at the picture."

The mouse had taken the bait. "Perfect. I'll wait here at the sheriff's office for you."

"I'm on my way."

Tally, ponytail swinging behind her, arrived at the sheriff's office with an equal mix of annoyance and trepidation. DeWayne sat at his desk, taking it all in. Francine was a little more proactive. She came up to the counter. "Care for some coffee?" she asked. I had to wonder if maybe Coleman had put her up to getting a DNA sample or something.

"I don't have time for coffee," Tally said. "I've got band rehearsal tonight. The Christmas parade is just around the corner and my students are going to blow everyone away." She looked around the old office, taking in the battered wooden desks, the worn hardwood floor, the general air of neglect that occurred in two-hundred-year-old buildings unless they were meticulously maintained. Her gaze stopped on Pluto, sitting on the counter watching her. "You have animals in the office. Is that allowed?"

Pluto shifted from his pose and sauntered over to Tally. He stayed out of range, but he fixed her with a glare. On the floor at Coleman's feet, Sweetie gave the sweetest doggie sigh and yielded to sleep.

"Oh, they're just here for a visit," I said. "Pluto is like a living, breathing lie detector test. When someone is lying, he knows it."

Poor Tally. Her life was about to unravel. Animals in a public office and the Christmas parade would be the least of her worries. She faced grand theft charges, if not worse.

"Show me the picture," she said. "I know I can't help, but I would never want you to think I didn't try. Pleasant is the most talented student I've ever taught."

"Is that why you stole her songs and sold them as your own?" I asked.

Tally didn't even attempt to defend herself. Her face crumpled and tears literally squirted from her eyes like some cartoon character. "I thought she was dead." She boo-hooed harder. I only wished Tinkie were here to witness the breakdown. In her current mood, she'd probably toss Tally to the floor and sit on her.

Coleman read Tally her rights and proceeded to list the

charges against her. When he had thoroughly terrorized her, he put the composite drawing in front of her. "Do you know this man? Before you answer, consider that you may do yourself some good by helping us find Pleasant. Right now, you aren't charged with anything relating to Pleasant's disappearance. That will change if something happens to her. You could be facing charges of kidnapping. Or murder."

"Oh, god. I didn't have a thing to do with her disappearance. I didn't." She looked from Coleman to me to Francine. She didn't have a friend in the room. "I didn't. I warned those girls—" Her eyes widened. "I want a lawyer."

"You're entitled to one," Coleman said.

I wanted to kick him. Or kiss him. I was torn. But I didn't want her to have a lawyer. "Sure. Go ahead. Call a lawyer. If Pleasant dies, you'll be complicit in a capital murder."

"Capital murder?" Tally's tears fell freely. "Why capital? Does that mean the death penalty?"

I lowered the boom again. "Yes, harming a pregnant woman is capital murder. That means the gas chamber!"

Tally went green. Behind her, Coleman signaled me to cease and desist. He was not kidding around, either.

"Who is this man?" I pushed the picture at her.

"I don't know his name." She struggled for composure. "I'm not involved in the kidnapping. I took her songs when she didn't come back. I'm a thief, but I didn't kill anyone and I wasn't involved in abducting Pleasant."

"But you knew about the plan to abduct her and you didn't stop it."

"Is that true?" Coleman asked her in a tone weighted with seriousness.

"I . . . uh, I can't . . . I—"

"You know who took her. You'd better tell us now!" I slammed the desktop with my hand. Papers and paperclips jumped, and so did Tally and Francine.

"Break it and you own it," Francine said under her breath.

While Francine wasn't impressed with my tactics, Tally almost peed her pants. "I only overheard them talking. I thought they were kidding."

"Who is *they*?" Coleman asked softly.

"Those girls. They hated Pleasant. Lucinda had it in her head that Pleasant would get the scholarship that should have gone to her. The full ride. Lucinda was furious. They were talking about detaining Pleasant until she missed the deadline to interview for the scholarship. I thought it was a joke."

"But when Pleasant didn't return to school, did you report this information to anyone?"

"It was hearsay. I didn't have any proof."

"It was information that could have saved a pregnant young woman. Now, where did those teenagers say they were going to take Pleasant?" Coleman was through being Mr. Nice Guy. "You'd better tell me right now."

"They didn't say. They really didn't. They were just talking about making her miss the scholarship deadline, which was a month ago. It was like an overnight thing, the way they were talking. I didn't believe they'd really do it. I don't know that they did."

"Who is the man in the drawing?" Coleman pushed it in front of her again. "Help yourself and tell us."

"He's some guy Lucinda knows."

"How do you know this?" Coleman asked.

"I don't *know* it. That's what Lucinda said. I saw her

talking to him a few days before Pleasant disappeared. They were arguing under the bleachers, so I asked her who he was and what he was doing on campus. He's too old to be a student." She forestalled my next question. "That's all I know about him. And I only saw him that one time. I did see her talking to another guy, too."

"This man?" I showed the photo of Alfred Uxall.

"No, not him. Rudy. That's Rudy Uxall's brother, Alfred."

"Do you know the Uxalls?"

"They were students, when they bothered to come to class. Rudy followed Pleasant like a lovestruck dog. Maybe he took her."

"Rudy Uxall is dead," I told her. Her shock seemed genuine, but Tally was an accomplished liar.

"Okay. Now what girls were in on the abduction scheme?"

"Lucinda, Amber, and Brook. Those are the ones I know."

"Any boys from the high school?"

She shook her head. "Those girls won't give Cotton Gin High boys the time of day."

Coleman stood up. "DeWayne, please escort Ms. Mc-Nair to a cell." He looked at Tally. "Make yourself at home. I have a feeling you'll be our guest for a lot longer than you want."

I thought Tally might make a break for freedom, but she followed behind DeWayne like a ghost.

Francine went to wash out the coffeepot. Her day was done. Coleman took the opportunity to step close to me. I thought he might kiss me again, but he had other things on his mind.

"You've solved the case, Sarah Booth, but we still don't

have a clue where Pleasant is. I do believe she's alive, though. I can't wrap my mind around the concept that three teenagers pulled this off without help from an adult. Rudy Uxall might have been inadvertently involved, but it sounds like he genuinely cared for Pleasant. From what I've learned, he doesn't sound smart enough to plan this. And who stabbed him? So far DeWayne hasn't found the scene of the stabbing. It might not have even happened in Sunflower County."

"As much as I want to figure out who stabbed Rudy, and we will do that, my first priority is finding Pleasant. If she is alive, imagine how anguished she is over her baby." I took a breath. "Charity believes Rudy took baby Libby to my house because Pleasant told him to. She believes Pleasant was trying to send a message for someone to come looking for her."

Instead of laughing, Coleman rubbed his chin in thought. "So maybe Rudy was duped into helping abduct Pleasant, and then he realized she was really in danger. So—"

"Amber is capable of stabbing someone." I didn't have a doubt. "Maybe Lucinda and Brook, too. If those girls are behind this, someone helped them. I think it was Carrie Ann Musgrove."

"Lucinda's mother? The Olympic gymnast. Man, a lot of the boys had some hot fantasies about her."

"More information than I want to know." I put my hands over my ears. "Too bad Carrie Ann is in Bolivar County or we could pay a visit on her. We'd be right on time for supper."

"She lives in Sunflower County. Just on the line, but in this county. June Bug community straddles the two counties, but her house is here. I had to go out there two years ago with the tax assessor. She threatened to shoot him."

"What are we waiting for?" I was starving and tired, but the thought of arresting Carrie Ann was like a jolt of pure adrenaline.

The fax machine beeped and Coleman hurried to Francine's desk. In a moment he looked hard at me.

"What?"

He printed off a sheet of paper and brought it to me. He handed it over without comment.

The photo was grainy, but it was evident that Gertrude Strom, in a Chinese-red Mercedes roadster, just like my mother's, was filling her tank with gasoline. In the distance were cotton fields that stretched forever. She was in a Delta area, in Mississippi, Arkansas, or maybe Louisiana.

"Where is she?" I asked.

"Bolivar County. The clerk at the station thought she looked familiar, but a tanker pulled in to fill the pumps and he got busy. This was about two hours ago. He checked the store's security cameras and compared the likeness with those on the wanted posters. He's after the reward."

"Then he should have acted more quickly." Two hours. Gertrude could be sitting outside the courthouse right now with a rifle and a scope.

"I'm going to take you home and stay with you." When I started to speak, he shook his head. "No arguments. I'll stay in a guest room." He was all business. Now wasn't the time for innuendo or teasing. "I want to keep you safe."

"Why can't someone catch her?"

"Sarah Booth, there are two, maybe three deputies in

most of the rural counties. We need ten or twenty to do the job properly, but the supervisors aren't going to fund law enforcement when roads aren't paved and bridges aren't maintained. Schools are falling down around our ears. The state can't help because they're in deficit spending. There are half a dozen highway patrolmen for the miles and miles of highway in the region. There's not enough manpower, and when the average citizen sees an antique car pass, they think, how nice. That's it. Gertrude Strom is the furthest thing from his mind."

"That's not comforting in the least."

"It isn't meant to be. DeWayne and I will do everything we can to protect you. So will your friends, but you have to be hypervigilant. You are the target. No one can take better care of you than *you*. Pay attention."

"She's like a force of nature. She can't be stopped. Do you really think she wants to kill me?" I'd done nothing to Gertrude. She hated me for an imagined slight my mother had made against her. In Gertrude's mind, my mother had given away the secret of her illegitimate pregnancy.

That was untrue and crazy, but even nuttier was that Gertrude had ended up killing her own son. Her target had been a pseudo-intellectual and academic, Olive Twist. Instead of killing the obnoxious Twist, Gertrude had poisoned her own child. Next, she meant to harm me. She'd made a few unsuccessful attempts, and she wasn't done yet. Gertrude had gone from a local kook with a mean streak to a full-blown sociopath.

"Let's get you home. It's too dangerous to be running up and down the roads in the dark."

"What about interviewing Carrie Ann?"

"It can wait."

I agreed with some reluctance. Pleasant's life could be

in jeopardy—we needed to focus on squeezing the truth out of Carrie Ann Musgrove, not hide out at Dahlia House. Would Carrie Ann be smart enough to cover her tracks? I didn't want to delay, but I was a coward. I was afraid of Gertrude.

15

Sweetie Pie led the way to the kitchen. While I put coffee on to brew, Coleman went through the refrigerator to see what supplies I had. All of us were starving. A sit-down at Millie's Café would have been my preference, but Coleman didn't want me in town, easily visible in the plate-glass windows of the diner. It was make do at home.

"Stir-fry," Coleman said as he pulled out vegetables. "I'll cook if you clean."

"You've got a deal."

While he busied himself with our meal, I heated some beef stroganoff for Sweetie and a bit of leftover amberjack for Pluto. Both appreciated my efforts and fell asleep under the table. As I set the small table in the kitchen, my heart thudded. Food preparation and cleanup would be behind us, and I would be with Coleman, alone, in my cold home—knowing that he had everything needed to warm me up.

My body was surely ready for the adventure, but was my heart? Coleman and I had gotten crosswise of timing in the past. I'd been free and ready, and he'd been married and ready. I respected him for refusing to engage in an affair while Connie wore his ring. Until it became abundantly clear that Connie had no honor. A fake pregnancy had brought Coleman home, and when her deception was revealed, it had ended their marriage.

It was too late for us by then. I'd hardened my heart and gone on to new relationships, the latest of which had ended in a broken engagement. I wasn't certain my heart was ready to try again. Rushing into a relationship, romantic or just plain sexual, was not what I needed. And I had to hold firm to that knowledge and not let Coleman seduce me—because he certainly could.

Coleman came up behind me as I leaned over to put napkins at our plates. His arms circled my waist and pulled me into him. At first I resisted, and then I relaxed. Coleman's arms were the safest place in the world.

"Dinner's ready," he whispered in my ear, sending chills over me.

"We should eat."

"We probably should." Coleman lifted the wine bottle I'd uncorked and poured a glass. He offered it to me, and I shared with him. Leaning against him, I let my worries drop away. Life offered so many wonderful opportunities.

"The food smells delicious."

"I can cook." He laughed. "I know that shocks you."

"You were always a grill expert, but I didn't realize you'd mastered Chinese cuisine."

"Mastered may be stretching the point." His hands spread across my rib cage, drawing me more closely to him as his chin tucked into my shoulder, the better to allow his words to tease my ear.

My body wanted to turn, to press myself against him. I could feel the blood thrumming through me, and I was short of breath. Coleman could read the signs. He knew he was having an effect on me, because he chuckled softly.

Unable to bear it any longer, I spun in his arms and lifted my face, anticipating a kiss.

"No, I don't think I will kiss you, although you need kissing badly. That's what's wrong with you. You should be kissed, and often, by someone who knows how."

I stepped back to find him unable to hide his amusement. "You are going to pay for that Rhett Butler rip-off. I am no simpering Scarlett waiting for a man to solve my problems."

"That's where you're wrong." The challenge had been thrown.

"Coleman Peters, what do you mean?"

"You're brave and fiery and capable."

"Oh." I'd misread his comment.

"And you're willful and rash and impetuous."

He was heading back into deep water.

"And very kissable."

Before I had time to think, he kissed me.

When he finally eased back, I was Jell-O kneed. This was a whole new Coleman. We'd shared passion in the past, but Coleman had never demonstrated such accomplished skills at making a woman tingle all over. He was confident, and that was like a live wire of desire right to my nether regions.

"You can't do this."

"Because you're a lady?"

"Dammit! Stop thieving Rhett's lines. I am no lady."

He handed me the wineglass. "Drink the wine before you throw it. Less mess to clean."

"What is wrong with you? Have you binge watched *Gone with the Wind*?"

"I'm patterning myself after a man that all Southern women love."

"Sit down and let's eat. The food is getting cold." In truth, I wanted the table between us. Coleman affected me, and there were no two ways around it. He was like a flame, and I was drawn to him, even knowing I might get myself torched. Judging from the fire Coleman generated, more like burned to a crisp.

We'd just taken a seat when Coleman's phone rang. He hesitated.

"Answer it. Maybe they arrested Gertrude."

"Hello, Sheriff Kincaid." Coleman slowly rose from the table and turned profile. "I see. Well I can assure you it wasn't Ms. Delaney. She's been with me most of the afternoon and this evening."

He kept his attention focused away from me.

"Yes, she's here right now. I appreciate the heads-up on Gertrude Strom, by the way. You will let me know if you apprehend her. I'll be on my way there shortly."

He put the phone down. "Carrie Ann Musgrove has filed charges against you. She said you tried to burn her house down."

"That's insane. I've been with you."

"It's time I have a chat with her."

I stood, too. "I'll go with you."

"No, you're staying right here with Sweetie Pie and Pluto to watch over you. And just for extra precautions, I'll send DeWayne over."

"That's not necessary. I'll be fine. I have a gun."

"And that's one of the things that worries me."

I gave him the Vulcan salute that I'd learned so long ago from *Star Trek* reruns. "Live long and prosper."

"Stay in the house. Lock the doors. DeWayne will be here shortly."

About ninety-five percent of me watched Coleman walk out with sadness. The other five percent, that small percentage that warned me to use caution, was relieved. The sexual pull between us was heady and dangerous. Not dangerous like Gertrude, but we both had the power to harm each other, and I had had enough heartache.

I filled my plate and sat down. I was famished, and Coleman's departure had done nothing to quell my appetite.

The stir-fry was delicious. I hadn't considered that Coleman had taught himself to cook since his divorce. Such talents might prove useful in the future, which stretched out before me, a long path fraught with possibilities.

I'd just stabbed a snow pea when I realized I was being watched. I pivoted in my chair and almost fell over. A beautiful young woman stood by the kitchen sink. I recognized her instantly, even without her crown. Millie, my tabloid-reading friend, was going to be pea green with envy. She had had a real thing for Princess Di.

"Only do what your heart tells you," the woman, who was once in line to be the future queen of England, said.

"Listening to my heart isn't so easy, Diana. It wasn't easy for you, either. The fairy tale often has a dark ending."

"Love can be treacherous, but it is the joy of life. You have many who love you, as did I. And I left two fine men behind to brighten the world."

"I have to know. Was the wreck a setup?"

She ducked her head in that classic shy maneuver. "That's behind me. The future is what you must guard. Be careful, Sarah Booth. You have much love to give, but there are also those who don't want love to flourish."

"Are you talking about Gertrude Strom?"

"Gertrude is not alone. There are many who disdain love and compassion and focus only on greed and acquisition. They will stop at nothing to get what they want."

She would not tell me who. The rules of the Great Beyond did not allow name-dropping.

"Are you happy?" I asked her. Millie would want to know this.

"I am. And proud of my sons and my grandchildren, though I will never hold little George or Charlotte. That is a hard thing."

"And you are eternally young." Not exactly compensation for the inability to hold a grandchild, but it was at least something.

"Your children are your legacy, Sarah Booth. Never forget."

Slowly she began to change, the blue eyes darkening to brown, and the pale skin taking on the mocha tones of my personal haint. Jitty was in the house.

"Jitty, I appreciate the artistry of using a beloved princess to try to get me to bed a man, but if my sole purpose is to breed a Delaney heir, you may be disappointed."

"How do you know that was me? Maybe I'm merely a vessel for the spirits who try to pound somethin' into that hard noggin of yours."

"It's you—in disguise."

"Are you so certain?" Jitty was back in full haint mode. Gone were the sequined gown and the blond bob. She wore my favorite jeans, a plaid flannel shirt, and my riding boots.

"You have an endless wardrobe. Why are you wearing my clothes?"

"What do Princess Di and Sarah Booth Delaney have in common?" she asked.

"Certainly not a sense of fashion."

"You can say that again," Jitty said. "But you both love life and try to help people."

"Jitty, my dinner is getting cold. I appreciate the visit, but I have bigger fish to fry than romance and errant sperm—like finding Gertrude Strom."

"Where is that deputy?" Jitty grumped. "He should have been here by now."

My phone rang and I answered DeWayne's call. When I looked up, Jitty was gone.

"I just got a 911 from a woman in Fitler. There's a shooting there and Coleman is on the other side of the county. I was on my way to stay with you, but I have to go to Fitler. Who should I call to stay with you? Scott? Harold? Cece? Tinkie and Oscar are out of town."

It was a quandary. Cece was likely at Playin' the Bones with her man, Jaytee. And that's where Scott needed to be also. "Harold would be great, if he isn't busy. He can bring Roscoe for a play date with Sweetie Pie."

It was pointless for me to attempt to escape adult

supervision. I would only make life hard for DeWayne if I protested or delayed.

"I'll give him a call. I'm sorry, Sarah Booth."

"Duty calls, and I'm fine. Sweetie Pie is right here with me. And Pluto, the cat with the killer claws. We're fine. I'll enjoy a visit with Harold. Have you heard anything more about Gertrude?"

DeWayne cleared his throat. "No other sightings. Sarah Booth, she's hiding somewhere close. She comes out to get the rumors started and then runs back in her hidey-hole. She's cunning, and she's planning something, and whatever it is, you aren't going to like it."

My gut clenched in a way that told me DeWayne's predictions were probably true. "I'm on alert." I slid the kitchen door latch as I talked. With Coleman in the house, I hadn't felt the chill of apprehension. Now, though, I was on edge.

"Harold should be there shortly. If there's a problem, I'll come pick you up and take you to Fitler with me."

"Okay." I'd made it to the front door and snapped on the porch lights. The day had slipped into darkness so complete the lights illuminated the porch and nothing else. I bolted the door until Harold arrived. As much as I hated to involve my friends in what could be a dangerous scenario, I didn't want to be alone.

Gertrude was crazy. And she hated me.

My hand was still on the door lock when Sweetie Pie materialized at my side. She growled and inserted herself between the door and me. When I looked down, Pluto was there, too, back arched.

Someone, or something, was outside my home.

16

I eased to the sidelight on the right of the heavy oak door and peered out. I'd never seen such a black night. Despite the inky darkness that seemed to drink all light, everything was normal. My car was parked at the front steps. The wind blew a few dead leaves across the gray boards of the porch. Typical November night. Everything was fine. My imagination had gotten the best of me.

I petted Sweetie and rumpled her ears. "Take it easy, girl. We're both on edge." Pluto was not a cat to be cozied out of his wariness. When I reached to stroke his sleek black fur, he growled low and deep.

"It's okay," I told him, pulling back the sheer curtain at the sidelight so he could see out unobstructed. "No one is there."

A long shadow stretched across the porch where none had been before. It moved toward the door. It had a head, torso, arms, and legs. The animals were correct—someone was on the porch.

I pressed my back against the door, my thoughts like rodents trapped in a cage, running madly. I'd foolishly left my gun in the trunk of the car. I was careless. I didn't bring it inside when I got home. I'd violated one of the first rules of those who kept a gun for protection: if it wasn't accessible, it was useless.

Footsteps scuffled at the door, and beside me, the brass knob turned to the right, then to the left. The door was locked and refused to open.

The knob rattled with such force I almost cried out. I jumped away from the door but knew better than to race up the stairs and trap myself on the upper floors. Instead, I rushed to the kitchen, Sweetie Pie and Pluto at my side.

The first thing I did was check the dead bolt and latch the doggie door so Sweetie and Pluto couldn't hurl themselves into the yard and possible danger. I found the biggest knife in the kitchen and gripped it tight. Close-contact defense wasn't what I considered a good idea. I far preferred the option of shooting the intruder at twenty paces. Without my pistol, that wasn't going to happen. The knife was the best weapon I had.

My cell phone was upstairs in my bedroom, and the only landline was in the detective agency office on the other side of the house. I wasn't trapped in the kitchen—I had options—but I wasn't in the best place, either.

Several of my coats hung in the mudroom, and I gathered my warmest clothes and changed into paddock boots. A flashlight was a necessity, and I slipped the brightest one into my jacket pocket. It was cold outside, and if I had to hide on the property, I wanted to be warm and able to see.

What I was doing my damnedest not to do was wonder who was outside my house. At the top of my dread list was Gertrude Strom. She was out to get me, and she had the courage of the insane. There was another possibility, though. What if it was someone involved with the baby? After all, the infant had been left at Dahlia House. Maybe whoever left her wanted Libby back? That thought was more frightening than facing Gertrude armed only with a knife.

Sweetie paced in the kitchen, going from the back door to the dining room door, which I had also bolted. It was a swinging door, and sometime in the past, when my father was a child and careened through the house, his mother had put a thumb bolt to stop the kids from knocking each other out with the door. Now it served the purpose of keeping anyone who'd gotten inside the house out of the kitchen. Of course it was only a wooden door. It wouldn't keep bullets out.

My watch showed only five minutes since DeWayne had called. My concern was that Harold would drive right into a trap. If this was Gertrude, she would shoot my friends, knowing that was as good as hurting me.

The shrill cry of one of my horses came from the field behind the house.

I ran to the window of the mudroom and searched the blackness outside the barn. The horses were not confined; they were free in the pastures. It would be hard for a stranger to catch them, but they were vulnerable if a madwoman meant to harm them.

Clutching the knife and with no further thought, I

stampeded out the back door and toward the sound. Horse hooves pounded into the dirt, and in the near blackness I could make out my three horses bucking and kicking. At what I had no idea. If Gertrude had done something to my horses, I would kill her. She would suffer death, even if it took me the rest of my life.

This was probably what she hoped to achieve—to force me out of the house where I was protected and into the open where I was a target. I didn't waste time figuring out her plan.

Reveler was near the fence, and he reared and pawed the air. I froze. If he came down on the wooden fence with his forelegs, he could be crippled for life. What in the hell was making the horses react so? I couldn't see anything in the pasture with them.

Sweetie had remained by my side, but she caught scent of something on the wind. Her hackles rose and a deep, fierce growl erupted from her throat. Then she was gone. She streaked across the open yard and jumped through the fence. In a moment I heard her hunting bay echoing from the empty cotton fields. She was in hot pursuit of something.

Pluto took a position at my right side. His arched back told me he, too, sensed danger. He turned slowly in all directions.

When we both turned back to the house, I saw her. Gertrude Strom stood on the back steps at the kitchen door. Her wiry red hair caught the yellow glow of the porch light. She wore a big coat and sensible shoes, and she had a gun in her hand pointed at me.

"Run!" I yelled to Pluto. I darted right, away from the horses, as the first shot rang out in the night. I heard the bullet smack into a fence post and I rolled like I'd seen on some crazy cop video. It had looked silly at the time, but now I realized, as a target, that it behooved me to duck, spin, tumble, and scramble.

"Gertrude!" I yelled as I ducked behind the barn. "I'm going to kill you."

"You can try."

If I'd doubted it was her, I recognized her voice. "You're insane."

"Isn't that your worst nightmare, Sarah Booth? I *am* crazy enough to do anything. Just like this—showing up at your house when you're unprotected. How about I kill you in your own yard?"

Talking to her only allowed her to draw a bead on my location. I eased into the interior of the barn. Pluto was a shadow as he raced ahead of me and jumped on the ladder up to the hayloft. I'd seen too many horror movies where the bad guy shot holes into the floor of the hayloft to want to follow the cat. There wasn't really another choice. If I stayed below, without a gun to shoot back, I was an easy target. Maybe there was something in the hayloft, like a pitchfork, that I could hurl at Gertrude.

"I wouldn't be counting on any of your friends coming to the rescue, Sarah Booth. This is between you and me."

She was a middle-aged woman with flabby arms, a bad dye job, and wire-rimmed glasses. How she had become the Leonarda Cianciulli of Sunflower County, I had no idea. All I knew was that if I wasn't very careful and extremely lucky, I would end up in Gertrude's bar soap and teacakes. Leonarda had devised truly clever ways of disposing of the bodies of her victims. Gertrude was just as diabolical and twice as nuts. And I was the prime target for her ire.

"Come out, Sarah Booth. Come out and take your medicine. I would hate to hurt one of those beautiful horses just to get your attention."

She was evil. And she was taunting me. I kept quiet. If she didn't know where I was, she might focus on finding me instead of trying to hurt my pets. Speaking of, Pluto nestled against me in the hay. He was not hiding—he was waiting for his chance. Pluto plotted his attacks. I could only hope Sweetie Pie stayed away. She'd sailed across the pasture chasing whatever had been frightening the horses.

Gertrude's voice cut through the night. "Oh, that pretty gray. That's the one you rode over to my house with that bitch partner of yours. I wonder what he'd fetch at the meat buyer. At least thirty cents a pound? Where is Tinkie? She and Oscar took a private plane ride this afternoon."

How the hell was Gertrude keeping tabs on us when she was a phantom? No one on the west side of the state seemed able to arrest her, yet she knew the most intimate details of our lives.

"Sarah Booth, I'm going to mess up your life. I came here in person to tell you. That movie star man threw you over after he realized I'd left him a cripple. I'm going to do the same to everyone who cares about you until you're all alone. Then I'm going to make you pay."

For what? I'd never done anything to her. She had a stupid idea that my mother had betrayed a confidence— but that had never happened. Never. I'd tried to talk to Gertrude, but it was pointless. Her reality came strictly from her own twisted thought processes. She was a victim. She'd been wronged. No matter that it was all a fantasy. She still intended to make me and all my friends pay.

Car lights swung down the driveway and swept across the barn. The purring motor of Harold's sports car stopped after he'd parked behind my car. I could hear the radio playing a new Jason Isbell song. Harold had impeccable taste in music and really bad timing for his own safety.

"Oh, company is here, Sarah Booth. It's that handsome banker friend. How about I give him the surprise of his life?"

I couldn't hide like a desperate rat while Harold walked into Gertrude's snare. I ran around the stacks of square bales and hurried to the loft widow. I pushed it open. "Harold, watch out! Gertrude is here and she has a gun."

Harold dropped behind his car, and a streak of frizz and gristle took off toward the barn. Roscoe was on the hunt. "Get Roscoe. Gertrude is insane!"

I ducked back in, expecting her to take aim and plug me. But there was nothing. Not a sound. Roscoe set up a bark, but he stopped at the barn. He stared into the night, jumping up and down with the ferocity of his barking. In a moment Sweetie Pie joined him, baying as if she were on the trail of a Baskerville.

Risking a hole in my head, I crept to the edge of the loft door and glanced down. Harold was behind his car. Sweetie Pie and Roscoe had stopped at the edge of the driveway and were looking toward the road. The chain of events was obvious. Gertrude had parked along the verge and walked across the front pasture to get to Dahlia House undetected. She'd left the same way. She'd come and gone with such ease.

In the back pasture, the horses had settled down. I don't know what Gertrude did to them, but once I was positive she wasn't playing possum and had truly vacated the premises, I'd check them over thoroughly.

"Sarah Booth," Harold called. "Are you hurt?"

"No. And you?"

"Embarrassed. I should have had my shotgun. DeWayne said Gertrude was on the loose, but I never believed she'd show up here."

"Did you see her?"

"No." He slowly stood up behind the car. "I didn't see anyone. And I didn't see a vehicle. Are you sure it was Gertrude?"

"Without a doubt. I'll be right down." I made my way back through the hay and down the ladder to the floor. Harold was waiting for me.

"Gertrude isn't a spring chicken." Harold put an arm on my shoulder as he flipped on the barn lights and examined the interior of the barn. "How is she running all over the place and avoiding capture?"

"That's the sixty-four-million-dollar question, isn't it?" Aggravation burned like salt in a wound. "She could have killed me, but she didn't. She's playing a game and having a great time."

I filled three buckets with grain and poured them into the horses' stalls. Reveler, Miss Scrapiron, and Lucifer came on the run. While they ate I examined every inch of them. The only thing I could find were a few scratches on Reveler's back legs. Tomorrow, when it was daylight, I would check the pasture for brambles.

Harold patiently watched as I finished my chores. When the buckets were back in place and the horses turned out, he put his arms around me. "Calm down. Everything is okay."

I realized then how terrified I'd been—for him and

my animals more than myself. Gertrude had damaged someone I loved. She'd changed his life irrevocably. Tears pushed against my eyelids, and I leaned against Harold and let him rub my back through my thick coat. "She is going to kill me if she can, and she's going to hurt every one of you. Somehow she knows what each of us is doing. She knew Tinkie and Oscar had flown somewhere."

"How is she finding out all of this?" Harold asked.

"I don't know."

"Come on to the house. I'll make us both a drink and you can tell me what's going on with Carrie Ann Musgrove."

"How did you know about Carrie Ann?" The grapevine in Sunflower County was humming and Gertrude wasn't the only one downloading info.

"Her ex-husband was in the bank for a construction loan. We've done business together for twenty years. He mentioned how she'd been howling about you and Tinkie. He said she was certifiable. The daughter, too. I quote, 'They both have a screw loose.'"

Oh, joy, two more nutcases to muck up my life. "You make the drinks. I'll do the talking." Arm in arm we left the barn and walked to the comfort of Dahlia House.

By the time my teeth quit chattering, I'd consumed two drinks and was sitting on the parlor floor at Harold's feet while he rubbed my shoulders. He'd reported Gertrude's assault to Coleman and the Mississippi Bureau of Investigation. Yet again, Gertrude was on the radar of the top state law enforcement officials. We'd done all we could do for the evening. As my muscles relaxed, my body slumped.

"This business with Gertrude has to stop," Harold said. He rubbed my very short haircut, which was growing out—and taking forever to do so. "How can she evade the law so easily?"

I repeated the things Coleman had said. "It's a big territory. The law officers are busy solving murders and robberies and other violent crimes."

"Gertrude is violent." Harold lifted me and eased me onto the old horsehair sofa beside him. "She is crazy *and* violent."

"She is." I hadn't really digested the fact that she'd come on my property, onto the porch and steps of my home, and fired a gun at me. She could have hit me, one of the horses, the dog or cat. She didn't care who she hurt in the process of getting her imagined revenge.

"She also has a source close to you, Sarah Booth."

That was the most troubling thing of all. "I have no idea who that might be." I'd thought about it, and no one came to mind. My friends were as loyal as my hound. No one would assist Gertrude in her quest for revenge.

"Who could it be, Harold? The people who know my business wouldn't tell her the time of day."

"Non-friends, then. Someone who might know these details? A bank teller? A dental hygienist? A florist? The postal delivery person? Someone you see or talk to without even thinking about it is watching you and reporting to Gertrude."

"I hate this." It put everyone I encountered in line as a suspect—perhaps even someone who wasn't intentionally revealing facts about my life. "I'm friendly, but it's Tinkie I'm worried about. She'll talk to a post. And she has been shopping all over town with Libby. No telling who she told about taking the baby to Boston."

Harold nodded. "That's likely the source. We'll caution her when she gets back"—he checked his watch—"in about twelve hours."

"Still, I can't think of anyone she might talk to who would relay the information to Gertrude."

"Perhaps accidentally, as I said." He put his arm around me and pulled me close. "Don't get all paranoid, Sarah Booth. That won't help matters."

Leaning against Harold, I felt better. He didn't lecture me on how dangerous my profession was, or how I put myself in the path of trouble, or about any of the myriad character traits I had that ended up with me in danger. He simply supported me. Emotionally and physically, as he was doing now.

The cotton of his multihued sweater was soft and warm, and I allowed myself a moment to gather my frayed nerves. Gertrude would be captured. She would be punished for the terrible things she'd done. My life would return to normal. And the most important thing on my plate—other than not getting killed—was finding the missing mother of a newborn infant. Focus. I had to focus.

As comfortable as Harold's shoulder was, I sat up.

"Before you get all businesslike, I want to tell you something," he said.

I gave him my undivided attention. "Okay."

"Sarah Booth, when the dust clears and you're ready to date again, I want you to consider spending some time with me. Romantic time. I'll always be your friend, but I want more."

The thing I loved about Harold was his directness, his ability to put his thoughts and feelings out there without making it my burden to carry. "I love you, Harold. Since

I came home, you've always been here when I needed you."

"I'll say again, I want more. If you can't love me with passion and commitment, I will be that friend. I just want a chance to see how deep our feelings run."

My thumb gave a weak throb. Once upon a time, Harold had proposed to me—with a four-carat diamond. He'd learned that baubles, even the gorgeous, expensive ones, couldn't entice me to do a damn thing I didn't want to do. And he valued me more because of it.

Since that unfortunate incident, we'd learned each other. Unlike Coleman, Harold wasn't a local "boy" I'd known my whole life. He came from wealth and another town. As the months passed, I found traits in Harold I admired, and he'd come to appreciate my independence and hardheadedness. I had to admit that while others saw me as mulish, Harold celebrated my iron will. His quick wit kept me laughing, and he had set a course with his courtship of me—I would go to him, not the other way around. He would not pursue or persuade or pamper or seduce me into anything. I had to want him, and I had to take action. It was a riskier position for him to hold, and I admired him for it.

Not to mention that he was extremely handsome and urbane. And kindhearted. And he loved my critters almost as much as I did.

He stood up. "Up and at 'em, Sarah Booth. We have some things to figure out. Let's make a chart."

"I almost flunked geometry and I did flunk statistics. Charts are not in my wheelhouse."

Harold only laughed. "We can make a chart or we can go to bed. The doors are locked. Sweetie Pie and Roscoe are on red alert, and Pluto is watching out the front window to be sure we aren't invaded.

"Coleman hasn't called about his emergency. I thought I would hear from him before bedtime."

"Let it go for tonight. Tomorrow, I'll fix breakfast for you and all your friends. If, and it's a mighty big if, you help me clean up the kitchen. What the hell happened in there? I recognize the remains of stir-fry, but what is that orange stuff everywhere?"

"Pumpkin," I mumbled.

"You realize Thanksgiving is right around the corner."

I shot up like I'd been electrified. "I forgot! I haven't prepared anything for our dinner."

Harold rose and put his hands on my arms. "Settle down, Julia Child. Thanksgiving dinner will get cooked. I promise. You want to do it all yourself—I grasp that. But a little help from your friends is a good thing."

His words calmed me. Harold knew how to make everything okay. I stood on tiptoe and kissed his cheek. "I do take you seriously, Harold. I promise. I just don't know what I want. That's as honest as I know how to be."

"This will be a hard decision for you, Sarah Booth. After all the losses you've had, commitment is hard. I hate what happened between you and Graf. You didn't need another loss like that. I understand it, and I appreciate his position. I'm not blaming him and you're right not to either. But you've lost so much. You are the last of your family, and that's a burden I understand."

Tears edged into my eyes, but I willed them back. A pity party wouldn't do me a lick of good, even though I deserved one. "You always understand."

"I hope when your heart has healed that will be enough to earn a chance with you."

I nodded. "I promise." I thought he might kiss me, but he was too smart. Harold knew the surest way to win me was to reverse the roles and make me chase him. "You're a smart devil."

"Just like Roscoe," he said. "Now let's cook or clean or chart. Take your pick."

17

My kitchen was usable and a Thanksgiving Day menu planned—by Harold—and the duties strategically allocated to different guests by the time we went to bed. I was so tired I didn't bother undressing. I simply fell onto the mattress and when I woke, I saw Harold had covered me in a family quilt. He'd taken the green bedroom across the hall from me.

Harold had created a pie chart, which might be as close as I got this year to making anything pie related. The chart showed the possible suspects in Pleasant's disappearance, and the percentage that Harold and I believed they might be guilty. It was a Jim Dandy little tool. The largest slice of pie belonged to Carrie Ann and Lucinda Musgrove. I felt there was a forty-five percent probability they were behind Pleasant's abduction. Tally McNair followed at thirty-five percent. That left another twenty percent for someone unknown to be the culprit. If there was such a person, I felt positive I would find him or her in Nashville. Pleasant's value was in her musical talent.

When I tromped down to the kitchen for some coffee to wake up, I found Harold already at work. "Cece and Jaytee are on the way for breakfast. The dynamic duo of law enforcement said they'd stop by if they could. Millie is running the kitchen at the café because a chef is out, and Madame Tomeeka has an eight o'clock client."

Whatever he was making smelled heavenly. I poured black coffee and settled into a chair. "Thank you, Harold. What's on the menu?"

"A grits casserole. Girl, you need to stock your larder. I had to make do with a lot of substitutions. How did you plan on cooking Thanksgiving without any supplies?"

"I know." Buying groceries, with the exception of critter food, was not a priority. But I had to get ready for Thanksgiving. I'd ordered a free-range turkey from Swift Level, a wonderful farm where the animals were all treated humanely and allowed to roam free. "Today I'll buy everything on the list you made."

Harold laughed. "And when will you cook it all?"

He was right. I had to find Pleasant. Defeat was hard to accept, but saving a young woman took precedence over being the hostess with the mostest. "I guess we won't have the holiday meal at Dahlia House."

"Wrong. We'll decorate to the nines here and everyone can bring a dish or two, just like we talked about last night. We'll have the best Thanksgiving ever, Sarah Booth. In honor of your folks and little Libby. By the way, Tinkie and Oscar should arrive home any minute."

The beauty of private air transportation was scheduling and convenience. "Tinkie and I need to go to Nashville today. I have an appointment with Benny Hester, a music producer."

"That's a good thing. She needs to be away from that baby for a little while. She and Oscar are dangerously attached."

"I know. I just don't know what to do to stop it."

He put a plate loaded with the delicious sausage, egg, cheese, and grits casserole and homemade biscuits in front of me. "Chow down."

"Shouldn't I wait for Cece and Jaytee?"

"Eat and then jump in the shower and get ready. By the time you're dressed they'll be here and you can drink coffee with them."

Harold was better at managing time and money than anyone I knew. If I stuck to his schedule, I'd have my mystery solved *and* Thanksgiving dinner cooked.

A hot shower put a whole different complexion on the morning. Outside my bedroom window, the sun was warming another bare November day. This was perfect weather for Thanksgiving prep, riding a horse, sharing a picnic, just about anything other than trying to find a psycho woman who wished me dead and searching for a young woman who'd just given birth and might be in a bad situation.

I tripped down the stairs, sniffing something wonderful coming from the kitchen, and stopped at Coleman's baritone. Harold was filling him in on Gertrude, and both men sounded upset.

"She's got a hideout here in Sunflower County, and

someone is helping her," Coleman said. "I'll find her if it's the last thing I do, and when I do, someone will be in a world of hurt. That murder at Fitler that DeWayne got called out on—it was a false alarm. It was a setup so that Sarah Booth would be here alone. Thank god you arrived in time, Harold."

"Gertrude had her timing down perfect. She arrived just after you'd left and before I could drive here," Harold said. "I'm certain she was at the bottom of that fake call."

"And Gertrude has a mole," Cece agreed. "She's on top of every move Sarah Booth and Tinkie make. We'll sniff out whoever it is." Excitement laced her voice. "Once Sarah Booth finds Pleasant Smith, I think we should plant some false information for Gertrude. You know, a trap. Lure her somewhere we can drop the net on her and put her away for good."

I pushed into the kitchen. "A brilliant idea, and we'll put that plan into motion as soon as Pleasant is found." I snared a strip of bacon. "Tinkie and I will be gone most of the day. We have an appointment in Nashville." I grabbed a homemade biscuit. My first bite almost melted in my mouth. "Harold, these are wonderful!" I turned to Coleman. "So what happened with Carrie Ann and Lucinda?"

Cece jumped up and pointed out the window. "Squirrel, Sarah Booth! Squirrel!"

Everyone laughed, even me.

"Speeding much?" Cece asked, but it was said with humor. "You are wired, girl."

I took a couple of deep breaths. They were right. I'd roared into the kitchen like a cyclone. Sweetie Pie slipped up behind me and stole the rest of my biscuit from my hand. "Better on your hips than mine," I said ruefully. "Okay, I'm sorry. Coleman, did Carrie Ann or Lucinda reveal how I magically set a fire from forty miles away?"

"Carrie Ann's accusation had no substance. Someone, presumably the mother or daughter, burned some old pine pallets behind a rundown shed. It would have done the neighborhood a favor if the whole thing had gone up in flames."

"Is it possible Carrie Ann is working in conjunction with Gertrude?" The two of them in collusion would be a match made in hell.

"It's possible," Coleman said, "but probable? I just don't see it. How would they even know each other?"

A prickling sensation swept over me. "Is it possible that Carrie Ann's house is Gertrude's lair?" Had she been hiding there the day Tinkie and I stopped by? We'd had Libby with us, and the critters. We could all be dead.

All conversation stopped.

"I insisted on checking the property, but Carrie Ann said no. She demanded I have a search warrant," Coleman said. "Such a possibility . . ." He stood up and drained his coffee cup. "I'll ask Sheriff Kincaid if he can spare a man to sit on that property. Her house is in Sunflower County, but the best vantage point is in Bolivar. In the meantime, I'll see about a warrant. If Gertrude is using the Musgrove house as a place to hide out, we'll know soon enough. We'll catch her."

The tension in my shoulders eased a little. "Since Carrie Ann reported a fire that didn't exist, what did she want? Other than to possibly clear the way for Gertrude to come after me."

"To talk about old times." Coleman put a finger in his

shirt collar and tugged to loosen it. He was uncomfortable, and I suspected why.

"Old times, like back in high school?" The very devil was on my shoulder, but Coleman had been teasing me a lot and now I had my chance for a bit of revenge. What was sauce for the goose was sauce for the gander, as my aunt would point out. "Like when you were having sexy fantasies of how she could contort her body?"

Cece and Harold beat the top of the counter and hooted. Sweetie Pie sidled over to the kitchen table and snatched another biscuit, then ducked under the table to munch down. Pluto was angling toward a platter of bacon Harold had fried. I deftly swooped it out of his reach.

"I didn't go to Sunflower County High," Harold said. "Tell me about this woman with the double-jointed hips."

Coleman took the teasing with good grace, but the spark in his eyes told me I was in for payback. "Did you learn anything from her?" I pulled the conversation back on track.

"When I started asking about Pleasant and scholarships, she developed lockjaw. But she did serve me a slice of fine lemon pie. Homemade. She can make crust, Sarah Booth. Just like my mama used to."

"I'll bet crusty would describe many things about Carrie Ann," Cece said.

"Bazinga!" I high-fived her. "So tell me what you learned, Coleman, other than that she's a wunderkind in the kitchen. Though I hope you got all your vaccines before you ate the pie. If the health department looked through her house, I'll bet they'd take away her stove. That's just based on the horrid condition of the outside."

"Okay, okay." Coleman held up a hand. "She insisted that Lucinda and her friends were only kidding around about preventing Pleasant from making the scholarship interview." He buttered another biscuit. "But Lucinda did get the scholarship that was meant for Pleasant. She got it by default."

"That's not fair." Pleasant had been cheated out of her future because she was kidnapped. How was that right in anybody's estimation?

"The scholarship is the least of it," Harold said gently. "I'm sure that Tinkie and Oscar will help Pleasant, once she's found."

He was right. The Richmonds had already mentioned that to Charity. "Those scuzzy girls—"

"I believe they're involved in whatever happened to Pleasant and Carrie Ann is, too," Coleman said. "When I began to press her for alibis, real answers, she slammed the door in my face. On the way home I drove over to Rosedale to talk to Hoss Kincaid."

"Did he know anything?"

"He knew Gertrude had been seen, and give the man credit, he had two deputies on Highway 1 with a roadblock. Of course the Delta is so flat there, Gertrude could have seen the roadblock a mile away and taken a hundred small turnoff roads through the interior of the county. It's just as well you and Tinkie will be in Nashville all day."

The kitchen door swung open and Tinkie stepped through. She wore some smart knee-high lace-up boots, trimmed at the top with faux fur, black jeans, and a red and black sweater that emphasized her petite figure. She had Libby, dressed in a matching outfit, in her arms. My best guess was that Tinkie had the baby's outfit custom-made to match hers. "We won't be gone all day. Yancy Bellow has offered to fly us to Nashville. His pilot will wait for us and bring us home. We shouldn't be gone longer than three or four hours."

"That's really generous." Yancy had been kind in the past, offering reward money for information leading to the person who killed the bartender at Playin' the Bones. He'd also offered to help Scott out of a jam with the blues club. Luckily, my friend had been able to hold on to the club without taking a financial partner.

"Yancy is sympathetic to our situation. He's worried about Pleasant. He just melted at the sight of Libby. Oh, by the way, Cece, he asked that you call him. He's going to offer a reward for information leading to Pleasant's safe return."

"That should bring in some leads," Coleman said. "Yancy's a strange fellow. I don't hear anything from him for months at a time, and then he pops up helping someone. He's been a real benefactor to the library and to several children's organizations, too."

Aunt Loulane would say, "Never look a gift horse in the mouth." It was an adage I was happy to obey. The private plane would save me ten or more hours of driving. While I loved the scenery, time was a precious commodity right now.

"Tinkie, we can't take the baby." I said it as gently as I could.

"I know, Sarah Booth. Madame Tomeeka will keep her. Oscar had to go to work."

"Thank god," Harold muttered under his breath. "It's about time. The bank won't run itself."

Tinkie acted like she hadn't heard. "I'm ready if you are, Sarah Booth. We can drop Libby on the way. The plane is waiting at the airport." Zinnia didn't really have an airport. What was called the local airport was a cluster of hangars and two landing strips for small planes. I was almost positive Yancy had his own private landing strip, but it was far more convenient to go to the little airport on the edge of town.

"Hit it, ladies," Harold said. "I'll clean up this mess. Or I may call Toxic Waste Disposal to remove that orange stuff. Is it breathing?"

"Leave it. I'll be back and take care of it."

"I'll help Harold," Coleman said. "I need more coffee, and this will give me a chance to have a cup."

"I'm half asleep, but after this great grub, I'll take care of all of it," Jaytee said. "The rest of you working men, take off. Cece, if you can catch a ride to town with Harold and leave me the car, I'll bring it to the newspaper when I finish here."

"Done and done," Cece said, kissing him on the cheek. "You fill my life with joy."

"Let's get out of here before our blood sugar surges and we stroke out," Harold said, but his smile spoke more loudly of his happiness for Cece.

We rented a car at the Nashville airport and drove straight to the Landbridge Building where Benny Hester maintained an impressive suite of offices. He was a big agent with a lot of power, and we were right on time for our meeting. For someone like Hester, time really was money.

Though we had an appointment, Hester had been called into an urgent meeting. We were told at the first floor reception area to check back in two hours. With time to kill, I called Rick Ralston and we met at Edgehill Café. I was stuffed from Harold's breakfast delight, but Tinkie and Rick ordered food and coffee.

"Sorry about the meeting. Hester's a busy man. Putting out fires. All of that." Rick sipped his coffee. He was blond-blond with bright blue eyes and a winning smile. He looked more like an art student or musician than a private eye. Then again, he played bass in a Nashville band as well as solving mysteries. Multitalented.

"Not a problem. Our appointment was originally for this afternoon. We rearranged because we caught a private plane up here," I said.

"So tell us how you came to track down Pleasant's songs," Tinkie said.

It wasn't a long story. Once Rick had the photo of the sheet music—and since he was a musician—he scouted the top venues where young talent played for tips. "Good material like the songs your missing girl wrote—someone would be singing it. There are thousands of talented people trying to break into the business. What they all must have is that song that will rocket them to the top. Pleasant wrote two songs that I'm willing to bet will hit the number one position."

"I'd love to hear someone perform them," I said. Reading music wasn't a talent of mine.

"Finish your coffee. I can make that happen."

Tinkie wolfed down her omelet and we left our rental and rode with Rick. The hills of Nashville were so different from the flat, flat Delta. Music City combined the gracious architecture of the South with a touch of the mountains. The city could easily seduce me.

We left Music Row behind and twenty minutes later pulled into what looked like a real dive. It was only ten in the morning. I had my doubts that anyone would be playing music at this hour. Musicians were notoriously night people who didn't stir until after noon. Cece could attest to that. Jaytee's schedule was taking some adjustment for a woman who was frequently made up, dressed to the nines, and out the door at six in the morning.

Rick parked in the rear of a building that looked like it might be a crack house or a front for the sex trade. Three young girls in minidresses, black stockings, and multihued hair stood outside smoking cigarettes. They watched us as we walked toward them. Tinkie and I shared a glance, but we followed Rick inside.

The building hummed with chatter and the wail of guitars. Someone clapped and silence fell. "Craig's got a new song. Give a listen."

A young man took the stage, guitar at the ready. Four minutes later he was met with loud applause. "It's a music co-op," Rick said. "These musicians meet, try out new material, critique each other. It's an unusual group of folks. And that," he pointed to a petite brunette who sparkled with energy, "is Laney Best. She's the next Taylor Swift." He signaled her over. "Laney, these women know the girl who wrote your song. Would you play it for them?"

"Sure. I want to get some opinions on the bridge." She picked up a guitar and took the stage.

When Laney started singing, everyone in the room stopped and focused on her. I discovered I was holding my breath. Laney had a big, big voice, and she had "it"— that indefinable quality that drew people to her. Emotion rippled through her voice, and I lived the song with her as she sang about lost love, the yearning for what once had been a dream, all of it.

"She's a dynamo," Tinkie said, while I gathered my

ragged emotions. Pleasant's song brought up a past I needed to leave behind. Pleasant had a lot of mojo as a writer, and Laney knew how to put her heart into a song.

"Yeah, Laney's a great singer who identifies with her material," Rick said. "Your missing girl wrote that song. Laney and Benny Hester are just smart enough to recognize the power Pleasant Smith created."

"How did Benny come by the material?" I asked Laney after she walked over to our table.

Laney didn't hesitate to answer our questions. "He told me he was approached at a music festival by a young woman from Bolivar County who said she'd written some songs. She e-mailed him the music, then took a meeting with him. They made the deal. I sure hope the songwriter doesn't pull out of the agreement, because we cut a music video of the song last week. It's ready for release." She looked from Rick to us. "We have the rights to the song, don't we?"

"I'm not certain," I said. "But I'm sure the songwriter will work with you—as soon as we find her."

"She's missing?" Laney looked really uncomfortable.

"Yes. Do you know something about that?" Tinkie pressed.

She released the strap on her guitar and put it on a stand. "I don't. Not really. I wish I could help."

"Me, too. Are you sure you can't?" Tinkie asked.

She looked longingly at the door for a moment, as if she might flee, but instead she answered Tinkie's question. "The day Mr. Hester called me in and gave me the song to rehearse, there were some girls in the lobby of the Landbridge Building. There was also a woman in his office. Not so old, but too old for the ponytail and the skinny jeans with holes she was struttin' around in." Her eyes squinted. "It was like she was trying to look like a teenager, but she failed. I was a little early for my appointment and Mr. Hester was busy, so I went downstairs to the coffee shop on the corner. I was nervous, and yeah, I know it doesn't make sense, but coffee calms me down. I thought I'd grab a cup to pass the time."

When she paused, I prompted her with an, "And?"

"Those girls and that woman were in the lobby high-fiving each other. One of the girls said something like "by the time that redneck bisnotch figures out how to get home, we'll be set.""

I showed Laney the photo of Tally McNair first.

"That's the ponytail woman." She identified Tally.

I'd taken a few shots of Brook, Lucinda, and Amber, so I showed them.

"Yeah, that's the trio. And that one," she pointed at Lucinda, "is the one who was talking. I remember it because they thought they were so cool with the whole *bisnotch* thing. Like slang was her special province."

"What about this guy?" I showed her the photo of Alfred Uxall.

"I didn't see any males. Just the girls and that ponytail woman."

I knew three girls who were headed for a stint in reform school or juvy if not outright adult prison, and the band director would be right with them. Sadly, they would learn that neither popularity, money, nor intimidation of their peers would keep them from time behind bars.

"Thanks, Laney." It was time for our meeting with the music agent.

"I hope you find her and she's okay." Laney was caught

in the middle of Pleasant's disappearance, like the rest of us.

The Landbridge Building was one of the premium office spaces in Music City. Rick walked us up to Benny Hester's office, then took off to work another case. While we waited for Hester to finish a meeting down the hall, we took in the mahogany paneling, the impressive number of framed gold and platinum albums hanging on the walls, and the waterfall that comprised one entire wall of his office. Lighting twinkled behind the water, which soothed my nerves even though I was eager to take the meeting and get back to Sunflower County and my search for Pleasant.

We were on the twentieth floor, and when I looked out the window I could see the area of Nashville where some of the great singers and songwriters had met fame. Music Row, the Ryman Auditorium, home of the Grand Ole Opry, and one of my favorite Nashville bars, Tootsie's Orchid Lounge, were all clearly visible.

I'd always enjoyed Nashville, and I knew the basics of the town's history—at least where country music was involved. The blues were my first love, but some country singer-songwriters had also captured my allegiance.

The Ryman had originally been built as a church and was known as the "Mother Church of Country Music." Stars such as Dolly Parton, Loretta Lynn, George Jones, and Porter Wagner had graced the stage with talent and glamour.

Behind the Ryman was Tootsie's famous watering hole, a place where "new" musicians were often discovered by music executives having a drink after taking in an Opry performance. Willie Nelson, among many, had gotten his first music break while playing for tips at the bar known as "the place where music begins." The music legends who grew from Tootsie's and the Ryman were staggering.

"This town could get in your blood," I said to Tinkie, who clearly wanted to be on the way home. She checked her watch every five seconds.

"I used to love to come here with Oscar when we were first dating. A lot of couples drove up to catch shows or meander through the bars, listening to new talent, singers like Laney Best. That girl is going places."

"She has the heart and the right material."

"I'm more and more positive Pleasant is alive but can't come forward. Someone is holding her prisoner."

"To what purpose?" I asked. "The scholarship thing is over and done."

"And Pleasant doesn't have a pot to pee in, as your aunt Loulane would say. It can't be a kidnapping for money. And they've stolen her songs."

"Jealous of her talent?" It worked as a motive. "Clearly Tally wanted the songs Pleasant had written. And those girls just hated her because they are eaten alive with envy. And they're all four stupid as a dead slug. They got her out of the way, but what now? Are they holding her hostage and forcing her to write new songs?"

"Maybe, but they can't keep her the rest of her life." Tinkie's eyes widened. "When they release her, what will they have gained? Pleasant can reclaim the rights to her songs. I'm sure she can prove they're hers."

The obvious answer was one I didn't want to say. They had no intention of releasing her. Ever. Tinkie had the same thought—it showed clearly in her expression.

My enthusiasm for the Nashville view had waned as Pleasant's terrible plight filled my imagination. I didn't know the teenager, and sometimes it grew too easy to think of her in the abstract. She was a missing young woman, one who had given birth and might not have received any medical attention. One who might be suffering from an infection, if the young man trying to get help from Betty McGowin was any indication.

Subdued by our thoughts, we took seats in club chairs beside the empty desk and waited. The rippling waterfall mesmerized me, and I tried not to think or check my watch.

Tinkie stepped on my toes. "We'll find her. Don't look so glum."

There was no time to answer. The door opened and a sharp-looking man in his fifties stepped into the room. "What can I do for you ladies?" Benny Hester asked. He checked his watch to let us know he had a busy schedule and that he'd made time for us.

"We're here about some songs," Tinkie told him.

"Yes, the McNair problem. The songs I'm representing are 'Too Blue' and 'Baby Love.'" Hester went through some files on his desk. He handed one to Tinkie. "Standard agent agreement signed by Tally McNair. She presented herself as the creator of the songs. I had no reason to believe they were stolen."

Our PI friend, Rick, had done a lot of the legwork for us and I was glad. "We're not blaming you," I said quickly. "When did Ms. McNair sign the contract?"

"October 15." Tinkie pointed to a page in the file. "Right here."

"Pleasant had been gone two days," I said aloud. "Tally didn't wait to see if she'd show up again because she knew she wouldn't. I don't care what that band director says, she knows plenty about Pleasant's abduction. She can pretend she only overheard those girls plotting, but she capitalized on the situation and she knows more than she's saying." I couldn't wait to call Coleman. He had Tally in a jail cell—unless she'd made bond.

"Rick Ralston filled me in on the situation. So the young woman who wrote the songs has vanished?" Hester asked. "Do you believe she's still alive?"

"Yes." Tinkie and I were in sync, as always.

"When you find her, I'd like to sign her. She's talented. She's got a great career ahead of her. Now I realize this isn't your problem, but I have a music video I've paid for that I can't release until the rights are clear on this song. I need to speak with Ms. Smith as soon as you find her. There's a bonus in this for you if you turn her up before Thanksgiving. Say twenty grand?"

When we found her. If we found her. There was a lot more at stake here than a music video or even Pleasant's career. Libby needed her mother. Tinkie was great. Amazing, even. If the baby was adopted by the Richmonds, she would have a privileged, secure, and loved life. But she would not have her natural mother.

"Thank you for your time, Mr. Hester. The date on the contract is very helpful. We'll be in touch as soon as we have any information."

We left his office and took the elevator to the lobby. I'd learned three bits of valuable information. Tally McNair had sold Pleasant's songs almost as soon as she disappeared; the high school trio was in this up to their ears; and Pleasant was the real deal. She was *the* one in a million who might break big in country music. It spoke to motive for her kidnapping, and not in a good way.

Pleasant's talent translated into money, and people did many regrettable things for money.

"Let's zip back to the plane," Tinkie said. She was itching to get home.

I pushed open the glass door and stepped on the street. And froze. Gertrude Strom was standing across Fifth Street glaring right at me. Incredibly she wore a khaki skirt and a red cardigan. She looked like someone's grandmother. Except for the malice that contorted her features.

Tinkie saw her, too. "I have had enough." She started to push past me, but the light changed and the road flooded with speeding vehicles. There was no way to cross. Gertrude made a crude gesture and walked into the crowd. By the time the traffic stopped, there wasn't a sign of her.

18

On the brief plane ride home, I called Coleman and told him about Gertrude. His anger warmed the cockles of my heart. He was furious.

"How is she moving so freely and so fast?" he asked. "It's a five-hour drive to Nashville. She must have left at dawn this morning, and how did she know you had a meeting with Benny Hester?"

"She could have driven up here after she left Dahlia House last night. But how did she even know I'd be in Nashville, much less the music agent's name. She knows what I'm doing before I figure it out." I took a breath and dove back in. "Flying around in Mr. Bellow's private plane has given me some new perspective. I'm working on the suspicion that someone wealthy is helping her."

"Good point. Any idea who that might be?"

It hit me. "Bijou LaRoche." In the not so distant past, Bijou had involved herself with some pretty skanky characters. She was a wealthy plantation owner and well-known succubus, who'd gone to the dark side and managed to escape real punishment for a number of crimes by cooperating with the feds.

"She was my first thought," Coleman agreed. "She doesn't much care for you, Sarah Booth. You have that effect on people."

His teasing note made me feel worlds better. The situation wasn't so bad that we couldn't laugh. "Thanks. So what are you going to do?"

"Sheriff Kincaid has agreed to put a deputy on watch near Carrie Ann's place. I'll ask Jaytee if he can bird-dog Bijou. She has a thing for good-looking men."

"He has to sleep sometime. He's at Playin' the Bones all night." I loved that my friends wanted to help, but the man couldn't play music all night and gumshoe all day.

"Scott and the rest of the band volunteered to share shifts. They adore you, Sarah Booth."

"If Bijou is harboring Gertrude, it could be dangerous work, and they're musicians. They aren't trained."

"They've promised to watch and report. No heroics."

I was still uncomfortable, but I didn't have a better solution. Coleman was woefully understaffed, and that wasn't going to change.

"We should be touching down in an hour," I said. "I know Carrie Ann let you into her house, but could you really search? Maybe there's evidence that Gertrude or Pleasant were there?"

"Waiting on the judge to sign a search warrant for her house. If there's any trace that either was there, I'll find it."

"What about the three men who were murdered in the farm shed?"

"Mississippi Bureau of Investigation and the Memphis Drug Task Force want to take over the investigation. I'm going to let them. This is bigger than Sunflower County. They have more technology, more men, more surveillance equipment." He chuckled softly. "They have drones, Sarah Booth. The really expensive kind."

"Dammit. I want a drone." I would be hell on wheels if I had aerial surveillance of Bijou's property. I'd find Gertrude Strom, hog-tie her, and deliver her to the county lockup.

"So do I. Not happening anytime soon; we barely have a budget for gasoline. When you land, be on alert. There are roadblocks up on every road leading from the Nashville area into Mississippi, but there are so many farm roads, and Gertrude knows this area well."

"Any luck identifying the young man Betty McGowin helped DeWayne with the sketch of?"

"We have a lead. I'll tell you when you get here. This might tie in to the stabbing of Rudy Uxall."

After we landed, I took Tinkie straight to Madame Tomeeka's, where Libby had Tammy's clients charmed. I swear, the baby recognized Tinkie when she walked in the door. Everyone said Libby couldn't really see, but Libby seemed to perk up at the sound of Tinkie's voice. They went to each other as if directed by some magnetic pull.

"This baby has a special mojo," Tammy said as she gave the baby over. "She hasn't cried at all. She's a happy and secure spirit. This little girl will bring great joy to the world."

"Great joy to me?" Tinkie asked.

"Doesn't she already?" Tammy sidestepped the question easily. I wondered if she knew that pain loomed in the future for Tinkie. Through dreams and tarot cards and visitations from the dead, Tammy sometimes had a line on the future, but she practiced caution dispensing her intuitions.

"Ladies," I had things to discuss with Tinkie. "I'm going to the sheriff's office. Want to come along?"

I hoped Tinkie might offer to come with me, but no dice. She held the baby and crooned softly to her. God save me from the brain mush of motherhood. If it happened to Tinkie, it could certainly happen to me.

Since there were no takers on my offer, I left Tammy and Tinkie oohing and aahing and I went to work.

Coleman was executing the search warrant at Carrie Ann Musgrove's house when I got to the SO. DeWayne hunkered over his desk writing reports. He threw the pen aside, eager to tell me the news on the composite he'd created with the midwife's help. The man who'd been asking for cramp medication had been identified as Luther Potter.

"Luther Potter!" I was surprised. "He was over at Charity's place asking about where Pleasant might be only a couple of days ago. He was also in a bar fight with Rudy Uxall about Pleasant."

"I've done a lot of background research. Potter's a bad dude, no way around it. The thing is, there's no evidence to connect him to Pleasant or her abduction. I'm not saying he's innocent, but folks are jumping to a conclusion here," DeWayne said, clearly worried.

I snapped a photo of the composite and also took a physical copy of the flyer DeWayne had created. Yancy Bellow was offering five thousand dollars for information leading to Luther Potter, who had a criminal record on the east side of the state in West Point and Starkville. Potter had flunked out of Mississippi State University some ten years earlier. He'd been in the agriculture program, and reading his criminal past, I thought I understood what his academic interest had been. Judging from the classes he took, if Mississippi ever legalized the growing of marijuana, he would be well prepared.

During his tenure at MSU, he'd been a highly celebrated tight end on the football team. He'd also been charged with rape by a coed, but she'd dropped the charges after she'd been badly beaten. The accusation had derailed his football career, and he'd ultimately dropped out of school.

Things just went from bad to worse. Potter had been convicted of armed robbery eight years earlier in West Point, and he'd done a stint in Mississippi State Penitentiary at Parchman. He'd been released six months earlier. He was not a good guy.

"It's easy to see how someone would automatically think he might be involved in a criminal act."

"What would this dude want with a pregnant woman and a baby?" DeWayne asked. "I'm just saying . . . there's not enough evidence to arrest him."

"Yet."

"I'm working on connecting him to Rudy Uxall," DeWayne said. "Then we'll have probable cause."

DeWayne had put the composite out on the wire and posted flyers around town. At least a dozen people had called who'd seen Potter or knew him, but none could pinpoint his whereabouts. Like Gertrude and other cockroaches, he had a good hiding place.

As a favor to DeWayne, I took the sketch of Potter and the information about the reward Yancy was offering over to the newspaper. Cece would do a story, and hopefully that would bring more leads to the sheriff's office. I needed a chat with Cece anyway. I found her buried behind mountains of notebooks, newspapers, and a new addition to the clutter of her office—high school annuals.

"You can learn a lot by looking at annuals." She flipped a Cotton Gin High School annual open to the junior class. "Recognize anyone?"

I sure did. It was the bitchy trio who tormented Pleasant. They were standing behind Tally McNair. To one side was the special honors band and on the other side the dance team. In several more photos, Tally and the girls were involved in projects. They looked buddy-buddy. It wasn't new information, but it confirmed my suspicions that the teacher-student cabal had been in place for a long time.

I filled Cece in on what I'd learned in Nashville. She was discreet and wouldn't publish anything that might harm our chances of finding Pleasant alive.

While I was at the newspaper, I decided to look up the events surrounding the day Pleasant disappeared. If Luther Potter was involved in Pleasant's vanishing act, there might be a robbery or some other illegal act that had happened in the vicinity.

"Can I look at some back issues?" I asked Cece. In the good old days, the newspapers were bound in huge books and it was easy enough to leaf through the back editions. Now, everything was on computer, and while

the digital system had some advantages, I missed the
smell of paper and ink.

Cece took me to a cubbyhole fitted with a computer
and a rickety chair. "This is the morgue now."

"It's perfect." I sat down and went to work. My target
dates were in the second week of October. I'd cull through
the news articles to learn what was happening around the
same time Pleasant disappeared. I was hoping for a new
lead, some event that might reflect on Pleasant's fate.

The *Zinnia Dispatch* was one of the last family-owned
daily papers in the state, and I was surprised at the in-
depth coverage as I rolled through the days and stories. I
read the newspaper daily, but the weight of all the stories
back-to-back reminded me how hard Cece and the other
reporters worked. City and county board meetings were
covered, weddings, funerals, sports. It was like peeling
time backward and drinking in the essence of life in Sunflower County.

As I skimmed headlines and lead paragraphs, I found
events that had slipped my mind. I'd forgotten the acci-
dental electrocution of a teen who climbed a power pole
trying to illegally hook up to cable. I'd also pushed to
the back of my brain the terrible traffic accident that
took the lives of two Ole Miss students who'd collided on
Highway 8. There were house fires, burglaries, and also
some wonderful stories of folks reaching out to help each
other.

When the Caledonia Baptist Church was struck by
lightning and caught fire, many churches in the county
joined together for an old-fashioned church raising. The
exterior structure went up in under three weeks because
the community worked night and day to help.

Clicking through the pages, I was proud of my town

and county. Tragedy happened, as it did everywhere, but Zinnia and the county knew how to pull together when it was necessary. Another example was the fish fry sponsored by the Rotary Club to buy radios for the sheriff's department.

While I'd found plenty of news, there was nothing that might relate to the disappearance of a pregnant teenager. I clicked to the next page and a headline caught my eye. DEWEY BACKSTRUM KILLED ON HWY. 12. That was the road near the Three Bs convenience store where Pleasant was last seen.

I read the news story, which was inside rather than on the front page because the accident occurred in Bolivar County. The *Dispatch* focused primarily on Sunflower County news, though it did cover other counties and had a regional page, which is where I found this article, but also why I might have skipped over it when it was first published. Coleman wouldn't have investigated the hit and run, either.

Dewey Backstrum was a fifty-two-year-old farmer whose truck had stopped on the side of the road. He'd been under the hood, working on the engine, when he was struck by a hit-and-run driver.

I checked the date, which matched the day Pleasant disappeared.

I didn't have evidence to link the two events—yet. But my gut told me they were somehow connected.

I scoured the paper for more stories on the hit and run. Two additional articles gave a few more details, but nothing striking. Sheriff Hoss Kincaid said a black pickup had been seen near the vicinity of the accident. Kincaid had pursued a lead to the Riverview Motel, but the truck and driver had checked out.

No leads were forthcoming, and the case went cold.

I researched Dewey Backstrum, who was a longtime resident of Bolivar County, known for good deeds and kindness. He'd operated a forty-acre truck farm most of his adult life. A widower, he'd never had children. There had been no one to fight for justice for him. Sheriff Kincaid, like Coleman, was overwhelmed with other crimes. Once a case went cold, the likelihood of solving it dropped to less than ten percent.

I printed off the story, thanked Cece, and headed to Dahlia House to pick up Sweetie Pie and Pluto. They would be ill-tempered because they'd been home by themselves all day. Spoiled didn't begin to describe them. When they were loaded in the front seat, Sweetie with an old aviator hat to keep her ears warm and goggles to protect her eyes when she stuck her head out the window, we took off for Three Bs and a chat with Frankie.

It was a beautiful autumn day, the earth a dark brown and the sky a deep, cloudless blue. It was a good day for justice, I thought. Driving through the flat vista of the Delta, my thoughts drifted to the upcoming holiday. Thanksgiving would be here before I had time to count to ten. Thank god for Harold and his ability to take over a party, even when it was at Dahlia House. No matter how the holiday happened, I would be surrounded by friends and love.

Where would Pleasant spend Thanksgiving? If I didn't find her, she wouldn't be with her daughter. That was unacceptable. Thanksgiving was *the* family holiday. That baby girl deserved to be with her mother.

I'd chosen to drive along Highway 12, which went past the turnoff to Fodder Gin Road, where Pleasant's family lived. This route made my journey a bit longer, but

I was working on a theory. I wanted to pinpoint the spot Dewey had been killed. Far in the distance, little more than a speck on the horizon, was the convenience store where Frankie worked. I slowed to a crawl, using my imagination to play out the death of the farmer.

I could easily visualize his pickup on the side of the road as he tinkered with the engine. A black pickup had come from the east. I didn't know if Dewey had stepped from behind the hood without checking the road or if the pickup had swerved into him for some reason. No one knew. If the driver was found, he'd be charged with homicide, though. He'd left the scene and hadn't reported the accident.

The question I didn't have an answer for involved Pleasant. Had she witnessed the hit-and-run? Had she maybe stopped to help Mr. Backstrum? Where was she when Backstrum was killed? My gut told me she was close. Involved. Was this the motivation behind her disappearance? Had she been in the truck that killed Backstrum? Or maybe she was a witness to the hit-and-run. I knew who to ask, and he was only a short distance away.

Frankie Graham was slumped behind the counter in the Three Bs reading another novel. He greeted me with a wry grin. "You're back. Have you found her?"

"No, I'm afraid not yet." I held up the drawing of Luther Potter. "Have you seen this guy?"

He took the sketch and studied it. "Yeah. I have." He met my gaze with a steady one of his own. "I didn't know his name. Did he take Pleasant?" He put a marker in *Go Set a Watchman* and put it aside.

"Why do you ask that?"

"He used to show up here when she was shopping. At first I thought it was just coincidence, but days would pass and I'd never see him. He never did anything. Pleasant would arrive, and he'd be here ten minutes later."

"Was he stalking her?"

"I can't say for certain. It was odd, though, and she noticed it and confronted him."

"What did he say?"

"He just laughed at her and made some crude remarks about her pregnancy and how no guy with a sex drive would be interested in her in the condition she was in. He made her feel creepy, though. When he was in the store, she would ask me to walk out to her car to be sure it started. Who is he?"

"His name is Luther Potter. He has a criminal record." I debated telling him about Potter's attempts to get something for "cramps" for a woman. Frankie cared for Pleasant, though he was adept at hiding his feelings. The implication in Potter's visit to the midwife was clear—that he had a woman relying on him for help. His criminal record did not reveal a man who had a lot of compassion.

"Do you think he took Pleasant?"

"I can't say. He is a person of interest, though. Do you recall what Luther Potter drove?"

"A black truck. I don't remember the details." Frankie gripped the counter to keep himself under control. "He was crass. He implied things about Pleasant. He said things that made us both believe he would hurt her." He'd gone completely pale. "If he has her, there's no telling—"

"We don't know that he's involved. What do you remember about the hit-and-run back in October? The farmer who was killed on Highway 12."

Frankie calmed a bit as he recalled the incident. "Mr. Backstrum was a nice man. He helped everyone in the area. He'd just been in the store before it happened.

He'd bought gas for his truck and some sodas to take to the church for 'the young people to drink.' He did stuff like that all the time, even though he didn't have a lot of money."

"Did he arrive before or after Pleasant?"

Frankie thought a moment. "Before. But not by much."

"Did he say where he was going?"

"Mount Zion Methodist is along Highway 12. I assumed he was taking the sodas to the church on his way home. There was a youth fellowship or something going on, or that's what I gathered. He didn't say that exactly."

I paid for a pack of gum. "Would Pleasant have been on Highway 12?"

"It's the route she would have taken home, and her car was found there. Only she was gone." His face drew in. "I should have followed her home, or let her take my truck. It was dark, and she was tired. That rust heap she drove was a POS. And those creeps had been in here pestering her."

"Those creeps meaning Rudy Uxall and the other two men. But was Luther Potter with them?"

"No. That Potter guy wasn't with them. And Rudy didn't come in. He stayed in the truck, until he realized his friends were bullying Pleasant."

"Did you ever see Rudy and Potter together?"

"Never. But they could have been engaged for all I know. I'm here working or helping on my dad's farm. I don't have what would be called an active social life."

"Thanks, Frankie."

"Did the DNA test come back yet?" he asked. "I stopped by and saw Sheriff Peters and told him I wanted to check. I've been thinking about that baby girl. Look, I lied to you about my relationship with Pleasant. We loved each other. The thing is, I begged her not to have the baby, but she wouldn't listen. The baby, me, we would be millstones around her neck. She could be somebody. She shouldn't have to drag Bolivar County behind her for the rest of her life." His face was white with emotion. "I didn't want to say I was the father because . . ." he shrugged. "She can do so much better than me."

"If you really love her, Frankie, and she loves you, that's a rare and special thing. You'll be the support that keeps her going. You don't want to walk away from Pleasant or your daughter."

"I never thought I'd want a baby, but you know, it's different when it's your kid." He choked.

To change the subject, I scrolled on my phone to show him Brook, Amber, and Lucinda. "Tell me about these girls."

"What's to tell? They rule the social scene at the high school. They were mean to Pleasant, but she ignored them. They were likes flies buzzing around her head; she just brushed them aside."

"That must have really ticked them off."

He grinned and looked away for a minute. "Lucinda does hate to be ignored. Yeah, it made her mad, but she didn't have anything Pleasant wanted or needed. None of them did. Amber has money, but who cares. She's empty here." He tapped his head. "And here." He patted his heart.

Frankie might be a kid with a passion for reading novels, but he had his head on straight when it came to what was important in a person.

"Are you going to take the baby if it's yours?" I had to ask. Tinkie must be prepared for what was coming at her.

"I want to." He flipped his hand at the shelves of potato chips, candy bars, canned spaghetti. "I can't support myself on what I make here, but I don't have reliable transportation to get a better job anywhere else. I won't take her unless I can support her."

"What would you like to do?" At his age, I'd wanted only to be a Broadway star. I'd set my sights high.

"I want to be a writer. Like William Faulkner."

While Frankie didn't appear to be on fire with ambition, he'd certainly chosen a big and difficult dream. Any creative pursuit was fraught with hardship and a lot of disappointment. I had a sudden image of Frankie, Pleasant, and the baby living in Nashville. Pleasant's success as a songwriter and singer would give Frankie the time to craft his first novel—and play daddy. They could be a happy family.

"Have you published anything?"

A grin broke across his face. "Next month, in the *Sewanee Review*. A short story."

I was impressed despite myself. Literary journals had thousands of short story submissions. Here was a young man with no mentor, no connections, no university background to offer a leg up, and yet his story had been accepted on merit. "Congratulations."

"I would never have submitted if Pleasant hadn't pushed me. She believes in me."

"The same way you believe in her."

He turned away. "Do you think she's still alive?"

I could hear the emotion in his voice, but he was strong. He might look like a beanpole with a shock of unruly chestnut hair and arms that could be snapped with a bit of pressure, but he had inner strength. He would work his shift, show up to keep the job, do the day-to-day chores that kept his life from tipping over, so that when Pleasant returned, he could be there for her.

"I do."

"Where is she? Do you have any idea?"

"I don't know for positive, but I have a sense she isn't far from here."

The hope that sprang across his features made me regret my words. I had no proof Pleasant was still alive, and this young man, for all of his stoicism, cared deeply for her.

"I'll call when the DNA results come in." If he was the father, Libby belonged with him. Unless he came to the conclusion that she would be better off with the Richmonds than with a single father unable to support himself.

19

Since I was in Bolivar County, I swung by the high school. Marcia Colburn was the girl I wanted to see. Classes would be dismissed in a few moments, and I wanted to catch Marcia before she got away. Actually, I wanted to follow her.

She was Pleasant's self-proclaimed best friend. Yet she'd painted Pleasant as a goodtime girl with easy morals and a taste for drugs. Not one other person had presented Pleasant that way—not even Tally McNair, who'd stolen from her. Why would Marcia turn on her friend in such a way?

When I checked in at the office, I was prepared for an earful from Principal Bryant. To my surprise, he didn't mention a word about Tally McNair's arrest. Five minutes later, I understood why. Tally came down the hall at a brisk walk, and at her side was Marcia Colburn. They were so busy gabbing they didn't even look in my direction.

The bell for dismissal rang, and they were out the front door like a shot. They both looked guilty as homemade sin, another of Aunt Loulane's descriptive terms I enjoyed. Homemade sin would be more treacherous than store-bought, I supposed.

I'd had the good sense to park in the middle of a clump of shrubs, so that when I followed the two out of the school and to a tan sedan, it was easy for me to fall into the flow of traffic and follow them.

On the way I called the Sunflower County sheriff's office. DeWayne told me that Tally had made bond early that morning. She'd obviously come straight to the high school to meet her classes. And now she was hauling boogie with Marcia.

When the school traffic thinned, I fell back a bit. They were headed toward Rosedale. A shadow of apprehension clouded my day when I thought about Gertrude. It wasn't possible she was working with Bijou, Carrie Ann, and Tally. That was crazy, and I sounded paranoid even to myself. Still, I kept an eye on all the side roads where she might be parked, ready to ambush me.

Tally drove like a bat out of hell, which was fine with me. Tally overshot the road to Rosedale and kept going. When she pulled down a pig trail that went back into deep woods, I pulled off, too. When I was satisfied my car couldn't be seen from the road, I got out with Sweetie and Pluto. Gertrude had me spooked, no doubt about it. I called Tinkie and told her where I was and what I was doing.

"Stop it right now, Sarah Booth. Don't you dare walk into those woods without backup." She was angry, but I suspected it was more with herself than with me. I was out here without backup because she had baby fever.

"I'll be careful. Call Coleman and tell him where I am."

"Don't you do it." Tinkie sounded a lot like her dog, Chablis. Small but mean.

"I'm turning the phone off now." And I did. I got my gun from the trunk, and I walked down the pig trail, alert to the sounds all around me.

The small brick house I came upon was another eyesore. What could have been a neat and attractive home had been neglected. Weeds choked the yard. Every living shrub or tree was dead. The only sign of life was smoke rising from the chimney. The place was blighted. The only vehicle near the house was Tally's sedan. Apparently Tally and Marcia were inside where it was warm. I was freezing.

With a low moan, Sweetie Pie nudged my leg. To my dismay, she sped toward the house. Pluto was hot on the dog's heels. I had no choice but to follow—cursing under my breath. It was broad daylight and there wasn't even a living shrub to hide behind. I pressed myself against the bricks as if I might somehow blend in.

Following Sweetie, I edged around the corner and came to a narrow window. At least I could maybe catch a glimpse of the occupants. I ducked down and peered over the window ledge into a nightmare out of the 1970s. The carpet, a dirty orange shag, stretched wall to wall. Tally, Monica, and a blond man reclined in beanbag chairs. The man waved a beer bottle angrily. He slammed it onto the floor so hard beer sloshed out and disappeared into the carpet.

I used my cell phone to snap a photo of the three of them. This young man looked to be in his early twenties, but his features were in shadow. He sprang out of the chair with the speed of a panther. His hand grabbed Tally's ponytail and he pulled her to her feet.

My impulse was to rush inside and stop him, and I did have a gun, but I forced myself to hold back. Marcia went to him and in a moment he let Tally go, but he was clearly irritated with her. He waved his arm and pointed at the door in an animated gesture. It was my cue to take off. I had to get back to my car and away.

Sweetie and Pluto, for once, followed behind me with perfect obedience as I ran through the weeds and trash until I put distance between me and the house. As much as I wanted to stay and eavesdrop, I couldn't risk it. I had a photo of Tally and Monica in cahoots with a young man who might be one of Pleasant's abductors. Coleman could work with Hoss Kincaid to get a search warrant and proceed with the proper legal authority. If there was evidence in that house, I didn't want to taint it.

The critters and I had just ducked into the well-hidden roadster when I heard a vehicle bumping down the drive. From my hiding place, I could see Marcia. Even in the cold she had the window rolled down so she could smoke.

"That bastard," Marcia said. "He's going to get us all sent to prison. And you!" She rounded on Tally. "You couldn't wait to sell her songs? You're an idiot."

They bumped past, and I didn't hear Tally's reply. In a moment they were on the road and headed toward Rosedale. I had two choices. I could sit here and see if the blond man left, or I could go to Rosedale and look up the property at the county tax assessor's office. I chose the latter, because I was freezing to death.

I wrote down the address from the leaning mailbox and took the same road Tally and Marcia had taken, but I turned off to Cleveland, the second county seat in Bolivar County. Rosedale had been the original county seat, but Bolivar was a large county and travel had often been difficult for many residents. As residents moved inland from the Mississippi River, Cleveland, a town named after President Grover Cleveland, had been named the second county seat. Cleveland boasted Delta State University as the jewel in its crown.

The clerk in the tax assessor's office took the address from me, and a moment later, I had a name for the owner of the property where Tally and Marcia had visited. Owen DeLong. I had plenty to tell Coleman when I got back to Zinnia, but while I was in the area, I decided to stop by Delta State and check into the scholarship situation that seemed to be the reason Pleasant Smith had initially been abducted.

Schools, like hospitals, were closemouthed about the students who attended, but I'd spent some pleasant hours on the DSU campus, and the Delta Music Institute was where I headed. DMI offered a unique opportunity for college students to taste the real business of the recording industry.

I was in luck. Tricia Walker, head of DMI, was in Nashville with several students, but a gaggle of young people hung outside the building. The students would be an unfiltered source of information.

I walked up and introduced myself as a private investigator, easily engaging their curiosity. When I mentioned Pleasant Smith, they were far ahead of me. They knew all about Pleasant's failure to appear for her scholarship interview.

"She is so talented," one young woman said. "Why would she do that? I heard the school offered her a full ride plus a stipend. She had only one other girl to beat out for a special scholarship created by Mike Utley, a big producer. She didn't show up for the interview and blew her chances. She would've left school debt free and with a ton of contacts in the music business."

My talkative student was named Ginger Ven. She was exotic, beautiful, and had her finger on the pulse of campus life. In other words, she could be a real asset. There was no point lying to her, so I told the truth. "I don't think Pleasant missed the scholarship interview on purpose."

"Was she sick? Is the baby okay? She was really determined to make sure her baby had a good life. I was assigned to show her around the campus when she came for the initial interview. I really liked her. She didn't strike me as someone who'd fail to show up like that."

"I believe she's been abducted."

Ginger stepped back. "She said folks were out to get her."

"Did she say who?"

"There were other girls here that day, and she made it a point to stay away from them. Prissy girls."

"Did you notice any boys?" I showed her the picture of Owen DeLong. "Maybe him? Or these guys?" I flipped through the photos to the composite of Luther Potter and the photo of Rudy Uxall's brother.

She shook her head.

"This one," I tapped Luther's photo, "may have given her a ride here."

"Maybe he did. I can't say for certain. This is a small campus. If they'd been hanging around, I would have noticed. They look kind of tough."

"An understatement," I said. "Who came to the campus with Pleasant?"

"As far as I know, she came on her own. The other girls had their mothers with them. They kept looking at Pleasant and laughing, like it was a big joke for her to be at DSU because she was pregnant. She wouldn't be the first or last girl who had a baby."

Ginger had a level head on her. "Who handles the scholarships?" I asked.

"It would be in the administration office. Dr. Beverly Moon will tell you what you need to know. She goes out of her way to help all the students."

I thanked her and left.

Sweetie and Pluto had been confined to the car for most of the day, so I took the opportunity to let them out to frisk about the campus. Sweetie loved the attention from passing students who threw a Frisbee for her. Pluto ignored them, allowing a privileged few to stroke his back and acknowledge his superiority.

I loved the feel of the campus in the brisk November weather, the students bundled in jeans, boots, and sweaters. Soon they would be leaving for Thanksgiving break. Again I felt a pang—the passing of time. Not so long ago I'd been walking across the campus at Ole Miss, wishing for classes to finish so I could go home to Dahlia House and Aunt Loulane. With each passing year, I realized more and more what she'd given up to be there for me. She'd put her life on hold to make sure I always felt I had a home.

While Sweetie frolicked in the crisp air, loving the tug-of-war and fetch with the college students, I sat on a bench and realized I wanted a cigarette. I'd quit—but with Gertrude's brutal treatment of my fiancé, the pressures of the last few cases, I'd fallen back into the habit. I hadn't thought of a cigarette for weeks, until now. And too bad. I wasn't buying a pack.

I pushed the thought out of my head and ran to join the fun with Sweetie. By the time I was panting and tired, the urge to smoke had departed. I put the critters back in the car and stopped by the administration office to see what was what with the scholarship.

Dr. Moon was as helpful and concerned as Ginger had said she would be, but because I wasn't a family member, I couldn't get a definitive answer. I gathered enough information to know that when Pleasant failed to appear for her interview, the school had had no choice but to pass her over and award the full ride to the next student in line, Lucinda Musgrove.

The dirty deed was done. So why wasn't Pleasant released?

I'd confirmed several important elements of the case, and I had Owen DeLong's address. What I didn't have was a solid tie between Owen DeLong, Luther Potter, and Pleasant. That Potter knew Pleasant was not in doubt. Had he given her a ride to Delta State, as her note indicated? Maybe. But so what? I dialed Coleman on my drive home and filled him in.

When I'd caught him up to speed, I asked the question nagging at me. "Any Gertrude sightings?"

"No. I paid a visit to Bijou LaRoche and found nothing."

"Gertrude could be anywhere on that plantation. There are farm sheds scattered over five thousand acres." My voice rose and I couldn't stop it.

"I know." Coleman's tone gave nothing away. "Bijou gave me permission to check every building on her property. Any time of the day or night. She said she hasn't seen Gertrude and won't associate with her because to do so would land her back in prison. She's right about that, too. She escaped a prison sentence by the skin of her teeth. If she's hanging out with wanted felons, she'll go straight to jail."

"I don't believe her." Stubborn. That described me.

Coleman's chuckle was soft and sexy. "That's a point we agree on. I don't trust her either. She was way too cooperative. She's hiding something. I just don't know what. Yet." I heard a commotion in the sheriff's office. "I have to go, Sarah Booth. Go straight to Playin' the Bones. Scott is expecting you. Take the dog and cat."

"What about the horses?" I wasn't leaving Reveler, Miss Scrapiron, and Lucifer for Gertrude to harm.

"Lee picked them up about an hour ago. They're safe with her."

"That's mighty presumptuous." If he were standing in front of me I'd be torn between kissing him or kicking him.

"I know. It's what I do when I care a great deal about someone. Now do as you're told."

My hackles went straight up. "Coleman Peters, don't you dare treat me like a child or a piece of property."

His laughter came through the phone, deep and satisfied. "Now that you're riled up, maybe some blood will flow to your brain and you'll see the wisdom of staying at the club with Scott and the band. You can't be alone, Sarah Booth. Not at night. It's dangerous enough during the daylight hours."

"What are you going to do?"

"Serve a search warrant on Carrie Ann Musgrove. DeWayne and I will tear her place apart."

"What about Owen DeLong?"

"I'll get Kincaid on that."

"Coleman—" I knew he couldn't step across the county line and conduct the search, but my confidence in Kincaid wasn't high.

"He's a competent lawman. Let him do his job. He's got a vested interest in this. Rudy Uxall was a resident of Bolivar County, and Mrs. Uxall is riding Hoss hard to find some answers."

"Good." This wasn't the time to argue with Coleman. He was bending over backward to protect me and help me find Pleasant. The least I could do was work with him instead of against him. "What about Tally McNair?"

"The judge set bail and someone paid it for her."

Now that was a lead to follow. "Thanks."

"Go to the blues club." Coleman's determination was clear. "It's that or spend the night in jail. You can't be running all over the place. Gertrude means to hurt you."

"And she's doing a damn fine job of it, too. I can't go home alone. My life is in upheaval, which is exactly what she wants to accomplish." I wasn't mad at Coleman, I was furious with the situation.

"I know that. We all know it. Until we grab her, the only course of action open to me is to try to keep you in a protected place. Besides, you love the blues club. You'd be happy to be there any other night. You just don't like being ordered around."

"True." He sounded exhausted. "I'm sorry. I'm grateful for what you're doing. I'll go to the club, but first I'm going to talk to Junior Wells."

"Okay. I can look out the window and see his place. I'll be watching. You'll get more out of Junior than I ever will. See if you can find out who paid Tally's ten-thousand-dollar bail."

"Will do, chief." I hung up before he could change his mind.

20

When I pushed open the door of Wells Bonding Agency, the smell of old wood, dust, and desperation enveloped me. The cement floor, once painted a green and gold pattern, was scuffed beyond recognition. Junior Wells's clientele wasn't all that interested in décor. Junior sat behind a giant, military-gray metal desk that was bolted to the floor. Because, I assumed, some of his "visitors" were angry and rowdy. I had no doubt he had a weapon at the ready. A bail bondsman was the ticket to freedom for someone who needed a bond signed. To someone who'd skipped out on his bond, Junior Wells would be worse than the devil himself.

He was a tall, thin man who often wore a large hat, giving him the look of a character from another time period. He'd run his bail bond business when my parents were alive and I would ride my bicycle around the courthouse square. A time or two he'd treated me to an ice cream cone from the little shop on Main Street. He was an acquaintance of my parents, and my father said he was an integral part of the judicial system, getting people out of prison so they could prepare their defenses.

"Mr. Wells," I said as I closed the door behind me.

"Sarah Booth Delaney, what brings you to my door?"

"I need your help." Junior had helped me in the past. He was a discreet man who ran his business by means fair and foul. Woe to the person who jumped bail, such as Gertrude Strom. I had difficulty believing he'd actually bonded her out, but he had. That was an emotional hurdle I had to jump if I expected his help with Tally McNair. Junior didn't see guilt or innocence. He saw money. Bonding Gertrude out wasn't an act of support for her, it was a business decision.

"Tread carefully. If you're here about Gertrude, it's a sore point." He tilted his chin at Sweetie Pie and Pluto, who'd followed me into the office. "There's no partner more loyal than a dog. Not so sure about the cat, though."

"Tally McNair is why I'm here."

"Perky little thing, isn't she?" His lean face was composed of wrinkles upon wrinkles, and I had no clue if he was provoking me or just making conversation.

"Perky and a thief. Who paid her bail?"

"Excuse me," he said.

I walked to stand directly in front of his desk. "I know you don't have to tell me anything. Let's skip all of that and jump to the important issue. A pregnant girl named Pleasant Smith was abducted over a month ago. Her baby was left on my front porch several nights ago, and the man who put the infant there is dead. Tally McNair is involved in Pleasant's disappearance. I realize this doesn't directly impact your world, but I know my daddy thought a lot of you. The service you provide is a vital one, because people are innocent until proven guilty. But sometimes, Junior, you put bad people back on the street."

"You think I need a lecture about that?" He sat up tall and his eyebrows shot together like a unibrow. "I'm going to lose my home and land unless I find Gertrude Strom. Do I regret bonding her out, you betcha. Can I undo it? No. Tally McNair is a schoolteacher. She ain't going far, I can promise you that."

Junior was as sore as an ingrown toenail. "I can't change your decision about Gertrude either, though she was at my farm the other night trying to shoot me. I guess we both have to live with your decision to set her loose."

He pushed back in his chair. The protest of the springs sounded like a catfight. "I'm sorry, okay. I made a mistake. I never figured Ms. Strom for a runner, much less a killer. She gave me a sob story about how she'd been framed and all she wanted to do was return to her B&B and keep it from going under. She made a fool out of me, okay? I admit it."

His explanation only served to make me madder, but I swallowed my anger. It didn't help me at the moment. Another day, when this was settled, I'd have a real sit-down with Junior and hash out the things Gertrude had done to me and others—things he should have researched before he cut her free. Right now, though, Tally and her benefactor were my immediate interest. To keep pounding Gertrude wouldn't help find Pleasant.

"Can you help me with Tally?" I asked.

"No."

I thought about begging him, but it wouldn't do any good. Junior's reputation for crustiness was legend. I pivoted on my heel. I had better things to do with my time. I couldn't compel him to talk, and he wasn't going to volunteer.

"Sarah Booth, I would help you if I could."

I spun to meet his gaze. "Then do it."

"I can't. The money was left anonymously. I came back from lunch and the cash was in a paper bag shoved through the mail slot."

"How did you know it was for Tally's bail? Surely there are plenty of other folks needing bail money."

"There was a note in the sack." He reached into his desk draw and handed me a slip of paper.

"Bail money for Tally McNair." To my bitter disappointment, it was typed, not handwritten.

"Did any of your neighbor's see—"

"You can ask. I never look a gift horse in the mouth."

Ask is exactly what I would do, though I had promised Coleman I would go straight to Playin' the Bones. Still, I would be only a hundred feet or so from my original destination.

"Thanks, Junior."

"You say Gertrude was at your place the other night?"

I gave him the details, watching his expression shift from distaste to sharp interest. "She's still in the area. That's hopeful. I've hired two bounty hunters, and they'll be here any hour to find her. I hope their fame doesn't get in the way of capturing Gertrude."

"What are they famous for?" Bounty hunters could earn headlines for good or bad, depending on how they handled their clients. In some states, bounty hunters had more leeway than an officer of the law. They could force entry, apprehend, and transport without worrying about warrants or the legal technicalities that sometimes hampered lawmen.

"They're pretty well known." His wrinkled cheeks lifted as what passed for merriment glinted in his eyes. "Duane Chapman and his crew."

"You hired those guys from television?" *Dog, the Bounty Hunter* had been a popular reality show as the public followed along behind Dog and his family as they brought bail skips to justice.

"Should be here today. Gertrude will be caught and put back in the pokey where she belongs."

My hard feelings toward Junior softened. "Thank you."

"Gertrude outfoxed me. I'm not proud of it. She made me believe it was a case of mistaken identity. I looked at her and saw a grandmother, a small business owner who'd lived in Zinnia most of her life. She snowed me. She's a cunning woman."

"That she is. Listen, I'm really glad to hear this." I wanted to clap and sing. "From what I've seen, those bounty hunters will have her rounded up in no time. Thanks for the lead on Tally's bond money. I'll check at the businesses next door." My step was considerably lighter as I left his office.

Stitch Witchery, the fabric store on the south side of Junior's business, had been closed for lunch when the money drop was made. At the newly opened vape shop to the north, employees had been stocking shelves. They hadn't noticed anyone coming or going at the bail bondsman's place. My frustration built as I checked three more stores, all with the same results. No one had noticed anything. The little stretch of businesses across from the courthouse was happily oblivious to the comings and goings of Junior's clientele.

When I'd asked everyone I could find and still came up empty-handed, I did as I promised Coleman and left Zinnia behind. I drove the short distance to the blues club. I would hang with my musical friends until someone could go home with me. I hadn't felt this helpless since I was in cotton panties with eyelet lace and ugly Mary Janes.

The minute I walked in the door, Scott Hampton swept me into a bear hug. "I've been worried about you." He rumpled my short, short hair then held me at arm's length. A lopsided grin lifted the corner of his mouth. "Oh, I remember mornings when we were lying in bed and your hair would be spread across the pillows. The way the light played in it—gold, chestnut, a hint of red. You have beautiful hair."

"Had," I corrected him, more self-conscious than I wanted to be. The new hairstyle disconcerted me. When I passed a mirror or window and caught an unexpected glimpse of my reflection, I wasn't sure who was looking back.

"The buzz cut is growing on me."

"I wish it would simply grow." I tried to rein in my vanity most of the time, but Scott made me keenly aware of my appearance. Not so long ago, as he recalled so vividly, he'd toyed with my tresses. The memory of his fingers trailing through the thick curls shook me to my toes. Scott's sensual nature, the deliberateness of his touch, worked on me from our first enounter. He evoked those memories with a few words and the brush of his hand across my skin.

I cleared my throat. "You've cultivated a nice head of hair yourself, Mr. Blues Blizzard." Scott's white-blond hair, long and sexy, was part of his trademark as one of the best blues players around. I ran my palm over my fuzz. "I feel like Woodstock."

"You're far from Woodstock." He kissed the top of my head. "In two months, you'll have a pixie. In six, you'll have a wedge. After that—"

"Hold on, Vidal Sassoon, where did you learn so much about women's hair styles?"

"I read," Scott said, but he fidgeted.

"Scott?" I gave him the stink eye.

"Okay, I was eavesdropping on Cece last night and that's what she said about your hair."

I punched him lightly in the arm. "You eavesdropped on Cece and Jaytee? You'd better be careful. Those two might teach you things you don't want to know."

He put his arm around me and walked me to the bar. "Let me fix you a Jack. And I put some pillows down in the office for Sweetie and Pluto. I worry that the bar will be too loud for them."

"Thanks. I'll take them home before the band cranks up." Sweetie loved the blues, but her hearing was six times more sensitive than mine, and it would be damaging to her ears to keep her in the club when the volume was cranked up and folks were boogying down. Pluto hated loud noise, so it was imperative I returned him safely to Dahlia House before the band took the stage.

Aside from the bedding, Scott had thought far ahead on other fronts. Curtis Hebert was cooking and he'd made a pulled pork sandwich, without sauce, for Sweetie. Pluto also had a plain serving of pork and half dozen lightly sautéed shrimp—more food than he could consume. Cats were like that. They wanted abundance, even if they couldn't eat it.

Curtis served Pluto with a tiny bow. I gave him a hug of thanks.

"Thank you, Scott." He was one of the most thoughtful men I knew. "And thank you, Curtis. You're going to give my cat an attitude."

"Too late to stop that, but I'm happy to do it," Curtis said. "I love that mutt. I've never been partial to cats, but Pluto is an exceptional puss." He stroked the cat's sleek black fur and was rewarded with a head butt from Pluto, the highest sign of his affection.

Scott went behind the bar and mixed a Jack and water for me and then came to sit beside me on a high stool. Even though it was hours before the music started, the club was doing a great business. The tables were filled with folks who were eating, laughing, and drinking. Many would stay until the band shut it down for the night, which might not be till two a.m. Zinnia had needed this club and didn't even know it.

Scott's fingers danced on my arm as if he were playing chords on a guitar, and I thought of the low-down and gritty sound he could bring forth from Lay Down Sally, his guitar. "I'll stay over with you tonight, as soon as the band finishes," he said. "I know it'll be late, but I want to."

"I hate this." Whining was unbecoming, but I couldn't stop. "I'm not helpless and I despise everyone having to disrupt their lives to look out for me."

"I know you do. It's only temporary. Besides, I'm glad for the opportunity to be with you. We seem to be running at cross-purposes these last weeks. I want to see you."

I hadn't spent the time with Scott that I would have liked. When he wasn't busy with the club, it seemed I was working a case. When I was free, he was on the stage bringing the blues to a packed crowd. In a few weeks, the reputation of Playin' the Bones as the premier club for music and food had spread across the South. International blues aficionados traveled to Zinnia and practically lived in the club.

"Are you avoiding me, Sarah Booth?"

"No." I answered honestly. "I'm not. But I'm also not seeking you out. I'm still in emotional limbo. I don't trust what I feel about anything except work and Dahlia House. I know it's crazy, but feeling numb or asleep, that's good for me right now."

"I'd like a chance to wake you up."

And he could do it, I had no doubt. "Not going to happen." I held up a hand like Diana Ross. "Stop in the name of love! I can't be pressured."

He laughed, but his eyes watched me closely. "No promises on that one. But I will respect your feelings."

To change the subject, I told him that Junior Wells had hired a famous bounty hunter to track Gertrude. Scott had the same reaction I'd had.

"Now that's brilliant. That crew can get 'er done."

I didn't feel all that jolly, but I had to laugh. "Do you really think they'll be able to apprehend her?"

"The law of averages. More people are looking, more people are aware, yeah, it's only a matter of time."

But the havoc she could wreak in that time was what worried me.

No doubt taking in my mid-range anxiety level, Scott took the initiative and shifted the conversation. "Tell me about Pleasant. What have you discovered?" He kindly took my thoughts off Gertrude as I filled him in on Owen DeLong, my trip to DSU, and the discovery that Lucinda Musgrove had indeed accepted the scholarship that would in all likelihood have gone to Pleasant. We talked and Scott's gentle teasing lifted my mood as night fell over the Delta.

Scott excused himself to take care of club business, and I sipped my third drink, put in front of me by the new bartender before I even asked. Curtis served me a sandwich with a tart dill pickle and chips, and I did my best not to show how antsy I was. I spied Jaytee coming out from behind the stage and zeroed in on him. I waved him over to the bar. He obliged with his slow, loose-hinged gait.

"Did you learn anything about Bijou?" I asked.

"She has lots of free time and lots of money."

"Meaning?"

"She likes to shop. She spent half the day in Zinnia going from shop to shop. I think she made it to every store in town before she was done."

"Did she go to the Stitch Witchery?"

"Yep." Jaytee yawned. He'd given up his rest to help me, and tonight he'd pay the piper with exhaustion.

"About what time?"

"Just before she went to Millie's for lunch. And thank god for that, I was starving."

I couldn't prove a thing, but I had a suspect for Tally McNair's bail benefactor. But why? Why would Bijou be involved in a case involving a missing teenager? It didn't make sense.

"Did she meet anyone?"

Jaytee perched one hip on a barstool. "I didn't follow her into all the shops. It would have been pretty obvious I was following her if I ducked into Betty's Boudoir."

I laughed out loud at the image of Jaytee traipsing behind Bijou into a high-end lingerie shop. If she caught him there, she might snare him with some fishnet hose and eat him alive. Bijou had a reputation for being something of a female spider—someone who cannibalized her mate.

"I don't blame you. Moth too close to the flame and all of that."

"I only have eyes for Cece. But I didn't want Bijou to know she was being tailed, so I was extra careful. If she met anyone, it had to be in that shop."

"Thanks, Jaytee. I know you're desperate for some sleep."

"No worries, Sarah Booth. I'll catch up on my shut-eye after our gig tonight. Cece promised to pamper me when we get home. She's very accomplished at pampering!"

I had no doubt about that. Once Cece set her mind to it, it was a done deal.

I finished my drink and was popping my knuckles to keep from drumming my fingers on the bar. I wanted to go home. As much as I loved the club and enjoyed the atmosphere, I had calls to make about Pleasant. And Tinkie. My partner had disappeared into baby-zombie land. I had no idea what she'd done with her afternoon—because she hadn't bothered to call and check on me or our case—and I was beginning to get worried.

I stepped outside the back door in the quiet of the evening and called my partner, who should long ago have checked in. She answered after half a dozen rings, and I could tell she'd been crying.

"Is everything okay, Tink?"

"Sure."

"Then why are you crying?"

A few seconds of silence gave way to a sigh. "I love this baby, Sarah Booth, and she isn't mine."

The reality of the future had touched the dream Tinkie had built in her mind. It didn't matter that the dream had never been sustainable. Dreams weren't founded on hard truth and reality. They were spun in the air of sunshine and hope. I'd had a few myself, and the loss of a dream was equal to a death in the family.

"Hold on, Tinkie. Don't get ahead of yourself." I cast about in my mind for something useful. What would Jitty say? Sometimes she offered wise counsel. I suddenly had it. "Whatever happens with Libby, she'll always be in your life. You and Oscar have bonded with that child, and when Pleasant is found, she'll view the two of you like fairy godparents."

She gulped down a lungful of oxygen. "Do you really think so?"

"I do." I wasn't lying. I believed it with all my heart. "Charity appreciates everything you're doing for Libby. She knows you're good people. She'll want you to share in that baby's life, and so will Pleasant."

"I don't think I can let her go." Tinkie whispered the words.

I walked a fine line. I could never condone the idea that Tinkie would be allowed to keep Libby. I didn't see that as a possibility. Charity or Frankie, if he proved to be the father, would exert their claims, and that was as it should be. Both, I believed, would be overjoyed to share Libby with the Richmonds. Share, not give.

"If she goes home with her grandmother, I'll bet you'll see her all the time."

"She has her own room here. Oscar and I have been looking at schools."

Oh, this was bad. Really bad. "You have to stop that, Tinkie. I thought Oscar had more sense than to indulge in things that are only going to hurt you both."

"We couldn't love her more if she were our blood."

"But she isn't." I had to make her understand what was coming down the road at her like a tank. "She is Charity's grandchild and Pleasant's baby. You are a temporary caregiver." I almost cried at the harshness of my words, but I viewed it like pulling the bandage off a sore with one quick jerk. She had to understand the limitations of her role.

"I have to go." Tinkie was wounded by my remarks and tone.

"I'm sorry, Tink. I am. I'm trying to keep you from getting your heart torn out."

"Too late."

That was like a blow to my own chest. I'd given her the baby to hold, to take home, because I thought it would be good for her and Oscar. I'd meddled in her life and set her up for devastation.

"Bring Libby to Dahlia House, please. Coleman won't let me stay there alone because of Gertrude. I need to do some work, and you can help. Maybe we can put up some decorations for Thanksgiving." It wasn't what I should do, but it was something to do with Tinkie that might take her mind off the inevitable loss of Libby. "Bring Oscar, too." He was an excellent shot, and so was Tinkie.

Might not hurt to have some firepower. "And bring some guns."

"Okay," she said with only a hint of reluctance. "I'll do that. Give me an hour. I need to clean up and pack some things for Libby."

I had a vision of an eighteen-wheeler pulling up to the front door of Dahlia House to unload Libby's "necessities." That child would lack for nothing if the Smiths allowed Oscar and Tinkie to provide for her. "See you in an hour. I'll cook something."

"I'll stop at Millie's. No offense, but I've had some of your cooking."

Now that sounded like my partner—a dollop of sass. "Bring me some turnip greens and cornbread, please." I hung up feeling a bit more hopeful.

When I sat back down at the bar, Travis Johnson, the newly hired barkeep, plopped another drink in front of me. Scott signaled "drink up!" from the stage where he was doing a sound check. "Be with you in a minute," he called out. And he was. A minute later, he strode over and accepted the Jack on the rocks Travis made for him.

"Things okay?"

"Tinkie and the baby." I closed my eyes. "Train wreck coming hard."

"You need to get away from your life and all the responsibilities, even if just for a few moments. You carry a lot of weight on those slender shoulders, Sarah Booth." He went to the jukebox and the song that defined so much of my love of the blues blasted out of the speakers. Percy Sledge sang, "When a Man Loves a Woman." Scott took my hand and pulled me up and against him.

"Scott, I—"

"No talking. Just dance. For three minutes forget

everything but this song." He leaned closer and whispered in my ear. "Forget everything except the way you felt when we were together."

Those were potent memories, and with Scott's body pressed against mine, moving to the beat of the music, it was impossible not to remember the passion Scott had stirred—and still did—in me. It was also impossible not to yearn for a time when the emotions generated by this song were the most important thing in my world. Once upon a time, finding love had been number one on my priority list. Now I had to worry about lost mothers, partners on the edge of emotional destruction, and a crazy woman trying to kill me. How had life become so complicated?

As Scott had intended, the music caught me in a current of emotion. When I'd come home to Zinnia from New York, I'd only wanted to save Dahlia House and the memories living within the walls, and to find true love. I'd done both, though the true love part proved temporary. I'd also started a career I'd never foreseen. When Scott happened into my life, I'd fallen in lust and in bed, in short order. I might have fallen in love had he stuck around. He'd gone to Europe to secure his title as number one blues guitarist, and I'd moved on emotionally. Sort of. I couldn't deny that I still had feelings for him.

Scott spun me around the floor, and my bones limbered and my body molded to his. Scott had all the moves of a dirty dancer. His body reacted instinctively to the music. As Jitty had said, he was sex on a stick. The thoughts I tried to hold on to fell away, and there was nothing left but the music, the lyrical passion of the song performed so well by Percy Sledge. And Scott, pressed against me.

When the song ended, Cece and Jaytee, along with

the rest of the band, applauded. "Get some cold water to throw on those two," Cece called out, bringing on another round of applause.

"Get a grip, Cece," Scott said as he seated me at the bar. His lips brushed my ear and traveled down my neck. If my body had been asleep earlier, now it was alive with electricity. Scott played it cool. "Calm down, Cece. It was only a dance to take Sarah Booth's mind off her troubles."

"Oh, yeah, I clearly saw that as a charity dance." Cece was incorrigible. "Don't tell me you're not affected." She arched an eyebrow, daring him to play innocent.

"We'll finish this later. You're making Sarah Booth uncomfortable."

"Right. It's Sarah Booth who's uncomfortable."

"Come have a drink," I said to her, partly to shut her up and partly because I had some questions. Cece sometimes turned up more information than anyone else. She had sources in every socioeconomic group and every social organization.

She took a seat beside me, leaving Jaytee and Scott to do a sound check and get ready for the stage. "Dirty vodka martini, on the rocks." She winked at the handsome bartender. We still missed Bo Shavers, the former bartender who'd been gunned down, but Scott had to have someone reliable and personable behind the bar. Travis was a good candidate. Judging from his physique, he could also double as a bouncer if needed.

"What's Bijou up to?" I asked.

"Missing from her social agenda. She's staying at home, according to my sources. She's missed garden club, The Club, and even her investment club meetings."

"Is Gertrude hiding out at Hemlock Manor?" I'd

nicknamed Bijou's huge plantation and the derogatory term had stuck.

"I can't say for positive, and neither can Jaytee, though he sat on Bijou all day." She rolled her eyes. "I love to shop, but how one woman could spend six hours trotting around Zinnia going to store after store . . . oh, yeah, I think Tinkie can do that, too."

"Tinkie's bought enough clothes for Libby to get her through until college." It was true. "Somehow there has to be a way to explore Hemlock Manor and see if Gertrude is there."

Cece swiveled on the bar stool and grabbed both my arms. "You are not to put foot on that estate. I'll tie you up and sit on you."

"*I* can't go to Hemlock Manor. Bijou would press charges against me." I gave her a dazzling smile. "But *you* can. How about a spread in the fashion section of the paper? Bijou would go for that. She's such a narcissist she'll invite you in if she thinks she'll be presented in the newspaper as someone with class and style."

"Don't you think she'd smell a rat?" Cece ate one big, fat queen olive from her martini. "She's not stupid."

"But she is a narcissist. She'd jump at it even if she suspects something. The lure of being lauded in the paper will outweigh the possibility that you have an ulterior motive."

Cece considered, and I signaled for another drink for her. I could be a lot more persuasive if Cece's common sense was dulled by alcohol.

"Ply me with liquor. That won't get you much except a huge bar tab. You know I have a hollow leg." Cece accepted the drink with a grin.

"So will you do it?"

"It won't do any good. Coleman checked Hemlock Manor. He didn't find a trace of Gertrude, but we both know there are hundreds of hiding places on an estate that big."

"I know." Defeat was hard to accept.

"I'll ask Jaytee to tail her again."

I had no doubt Jaytee would attempt to spin the earth clockwise if Cece asked him. "I think Bijou is a dead end. I'm just desperate."

"I know." Cece clinked her glass against mine.

As exhaustion and alcohol finally began to take a toll, I relaxed and enjoyed a chat with my friend. Cece was all ears about the hiring of Dog and his crew of bounty hunters. She whipped out a pad and made notes. "Do you think Junior Wells will talk to me about it?"

"He was mighty pleased with himself. Maybe."

"That would be a great story. Is Dog's wife and family coming?"

"Hold on. I'm not certain Dog is personally coming here himself. He may send employees. Junior will have to tell you about the arrangement."

"Did you talk with Betty McGowin and tell her I'd like to interview her?"

I wasn't slacking on my friend duties. "In fact I have. She said after Thanksgiving she'd consider it."

"Thanks, Sarah Booth."

"We work well together." I finished my drink and felt the return of anxiety. I hated being forced to sit and watch the clock wind down. There was so much left undone, and I was hamstrung by Gertrude. When Cece excused herself to assist Jaytee, I called Coleman.

"What did the search of Carrie Ann's house turn up?"

"No sign of Pleasant or Gertrude."

He sounded tense. "What's wrong?"

"Carrie Ann isn't right. In the head."

I could have told him that from my brief visit. She'd displayed all the loon behavior I'd needed to see. I could only imagine how much angrier she was that Coleman had invaded her home.

"But you didn't find anything relating to Gertrude or Pleasant?"

"Nothing that would count as evidence in a court-room. But—"

My heart leaped. He had found something.

"I have information on the blond young man Tally and Marcia were talking to."

"What did you find?"

"Owen DeLong did time with Luther Potter at Parch-man."

This was the link we needed. "He'll know where Pot-ter is."

"My thoughts exactly, which is why Hoss is picking him up right now for questioning."

"I need to drop Sweetie and Pluto off at Dahlia House. Tinkie and Oscar are meeting me there with Libby. Can you stop by later?"

"I can," Coleman said.

"I found some things today, too. We can compare notes."

"And take care of some other business."

He hadn't said anything inappropriate, but the tone of his voice made me flush. Thank goodness Tinkie and Oscar would be there to protect me from myself. "I'm heading home in fifteen minutes."

"Just as long as you aren't alone."

"I promise."

"And steer clear of Bijou's place."

I was about to ask how he knew I'd even discussed Hemlock Manor with Cece, but it was pointless. Coleman had great intuition.

I finished my drink, thanked Curtis and Scott, and said good-bye to my friends before I whistled up Sweetie Pie and cajoled Pluto into leaving. Sometimes my pets reminded me of a good daughter and a James Dean rebel. One wished to please and the other was too aristo-cat-ic to even take notice of my requests.

21

By the time I pulled in front of Dahlia House, the long day and roller coaster of emotions had begun to take their toll. I was relieved to see Tinkie's Caddy there, the trunk still open and Oscar coming down the steps to retrieve more of Libby's "necessities." I wondered if there would be room to sit in Dahlia House with all of Libby's new gear.

When I got out of the car, Tinkie was standing in the doorway holding Libby. Chablis was nowhere in sight. Sweetie and Pluto took off at a run, scooting past Tink and baying through the interior of the house. They were looking for their furry friend.

"Where is Chablis?" I asked when I made it up the steps.

"She's here."

"Where?" Chablis was always eager to greet me.

"Around."

My hackles went up and I walked past her and began to scout the house. What I found sent steam shooting from my ears. Chablis was curled in a corner of the music room. She was so despondent that she didn't even move when I called her name. Sweetie nosed her, and Chablis ignored her best playmate. Not even Pluto, testing with one black kitty claw, could get a response.

"Chablis," I whispered, kneeling beside her. I stroked her trembling body and checked her for a wound or illness. She wasn't hurt—physically.

I scooped the dog into my arms and marched back to Tinkie. "Put that baby down this instant. There's someone here you're neglecting."

Tinkie's expression went from shock to fleeting anger and then sudden remorse. "I have been ignoring Chablis."

"And it will stop now." My friend was tenderhearted and loved her dust mop of a dog, but baby fever had clouded her judgment. Tinkie would never, ever do a single thing to upset Chablis or hurt her feelings. Yet she had. And knowing my partner, she would suffer guilt until she made amends with her pooch.

Libby was oblivious to all of it. When Tinkie put her in the playpen, the baby turned to look at Sweetie, gurgling with joy.

I handed Tinkie her pup. "You need to do some serious making up."

Tinkie sank into a chair beside the playpen and rocked Chablis back and forth, crooning apologies to her. I went to the front door, where Oscar, loaded with even more baby stuff, struggled up the steps. Some of the products I'd never seen or heard of. Baby-ramas, Johnny jumpers, cuddle clothes. I'd grown up knowing about pacifiers, teething rings, diapers, and baby rash ointment. In the years I'd failed to pay attention, there'd been an explosion of things for doting parents to spend money on. Much of it useless, in my opinion.

"Oscar, put that stuff back in the car. Libby has everything she needs right inside."

"But she might want—"

"This excess has to stop. It isn't good for you or the baby. And while I'm laying down the law, you have to stop neglecting Chablis. Her little heart is breaking."

He slowly lowered the goods, a chagrined expression on his face. "I hadn't realized how we were leaving her out."

"She was your first responsibility. Sure, the baby needs constant attention, but Chablis needs to know she's loved, too. You can balance the two."

Oscar left his bundle at the door and hurried inside. He joined Tinkie, who still cuddled Chablis. The pup looked a thousand percent more chipper, and after a few minutes of love from both her humans, she jumped to the floor and romped off with Sweetie.

Crisis averted.

"Thanks for the wake-up call," Tinkie said as she shifted to sit on the floor beside the playpen. She lay down on her side so she was eye to eye with Libby, who watched her with absorption.

"Chablis is a sensitive soul. She's fine now. She will love Libby just as much as she loves you two." I stifled a yawn. My day had been long and worry had settled heavy on my shoulders. The long hours of the night stretched ahead of us.

Famished, we dug into the food Millie had prepared, and Tinkie and Oscar regaled me with stories of Libby's intelligence and ability to understand English, French, and Spanish vocabulary words. They raved about her discerning palate. I didn't say a word. How a baby who drank only formula could be such a prodigy of taste, I didn't know and refused to ask. It was just fun to hear them brag so outrageously over the infant.

The critters enjoyed the special treats Millie had sent them, and they stretched out on the floor beneath the kitchen table.

I'd locked all the doors, windows, and even the doggy door. Sweetie, Chablis, and Pluto were fearless. I was filled with fears. To keep them safe, I made sure they couldn't charge out into the night—should Gertrude show her face. Before it got any later, I called Lee McBride, my horsey friend, and checked on my herd. Reveler, Lucifer, and Miss Scrapiron were grazing in a lush winter pasture, content and well attended.

After Gertrude's surprise visit, when she recklessly shot up my place, I was glad the horses were safely away from Dahlia House, at least until Gertrude was brought to justice.

As the hours passed, Coleman called twice to check on me. He didn't explain his absence, and I was honestly too tired to question him thoroughly. Tomorrow. Tomorrow.

"Sarah Booth, you should go to bed." Tinkie knelt in front of me. I'd fallen asleep sitting up on the horsehair sofa.

"Scott said he'd spend the night." I yawned again. "Watchdog."

"You jump under the covers. We'll let him in. I promise." Tinkie put the back of her hand against my forehead as if she were testing for fever. "You're so tired your body is cool to the touch. You need rest."

I covered a yawn with my palm. She was right. I'd get a crick in my neck if I continued to sleep with my head cranked over. "Thank you both."

"See you in the morning," Tinkie said. "And thanks for pointing out how left out Chablis felt."

I nodded and trudged up the stairs to my room, barely aware of what I was doing.

The next morning I woke up with the sun in my eyes and someone sitting on my bed. When I finally focused on the towering blue beehive hairdo, I scooted against the headboard. "What the hell?"

"It's going to be a lovely day, Sarah Booth. Friends and family gathering round."

I leaned toward the bedroom door. If I could get away from the apparition with the huge blue hairdo, red necklace, and voice that sounded like gravel, I was going to make a break for freedom.

"Don't be in a rush, Sarah Booth. Rushing is bad for your digestion. Homer never rushes."

"Marge Simpson." I meant to speak under my breath but failed.

"Yes, it's me. Marge. Here to keep you on the straight and narrow."

I'd seen Jitty take on the form of cartoon characters, in particular Betty Boop and Wonder Woman, but to see her as Marge was disconcerting. Marge was a long way from beautiful or sexy, which were Jitty's preference. Marge tolerated Bart's mischief and Homer's mediocrity. She was loving and kind and forgiving, which was also far down the list of Jitty's character traits.

Marge loved her family above all else.

At last I got it—why Jitty presented as Marge Simpson. She was the mother of unconditional love.

"You got it, cupcake," Jitty/Marge said in that voice that could drive me straight up the wall. "Mothers love. That's their job. You're a mother to Sweetie Pie and Pluto. And one day, you'll be a mother to your own little Delaney."

I braced myself for the shriveling ovaries lecture, but Marge was kinder and less repetitious than Jitty. She moved on to other areas.

"You don't have to be smart or famous or even pretty to be the best mother around. I know. I'm none of those things. But I got love."

In the crazy way that Jitty worked on me, I began to miss the idea of common, plain old motherhood. I didn't have to be a genius, or the best private eye, or the prettiest Delta gal, or even the best cook. I could be Mom, and that required the capacity to love. It was a job description that suddenly held gargantuan appeal. My mother had been an exemplary mother. She fought for her community and to change the world. She married the smartest man in the South, a man who stood for something. But I didn't have to match her. I could just be a mom in my own way.

"Don't compare yourself to the past. Remember, history's like an amusement park. Except instead of rides, you have dates to memorize."

That statement was like a slap in the face or a glass of cold water tossed on me. I snapped out of it. Throwing the covers aside, I leaped out of bed. "Stop it, Jitty. You're turning my brain into mush. Of course I have to be the best mom ever—just like my mama. I can't be a substandard vessel for the last Delaney spawn." I knew that would get her goat.

Her blue beehive jumped a foot taller. "Stop that, Sarah Booth. Spawn is an unacceptable term. Just get pregnant. Look, roll the dice. DNA is a crapshoot anyway. Maybe you'll get lucky and get a good baby like Libby."

"In contrast to a bad baby?" I had her on the ropes.

"You haven't lived until you have a baby that cries or won't thrive or stays sick and worries you to death. Yes, a *good* baby is one that is happy and joyful and will grow up to be a happy, joyful adult. Like Libby. That's the kind of baby you want."

That was true, so instead of arguing, I grabbed my clothes from the floor. I had no idea if Tinkie and Oscar had left or what had happened while I was drifting along the River Lethe, unmindful of anything around me. Gertrude could have slipped into the house and slit me from gullet to stern.

"Right now, Marge, I'm not interested in a baby. I have work to do. You know, that occupation that keeps a roof over our heads."

"You think you're so different from Marge." My beautiful haint, still sporting blue hair but completely herself, stood up. "That's a problem in this world. Folks see the differences. Just remember, our differences are only skin deep, but our sames go down to the bone."

With that she was gone on the lingering scent of baking sugar cookies. I had been handed a lesson in humanity by a blue-haired cartoon.

I took a steaming shower, put on jeans, boots, and a flannel shirt and went down to the kitchen. Coffee smelled heavenly, and I poured a cup of black and grabbed a strip of bacon. Someone had been busy, but now there was no evidence of anyone in the kitchen or the house. Not even my hound was around to wish me good morrow.

"Where the heck is everyone?" Since I'd been abandoned, I was forced to talk to myself. Coffee in hand, I stumbled back through the dining room and halted. Someone had made pinecone turkeys, and a huge cornucopia graced the dining room table, which was set with my mother's Thanksgiving bone china plates edged in gold. Autumn leaves were scattered about the center of each plate, and Native American designs rimmed the edges. I loved this china set, and someone had taken the time to put a beautiful forest green tablecloth under the china, crystal, candles, and other elements of a proper table setting.

But where had everyone gone? It was as if the decorator fairies had come, spruced up the house, and stolen my friends and pets.

And then I heard laughter. I rushed to the front door where Harold was unloading bales of hay, pumpkins, and two dancing scarecrows to stage the front porch. Keeping him company were Tinkie, Oscar, and Scott. Libby, only her eyes exposed beneath the bundle of clothes, gurgled happily in the playpen, which had been moved to the porch where Tinkie could watch her.

"Morning, sleepyhead," Scott said.

"You guys! This is wonderful."

"Thanksgiving isn't going to just happen, Sarah Booth." Harold loved to tease me, and he did it with great style. "You have to make the holiday arrive."

"I have the best friends ever. Come inside and have some coffee." I wanted to kiss them all.

"Do you like it?" Harold asked as he arranged the scarecrows and plugged them in. They ran through a fine do-si-do and then started over to the catchy music.

"Where in the world did you find this?" I was amazed. Harold could find anything.

"At the gettin' place. I wanted to be sure this Thanksgiving gathering was festive. I've also arranged for square dance lessons for all of us. Something to burn off some of the calories we're going to eat."

In a million years I'd never have thought of square dance lessons, but it was the perfect treat for a day devoted to gluttony. We could eat and then dance, and then eat again.

"Harold, you are the party prince. You think of everything."

"I know how much it means to you for this Thanksgiving to be special. I'm happy to help. You've got your hands full with the search for Pleasant and the manhunt for Gertrude."

I'd missed god-knew-what while I was sawing logs. "Speaking of the devil, any updates?"

Tinkie sat up. "Two bounty hunters, a man and a woman, checked into The Gardens B&B. Pretty ironic that they're living in Gertrude's former business. And they are not shy about telling folks their business. In fact, they're passing out flyers of Gertrude with reward money attached. That, combined with what Yancy Bellow offered, has upped the ante."

"It will be a bitter irony if they catch her, maybe in the flower beds." Gertrude, whatever her faults, had an amazing green thumb. The grounds of the B&B were some of the most beautiful I'd ever seen, ablaze with the fall colors of gold, purple, maroon. Each season presented with showy blossoms, and the autumn belonged to the mums. "Is it Dog and Beth?"

Tinkie shook her head. "Junior was pulling your leg. He hired some bounty hunter named Clete Purcell and his partner Dave something from New Orleans. This has nothing to do with Dog and Beth."

"That Junior. Daddy always warned me he was a card. It's too bad, though, that Dog isn't in town. Gertrude would make an excellent TV episode." Frankly, I didn't care if Scooby Do brought her to justice, as long as she was caught.

"You'd better get cracking if Pleasant Smith is going to make it home to spend Thanksgiving with her family." Harold avoided looking at Tinkie or Oscar as he spoke. He wasn't being cruel. It was merely a reminder for them to keep their hearts as protected as possible.

We trooped into the house and cleaned up a breakfast that would have filled three-dozen hungry farmhands, and then I picked up my keys. "I'm going to work."

"We're almost done decorating," Harold said. He checked his watch. "I have to go to work, too. How about we finish this evening?"

"Great." Since I was in need of babysitters, it would be nice to have something productive to do with our time.

"Would you mind dropping Libby by Madame To-meeka's?" Tinkie asked Oscar.

"Sure."

Oscar kissed her cheek with such gentleness my heart twitched. "I'll be at the bank. Call if you need me."

"And I'll be at the club," Scott said. "We'll meet back here when we can."

We all nodded. It would be a great Thanksgiving celebration, but only because I had such incredible friends.

With the baby safely delivered to Tammy, and the critters in the backseat of the Cadillac, Tinkie and I were ready to find Pleasant. Although my gut knew beyond a doubt that Carrie Ann, Lucinda, and Tally had engineered Pleasant's disappearance, I couldn't figure out where they'd taken the young woman or why they were still holding her.

Tinkie was all in the game as we drove to the spot on Highway 12 where Dewey Backstrum had been killed. I wanted her to examine the scene of the crime, even though there was nothing there to see but a bare stretch of road and empty fields. I also wanted her to meet Frankie. The DNA test results for Frankie's paternity weren't in yet. A backlog in the state lab was working in Tinkie's favor. But I thought if she met the young man, she'd see he was kind and decent. It might help, when the time came.

Off to the west a storm was brewing, and a massive thunderhead loomed, but it was far in the distance. Storms could sweep across the flat land of the Delta in record time. The assault was often quick and short-lived, but sometimes the black clouds moved slowly, a behemoth of rain, thunder, and lightning. I hoped this storm stayed to the west and moved north or south rather than on top of us.

We exited the car into a stiff easterly wind, blowing away my hopes of avoiding the rain. The storm would be here, and if the wind was any indication, it would be here quickly. As I diagramed what I thought had happened with Dewey Backstrum and Pleasant, Tinkie visualized it.

"If Pleasant had stopped to help Mr. Backstrum, it's possible she may have witnessed the hit-and-run. Her abduction may have nothing to do with the Delta State scholarship," Tinkie said.

She was dead right. "I believe those men, Rudy, Owen, and Luther took her. I'm still not certain about Rudy's role in this. But I believe Owen and Luther still have her. While these men may have done the kidnapping and hostage holding, I think those little high school bitches and Carrie Ann masterminded the operation."

"We need to focus on two questions. How can we prove it and where can we find her?"

She was exactly right, and I knew where to find a source who might give some insight into Potter. "Let's take a drive to Parchman."

Tinkie blanched, but she didn't refuse. "What do you hope to find there?"

"Owen and Luther both did time. Maybe someone at the prison knows about their habits, places they might hide out. There is reward money on this, and it's enough to maybe bribe someone to talk."

"Oscar isn't going to like this one bit," Tinkie said as she got behind the wheel. I slammed my door and she was grinning. "A prison adventure. Makes my heart go pitter-pat."

Sometimes I underestimated my partner and I needed to stop doing it.

We dropped by the Three Bs grocery first, and I introduced Tinkie to Frankie and gave them a few minutes to chew the fat about Libby. Tinkie seemed somewhat relieved when we left the store for the short drive to the state penitentiary.

"He's a nice young man, isn't he?"

"He loves Pleasant. I'm pretty sure he's the father."

"Yes, I can see it. Libby has that same tender look."

We drove the rest of the way in silence, but it was not uncomfortable. Tinkie seemed to be processing Frankie as Libby's father, and I was figuring out what to say to the prison warden that would win us an interview with anyone who knew Luther or Owen and who would voluntarily talk to us. A call from Coleman might smooth the way, but I thought we'd try it on our own first. I'd resort to Coleman as a last ditch effort.

We had no difficulty getting past the guard station, after an assistant warden agreed to meet with us. I'd been to Parchman on several occasions. My father had worked with clients there, men and women, before a separate female prison was built. My father believed that some inmates had been railroaded in a system that punished blacks and the poor far more severely than others. Daddy had saved two men from the gas chamber, which was the means of execution at the time. In more modern times, Mississippi had upgraded the state-administered death system to lethal injection.

Prisons are bleak places no matter the season, but winter is particularly depressing in a prison that stretches across twenty-eight square miles of some of the most fertile land in the world. While the warden's office was warm and sunny, the land seemed drenched in desperation and despair. The blues were born at Parchman, and if not born, then nurtured into a musical form that expressed both the joy and sorrow of life, the love of a good woman and the temptation of a bad one, the injustices yet also the small pleasures that make life worthwhile.

As Tinkie and I waited in the small but comfortable office for the deputy warden to personally hear our request, I thought about my father, who'd been greatly taken with Alan Lomax's work in collecting blues from Mississippi prisoners.

"Parchman is a place where the blues find you, no matter how hard you hide," was a quote my daddy said often enough for me to remember it all these years. While Parchman had a terrible reputation for abuse in the early and middle decades of the twentieth century, it was also the first prison in the nation to allow inmates conjugal visits, though not to female inmates, who had no such rights. Mississippi was, and will always be, a state of great disparity and conflict when it comes to justice and equality.

The office door opened and a pleasant-featured young man with blue eyes and sandy hair introduced himself as Deputy Warden Kim Lambert. "I understand you're requesting to speak with inmates who knew Luther Potter and Owen DeLong."

I explained about Pleasant, the baby, and her run-in with the men. "There is a reward, and the donor who put it up would be glad to send it to the inmate's family."

"Wait here. I'll check and see what I can find. I know a couple of guys who were buddies with those two."

Cooling our heels in the administration building, I worried about Sweetie, Pluto, and Chablis out in the car.

The windows were cracked and the day was mild. Still, I didn't like to leave them for long. As it turned out, we didn't have to wait. Lambert returned with two names, but only one man had agreed to speak with us.

We followed the warden, wondering if we'd have to use the phones behind glass partitions that I'd seen in movies. We didn't. Lambert showed us to a small room with a table and three chairs.

"Jimmy will stay with you," Lambert said, indicating a muscled guard who stood in the corner at parade rest. "Do not pass anything to the inmate. Do not attempt to touch him or make physical contact. Stay in your seats. Got it?"

"Yes, sir," we said in unison, and we weren't being smart alecks, either. I had one criminal on my butt and I didn't need to get in Dutch with another.

When we were alone in the room with Jimmy the guard, I turned to my partner. "Are you ready?"

"As I'll ever be." She squeezed my wrist lightly. "This is the break, Sarah Booth. We'll find Pleasant today and have her home for Thanksgiving."

I searched her face for the distress those words were bound to give her, but I saw only peace. Somewhere in the long night, Tinkie had finally accepted that Libby would live with her birth mother.

"You'll see her every day," I whispered. "I believe that."

Tinkie's smile held a tiny drop of sadness. "I believe it, too."

22

Buster Beech, shackled at the wrists, waist, and ankles, clanked into the interview room looking bored and sleepy. He wasn't a big man, but he carried himself with pride. His head was closely shaved, and his prison jumpsuit was neat. When he sat down across the table from us, I couldn't help but notice the prison ink that showed a skull on one bicep and a snake on the other. The guard linked his handcuffs to a chain that went to a bolt in the floor.

Buster got right to the point. "The guard said there's a reward. How much? How do I know you won't cheat me?"

Using my cell phone, I looked up the newspaper article that showed the flyer of Luther Potter and the five thousand dollar reward. With the guard's approval, I showed Buster the article. "I told the warden we'd give the reward to your family," I said. "I promise."

He snorted. "Like yours would be the first promise made and broken."

I understood his reluctance, but my patience had thinned. "Either you talk or we leave." When he didn't answer, I pushed back my chair. "Let's go, Tinkie. This is a waste of our time."

"Wait a minute." He looked at the guard. "Can you make them sign a piece of paper saying I'll get the reward money?"

The guard shrugged.

"I can call the Bank of Zinnia and have that money transferred into your wife's account," Tinkie said. "But you won't get a dime unless you start talking."

I'd never have thought to call the bank. Tinkie was a flipping genius.

Once the deal was struck, Buster was eager to talk. "Yeah, I bunked with Potter. What do you want to know?"

"Did he ever talk about his past?" I asked.

"What? You think I'm Dr. Phil?"

Tinkie snort-laughed and I drilled her with a glare, but she was unrepentant. "It's funny, Sarah Booth. I don't think guys in prison talk much about the past. Except maybe their crimes."

"I'm not interested in hearing about Potter's emotions," I said through gritted teeth. "Specifics, like did he have a favorite bar or was there a special place he liked to poach, or some of those things."

Tinkie was still grinning as she leaned forward. "Did

he talk about his family, where he grew up, anyone he might still be close to on the outside?"

Buster thought about it, chewing on his bottom lip. "He talked about playing football."

It was at least a start, though not where I wanted to begin. "Tell us."

"He said he was a good player, but that some girl lured him into having sex and then called it rape." He glanced at the guard. "He was still angry about it. All these years later. He said that girl ruined his life. He said women were cheap whores and had to be taught who was the boss."

"His criminal record might have had a bit to do with a ruined life," I said.

"He was a tough guy. He liked to talk about himself, and he made it clear he liked to hurt the other players on the football field. He was on the prison boxing team, and he went after his opponents hard and without mercy. He had a reputation for being a bulldozer. Said he could go through anyone or anything, and he was happy to prove it."

"Did he ever talk about family?"

"Not that I recall. And nobody ever came to visit him, as far as I know."

"Where did he live?"

Buster's eyebrows jumped. "Yeah, yeah. I remember something he said. There was a cabin. In that national wildlife refuge over by Rosedale. He said he could live off the land there and stay completely off the grid." Buster leaned forward, but when the guard stepped toward him, he relaxed back in his chair. "He said all he lacked was a woman to serve his needs."

Tinkie carefully put her hands on the table. "Where was this cabin? Be as specific as you can."

"It was federal land right around here."

"Dahomey National Wildlife Refuge?" I asked.

"I guess. If that's the one by Rosedale. That's all I know. It was close to here. He said he could kill a deer most any time of the year, and there were ducks and fish and squirrels and rabbits. He said he could live without ever goin' into town for food or supplies."

My brain was racing. A hunting cabin would be the perfect place to hold a hostage. So isolated that even if Pleasant could escape, she might not find her way to civilization. "Where is the cabin? That refuge is ten thousand acres."

"Do I look like a freakin' GPS?" Buster asked.

"Did he say anything about the terrain? Was there a creek nearby? How did he get water?" Tinkie asked.

"There was a creek. Just down a little hill. He said sometimes the land flooded if the winter rains were bad, but the cabin was built up." He ignored me and focused on Tinkie. "Do I get the money?"

She glanced at me, and I nodded. "Okay." She dialed Oscar. "Please assure Mr. Beech that I'll personally guarantee the transfer of five thousand dollars into his wife's account when the information leads us to Potter."

"Hey, you said you'd do it while we were sitting here."

Tinkie arched one eyebrow. "The information has to pan out. And we need some information from your wife. I can't magically make the money fly through the air. We need a bank account and routing numbers." She put the phone on speaker. "Oscar, please tell Mr. Beech that you guarantee the money."

Oscar's voice came through loud and clear. "You will

get your five thousand dollars if Luther Potter is found," Oscar said.

"I don't like the way this came down." Buster was agitated. "I've been tricked."

"You'll get your money," I assured him. "If Potter is in that cabin and we capture him, you'll have the money within the hour."

We stood up, and the guard unhooked Buster's handcuffs from the table and led him out. Tinkie and I sprinted for the door. We needed a map of Dahomey National Wildlife Refuge, and I knew exactly where to get one.

Tinkie idled the Caddy as I slid out of the front seat at one of the entrances to the largest remaining tracts of bottomland hardwood forest in the state. Dahomey was a relatively new refuge, and one my folks had supported creating.

A bulletin board held maps and a list of hunting and fishing seasons and licensing procedures. I grabbed a map and jumped back in the front seat. Spreading the detailed chart out on the seat, I studied the topography to find the area that best fit the vague description Buster had given us. I did believe the inmate had told all he knew—it just wasn't enough to pinpoint an exact location.

I tapped a section of private land between Stokes and Belman Bayous with my pointer finger. "The cabin could be there. I don't think the Wildlife Services would allow a private citizen to maintain a cabin on federal land, but you never know about the good old boy club.

"The private land looks more plausible," Tinkie agreed, "and it's smack-dab in the middle of the refuge. That's what I'd call isolated." She turned the Caddy

down a rutted dirt road that led into the interior of the
refuge. Maintenance of the road had been neglected, and
washouts and sandy pits, where the tires were almost
trapped, were the norm. I didn't say anything, but the
Cadillac was not the vehicle for this job.

I whipped out my cell phone. "I'm going to call Coleman. He'll have to get Kincaid to help, but we need to do
this right. They can bring some ATVs. If Potter is hiding
out in here, we'll need manpower to bring him in."

"Good idea." Tinkie stopped beside a cypress pond
covered in a brilliant green algae. Even with the sun hiding behind clouds, the pond seemed lit from below in a
light so intensely green that it looked unnatural.

"Green, green, green," I said, remembering Madame
Tomeeka's words. She'd said Pleasant was somewhere
surrounded by green. "This is the place, Tinkie. We're on
the right track."

"And we can't go any further."

Up ahead a giant tree had fallen across the road. There
was no way the Caddy could plow through the small
trees that crowded the road on either side.

"And we don't have a cell signal here." I held up the
phone, which clearly said no service. We were caught
between a rock and a hard place, as my aunt Loulane
would say.

"Let's ditch the car and walk in," Tinkie said.

"Wait!" She wasn't going to like this plan, but it was
the best one I had.

"Wait for what?" She looked at me.

"Take the car and drive until you get a signal. Then
call Coleman for backup."

One eyebrow arched. "And what do you think you're
going to do? Go in there alone? Not in this lifetime."

"Only to observe." I put on my most noble and trust-worthy expression. "I'll mark the trail so you can easily follow me. I'll break limbs and draw arrows in the dirt to show which way I've gone. It might save us several hours. If I find a cabin, I swear I won't go close."

"As if I would believe that." Tinkie wore her stubborn face. "I'm not going anywhere and leaving you alone to traipse into danger."

"I brought my gun."

"And I'm the better shot. You take the car and leave me."

That wasn't going to happen in a million years. "Look, I won't get far from this road. Ask Coleman to bring some ATVs and hurry back. I'll just scout around a little." I pointed to her stylish shoes, some lovely red velvet flats that perfectly matched her red shrug and black leggings. "I have on sturdy paddock boots. There are big snakes in the woods. Timber rattlers. Copperheads. They're aggressive and fast." Snakes would likely turn the tide.

"I'm not afraid of snakes."

"And alligators."

"Pffft." She waved the gators away.

"And this is the home of the three-inch palmetto roaches that fly and are attracted to hairspray. Remember when Ruth Ann Scott went camping with her boyfriend and that cockroach flew into her hair? She knocked herself out on a tree running in the dark. She said his little legs were digging into her scalp, pinching. She could hear it gnawing her hair roots."

Tinkie's head swiveled toward me like Linda Blair's in *The Exorcist*. "You're making that up."

"I am not. And these big bugs have those long legs

that grasp and hold. If you put them on something shiny and hard they make that terrible clicking and scratching noise."

"Stop it, Sarah Booth. I'm not afraid of a few flying bugs."

"You will be if they get in your hair and start chewing at the roots. Did I say they're drawn to hairspray?"

"I don't believe a word you're saying."

But she did. I'd finally figured out how to keep her safe, and I didn't feel bad about the deception at all.

I found a pen in the glove box and marked an X where I thought the cabin might be. "This is where I'm headed, but I promise not to approach the cabin until you guys get here. Just hurry. If I find her, I'll try to let her know help is on the way."

"I don't like this one bit." Tinkie's bottom lip protruded in a pout.

"Please, Tinkie. Drive like the wind. The quicker you go, the sooner you can bring Coleman back."

"If you swear you'll stay safe."

I held up the three-fingered scout pledge we'd learned in grammar school. "You have my word. I'll just be able to save some time by moving on this while you get help."

"Coleman is probably going to kill me."

But the argument was won. I retrieved my gun from the trunk of her car. I considered taking hers, too, just for the extra firepower, but I didn't want to leave Tinkie without protection. I handed her pistol through the driver's window. "Just in case. You might run into Potter on your way out. There are a million little pig trails through here that a powerful pickup with four-wheel drive could manage. Be careful."

"And you, too." She reached through the open window

and grasped my hand. "I love you, Sarah Booth. Keep yourself safe. You're the best partner ever." She choked up.

"Tinkie, I promise not to do anything rash. You act like we're saying good-bye forever."

"I do love you."

"And back at you." I turned and walked to the downed tree. It was a simple matter to climb under it, but I checked for snakes first. It was November, and most limbless reptiles were likely hibernating, but it always paid to be careful in the woods. I heard Tinkie's car door slam and whipped around to see she had loosed the hounds and Pluto on me. She wasn't leaving me to face danger alone.

Tinkie did a neat turnaround and headed back to civilization. Though the day held patchy sun, the big storm had moved closer. As I stepped into the dense growth of trees, I felt the temperature drop. I loved Mississippi's beautiful woodlands, but I was no fool. The woods could be dangerous for those who failed to pay attention. And not necessarily because of the wild beasts. Luther Potter was a lot more deadly than any wild animal I might encounter.

An hour later I figured I'd covered three or four miles at a brisk pace. The first pitter of rain sprayed across the road in a gust that shook dead leaves from the hardwoods and sent them flying. In the proper gear, I'd enjoy a walk in the rain. Not so much without a waterproof slicker, which I didn't have. This was going to be nasty.

I'd explored a couple of deer trails that I thought might be a secret entrance to a cabin, but I'd ended up at one of the creeks in a dead end. Still, I had the sense that I was closing in on Potter. When I came to a mud track with tire marks, my gut sent out a warning that made me take cover and drop into a crouch. The tracks were fresh. Danger was near.

I picked my way through the mud, hoping I wouldn't slip and break a bone. Thick layers of claylike soil stuck to the bottom of my boots and made my feet feel like cement blocks. Somehow the critters knew exactly where to step, and they crossed the bog without incident. The ground tilted slightly downward, an indication we were heading for water.

While the area was mostly flat and filled with small lakes, ponds, creeks, streams, and swamps, the area on either side of the creek was sloped. As I pushed through the dense undergrowth, I could see watermarks where flooding had pushed the creek out of its banks. Such a flood could happen in an instant if the rain was heavy enough. The cloud that had drifted atop me was pregnant with water. Any minute now the bottom would drop out.

Pluto scampered up to me and jumped on my leg, all four paws digging in. I hopped and choked back my cries of pain, and finally picked him up and tucked him into my warm jacket. He sensed the approach of the rain and—typical cat—he wanted inside my coat. He wouldn't be totally dry, but it was a lot better for a black kitty than slogging through mud. Sweetie Pie and Chablis were oblivious to the horrors of impending wet.

The crazy thing about my dog was that she could swim in the icy creeks and rivers and never feel it. A good hot bath, on the other hand, left her shivering and acting as if I'd been terribly cruel to her.

I'd just cleared the bog when Sweetie stopped in front of me, a low growl vibrating from her throat. The trees on either side stood like sentinels, so thick in places they actually blocked the daylight, which was dim at best due to the storm.

Hushing the animals, I listened in all directions. The woods were quiet. Too quiet. The natural world had been silenced by something or someone. Something dangerous. The birds and small mammals knew when to hide, and I took their lead and ducked behind an old stump until I could determine where the danger came from.

I heard it then, the long, thin wails of a woman crying. The sobs raced up my spine, tingling every nerve along the way. This was the sound of total depression and hopelessness. This woman had given up all thoughts of rescue.

It had to be Pleasant. I knew it instinctively. And if this was the prison where Pleasant was being kept, then Luther Potter and Owen DeLong might not be far way.

I slipped through the woods silent as a shadow holding Pluto under my coat, with Sweetie Pie and Chablis in lockstep with me. The storm drew down on us, and the wind kicked up. Leaves whirled through the air and another shower of rain spattered like buckshot all around me, propelled by a wind so strong the drops stung like pellets.

At last a cabin came into view. Smoke curled from the chimney, and the thought of a nice, warm fire was tempting, but not enough to draw me out of my cover. I had no idea who might be in the cabin. Or what firepower they might have.

I gripped my pistol and automatically checked to be sure the safety was off and the gun ready for use. I'd never taken to the idea of shooting anyone, but I would protect myself and the critters with necessary force. If someone tried to hurt us, I'd do my best to hurt him first.

I duckwalked closer to the rustic cabin, taking care to stay below the top of the scrubby undergrowth that offered cover. The cabin seemed to contain no more than four rooms. The cypress wood, decay resistant and unpainted, was a dark gray that blended perfectly with the tree trunks.

When I'd watched the cabin for fifteen minutes and saw no movement, I moved closer. The storm wouldn't hold off forever, and I needed to find out who was in the cabin with the sobbing woman. If she was alone . . . I had to gauge the danger versus the opportunity of saving Pleasant.

I stepped forward and felt a sickening snap as the ground gave way beneath me and I sank up to my hip in a hole. I'd stepped into deadfall that gave way beneath my weight. I wasn't injured, but not four inches from my foot was a cottonmouth moccasin as big around as my upper arm. It was a granddaddy of a snake, with enough poison to kill me if I couldn't obtain immediate medical attention. The lidless eyes of the snake stared straight into my quaking soul.

23

Pluto abandoned my coat, leaping across the hole to the other side in classic Halloween stance. He saw the snake and he didn't want to be friends. Sweetie Pie eased to my side and growled. I grabbed her collar and held on to prevent her from jumping into the hole. She'd risk her life to save me. The venom from a snake that size would kill a ninety-pound dog quickly, and tiny Chablis wouldn't stand a chance. The little dust mop tiptoed closer and I stopped her with a low command.

What I hadn't expected was Pluto. Like a streak of black lightning, Pluto darted into the hole and smacked the coiled snake on top of its head. The snake darted and wove as Pluto jumped to the side seconds before the snake struck. The cold weather had slowed the serpent's reactions, but it was waking up, and the muscles beneath the brown, red, and black skin tensed and contracted as it coiled tighter, giving it a longer range to strike.

Terror almost paralyzed me—for myself and my cat. Pluto yowled like a tomcat ready to fight.

"Pluto, no!" If I reached down to grab the cat, I might provoke the snake to strike again.

Pluto crouched to make another foray against the snake. The fetid odor of a stinky gym and rancid cheese hit my nostrils, trademarks of the cottonmouth. There was no doubt this was a poisonous reptile, and one of the most territorial snakes in the world. He would not tolerate our sudden intrusion into what appeared to be his den. Pluto and I were in serious trouble.

I inched my hands down, ready to grab Pluto and throw him to safety, but the snake opened its jaws, a signal of impending attack. My paddock boot, good leather, protected my foot and ankle, but if the snake aimed for my calf or above, I would be a goner. To my surprise, though, the snake waited. Perhaps he would allow us to retreat.

I shifted slightly, and the snake responded by opening its mouth again, showing the white "cotton" interior and its fangs. To withdraw, I had to move, but it was my movement that would provoke the snake and make him feel threatened. It was a standoff, and one I couldn't win. The cat or dogs would soon take action and one of us would be bitten.

I eased my gun from my waistband. I had one chance. I wouldn't get a second shot, and a wounded snake could still bite. I had to hit the snake's head if I meant to escape without being struck.

"Pluto, stay still." I cocked the gun and aimed, trying to clear my mind of everything except focusing on the snake's head. If Pluto jumped suddenly, I might kill him. Or hit my own foot. A .38 would do some major damage to a foot. I was suddenly very fond of my feet. While they were long, skinny, and somewhat unattractive, they were perfect for walking, standing upright, and dancing.

There was also the problem that if Luther Potter or Owen DeLong was in the vicinity, a gunshot would be as effective as a marching band in letting them know company was a-comin'.

Sweetie Pie lunged forward, and I lowered the gun. "Stop!" I pulled backward on her collar with all my strength. The hound reversed and the momentum of her reversal pulled me clear of the hole before I could even think. As if the critters had choreographed the action, Pluto leaped out, landing on my stomach with enough weight to expel the air from my lungs. I uttered a loud *ummmmptf.*

Even though I had fifteen pounds of kitty on my solar plexus and no oxygen, I managed to get my heels and elbows under me and execute a backward crawl like something from *The Grudge.* I didn't believe the snake would chase us, but I wasn't taking any chances.

Chablis ran to the hole and growled a warning at the snake to stay down there. I was very sure Mr. Moccasin was as glad I was gone as I was to be free of his home. I forced myself to my feet, still sucking in air and wheezing. No matter, I wanted to leave the snake behind me. In front of me was the rescue of a terrified female.

The long wails of the woman had stopped. The only sign the cabin was inhabited was the curl of blue smoke that lazed out of the chimney and into the wind. My watch showed an hour had passed since Tinkie dropped me off and went for help. My partner and the cavalry should be arriving any minute. If I was going to have something to report, I needed to investigate the cabin. Instead of a frontal assault, I decided to circle behind the cabin, hoping the back had more windows or exposed areas than the front did.

I followed a slope, careful to avoid bogs. Big tire imprints indicated solid ground, and I counted my blessings that the storm continued to hold off, else the tracks would be washed away.

By the time I made it to the edge of an amber creek I'd caught my breath and stopped long enough to give the animals some much-deserved petting and praise. Sweetie Pie was a stout hound, but it was her iron will, not her strength, that had pulled my weight out of the snake hole. And Pluto—he was normally filled with disdain for all humans, but he'd risked his life. Chablis would have been down in the hole in two second flat if I hadn't stopped her.

While I praised the pets, I took inventory of my surroundings.

The rear of the cabin was visible from my hiding spot in a thicket of scrub underbrush. The light had grown so dim due to the storm and the fading afternoon, that I had an advantage. The place seemed abandoned. I'd never have noticed it, except for the cries of the woman within. If Pleasant was in there, alone, now might be my best opportunity. I took it and crept to the back of the house, after I'd admonished the dogs to stay back.

As I closed in, I saw movement in one of the windows. I hurried there and peered inside. Pleasant Smith, a one-inch-thick chain locked around her waist, cooked something at the stove. Owen DeLong sat in a rustic chair at a small wooden table. He drank rotgut whiskey neat and smoked a cigarette.

Owen looked rough, and Pleasant, for a woman who'd

just delivered a baby, was rail thin. Her red hair, so beautiful in the photos I'd seen, was matted to her head, and
her clothes didn't fit. She wore a dress two sizes too large
for her and designed for a grandmother, not a teenager.

Owen said something I couldn't understand, but Pleasant's response was clearly not to his liking. He stood up
and drew back his fist, threatening her. I gripped the gun
tighter. If he tried to hit her, I'd shoot him in the leg.

"Hit me." I heard her clearly now because her voice
was raised. "Do it again and I swear, when I get a chance
to pay you back, I'll give it to you ten times over."

"You'd best shut up," Owen said. "The only value
you ever had was that baby. Now that she's gone, Luther
won't have much use for you. You can't cook for shit.
And you know he can't let you go. He ain't goin' back to
prison and neither am I."

She gave the pot a vicious stir. "Shit is what you deserve to eat."

"Shut up. That's your last warning. Keep clanging that
tongue against the roof of your mouth and I'll smack you
in the jaw hard enough to break it. That'll shut you up."

She didn't back down. She thrust out her chin and
essentially dared him. When he stepped away and sat
down, she returned to the pot on the stove, revealing a
black left eye.

My fingers itched on the gun grip, and I brought it up
again. If I could get the drop on Owen and wound him,
I could free Pleasant, tie him up, and wait for Coleman to
come.

But I had promised Tinkie I would wait. I'd given my
word, and in the past I'd taken far too many risks. I'd put
myself and others in great danger. I owed it to those who
cared for me to wait.

I drew in a long breath and accepted the limitations before me. Moving with great care, I left the window and ducked back into the underbrush about twenty feet from the cabin. I was close enough to hear anything happening inside, but not a sitting duck outlined against the cabin wall if someone unexpectedly stepped out the back door. I could wait it out. It wouldn't be long. Coleman would be here any minute. I'd left my path clearly marked by breaking branches and drawing arrows in the dirt, just as I'd promised. Coleman could follow those tracks with a blindfold on.

The wind kicked up and whipped the tops of the trees into a frenzy. This time the bottom was going to fall out for sure. Sweetie whined, her nose in the air. Chablis came to my side, her underbite fierce as she growled.

"What's wrong?" They sensed something that I couldn't hear, see, or smell. Before I could grab her, Sweetie shot across the cabin yard just as I heard the rattle and squeal of a vehicle bumping over the rutted road. For a moment my heart lifted. Coleman was on the way. But my hopes were dashed. A black pickup inched out of the dense trees and pulled into the front yard.

Luther Potter got out, and he held a shotgun at port arms.

Before I could even call her name, Sweetie Pie shot across the front yard and slammed into Potter so hard she knocked his legs out from under him.

"You damn dog," Potter screamed, scrabbling for the gun, which had gone flying into the dirt. I wanted to rush forward, but there wasn't time. When Potter had the shotgun in his grasp, he rose to his knees and fired both barrels at Sweetie.

I had no time to think or calculate risk. I ran for the back door, praying Owen would rush out the front to see what Potter was shooting at. I edged inside and found myself in a pantry with rotting garbage in one corner. Holding my breath, I creaked open the back door.

Pleasant had her hands on the chain, struggling to push it down her hips. She saw me and her eyes widened, but she didn't make a sound.

"I'm here to help you, but we have to hurry."

She nodded, pressing harder on the chain that seemed hung at the widest point of her very narrow hips.

"Where's the key?" I asked.

"Luther. He keeps it on him. What's he shooting at?" Another two blasts made me cringe.

"My dog." Fear for Sweetie zipped through me, but I had to get Pleasant free and away.

The chain was attached to a bolt in the floor, and I was reminded of my interview with Buster at the prison. Potter's time in Parchman hadn't been completely wasted. He'd learned how to bolt a human being down.

The chain was too thick to smash with a hammer, and it was closed with a padlock stout enough that I'd need a key or a bolt cutter, neither of which was in my possession.

"Help me push down on the chain. I've lost a lot of weight since Luther checked it. I think I can wiggle out."

Pleasant was painfully thin. Her stomach was barely bloated from the baby weight, and her arms and legs and face were almost bone and skin. I tried to roll the chain down over her hips. "It's too tight," I said.

"Keep trying. We can force it."

"And take your hide with it."

"I don't care. I have to get away. I have to find my baby."

I realized then I could tell her one thing that would make all the difference in the world.

"The baby is safe. I swear to you. She's in great hands and as soon as I get you out of here I'll take you to her."

Outside, the shotgun blasted again, and I wanted to rush to the front of the house and shoot Potter and Owen. In fact, I didn't actually have another option. If they came in and caught us trying to escape, they'd kill us both. I didn't doubt it for an instant. I had to act while I still had the element of surprise.

"Stay here."

Pleasant grabbed my arm. "Don't take them on. They'll kill you without blinking an eye. Rudy was helping me and Potter stabbed him. They were going to sell my baby, and Rudy took her. He was going to leave her where I knew she'd be safe. Luther chased him into the yard and stabbed him, but Rudy got away and took my baby with him."

I didn't tell her anything about Rudy, but she read my face. "He's dead, isn't he? I knew when no one came to help me that he'd died. Rudy was my friend. He's dead because he took the baby to save her. Potter was going to sell her to some lawyer who had a family to buy her. I told Rudy to take her to Sarah Booth Delaney, because I knew she'd come looking for the mother." She nodded. "That's who you are, isn't it?"

"Yes, but let's exchange introductions later." I gave a ruthless tug on the chain. "This chain isn't budging."

"Oh, it will." She tightened her body and pushed. The

chain moved an inch down her hips and I sat on the floor and pulled with all of my might. The links dug into her tender flesh, but Pleasant never even whimpered. Any minute Potter and Owen would come inside. It was now or never.

With a grunt of desperation, Pleasant tore at the links, and five seconds later, the chain hit the wooden floor with a clatter. She was free. And just in the nick of time. The front door squealed open.

"If that dog comes out of the woods again, shoot it," Potter commanded. "I'm going inside for more shells."

We raced for the back door. There was no point trying to be quiet now. We took the steps in three strides and aimed for the underbrush where Pluto and Chablis paced. At the moment I dove into the bushes, the bottom dropped out of the clouds. Rain fell in sheets so thick it was as effective as fog. Pleasant and I crawled deeper into the woods.

I searched for Sweetie Pie, but there was no trace of my hound. I couldn't help but fear that one of the shotgun blasts had hit her and she was wounded somewhere, maybe bleeding to death. The rain came down so hard, I couldn't see four feet in front of me.

"Keep moving," I told Pleasant. "There's a creek. We'll go there and follow it north."

How Coleman would find us now, I didn't know, but we couldn't remain at the cabin. While I'd broken my word about remaining outside the cabin, I had rescued Pleasant.

Wearing only the sacklike dress and tennis shoes, Pleasant shivered in the cold. Her teeth chattered so loudly I could hear them. Hypothermia was a danger if I didn't find a dry place for her quickly.

"Stay here." I had a thought. "Chablis, Pluto, keep her safe here."

"Don't go back." She clutched at my arm. "They will kill you. I'm not exaggerating."

"If Potter left the key in the truck, we can have transportation out of here. If the key isn't there, at least I can disable the vehicle."

She saw the reason in that and stopped arguing. "Be careful. Those are two mean men."

"Stay here—and stay low."

Using the rain for a shield, I ran toward the parked truck. I was almost there when the front door burst open and Potter came out. He wore a slicker and boots, and he carried the shotgun and a high-power cue beam. He meant to track us. And I had no doubt he had years of experience in running his prey to ground.

I hid behind the truck, fully aware I'd miscalculated. I'd assumed Potter and his cohort would go out the back door and look for us where we'd disappeared. No such luck. Now I had a choice. I could run for it and risk getting shot in the back, or I could check for the truck key. I inched up and looked in the passenger window. The key wasn't there.

Edging the door open, I stuck my hand inside and ripped all the wiring loose that hung beneath the steering wheel. My mechanic's experience was limited, but surely I'd snatched something vital.

I didn't bother closing the door. I moved to the back of the truck, anticipating a dash into the nearby woods. To my consternation, the rain began to slack off. I was trapped.

24

I had no choice. I had to make a run for it, but I went in the opposite direction from Pleasant. If Potter got me, I didn't want to lead him to Pleasant. I'd told her to follow the creek. That was the best way out. I'd studied the map and the creek would lead her to the road. Potter couldn't use the truck, either. He'd be forced to walk, just like Pleasant. I'd done the best I could for her.

Expecting any second to hear a blast and feel the buckshot penetrate my back, I made for the woods.

"Hey! Stop!" Potter had seen me. "Stop or I'll shoot."

I kept running.

"Hey, POS, I'm the one you want." Pleasant stepped out of the woods. "You're going to prison, asshat. I'll see to it."

Holy cow, that girl had a set of brass ones. And she was going to get herself killed.

I'd made it to the edge of the woods. I turned around, my pistol ready at my side. "Sheriff Coleman Peters is on the way. He reserved your bunk in Parchman. Let's go."

Potter shifted the gun from Pleasant to me. We were both valueless to him, and I didn't doubt he'd shoot us if he had a clear opportunity. It had never occurred to me that Pleasant had been taken for her child. That Potter and DeLong were going to sell her baby made me furious. I still had my gun, and if he lifted the shotgun, I would shoot him.

As if he read my mind, he lifted the gun to his shoulder. "You've been begging for this a long time." He aimed at Pleasant.

I braced myself as I'd been taught, aimed, and fired. The bullet missed Potter's crotch, but not by much. Wood chips flew from the house. He was so shocked, he stumbled backward and dropped the gun. I took another shot, deliberately high.

"Run!" I yelled at Pleasant. We took off in opposite directions.

A crashing from the woods to my right sent my heart into my throat. When I realized it was Sweetie Pie, the relief was so delicious I wanted to cry. My hound was unharmed. Potter had missed.

I'd never been a fan of jogging and I hated sprinting even more, but I put everything I had into a long, fast stride as I ran for my life. Limbs slapped my face and my boots skidded in the mud, but nothing slowed me down. It was run or die, and I really, really wanted to live.

Sweetie edged me toward the creek, and I let her pick the way. She had a homing device in her hound dog brain, and while I might guess the correct direction, she was true as a compass. Fifteen minutes later, huffing painfully for breath, I heard something else in the woods. I prayed it was Pleasant, and my prayers were answered when she crashed through a thicket. A long streak of blood covered her hip, and her legs were a mess of scratches and bruises, but her face held radiance. She was free, and her baby girl was safe. I shrugged out of my jacket and offered it to her but she refused.

I signaled her to keep going and I forced myself to jog. We stumbled through more deadfall as we drew close to the creek. The rain was petering out, but night had begun to kiss the eastern sky. Darkness might be a helpful cover, if we didn't freeze to death. Where in the hell was Coleman? He'd had plenty of time to arrive. We weren't so far off the path that we wouldn't hear the four-wheelers.

Had something happened to Tinkie? Had she met Potter coming in as she was going out? Surely word was all over town by now that Tinkie and Oscar had a new baby. If Potter felt the Richmonds had thwarted his plan to sell Libby—and I had no doubt he could get ten to twenty thousand for a healthy baby girl so beautiful— then he might have taken his wrath out on Tinkie.

"Did you say the sheriff was coming?" Pleasant gasped out as we struggled through the woods.

"Yes, he's coming." There was no point sharing my doubts with her. "He'll find us any minute now. Just keep going."

I stumbled and went down just as the tree I'd been beside exploded. The gunshot blast made my ears ring.

Luther Potter was not fifty yards behind us—and he was closing in. He had no incentive to keep either of us alive. If he dropped us in the woods, he could leave the bodies for the animals to scavenge and wouldn't even be bothered with disposal of our remains.

Pleasant was panting with exertion, and her body trembled from the cold. We didn't have much time left for a rescue. She was about to fall in her tracks. Hypothermia would kill her as effectively as a bullet. What the hell had happened to Tinkie and the cavalry?

I judged we'd made it half a mile from the cabin. The terrain was brutal, and the wet, slick ground often made us trip and slide. Potter faced the same elements, but he wasn't afraid, freezing, and exhausted from having had a baby and being mistreated for weeks.

To Pleasant's credit, she never complained. Her gaze remained on the ground in front of her, and she was focused on the extreme will it took to put one foot in front of the other. She faltered and almost went to her knees, but she caught herself on a small tree, pulled up, and forged ahead. She had a baby to live for. I'd never seen anyone display such courage and determination.

"Give it up," Potter yelled. "I'll make it quick and painless. If I have to keep tracking you, I'll shoot you in the gut and leave you for the coyotes."

Pleasant sobbed. She stumbled and fell, hard, onto her knees and hands. She tried to get up but couldn't.

"Go," she said. "Leave me."

"I'm not leaving you here." I wasn't courageous, but I couldn't leave a helpless woman to the abuse I was certain would befall her.

She tried again to rise, lost her footing and tumbled to her side, and I knew she was done for. "My baby. I never got to hold her."

"Get up." I tugged her arm. "You can't quit. You have to make it. Libby needs you."

Her eyes had gone dreamy, and the shaking had stopped. She was dying right in front of me. "Libby." She whispered the name. "I like that."

I didn't have cell phone reception, but I damn sure had pictures of Libby. I whipped out the phone and found the cutest one where she wore a red and white polka dot onesie with a big matching peony bow on her red hair. "Look!" I commanded Pleasant, shaking her back to consciousness. "This is your baby. Get up and fight for her."

For a moment life came back into her eyes as she stared at the picture. "My baby. Love her for me and tell her I'm sorry," she said, and that was it. The black tide of unconsciousness pulled her under. Her breathing was so shallow and her body so cold I knew it was only a matter of moments before she was dead.

Rage consumed me. The injustice of what had happened to Pleasant washed red behind my eyeballs. I gripped the pistol and faced toward where I knew Potter was. "Luther Potter, I'm going to kill you." It was wrong and I knew it. Vigilante justice wasn't my normal operating procedure, but this man had tortured and imprisoned a young woman. A child, really. She would die in the woods because of this man. He'd generated a world of suffering for a lot of people, and he stood between me and rescue. If I had to kill him, that was fine by me.

"Little girl with a pop gun, you'd better watch your step. I'm gonna have some fun with you before I gut you."

He was a stupid, stupid man. And arrogant. And a misogynist, among many other unpleasant things. I wanted to stay with Pleasant, to hold her hand as she moved from this world to the next. I grasped her fingers, which were icy cold. She didn't seem to be breathing. She was already gone. The realization that I might have played a role in her death by dragging her into a freezing November rain when she could have stayed in the cabin, chained but warm and safe, was the final blow to my reason. I would kill him.

Potter was so self-confident, he stepped out from behind a tree. Either he'd forgotten I was armed, figured I was a bad shot, or was so deluded he didn't think I'd pull the trigger. He failed to consider the red rage that blinded me to everything, even danger.

Holding the pistol at my side and hidden by my jacket, I walked toward him as fast as I could move.

Concern flitted across his face, but it didn't stay.

"You'd best back up, girlie. I ain't playin'." He brought the shotgun up.

I'd closed the distance between us to within thirty feet. I brought up the pistol and pulled the trigger in one smooth motion. I didn't aim. I didn't have to. Righteous fury sent the bullet deep into his thigh.

Disbelief crossed his face, then fury, then pain. He dropped to his knees. When he tried to bring the gun around, I kept moving forward until I was on top of him. I put the barrel of the pistol against his head. "Drop the shotgun."

He did, immediately.

I'd never considered myself irrational. Or capable of killing someone in cold blood. But Luther Potter was the exception to many things. Pleasant Smith was dead because of him. She'd had her child stripped from her moments after the baby's birth. She'd never even held her infant girl. Potter's crimes extended beyond Pleasant to Charity, Faith, the Smith clan, Frankie, and Rudy Uxall's murder, and Tinkie's heart would be broken because of Luther Potter and the crimes he committed.

I cocked the hammer. In the middle of a hardwood forest in Bolivar County, Mississippi, I intended to take a man's life. The reasons were numerous and correct.

"Don't kill me." Potter's fear stank. Now that he was the victim, he was a coward. "Don't! You can't just shoot me."

"Yes, I can." My finger tightened on the trigger.

He started crying, which only made me want to pull the trigger more. My hand was steady. I didn't want to mess this up. One clean kill shot.

"Please, don't do this."

His sobs didn't touch me. Watching his blood spill from the hole in his thigh and seep into the forest floor didn't mean a thing to me. I felt nothing but a desire to end him.

I inhaled and pressed the barrel harder into his skull. He wailed. I began to squeeze the trigger.

I had no clue what hit me, but I went flying and the gun went off in a wild shot. I landed on my side, but the barrel was still trained on Potter. He looked longingly at his shotgun, some five feet away, but he didn't try for it. He finally believed I'd shoot him.

When I glanced around to see what had happened, Sweetie Pie stood beside me. I sat up, my weapon still on Potter. In the distance ATVs roared through the woods toward me. At last, Coleman was here. It was too late for Pleasant, but Sweetie Pie had saved Luther Potter. The moment when I'd been capable of pulling the trigger had passed.

My hound gave a sharp howl and took off through the woods. Chablis and Pluto were hot on her heels. They disappeared into the underbrush without a backward glance.

The shaking started in my hand and then moved into the rest of my body. Aunt Loulane would say that I suffered from Saint Vitus Dance. Had Potter been less of a coward, he could probably have gotten up and run away, because I was incapable of stopping him. The bullet hole in his leg, which was actually bleeding a lot, was as effective as a chain around his waist. A pale blue tinge had settled on his features, from either cold or blood loss. I didn't really care. If Coleman took much longer, maybe the bastard would bleed out.

Alas, it was not to be. A four-wheeler crashed through the underbrush, and Coleman zoomed down the slight hill toward me. He jumped off the ATV and rushed to me. "Are you hurt?"

"No, I'm good." I pointed at Potter. "He's shot and Pleasant is dead. She's over there. Owen DeLong is back at the cabin." And then I burst into tears.

Coleman clutched me to him, but he was taking no chances with Potter. As soon as DeWayne came to a stop, Coleman told him to radio the sheriff's office and ask Francine to call the air flight helicopter service out of Memphis immediately. "Then cuff Potter."

"He doesn't look like he's going anywhere," DeWayne said.

"Cuff him anyway."

I'd managed to compose myself, and I pushed back from the comfort of Coleman's arms. "I'm sorry. I'm okay."

"Can you show me where Pleasant is?" he asked.

I didn't want to, but I had no choice. We needed to get her body out of the woods. Someone would have to tell her grandmother. And Frankie. It was going to be a long, hideous evening.

When I saw Pleasant stretched out on the ground where I'd left her, I was shocked to see all of the critters around the body. Sweetie was lying on top of her back, and Chablis was on her thighs. Pluto had curled up on her calves. They were protecting her, and that made me burst into tears again.

"She was so cold, and we got wet. She'd been starved and was weak." Fury gave me strength. "She died because of the way they treated her. I should have shot Potter while I had the chance."

"No, Sarah Booth."

"I meant to. I had the barrel against his head and my finger on the trigger. Sweetie knocked me down. I was going to blow his brains all over the woods."

"I know." He put an arm around me. "I saw you. I was terrified you'd pull the trigger. Thank god Sweetie Pie stopped you."

"He needs to die."

"But not by your hand. You are not judge and executioner. You are not. You would never have been able to live with that. You owe your future to your dog."

I knelt down beside Pleasant. "Sweetie, you can move now. We'll take care of her."

Coleman knelt beside me. He checked her pulse, a routine action.

"She's alive, Sarah Booth. Just barely, but alive. The animals are warming her body." He stood and took off his dry jacket and wrapped it around Pleasant's still form. Sweetie returned to the job of body heat exchange.

"DeWayne, get that helicopter here now! She's alive. Hypothermia."

Moving quickly he gathered sticks. They were wet, but Coleman had built more bonfires and campfires and marshmallow roasting fires than anyone I knew. In a few short moments he had a blaze going beside her, and I had my jacket off drying and warming it over the flames. When it was heated, I put it on her legs and we warmed Coleman's jacket and returned it to her shoulders.

"Bring Potter's jacket," Coleman called out to DeWayne.

"What?" the deputy said.

"Bring him over here. He can sit by the fire. I need his jacket. And yours."

In five minutes Coleman had organized a rotation of warm coverings for Pleasant. He'd hold the jackets by the fire until they were toasty and then apply them to her body, exchanging them as they cooled. Luther Potter hunkered by the fire, weak and defeated. To my dismay, DeWayne had fashioned a tourniquet and stopped Potter's bleeding.

As Pleasant's body temperature began to rise and the outlook for her survival improved, my anger began to seep away, leaving me shaken by what I'd almost done. I kept looking at Potter, imagining him dead by my hand. Coleman was correct. I would never have been able to live with myself. Taking another's life, except in self-defense, could only be called murder, and I was no murderer. Had Sweetie not stopped me, though, I wondered if I would have been able to stop myself. That question would stay with me for the rest of my life.

I shifted over to sit by Sweetie Pie and stroke her long, silky ears as we waited for the helicopter. Pluto curled up in my lap, and Chablis nuzzled under my arm. It was only then that I thought to ask, "Where's Tinkie?"

"She called me and told me how to find you. She said she'd be right behind me."

Coleman frowned. "We'll call and be sure she's okay as soon as we get somewhere with a signal."

"What about Owen DeLong? He's back in the cabin." The cohort, who was just as evil as Potter, could be on the loose in the woods and he might have grabbed Tinkie. Such a scenario made me stand up.

Coleman patted his radio. "Not anymore. Sheriff Kincaid picked him up about ten minutes ago. DeLong's telling everything he can to Hoss. Hopes to work a deal."

"Don't give him anything. No deals. He beat Pleasant whenever he felt like it."

"Don't worry. These two are going away for a long, long time. Probably the rest of their lives. We have enough on them to put them away, and Pleasant's testimony will be the red ribbon on top of the package. I believe we'll prove Potter killed Rudy Uxall, and that's an automatic life without parole."

And while it was justice of a kind, it wouldn't undo what they'd done to a mother and child and all the rest of us. Even me. I'd carry the scars of this day.

25

Coleman had given the helicopter specific landing instructions for an area that had been clear-cut by illegal timbering. While the rape of the land upset me, this was one time I was glad to have a cleared area for the chopper to set down.

In no time at all, Pleasant was loaded and on her way to the hospital in Zinnia. With Coleman's care, her condition had improved to the point that the EMTs felt the long trip to Memphis was unnecessary. She could stay at the local hospital, and as soon as Doc said her condition was stabilized enough, I would put her baby girl in her arms.

Potter was in no danger, so his transport to the local hospital would be on a four-wheeler and then in the backseat of a patrol car. I only hoped that he felt every bump along the way. While I was immensely glad I hadn't killed him, I was not over wanting him to suffer.

Coleman and DeWayne stood on either side of me as we waved the helicopter off. Potter was cuffed to one of the ATVs. I heard the sound of additional machines, and Hoss Kincaid and two deputies came out of the woods. Owen DeLong rode behind the Bolivar County sheriff. When he saw Potter, he cursed a blue streak. I couldn't tell who his spleen was directed at and didn't care to investigate. If I saw a chance when someone wasn't looking, I'd kick him in the crotch as hard as I could.

Hoss pulled up beside us. "Want me to take the other one?"

"Sarah Booth shot him in the leg. I'd better take him to the hospital."

Hoss laughed. "You're a tiger, Ms. Delaney. I underestimated you, but I won't ever do that again."

"He meant to kill me. It was self-defense."

Hoss shared a long look with Coleman. I could almost read his mind. Was it really self-defense?

"Potter was tracking Sarah Booth and Pleasant Smith. He meant to kill them—said as much to Sarah Booth. *He* also underestimated her."

"Sometimes good things happen to bad people," Hoss said with a grin that lifted the corners of his big mustache. "Good job, Sarah Booth."

Coleman filled Hoss in on the rest of the case. "We almost lost the missing girl. She'd been beaten, starved, and abused. Hypothermia almost finished her off. But Sarah Booth got her out of that cabin and away. Potter took her captive so he could sell her baby. He had a buyer lined up, and as soon as I find out the lawyer who was handling the sale, I'll let you know. Charges there, too. I'm still checking into the role those teenage girls and Carrie Ann Musgrove played in this whole mess."

Hoss leaned toward me. "Men like Potter and DeLong don't learn. They want someone to abuse, whether it's a dog or a woman or a kid. They hate themselves, and so they want to crush anything of joy in whoever comes under their authority. There was a time in my law enforcement career that I would have been tempted to take them out. I mean there's a standoff in the woods, it's kill or be killed. And even if it didn't play out exactly that way, justice would be served."

What he described was familiar enough to make me blush. "I wanted to kill him. I would have if my dog hadn't knocked me down."

"Buy that dog a T-bone," Hoss said. "Taking a life never leaves you. Even when you have no other choice. All in all, I'd say you did a good job. Oh, and by the way, we have a lead on that bail skip, Gertrude Strom."

"What?" I thought maybe I'd heard him wrong.

"She checked into the Riverview Motel under a false name, but the young girl at the desk recognized her from the wanted flyer. The clerk knows you, Sarah Booth. Said you were a good egg. Anyway, a couple of bounty hunters had stopped by the motel asking questions and offering a reward on top of what Yancy Bellow offered. The clerk called the bounty hunters."

"Did they get Gertrude?"

He shook his head. "She got away, but someone saw her driving on Highway 8 through Sunflower County. The bounty hunters are about twenty minutes behind her. Highway patrol has put up roadblocks, and the bounty hunters are hard after her. They won't stop until they have her in custody."

Could it really be coming to an end? Coleman nodded encouragement at me. "She can't escape now," he said.

I hadn't been aware of the heavy, heavy weight pressing down on my shoulders until it lifted. I stood up taller. Pleasant was saved, and Gertrude would be behind bars. "Thank goodness." I wanted to say a lot more, but I was too tired to speak.

"I'd better transport Potter to the hospital," Coleman said. He gave Hoss a salute and motioned for DeWayne to lead the way out. Coleman tucked Chablis in his jacket and I took Pluto. The cat wasn't happy with the idea of a four-wheeler ride, but he knew which side his bread was buttered on and curled up against my chest.

I climbed on behind Coleman, glad for his solid warmth as we headed for civilization. Careful not to crush Pluto, I pressed my face against the back of Coleman's leather jacket and allowed my brain to empty. The only thing that mattered was hanging on to the man in front of me.

When we made it to the main road, a Ram 350 with a trailer for the ATVs was waiting for us, along with a patrol car. Coleman put Potter in the backseat of the patrol car and DeWayne wasted no time heading for the emergency room and Doc Sawyer. Potter was in no danger of dying, but he needed medical attention, and Coleman would never compromise the case against him by neglecting to provide it.

I helped Coleman load the four-wheelers on the trailer

and tie them down and then secured the critters in the backseat of the truck. Sweetie Pie loved to ride up high in a big truck. I slammed into the front seat. When Coleman cranked up the thermostat, I thought I might faint with the first blast of real heat. I'd been cold for so long, the warmth was a shock.

Coleman pulled me against him and held me close as he drove to town. For a moment, it took me back to high school days, when riding next to the boy of your dreams was a Friday night happening.

He dropped the truck and trailer off at the courthouse, tucked me and the pets into a patrol car, and drove to the hospital.

The hospital parking lot was mostly empty. The holiday was hard upon us and those patients who could go home had been released. Scanning the area, I frowned. "Where is Tinkie?" I'd expected her to be with Doc, but there was no evidence of her Cadillac anywhere on the hospital property.

Coleman checked his phone. "She was supposed to catch up with us in the woods. I wasn't concerned when she didn't show, because she doesn't have access to an all-wheel-drive vehicle. The Caddy wasn't designed for those conditions, but she hasn't even called to check on you."

Worry ate at me. Pleasant had been found. Tinkie had surely heard the news, yet she was absent. She should have been here, with Libby. I remembered her good-bye in the woods, just before she drove away. A terrible suspicion took root in my brain.

"Are you okay?" Coleman asked when he opened his door and got out of the car and I didn't move.

"I am." But I wasn't. "I'm still a bit frozen. I'll sit here a little while and get good and toasty, then I'll be right behind you."

He looked back in through the open door, assessing me. "Are you sure you're okay?"

"I am."

He gave me the key so I could start the motor and heater. "If I see Tinkie, I'll send her out to you."

"Perfect." I forced a smile. But he wouldn't find Tinkie. She wasn't in the hospital, and she wasn't at Hilltop. In fact, I would be willing to bet she wasn't in Sunflower County any longer. Possibly not Mississippi. I calculated the time from when she'd dropped me off to the present. She had a three or four hour lead. She was on the run with baby Libby.

I tried her cell phone—no answer. I hadn't expected her to respond, and I wondered if she even had the phone with her. She knew she could be tracked through the GPS on the phone. Likely, the smartphone was sitting on the foyer table at Hilltop ringing away.

I slid behind the wheel and drove to the Richmond house. If Tinkie was there, all of my suspicions could be put aside, and we could bask in the knowledge we'd solved our case and Libby and her mother would soon be reunited.

If she wasn't there . . . my choices became much more complicated.

When I pulled up at Hilltop, there was no sign of the Caddy or of Oscar's car. It wasn't yet five, so the bank hadn't closed. Oscar was still at work. I knew the worst when Chablis leaped from the car and ran yelping to the front door. She sounded as if someone were torturing her. She jumped and clawed at the front door. I understood. Chablis sensed that Tinkie was gone.

Trying to comfort the little dust mop, I lifted her into my arms and slipped into the house with the key Tinkie had given me so long ago. My worst suspicions were confirmed. The house was empty, and it looked as if a tornado had come through. Baby things were tossed everywhere. When I went upstairs to Tinkie's room, the floor and furniture were littered with clothes. Tinkie had gone through her things and packed in a great hurry.

Chablis ran around the bedroom, sniffing everything. At last, she sat in the middle of the room and howled. I'd never heard her make that sound. Sweetie Pie went over to nuzzle her, and even Pluto attempted to show sympathy by rubbing against Chablis's face.

There was no doubt now. Tinkie and the baby were gone. My heart ached for Chablis, but I had to focus.

My next call was trickier. I wanted to talk to Oscar without alarming him. As much as Oscar loved Libby, he would never condone kidnapping. Once he realized what Tinkie had done, he would be crazed. I didn't want to upset him and start a ball rolling that I couldn't stop. I needed to find out what, if anything, Oscar knew, and then I had to find my partner and the baby and bring them back before anyone realized they were gone.

It was a tall order, but this was one instance when I couldn't fail.

There were people I could trust, and I called Harold. "Do you know if Oscar has seen or heard from Tinkie in the last four hours?"

"Where is she?" Harold was nobody's fool, and he knew how attached Tinkie was to the infant. "She's taken off, hasn't she?"

"I think she's on the run. Pleasant Smith has been rescued and is safe at the hospital. Tinkie is nowhere to be found."

"Tinkie called and said she was leading Coleman into the woods to find you and Pleasant. That's what Oscar told me. As far as I know, that's where he thinks she is."

"She sent Coleman to the rescue, but she never showed."

"She left you there? In possible danger? That's not like Tinkie."

How right he was there. "If she's taken the baby—"

"That's kidnapping." Harold sounded as worried as I felt. "What are you going to do?"

A better question would be, what could I do? She could have gone in any direction, but my guess was she'd head for Memphis with the thought of a flight to New Orleans or Atlanta, both international airports. Tinkie was one of the smartest people I knew. Her only hope of keeping Libby lay in getting out of the United States and ultimately landing in a place without extradition. Dubai or Croatia might have the most advanced technology or beautiful terrain, but they were too far from Oscar and Zinnia, Mississippi. And from me.

I had to stop Tinkie before she made a mistake she couldn't take back. Much like my moment of darkness in the woods with a gun barrel to Luther Potter's head, Tinkie was acting on a dark impulse. Before my turn with Potter, I might not have understood. But my aunt Loulane would say, "The heart wants what it wants."

I'd heard that all my life, but I also knew the conclusion of the Emily Dickinson quotation. "Or else it doesn't care."

And boy did Tinkie care. Libby had become her whole

life. From where she was sitting, there was no future without that baby.

I only hoped that I could find her and bring her home before she wrecked her marriage and her life. Oscar might agree that Libby made the world go round, but he would be devastated that Tinkie had left him behind in a quest to keep the baby. I had to make this right before it was too late.

Where had Tinkie gone and how could I get ahead of her?

I left Hilltop with all the critters in the front seat of the patrol car. Chablis was pitiful. She curled into the smallest ball of glitzed hair and trembled violently. She wasn't cold; she was having a fit of despair. I tried to console her, but she only whimpered and crawled away from me. Her little doggie heart was breaking.

Tinkie was in danger of losing everything she loved, but she couldn't see that. She was driven by the maternal instinct to protect her child. It didn't matter that Libby was not her blood. Nor did it matter that Libby had a mother who would love her. For Tinkie, this was a case of life or death.

I had to make a call to the sheriff's office—after I returned the patrol car. Or sort of returned it. I drove straight to Dahlia House and transferred the animals to my car. I would call DeWayne and ask him to pick up the patrol car at my house and return it to Coleman. I didn't want to inconvenience Coleman, but I also couldn't go to the hospital. If he took one look at me, he'd know something was amiss. I had to hit the road.

When I pulled up at Dahlia House, I was shocked

to see an attractive blond woman in a wheelchair on the front porch. I jumped out of the car, worried that whoever she was, the bitter cold must certainly be affecting her.

"Just a moment and I'll open the door," I called as I let the pets out. My first clue was when Sweetie Pie and Chablis charged down the front porch, ignoring my guest. Pluto slowly walked up the steps and sat in front of the woman, staring at her with his green, green eyes.

"Ma'am, are you lost?" What were the odds of finding an infant and a woman in a wheelchair on the front porch of Dahlia House all in one week?

"I'm exactly where I'm supposed to be. I'm here to see you, Sarah Booth Delaney."

I didn't have time for this interruption. Where had this woman come from and how was she going to leave? There wasn't a vehicle in sight. "Let's go inside. It's freezing out here." Though I normally didn't invite strangers into my home, this beautiful woman didn't seem to pose a threat.

When we were inside, I held open the swinging kitchen door so she could wheel herself into the warmest room in the house.

"Would you care for something hot to drink?" I really had to get on the road, but I couldn't abandon the woman. "Can I call someone for you?"

"No, I'm exactly where I need to be."

"Why are you here?" I rounded up some cans of cat and dog food for the four-legged kids. I didn't know where I would end up or how long I'd be gone. They had to have provisions.

"To bring you a message."

It was only then that I realized who she really was.

I'd read the news story about her—though I couldn't remember her name—Stephanie something or other. Her heroics had been all over the television and Internet.

"You protected your children with your own body during a tornado. You saved both of them. They survived without a scratch, and you lost the use of your legs."

"A small sacrifice for my children."

A really bad feeling knotted in the pit of my stomach. Jitty always came with a purpose, and this one scared me. "What is Tinkie going to have to give up?"

"She's a mother. Whatever sacrifice is called for, she'll make it."

The beautiful blond showed not a whit of regret at what she'd given up to save her children, and while I knew the woman was an apparition—another guise for my haint, Jitty—I couldn't help the tears that formed. "Tinkie has given up enough."

"Her willingness to sacrifice tells me how deeply she can love."

"This isn't right, though. Taking Libby is wrong. I know Tinkie loves her, but she was never Tinkie's to fall in love with. And now she's kidnapped the baby. I have to save her."

"You can't." The blond shifted and morphed until Jitty sat in the wheelchair. "You can't save her, Sarah Booth."

"I have to try."

"Yes, you do." She stood up and pushed the wheelchair across the room. It evaporated before it crashed into the wall. "But you can't save her. She is desperate and willing to sacrifice anything and everything to save Libby."

"But Libby isn't in danger. Tinkie isn't *saving* her. Libby is happy and safe and she will have her mother back."

"That is danger, to Tinkie. You have to put yourself inside her skin. She is that little girl's mother now, and anyone who wants to take her is a threat. Tinkie has convinced herself that she can give Libby what no one else can, that primordial mother love."

"Pleasant will love her baby. She stayed alive in terrible conditions just because she hoped to hold her little girl."

Jitty sighed. "This is a case for King Solomon."

I knew the story of the two women who claimed the same baby. Their case was brought before King Solomon, who ruled that the baby should be cut in half so that each woman got a part of the child. When the real mother yielded her claim to save the baby, she was given the child because King Solomon recognized the true mother's willingness to sacrifice her heart to protect her son.

"Not even the wisdom of King Solomon can save Tinkie," I said. "This is Pleasant's baby, and she is a capable, responsible young woman who deserves to have her little girl."

"Then you must convince Tinkie to do the right thing."

"First I have to find her."

Jitty pointed out the kitchen window where the moon had come up over the empty horse pastures. "Times a-wastin'. If you want your partner home for Thanksgiving, you'd best find her and bring her back."

26

Memphis was the city I settled on. Tinkie would go for the place most likely to have a flight. Jackson, Mississippi, had an airport, but there were longer delays and fewer flights. With Thanksgiving right around the corner, more frequent flights would work in Tinkie's favor, because she would be on standby.

How I would find her or stop her, I didn't know. I only knew I had to try.

With the accelerator to the floorboard, I flew toward Memphis, regretting my decision to bring the critters along. They were no trouble, but I didn't know where I'd end up. Which was why I'd brought them in the first place; I didn't know when I'd be home. But they would have been safe and more comfortable at Dahlia House, at least my two would. Chablis would not be happy anywhere but in Tinkie's arms.

If luck ran with Tinkie, she'd have caught a flight and be on her way. I had no idea what security measures were in place for infants. Did she need identification? Would Libby need a passport to get out of the country? Tinkie was far better versed in such things. International travel with a kidnapped baby wasn't part of my normal world.

It occurred to me to call the airport security and have an amber alert put out for Libby. I might catch her in that net, but such a move would effectively ruin Tinkie's life. I couldn't bring myself to do it. Not yet. Maybe I could catch up with her, reason with her, and bring them both home.

To that end I drove too fast and reached the Memphis airport in record time. I left the animals in the car in the parking garage. As long as I hustled, they wouldn't get too cold. When I entered the airport lobby, I took my bearings. As I'd assumed, it was crowded with holiday travelers.

Tinkie would be easy to spot. She was fashion perfection, and wherever she went, men turned to watch her walk by. But there was no sign of my petite partner in the lobby. I went to the boards and checked the flights to New Orleans and Atlanta. Two airlines had planes boarding.

Without a ticket, I would never get past the TSA agents. I went to the check-in desk of one airline.

"My cousin is on a business trip, and I can't remember whether she's going to New Orleans or Atlanta to catch a flight to Europe. Her Aunt Loulane has taken a turn for the worse and is dying. Could you check your passenger manifest and get a message to her?"

It was a long, long shot. The agent looked through the computer and shook her head. "I don't have a Tinkie Richmond ticketed."

"Thanks." I hurried to the next carrier's counter and went through the same process.

"I'm sorry, we don't have a person booked with that name."

"Could she be on standby?"

The clerk checked the screen again. "I'm sorry. She isn't ticketed."

Turning away, I walked toward the exit that would take me back to the parking garage. I'd chosen wrong and wasted nearly two hours. Tinkie had obviously gone to the Jackson airport. By the time I got back to Zinnia, it would be too late to do anything to stop her. Everyone would know Tinkie had kidnapped the baby and run away. The fallout would be terrible.

The best thing I could do now was to get home as quickly as possible so I could support Oscar. I didn't think criminal charges would be brought against him, though Tinkie would surely be a fugitive from the law. Oscar wasn't involved in this baby-napping, and I had to make sure he was viewed as an innocent bystander

I called Harold and gave him an update. "She probably went to Jackson," I said.

"I'll call and see. I'm sure if she did, she's caught a flight, but we can begin to track her, at least," Harold said. "I have all of her account information, so they may give me some help on the phone. Should I put a hold on her ability to access money?"

At this stage, I didn't know the right answer. If she was caught, she'd go to prison. If she left the country, little Libby would never know her real mother, and Coleman and I would be held responsible since we'd both insisted that Tinkie keep the infant until Pleasant was found.

"Cut off her funds," I said. "If she hasn't left the country, we have to stop her and maybe we can patch this back together somehow."

"Have you checked the private airstrip?"

Harold was a damn genius. "I hadn't thought of that, and I'm right here. You're a god, Harold. Of course, Tinkie would go private if she could."

"With the right plane, she can get to Central America, and from there, she can go anywhere."

"Harold, thank you." My gut reaction told me Harold had hit the nail on the head. I'd never have thought of a private plane. "But wouldn't she have just asked Yancy to take her? He flew us to Nashville."

"She needs a plane with a longer reach, which requires a longer runway. The private planes so many plantation owners fly are perfect for short hops. If she wants to jump the border and land somewhere without extradition where she'll have half a chance of being welcomed, she needs a bigger plane."

When he explained it that way, it made perfect sense. Tinkie would know these things, too. "Do you think someone is giving her a ride as a favor?"

"Tinkie knows a lot of wealthy people. Maybe. Could be she's hired a charter. Do you know where she'd go?"

I hadn't considered Central America, but Costa Rica would be my first guess. I told him my thoughts.

"I'll check with the air traffic controllers to see if a flight has been scheduled for Costa Rica. If we can stop her in the States, that's the best outcome. If she's in Memphis, whatever it takes, bring her back to Zinnia. I'll stall everyone until then."

"How?"

"I don't know," Harold admitted. "I'd give my life for Oscar and Tinkie, and for you. I'll come up with some reasonable explanation for her absence. Just find her and drag her home."

"I'll do my best."

The private section of the airport was secluded and not easy to access. When I finally figured out where to park, I regretfully left the animals in the car once again. On second thought, I took Chablis. She might be my best bargaining chip with Tinkie. I knew my partner loved her husband and her dog. Maybe seeing Chablis would snap her out of the baby fog and force her to realize what she was leaving behind.

If she was even there.

The regulations for private flights were much different, though security was no less thorough. I was stopped the moment I entered the large building that served as a check-in and -out. No one said a word about Chablis, but I was ushered into a side office.

"What can we help you with?" a tall, mustached man who was obviously in charge of security asked.

"My partner is here with a baby. She's confused. She thinks the child is in trouble and I suspect she's headed out of the country. I have to stop her." There wasn't time to concoct a story more palatable. "If you know where she is, the best thing for everyone is to find her and stop her from taking off."

He got on the phone and made some calls.

"She's here. The plane is almost ready to taxi to the

runway. I've told the pilot to hold up and to keep the loading ramp in place. What do you want to do?"

Now that was a good question. "I have to talk to her."

"You can't take an unleashed dog—"

"This dog may be the thing that wins her over. I don't have a leash. Do you?" I wasn't about to give up on having Chablis with me. Now that I knew Tinkie was near and that I was the person who would step between her and the future she perceived as hers, I would need every asset I could muster.

He sighed. Obviously he'd dealt with a lot of cranky wealthy people, and though I was far from rich, I was pretty darn cranky. "Keep the dog in your arms. I'm going to ask the pilot to make her and the staff disembark. He'll say it's a mechanical problem with the plane."

"Thank you."

He marched away, leaving me and Chablis with our doubts and fears. I cuddled the dust mop and assured her Tinkie was all but on her way home. I spoke aloud to bolster my courage as much as to comfort the pup.

When I saw Tinkie coming down the stairs and onto the tarmac, where all of the luggage had been disgorged from the plane, I felt my heart drop to my knees. She was sporting black hair and wore off-the-rack dungarees and a flannel shirt with a ball cap. Libby was wrapped in a tacky pink and blue plaid blanket.

Tinkie stood beside her luggage, checking her watch, obviously anxious. I pushed open the door of the terminal and stepped into the night. To my horror, Chablis jumped from my arms and ran across the landing strip to Tinkie. Though I was hustling to catch up, I was still fifty feet away when Tinkie saw her dog. She put a hand to her mouth to stifle her cry, and she held out one arm to invite Chablis into her embrace, careful to protect the baby.

She faced me and I could see her features harden. "Stay away from me," she said. "I'm getting back on that plane and—"

"You're not."

"It's what I have to do."

I kept walking toward her. I had to get close enough to grab her. She wasn't reboarding. No matter how furious she got with me, her whole life depended on my ability to keep her in Memphis. She hadn't gone so far she couldn't turn this around. If she flew away, it would be a different story involving the feds, charges, prison time, and a lot of other really unpleasant things.

"Pleasant is going to be fine, Tinkie. She fought to stay alive under brutal conditions because of her baby girl."

"I don't want to hurt Pleasant or Charity, but Libby is my baby now. I'm the one who can take care of her, provide for her. No one could love her more than I can."

"At what cost?" I pointed to her wedding ring. "Oscar doesn't know what you're up to. I'm the only one who does. We can head back to Zinnia, make up a plausible reason why we were in Memphis, and all of this can go away."

"You know I won't do that. I can't. I've never loved anyone or anything with such intensity. With such pure joy. I'll die before I lose her."

I thought of Jitty's last incarnation in the kitchen, the woman who'd sacrificed her legs for her children. The story of King Solomon. I knew what I had to do. Chances were high my friend would never forgive me, but I had no other play.

"This blast of maternal love you're feeling isn't about what's good for Libby. This is all about you, Tinkie. This fills a hole in your life, and so you want it. And obviously you don't care who you hurt to get it. This isn't the partner I've grown to love like a sister. This is the selfish girl from college."

Tinkie could not have been more shocked if I'd slapped her. "How can you say that? You don't know what it's like to love a child."

That one stung, too, but I couldn't be defeated by my own hurt feelings. "The time may come when I consider having a child or adopting, but I won't steal someone's baby. Pleasant has every right to her little girl. What you're planning to do is worse than murder."

"You don't know what you're talking about."

"Oh, I do. I surely know. Everyone was so angry at Graf when he chose his daughter, when he put her first. I heard the whispers and the comments. Because he hurt me, you were all ready to string him up. But he made a choice for love, for his child. *His* child. Just as Libby is Pleasant's child. He chose his blood, and that's never the wrong choice."

"That's exactly what I'm doing and you're trying to stop me."

I stepped closer. Tinkie trembled in the cold wind that whipped across the open landing strip. "No, you're making up excuses for stealing another woman's child. Loving Libby is not the reason for your actions. This is for you, all for you. It has nothing to do with what Libby wants or needs."

"You're a mean person, Sarah Booth. I never saw it before, but I do now."

I knew the risk when I started. I knew Tinkie might

end up hating me forever. Even when she finally realized that I was correct, it was possible my harsh words would end our friendship, our partnership. Any future together.

While I asked Tinkie to make a sacrifice, I, too, was willing to make one. I would give up our friendship to save her from committing a terrible crime and going to jail. Before she cut Oscar's heart out and left it on the kitchen counter, I would give up whatever I had to surrender to see her safely home.

"Chablis's heart was broken when we went to Hilltop and you'd left her. How could you leave Chablis?"

Tinkie started to speak, but her voice broke on a sob. "She has a good life here. I didn't know where I was going or how I'd live. I took some money, but not enough to live on. Besides, Oscar loves Chablis. I couldn't take everything from him." She was crying in earnest when she finished speaking.

"You don't have to take anything. Come home, Tinkie. We'll come up with an explanation for why you were in Memphis. We'll give Libby to her mother, who has been through far too much. You and Oscar will see Libby all the time. The alternative is that you'll go to prison, Oscar will be heartbroken, and you'll never see that baby again." I picked up her luggage and motioned the clerk to help with the rest as we hauled it across the airstrip.

"Mrs. Richmond won't be taking a flight," I said.

"I called the police," the clerk said.

At first I didn't believe what he said. "You did what?"

"She was kidnapping that kid. That's not her baby. I called the police."

I got in his face. "You'd better cancel that call and say it was a misunderstanding right this minute. The baby is going home. I don't care how you walk this back, but if you're a smart man, you'll figure out how to do it. Now."

I grabbed Tinkie's arm. "We have to go. Our only hope is to get back to Sunflower County and put that baby in her mother's arms. Everything can be explained as a misunderstanding." If only we could get home before some branch of law enforcement snared her.

Because the Caddy had a bigger engine and a better heater than my roadster, I transferred the dogs and loaded Tinkie and the baby in. Within five minutes we were tearing out of the parking lot. We'd have to take the back roads home, which would slow us down some, but on a cold November night, there wasn't likely to be any traffic.

Sweetie and Pluto nuzzled Tinkie's neck and checked on the baby while I drove like the wind, this time in the opposite direction.

Tinkie cradled the baby in one arm and Chablis in the other. The child remained undisturbed by all the events. Chablis's heart was wounded, but she would forgive Tinkie. Dogs were the ultimate givers of unconditional love. Only a mother and a dog could dispense love with such an open heart.

I took Highway 3, because I wasn't sure the clerk at the terminal could actually stop the ball he'd put in motion. I had one chance to save Tinkie from the conflagration she'd started. If I got her back to Sunflower County and returned Libby to her mother, maybe, just maybe, this Memphis episode could be forgotten. As far as I was concerned, no one would ever know the true details about how close Tinkie had come to wrecking her life.

I didn't know how to broach the subject of Libby's mother, but I had to start somewhere. "Pleasant almost died, but she'll recover."

"I'm sorry I abandoned you in the woods. I knew Coleman would find you."

"It's okay." I wasn't sure that it was, but Tinkie was not the only person in our friendship who'd taken a regrettable action. When I first came home to Zinnia, I'd dognapped Chablis and ransomed her back. The money had saved Dahlia House, but guilt scalded me on a regular basis. More than anything I wanted to confess my sin to Tinkie, but to unburden my conscience would hurt her and our friendship. So I chose to live with the guilt.

"I knew you'd be okay. I really did. I have total faith in Coleman when it comes to protecting you."

"I almost killed Luther Potter in cold blood. I shot him in the leg and when he couldn't get away, I put the barrel of my gun to his head. If Sweetie Pie hadn't knocked me down, I think I would have killed him."

Silence stretched between us for a long time. The miles spun beneath the wheels. We drove in a tunnel of darkness, the headlights illuminating the road ahead of us, and the darkness gobbling up the light behind us. On either side of the narrow two-lane highway, empty fields stretched into the velvet night.

"You aren't a killer," Tinkie finally said.

"And you aren't a kidnapper. Yet here we are, both of us. The trick to survival, Tinkie, is to come to terms with our actions, accept them, and understand what we're capable of. I'm not saying we shrug it off, but we forgive ourselves and move forward. We both faced a set of circumstances that brought out the worst in us."

"You pack a lot of wisdom for someone who can't match socks and slacks."

It was such a relief to laugh out loud. I'd feared my friend and partner was lost beneath emotions and actions. "Tinkie, I could wring your neck."

"Oh, get in line. I'm sure Oscar is mad enough to divorce me." She inhaled sharply. "Do you think he will?"

"No, but we'll minimize this. The two of us. We need a white lie."

"Such as?"

"Maybe you got a call saying the baby was in danger. You were acting to protect Libby."

Tinkie thought a moment. "You would lie to Coleman?"

"And Oscar and Cece and everyone else. Tinkie, you lost your head. You did something so far outside your normal conduct that I can't see punishing you for it. Let's clean this up."

"Does anyone else know what I did?"

"Just the folks at the airport. And Harold."

"Can we really fix this?"

"We have to."

Sweetie gave a low howl, concurring with my statement.

"It's settled then. The story is Libby was threatened. You acted impulsively not to steal the baby but to protect her."

"I don't know that I can live with this."

I reached across the seat and pinched her arm really hard, until she squealed. "You don't have a choice. You have to live with this. You owe it to Oscar and everyone else who loves you. Think how Oscar will feel if he knows you were willing to abandon him to have Libby. You can't hurt him that way. I won't let you."

She brushed a tear from her cheek. "I wasn't thinking clearly."

"Exactly. And now you are. This is settled."

"Coleman will want to investigate the call. He'll check my phone."

I reached across and snatched her phone from her purse. "Pull out the guts. Kill it and throw it out the window."

She did as I ordered, smashing it to bits and tossing it.

"Now just hold to the lie. We'll slide through this." I had to take this one step further to be sure she understood what faced her. "You have to give Pleasant her baby, and you have to do it with a smile."

When she finally answered, it was in a whisper. "I can't."

"Oh, yes you can. And you will. And you will be delighted that they are together as a family. Pleasant is a good kid, and she's going to be a great mother. She and Frankie will provide the perfect home, and you and Oscar will be part of it. Those kids will share Libby with you and Oscar. They will. *If* you play your cards right."

"Okay." She sounded defeated, not convinced. But only time would prove how right I was. In my heart I knew Frankie and Pleasant would come to view Tinkie and Oscar as extended family. Libby would always be a part of the Richmonds' life.

"What's that up ahead?" We were still thirty minutes from Zinnia, and far ahead it looked like something was on fire.

"There aren't any houses out here." Tinkie leaned forward.

"It's a car." The closer we got, the more detail I saw. A car had somehow managed to flip and burst into flames on a dead straight road.

"Sarah Booth, that's a sports car. It's a . . ." Her voice held dread.

"Yeah, a convertible."

I slowed when we got close. The car had flipped on its side and burned in the ditch beside the fallow cotton field. There was no sign of the driver or any passengers. When I was very near, I slowed almost to a stop. I reached for my phone to call 911, but Tinkie grabbed my arm with fingers of iron.

"Don't stop," Tinkie said.

"We have to stop." I couldn't drive by an accident that had obviously just happened without stopping to make sure someone wasn't injured.

"Look at the car."

I could hardly make it out because it was so damaged. "It's a convertible. The driver could have been thrown clear."

"It's a Mercedes roadster, Sarah Booth."

I felt my lungs contract. She was right. It was a car exactly like mine.

"This is a trap." Tinkie reached for the wheel as her window exploded and glass flew everywhere.

27

I hit the gas, but the Caddy moved too slowly and another bullet shattered the back passenger window where
Sweetie was sitting. I cut the wheel sharply left, and for
one brief moment, Gertrude Strom was illuminated in
the headlights, a rifle to her shoulder.

"Hit her!" Tinkie commanded.

I jerked the wheel right and a bullet thunked into the
driver's door as the wheels gained traction and the car
shot forward. The front wheels hit the thick gumbo soil
of the field and the car slewed left, then right. There was
a thud as the heavy Cadillac struck something. I had no
idea what as I struggled to get the car on the road and
prevent it from flipping. The gumbo held the wheels like
cement, making the car impossible to guide.

At last I steered up onto the road and stopped. "Is the baby okay?" Glass had showered Tinkie, the infant, and Chablis.

"She's fine." Tinkie sounded a lot less shaken up than I did.

"Check the pets," I said, my voice weak.

Tinkie put Libby on the seat between us before she leaned over the front seat. "Sweetie has a bad cut on her back, and Pluto has a shard in his paw. He won't let me touch it."

"Are they okay until we get to Zinnia?"

"I'm pretty sure. I'll watch them. You drive."

"I hit something. It could have been Gertrude." I looked behind us but there was only the burning car and darkness.

"You are not going to check." Tinkie grabbed my wrist. "You are not. She could be waiting there with her rifle, ready to take you out. Then she'd come for me, the baby, and the pets."

She was right. I couldn't risk those in my care. "Call Coleman." I nudged my phone toward her as I focused on the road ahead. I stomped the gas and the wheels squealed as we tore down the highway. As fast as I was going, I had to be extra careful.

Tinkie got my favorite lawman on the line and gave him a full report on Gertrude, the burning car, the shots fired. "How does she always know where we are and what we're doing?" Tinkie asked.

She'd put Coleman on speaker so I could hear. "That's a good question, Tinkie. Oscar has been looking for you for the past eight hours. He's worried sick and he didn't have a clue where you'd gone. What are you two doing driving on back roads?"

"Coming home from Memphis," Tinkie said, and I admired her cool. "I'll explain when I get there." She gave him the location of the accident on Highway 3 so he could call the state troopers to the scene. "We might have hit Gertrude with the car. We couldn't stop and check because she was armed."

"That was the proper decision. You say the car was burning when you saw it?"

"That's right. In the middle of a stretch of straight, empty highway."

"It's possible Gertrude has some kind of tracking device on your car. Possibly on both of your cars." Coleman sounded upset and worried. "We'll check when you get home. Where have you been, Tinkie? Where could Gertrude have located your car to put something on it?"

"The Memphis airport."

Give my partner credit, she was sticking as closely to the truth as possible.

"So the car was left in a parking garage?"

"Yes."

"Is Sarah Booth okay?"

"She's fine and we're taking Libby to the hospital. Please alert Doc that Sweetie Pie is cut and may need a stitch or two."

"Will do."

Tinkie disconnected and leaned back against the seat. "This entire night has been surreal. I can't believe I was going to skip the country and go to Central America. Then we start home and Gertrude almost kills us."

"I know. She's after me, but she doesn't care who else gets hurt."

"I hope you hit her, Sarah Booth. You should have

driven back and forth over her body to make sure she was dead. Freaking Jason."

I grinned at her horror reference. "I was afraid the Cadillac would get stuck in the field. If we'd been stranded, we would have been sitting ducks for her."

"She's stuck out there now, without transportation. She burned up her car just to set the scene so you'd slow down."

There was no doubt. Gertrude was totally insane. "Gertrude stole that car from the dealership. It was always just a way to torment me."

"If she's on foot, they'll get her."

I wasn't sure that was true. So far, Gertrude had eluded all attempts at capture. But with what Tinkie had facing her, I kept my thoughts about Gertrude to myself.

When at last we pulled up at the hospital, Doc came out to check Sweetie Pie. I hung back with my dog, but Doc whispered in my ear. "Go with Tinkie. I'll take care of Sweetie, and your partner needs you now more than the dog does. I've deadened the area, and I can take care of this right here in the car. It won't take but a couple of stitches to close the wound. And I'll take care of Pluto's paw."

Like it or not, I was in for the whole ride. Tinkie would have to act her way through this encounter, and I would have to be the supporting actress. I caught up with Tinkie in the corridor and walked beside her to Pleasant's room.

When she pushed open the door, we were greeted by Pleasant, who was sitting up in bed. Beside her were her mother and sister. Frankie Graham, whose wide grin was a billboard for his happiness, hung back in the corner.

I knew then the DNA test had come in and proven conclusively that Frankie was the dad. The Smith clan had accepted him. They all rushed forward with a cry of joy when they saw the baby.

"She's perfectly fine," Tinkie said. She walked to the bedside and put Libby into her mother's arms. "Just like Sarah Booth promised. Here's your baby, safe and sound."

Pleasant's tears fell on the baby's forehead. "She's perfect," Pleasant said. "Absolutely perfect."

"She is," Tinkie agreed. "I'm sorry I was slow getting here with her. We had some complications."

"I wasn't worried. I knew she was in good hands," Pleasant said. "Mama assured me you were the kindest people on the planet. She told me how good you've been to Libby. I want you and Mr. Richmond to be her godparents, if you will."

I didn't have to hear the answer. I slipped out of the room so Oscar could enter. Tomorrow I'd figure how to retrieve my car from Memphis. Tonight, I wanted to go home and dive into my bed. I couldn't think about Tinkie's near defection or the possibility of Gertrude's body lying broken in a bare cotton field. Too much had happened too quickly. I'd gone from near murderer to savior and possibly back to murderer. I'd sort it out tomorrow, when I knew the facts.

I woke up the next morning to the sound of laughter echoing from downstairs. My bedside clock showed seven in the morning. Who was in my house? And what smelled so wonderful?

I tiptoed to the stairs and sneaked a peak into the parlor where Harold, who'd driven me home and spent the night, bounced Libby on his knee. Beside him were Pleasant, Charity, Faith, and Frankie. The front door opened and Coleman and DeWayne came in, both carrying grocery bags.

"Sarah Booth is still asleep," Harold said. "Tinkie, Millie, Cece, and Jaytee are in the kitchen. Madame Tomeeka is on the way. I think Sarah Booth forgot today was Thanksgiving."

And I had. But my friends had not. And thank god Tinkie was here to celebrate with us. What a wretched holiday it would be if she weren't.

I hustled back up the stairs, showered, and brought my brand new, extra-special Thanksgiving sweater from the box it had arrived in. It was pumpkin orange with fall leaves embroidered down one sleeve and across the chest. On the back was a handstitched rendition of a pumpkin pie. It would absolutely send Tinkie up the wall, which was my intention. I also had a little orange hat with a green stem, which I perched atop my fuzz of new hair.

I sauntered down the stairs and into the parlor. Harold burst into laughter, which startled Libby, who set up a wail. Tinkie came running out of the kitchen like she was on fire. When she saw me, the first thing she did was rush to Libby and cover her eyes.

"Don't let her see! Don't let her see! That baby will be scarred for life!" she said.

Everyone erupted into laughter. My shopping had been well worth the effort.

"Something smells wonderful." I sniffed in the scent of cinnamon and spice.

"Millie is cooking," Harold explained. "With some help from Cece and Jaytee. I think they're actually sampling everything she cooks. They can't wait for lunch."

"Thank you for inviting us," Charity said. "This is a special treat."

"It wouldn't be a holiday without Libby and her family," I said. Tinkie's quick, hungry look at the baby told me a lot, but she had herself under control. She might weep for Libby, but it would not be in public.

The lie we floated about someone threatening the baby was accepted by everyone, though Coleman cocked an eyebrow and nailed me with his penetrating gaze. Harold excused himself and left the room.

"Sarah Booth, may I have a word?" Coleman said. He motioned to the front door. "We should take a walk."

"I should do something to help." I looked around, hoping someone would suggest a chore that urgently needed to be done.

"Everything is under control," Pleasant said. "Someone has already set the table with beautiful china, but I can fill the water glasses and things like that. You go ahead, Sarah Booth. I'll take care of anything that needs to be done. I owe you my life."

"I'm just glad everyone is healthy. Did you get things worked out with Benny Hester about your songs?"

"He was wonderful. Everything is good on that front. Ms. McNair is charged and will go to trial."

"What about Lucinda and Carrie Ann?"

"They instigated the kidnapping," Coleman said. "They paid Potter and DeLong to abduct Pleasant with the intention of holding her long enough for her to miss her private interview with the donor who sponsored her scholarship. Unfortunately, Potter ran down Dewey Backstrum when he had Pleasant in the car. That's when he devised the plan to hold her until she had the baby. He found a buyer for the infant."

It was pretty much the way Tinkie and I had figured it out. "But Rudy saved the baby."

Pleasant teared up. "He did. He wasn't part of the plan. He just happened to be riding with them. They never told him anything. Rudy was a sweet guy. At least he did little things that made it easier for me. And he saved Libby."

"He did indeed." I edged toward the kitchen, hoping to avoid the confrontation with Coleman. He could always see through my lies, and he'd know there was more to the Tinkie story than I was saying.

"And Pleasant has some wonderful news," Charity said. She motioned her daughter to speak.

Pleasant blushed, but she took the center of the room. "Beverly Moon with Delta State University called last night. A donor has offered a full scholarship for me. Tuition, room, board, and child care for Libby. And we've decided to keep her name. Elizabeth Marie Smith-Graham. So she'll be Libby Marie."

"Wonderful news!" I clapped and whistled.

Coleman was not to be avoided, though. "Out front, Sarah Booth. Now, please."

When he used that voice, I had to obey.

The day was sunny and brisk and the light golden. Coleman steered me across the drive and toward the barn. It was a perfect day for a ride, but my horses were still at Lee's, where they were safe from Gertrude's evil schemes. Except I heard the thunder of hooves and my three beauties crested a hill, squealing and bucking and farting. Only a horse could make a fart charming.

"They're home!"

Coleman was pleased with himself. "I called Lee and she brought them this morning."

"What about Gertrude?"

"That's what I want to talk to you about."

"She's dead? Did I kill her? I honestly didn't mean to." I sounded a lot like Dorothy, who hadn't meant to melt the wicked witch.

Coleman put a finger on my lips. When he gently touched my chin, lifting it so that my gaze met his, I connected with such a jolt that I put my hand on the pasture fence to steady myself.

"She isn't dead, but based on the blood the highway patrol found in the field, she's hurt pretty badly."

"She escaped?" How was that possible? She had no means of transportation and she'd been hit by a car.

"Someone stopped and picked her up. And someone had planted a tracking device on Tinkie's Cadillac. DeWayne took it off and sent it to the state lab for analysis. I doubt we'll learn anything except the brand and maybe where it was bought. There weren't any prints."

"Gertrude's had help all along. Bijou," I whispered.

"Maybe, but I can't prove it. A state team from the Mississippi Bureau of Investigation is tearing Hemlock Manor apart right now. The main house and every outbuilding on the property. If Bijou is guilty of harboring Gertrude, she'll pay a hefty price. Wherever Gertrude is, she won't be bothering you."

"How can you be sure?"

"She's not a young woman, Sarah Booth. She's seriously injured. If she values her freedom, she won't come at you again."

He knew something else. "What aren't you telling me?"

"Maybe I'll spill if you tell me what Tinkie was really doing in Memphis."

"Keep your secrets. Fiddle-dee-dee, who wants to know anyway?" I assumed my best Scarlett persona.

"I figured you'd protect Tinkie to the grave. But I don't want to know, because then I'd have to charge her. Just leave it. And those bounty hunters are gone, too."

Awareness widened my eyes. "You think they picked up Gertrude?"

"Maybe."

"But they'd take her to Junior Wells. They were working for him."

"Unless they weren't."

I frowned. "What are you saying?"

"Gertrude has had help all along. You're right about that. Someone has been giving her money, information, places to hide. And to that person, she was a real liability. She was reckless and foolhardy and dangerous. Whoever was funding her would be revealed if she were captured."

"You think they snatched her up to do away with her?"

He focused on the bucking horses as they frolicked around the pasture. "I do, actually."

"Who?"

"I don't know. That's what I want to ask you. Who benefits from having Gertrude on the loose to torment you? To possibly hurt you?"

"I don't know anyone who hates me that much."

Coleman sighed. "Someone does. And we have to find out who that is."

"How?"

"By watching and listening and digging into your past cases."

"You think it's someone from a past case?"

"Who else could it be?"

He was right about that. Prior to becoming a private
eye, I'd led a life without conflict. There were jealous ac-
tresses in New York, but none had a reason to take out
a vendetta on me. I'd never been that successful on the
stage. Maybe some crazy fans of Graf Milieu, my former
fiancé, would want to take me out—but Graf and I had
broken up. I was no longer part of his world. It had to be
past cases.

"After Thanksgiving, we'll get Tinkie and go over
each case. There's a loose end somewhere. Someone with
money and a motive to hurt you."

"Okay." I didn't look forward to this, but I was glad
to have Coleman on my side.

"Would you do me a favor?" Coleman asked.

"Sure."

"Take off that ridiculous pumpkin stem hat?"

"Why?"

"I can't kiss you when you're wearing that thing.
Makes me feel like I'm abusing a vegetable."

I laughed and removed the hat just as Coleman swept
me into his arms and delivered on his promise of a kiss.
"I'll find out who's behind this, Sarah Booth. I promise."

And I knew he would.

When we ended the kiss, I needed a moment to compose myself. Scott and the band were on the way. Harold
was in the house. Both were men who'd stated their interest. And they were my friends who deserved fair treatment. "I want to feed the horses. Alone," I said softly.

"Don't be too long. I'll see you inside."

I watched him walk away, aware yet again of my attrac-
tion to him. I hurried to the barn, glad to see my ponies
filled with piss and vinegar and ready for breakfast.

I'd just filled their feed buckets when I sensed a presence behind me. Still raw from Gertrude's sneak attacks, I whirled, swinging an empty bucket like a weapon.

"Lawsy mercy, Miss Sarah Booth, you 'bout took your mammy out."

"Oh, no! You cannot do this." Before me stood Hattie McDaniel in her maid uniform and doo-rag. "This is politically incorrect, Jitty. Stop it now. Really, you must stop it now."

"I made you some breakfast and I want you to stuff it in right this minute." She magically held a tray filled with pancakes dripping in butter and hot syrup. "Then when you go in that house with all your gentleman callers, you eat like a bird. You hear me, don't go in there and shovel food down like a field hand."

"What is wrong with you!" I had to get her out of the Hattie guise and back to herself. "Please, Jitty. Why are you doing this?"

"Who took care of Scarlett?"

She had a point. Mammy took care of Scarlett even when Scarlett was a terror. And Jitty took care of me, but she wasn't a mammy figure. Jitty had more style in her little finger than I had all over my body. "You do take care of me."

She shimmered in the dim light of the barn and suddenly was my familiar haint, all svelte and stylish in my black jeans and a red cotton sweater. "Sarah Booth, you've had some hard lessons this past week."

I couldn't argue that. "Tinkie and me both."

"You didn't fail me or your parents. You lived up to your raisin'."

"I almost didn't. I came close to killing a man in cold blood." This was going to eat at me for a long time to come.

"Close only counts in horseshoes and hand grenades."

"Is that an Aunt Loulane saying?"

Jitty laughed. "No, I heard that on Johnny Carson, back in the day. I'm not sure where he got it."

"I can't believe you're quoting Carson."

She lifted her head and listened. "There's joy in Dahlia House today. Your mama and daddy are happy. I want you to know that. Now get up to the house and tend your company like you were taught."

"I wish you could eat with us, Jitty."

"Girl, I don't need food. If I ate like you, I wouldn't have a figure at all."

She was a devil, but I loved her. "Happy Thanksgiving, Jitty."

"And the same to you."

The barn door cracked open and a shaft of pale gold light revealed only emptiness. Jitty had skedaddled. "Are you coming up to the house?" Tinkie asked.

"The horses have finished eating. I'm ready."

We linked arms and walked through the golden morning light toward the house that I loved and the friends that I cherished.

Sticks and Bones

The chill December wind rattles the windows of my bedroom at Dahlia House. Old Man Winter has a grip on my ancestral home, but I'm not about to let the cold keep me from this evening. I lean into the vanity mirror that has reflected at least seven generations of Delaney women and adjust my mother's diamond and pearl earrings. They're the perfect accessory for the white tulle dress I've chosen. It is by far the most beautiful gown I've ever worn, and though I'm a bit long in the tooth to play Cinderella, I feel like I've been tapped by a fairy godmother's wand. I do a little twirl and watch the dress float around me à la Disney animation. It is perfect for the approaching celebration marking the end of one year and the beginning of a new one.

"Glamour is nothing without intrigue, Sarah Booth Delaney." A husky voice comes from the doorway.

Without looking I know it is Jitty, the ghost who shares the Delaney family home with me. During the Civil War, Jitty was a nanny, but since she's taken up residence at Dahlia House with me, she is more of a bane. Nurturing is far down her list of talents—way behind tormenting, torturing, annoying, bossing, heckling . . . Did I say bossing?

I turn slowly and discover that Jitty too is dressed for the occasion. She's encased from head to toe in a beautiful black and gold sequined gown with matching skullcap that reflects an era long past. I recognize her instantly. My nearly two-hundred-year-old ghost is vamping as Greta Garbo in Mata Hari, a film about a female spy. Oh, Hollywood, gird your loins.

"You look marvelous, darling," I say. "Where did you steal that gown and that body?"

Jitty is beautiful on her own, but she is something else as Greta. She moves and the gown is like warm, molten gold. There's no doubt she could worm the most secret information from any man. As she slithers across the room toward me she is leaking sexuality all over the floor.

"You should practice your interrogation skills, Sarah Booth. I believe they'll come in handy."

"Is that a hint that I'm about to have a new case?"

"I don't give hints." She looks down her nose at me as I secure the last earring.

I stand up and reach for my wrap. "Good, because I don't have time for your hints and teases."

"My, my, my but don't you look feminine." Jitty circles me. "Sarah Booth, this is the dress that could do it. Uh, huh! This dress could offset that annoying mouth of yours. Wearing this, you should be able to throw a man to the ground and catch some little swimmers. I'll have me a Delaney heir before the new year even gets a jumpstart."

Protesting would only make her more outrageous so I pick up my purse and walk to the door. "Happy New Year, Jitty. Don't wait up, and take care of Pluto and Sweetie Pie."

"The cat and dog will be just fine. Don't come back until you're pregnant," Jitty calls out, followed by a cackle.

As I get into the car, I look up at my bedroom window. Jitty is there, her silhouette classic Garbo. I'd have to give some serious consideration to what she was up to. Jitty never gives hints, but she often uses symbols. Was my haint trying to tell me something or just having a frolic? Only time would tell.

The drive to town was short but cold. The party was in the Prince Albert Hotel ballroom, and I stepped inside and stopped. Winter Garden was the theme, and Harold Erkwell, the best party thrower in the Southeast, had truly created an enchantment with billows of blue silk decorated with twinkling stars forming the ceiling and frosted foliage and tiny white lights everywhere.

The words of "Unforgettable" swirled through the glittering ballroom on the strings of a small orchestra. Harold had done himself proud. This New Year's Eve party served a dual purpose—celebrating the coming year and the grand opening of the exclusive boutique hotel.

I was greeted with a chorus of well wishes from my friends and swept into the party where the champagne flowed and the orchestra took me back to the 1940s. I love the dances of that era, and I danced until my shoes were smoking.

At last I leaned against a marble column to catch my

breath and watch the glamorous couples spin around the dance floor. The gowns were all white and the men wore white tuxes, giving the party an Old World elegance. I spotted Harold across the room and waved. He was at my side in an instant.

"Happy New Year, Sarah Booth. I've been trying to flag you down for a dance but every time I get a break from my duties as host, I can't find you."

"It's almost a new year. Can you believe how fast time slips by?"

"It's terrifying how quickly the months roll past." He nodded toward the far side of the room. "There's your partner in crime."

Tinkie Bellcase Richmond, in a flowing gown of white silk with a diamond belt at the waist, was my partner in solving crime at the Delaney Detective Agency. She waved and came toward us. "Sarah Booth, you look beautiful."

"She does," Harold said, "and so do you, Tinkie."

"Ditto," I said.

"It's a lovely party, Harold. Millie is having a great time, and Cece has taken enough photos to fill the *Zinnia Dispatch* for the next year." Millie Roberts was the proprietress of Millie's Café, the finest eating establishment in the South, and Cece Dee Falcon was society editor of the local newspaper.

Cece came toward us, a waiter in tow with a tray of brimming champagne glasses. "Grab a drink everyone. It's almost time to toast in the new year!" Cece, though she was once Cecil, was the prettiest woman in the room. She wore an off-the-shoulder gown that hugged her slender form. Millie wore a white sheath overlaid with gossamer lace. With her hair swept up she looked ten years younger.

We each took a glass, and Cece was about to propose a toast when the door of the ballroom burst open in the tradition of all bad fairy tales—the grand entrance of the witch, sorcerer, villain, or in this case, troll. Frangelica "Sister" McFee stepped into the ballroom. Her gaze drilled into Tinkie.

"Well, well, if it isn't Stinky Bellcase Richmond." She sniffed the air. "Doesn't anyone else smell that awful stench?" She curled her lips in a nasty smile.

I'd never seen Tinkie intimidated by anyone, but she took two steps backward before she bumped into me. I tried to push her forward, but she balked.

"Oh, holy Christmas," I whispered. "It's Sister McFee." I pronounced the name properly for the Mississippi social elite—Sista.

"What the hell is she doing back in Zinnia?" Cece asked just before she blinded Sister with some flashes of her camera. "Run, Tinkie, run, before she regains her vision."

Tinkie had finally found her backbone. "I'm not running anywhere."

"Frangelica," Harold said, trying to step into the breach. "I had no idea you'd be in Zinnia or I would have sent you an invitation to my party."

"I figured it was an oversight," she said. "I hate this Podunk town and this backward county, not to mention this third-world state. And call me Sister, please. Only my classy New York friends call me Frangelica. Right, Stinky?"

I looked around for Oscar, Tinkie's husband, but didn't see him. This confrontation was headed south at a rapid pace. Coleman was supposed to arrive before midnight, but he would be too late to stop the bloodshed. Tinkie hated Sister McFee. I didn't know the details, but my normally cool and collected partner couldn't talk about Sister without becoming spitting mad. Something had happened in the sorority house at Ole Miss that Tinkie couldn't forgive or forget.

"Get out." Tinkie squared her shoulders and walked over to Sister. "Get out right this minute."

"Or you'll do what, Stinky? Gas me to death?" She laughed like a sweet Southern belle. "You're too cute." She reached to pinch my partner's cheek, and Tinkie snapped. Her teeth clicked on empty air with an audible sound as she tried to bite Sister's hand.

"Stinky and rabid," Sister said with a merry laugh. "Good to know you grew into my predictions."

"Get out!" Tinkie roared the words.

Harold stepped between the two women and grasped Sister's arm. "It was so good of you to drop by, and I'm sorry you have to leave." He propelled her out of the ballroom like a paper sack before a hurricane.

Two hotel staffers closed the doors as soon as the witch's hasty exit was complete. I put a hand on Tinkie's trembling shoulder.

"I hate her," Tinkie said, almost in tears. "She is the biggest biyotch on the face of the planet!"

I couldn't argue with that assessment so I didn't try. At last Oscar noticed Millie's frantic attempts to get his attention, and he hurried over and immediately saw Tinkie's distress. "Are you okay?" he asked, looking at all of us.

"I'm fine," Tinkie said, and with those words she seemed to expel the miasma that Sister had cast upon her. "Sister McFee made an appearance."

"She's a total bit—" He didn't finish because Cece elbowed him in the side.

"What is Sister doing in our *Podunk town*?" I asked.

"Her new book about the death of her mama and brother has been at the top of the bestseller list for several months now. I heard some gossip about a movie," Millie said. "I thought it was just big talk, but maybe not. Maybe she's here because they are going to film."

"Refresh me on what happened with Mrs. McFee and Son." Cleo, Sister's mother, and her son Daryl, better known as Son, had driven into the flooded and raging Sunflower River during a terrible rainstorm five summers earlier. Cleo's body was found trapped in the car, but Son's body was never recovered. The presumption was that he had also drowned and then been washed down river. Son had been driving the car.

Millie gave the short version because she had the best memory for local history. "Son was known to use drugs and drink," Millie said. "His father, Colin, insisted that Son had killed his own mother and himself, either by accident because he was drugged up or in a murder suicide scenario."

"What a terrible thing for a father to say about his child," Tinkie said. She'd regained her composure, and now she was about to lose her temper.

"How could Colin know that to be true?" I asked. "Son's body wasn't recovered. The investigators couldn't do a tox screen. It was raining cats and dogs. It could truly have been an accident."

Millie held up a finger, considering. "Colin couldn't know anything for a fact, but it didn't stop him from publicly blaming Son. And Sister's book does the same. I've heard rumors for the past several weeks that the book had been optioned for a movie." Millie always had the scoop on Hollywood. She read tabloids religiously, and she consulted Zinnia's famous psychic and one of my best friends, Madame Tomeeka, aka my high school chum Tammy Odom.

"Great," Tinkie said. "Just great. She'll be in town for weeks."

"Colin is running for the U.S. Senate from Mississippi," Harold pointed out. "This might be a manipulation to gain sympathy votes. You know, the poor guy whose loaded son killed his wife."

"Didn't he marry, like, six weeks after Cleo was buried? She was barely cold." Tinkie was no shrinking violet in the arena of gossip.

Before anyone could respond, the bandleader rapped for attention on his music stand. "And the countdown begins! Ten, nine, eight . . ."

The doors opened and Coleman walked into the room.

"Seven, six, five, four, three . . ." The bandleader marked off the time.

Coleman strode toward our little group.

"Two, one! Happy New Year!"

Harold swept me into his arms and laid a kiss on me that I wasn't likely to forget in the next twenty years. "Happy New Year, Sarah Booth."

"Happy New Year to you, Harold." I was flushed and breathless.

"You know your aunt Loulane would tell you that whatever you do on this day, you'll do for the rest of the year." And he kissed me again.

I'd forgotten how powerful Harold's kisses could be until my thumb gave a strange tingle.

Just as he released me, I felt a hand on my shoulder. When I turned, Coleman lifted my face with a gentle hand.

"In that case, I need to greet the new year myself." He kissed me too, but very chastely on the cheek.

"Happy New Year," I said to both men, because I was too flustered to think of anything original to say.

Tinkie at last stepped up to defend me. "That's enough, Romeos. Now let's forget about all the McFees and celebrate the new year. Oscar, can we contribute heavily to whoever is running for that Senate seat against Colin? Surely he doesn't stand a dog's chance of winning." But a tiny line of worry tugged at her lips.

When, an hour later, I managed to pull her away, I asked, "What's wrong?"

"It's Sister. Why is she back in town? Do you really think it's a movie deal?"

"I don't know, but I'm positive we'll find out sooner rather than later." I grabbed two glasses of champagne from a passing waiter. "Don't let her ruin this evening for you."

"You have no idea how much I loathe her."

"Why? I mean she's awful, but you handle awful people all the time."

Tinkie only shook her head, and her blue eyes teared up. "I have my reasons."

"Tinkie, I'm your best friend. You can tell me anything."

She shook her head harder. "I can't. I've never told anyone and I can't. Just know that Frangelica is the meanest bit—"

She never got to finish because Scott Hampton and his band, including Cece's squeeze, Jaytee, burst into the party. "Happy New Year," Scott said grabbing me and Tinkie and pressing a kiss on each of us. "And the new year is off to a rip-snorting beginning."

Before we could finish our conversation we were pulled
to the dance floor. It was impossible to stop Scott's infec-
tious good spirits, so I let go and partied as hard as I could,
dancing again and again with Scott, Harold, Coleman, and
a dozen other men.

As Jitty would have told me had she been there, mag-
ical evenings don't come around all that often. I took full
advantage.

New Year's Day rang itself in with a hangover from
too much champagne, but the wonderful memories from
Harold's party offset the Thor-like headache. I'd picked
up the phone to call Harold and thank him for the lovely
evening when I glanced at the time: 11:10. I was due to
meet Tinkie and the gang at Millie's Café for the traditional Southern New Year's Day fare of black-eyed peas
cooked with hog jowl or a ham bone, greens, and cornbread. The peas were for luck and the greens for money. I
wasn't about to miss out on luck or money.

I jumped in the shower, slapped on makeup and clothes,
loaded my hound dog and cat into the antique Mercedes
roadster, and tore down the driveway. The day was cold,
and I left the windows rolled up, much to Sweetie Pie's
consternation. She kept nosing the cold glass, but I wouldn't
give in. If I let the window down so she could hang her
head out, my eyelashes would freeze and break off.

"Millie said you and Pluto could hang out in her office," I told the critters. "She made a special dish for you
both. A pesky pet celebration for the new year. Roscoe
will probably be there too." Roscoe was an evil little dog
I'd ended up with while working a case. Harold adopted
him—and adored him. Every vile thing Roscoe did,
Harold enjoyed.

I whipped into the parking lot. The parked cars told me every one was already there. Millie had closed the café for us to have a private lunch. She would reopen at two for her regulars. A lot of people didn't cook and relied on Millie's delicious and nutritious offerings to keep themselves fed.

"Happy New Year. Sorry I'm late," I sang out as I rushed into the warmth of the small café that faced an otherwise empty Main Street. The most delicious smells made me sigh with pleasure.

"Champagne?" Harold asked wickedly as he approached me with a crystal stem and a bottle.

"Back!" I made the Sign of the Cross. "Coffee. Please."

Everyone laughed and Cece pushed a mug filled with strong black coffee into my hand. "Caffeine and something greasy and filled with carbohydrates will do the trick."

Tinkie nudged me into a chair and Millie put buttered toast and a side of hot grits in front of me. "The New Year's food is on the way," Millie said. "Eat this now and you'll feel better."

Of course she was right. As soon as I ate, my stomach settled and the little man with a sledgehammer tapping on my optic nerve stopped. "Thank you," I told them.

"Too bad you can't have a toast with us," Harold teased.

"I can toast. There's no law that says it has to be alcohol." I raised my cup of coffee and clinked with my friends as Oscar proclaimed the word for the new year to be *positivity*.

The lunch at Millie's had become a tradition since I'd returned to Zinnia. I looked around the room with gratitude. I was rich in friends. Good friends, and that was the greatest gift of all. But people were missing.

"Where's Coleman, DeWayne, Scott, and Jaytee?" Cece almost never left Jaytee's side.

"They're coming," Cece said. "I told the band to relax a little bit. After Harold's party they went back and closed down their club. The work of a musician is never done."

"Or a lawman," Millie threw in. "But here they all come."

Two cars pulled into the parking lot and the missing men entered the café to another round of hugs, greetings, and a toast.

Surveying the smiling faces of my friends, I saw the ghosts of the past standing close behind them. My parents, Aunt Loulane, the people who'd loved and cared for me. But I pushed those sad thoughts aside and lifted my mug. "To the best friends ever."

As we all raised our drinking vessels to toast, the door of the café slammed open so hard the jangling bell fell to the floor. Tinkie gasped as Sister McFee stepped inside. The Wicked Witch of the South grand entrance redux, and she eyed Tinkie like she was Toto.

"Well, well, if it isn't a little celebration, and they've let Stinky attend. What's with you? Have you all gone nose blind?"

Oscar put his glass down and stepped toward Sister. "Either apologize to my wife or get out."

"This is a private party," Millie said. "You should leave."

"The door was unlocked. If you want privacy, maybe you should lock your door." Sister sauntered deeper into the room and picked up the bowl of grits I'd been eating. She sniffed it. "Someone loves clogged arteries, don't they?"

"Leave now, before I arrest you." Coleman grasped her arm.

"For what? Entering a diner? Oh, please, you might humiliate me by tattling to the tabloids that I set foot in a place like this, but you can't arrest me."

"This is a private party. You're trespassing." Coleman was deadly serious and Sister was a fool if she didn't heed his warning.

Cece pushed her camera in Sister's face and took at least a dozen photos. She checked the shots. "Very flattering. Have you checked your nose lately? I think I have photographic evidence you've been practicing obsequiousness with someone."

I couldn't help it; I burst out laughing. "Good one, Cece."

"What do you want, Frangelica?" Tinkie was the only one to ask the obvious.

"I was checking this dump for a location for my movie, but I can see that if I brought a camera in here, the lens would fog with grease."

"Making a movie of that awful book that paints your dead brother as a murderer?" Tinkie asked. "The dead brother who can't defend himself against your unfounded accusations?"

"So you've read my book." Sister grinned. "Like millions of others."

I put a hand on Tinkie to keep her from jumping the table and tearing Sister's throat out. The animosity between the two was palpable.

Coleman tightened his grip on Sister and escorted her to the door. When she was outside, he closed and locked the door and closed the blinds. "I took the trash out," he said to Tinkie, who burst into tears.

"She is just so damn mean," Tinkie said, wiping her cheeks angrily. "I shouldn't let her get to me, but she is the meanest person I've ever known."

"She's pretty mean," Cece said. Her wicked grin told me she wasn't above a bit of mischief. "So let's pay her back in kind."

"Do you have a plan?" I asked.

"Oh, you bet I do. We'll plot together at a later date. I think Millie is ready to put the food on the table."

In ten minutes we'd brought out the holiday fare from the kitchen, formed a buffet, and filled our plates. Sister and her attitude were forgotten. We laughed and joked and told stories of the past year. Scott rubbed my short—but growing—hair and thanked me and Tinkie again for saving his blues club. Everyone put Oscar's word, *positivity,* to good use.

We'd just dug into the pièce de résistance, Millie's incredible Amaretto chocolate cheesecake, when we heard the sound of a glass-pack muffler or a motorcycle in front of the café. A loud knock followed.

Millie went to the door saying, "We'll be open to the public at two—" She stopped in midsentence when she saw a tall, very handsome man wearing leather everything. Right behind him was a strikingly beautiful woman, also in black leather.

"Oh, my, God!" Millie squealed. "It's Marco St. John and his wife, Lorraine. Come in, come in." Millie ushered them into the room and to the table, where Harold pushed forward two more chairs. "Have a seat and join us in a New Year's Day celebration."

"Smells delicious," Marco said. "I love Southern cooking."

Lorraine walked around the café examining everything.

"This is perfect," she said. "The light, the ambience . . . It's the place to bring Cleo alive. It's the perfect setting. This is a place she'd come and talk about her ideas for Mississippi education. She'd meet with the man on the street. She'd mingle with the real people here. Not at that old mausoleum they call Evermore."

"Cleo McFee often stopped by for breakfast or coffee and a slice of pie," Millie said. "She was a lovely woman."

"Who are those people?" I whispered to Tinkie.

"He's a movie director. She's a cinematographer. They're the hottest film couple in Tinsel Town. *Oblique, Touched, Fever Moon, Morgan Creek, Dead at Midnight.*"

I knew the movies and they were some of my favorites. "What are they doing in Zinnia?" I asked.

"I'm afraid I know exactly what this is about," Tinkie said. "It's Sister's book, *Dead and Gone.* They really are making a movie." She sounded defeated. "I thought it was all a big bluff, but it isn't. She's going to have a movie made of her book. How is it possible that someone who is such a bully could be so talented?"

Oscar brought his wife another glass of champagne and gave me a concerned look. I was worried too.

Marco and Lorraine dug into the holiday food with gusto. The moviemakers were surprisingly open about everything except the name of the movie. "We can't say," Marco said. "Once the deal is signed, we'll tell you everything, because we're going to need your help."

While Marco and Lorraine ate, we peppered them with questions. Finally, Marco pushed back from the table. "Thank you for such wonderful food, but I'm here on business. I'm looking for Sarah Booth Delaney."

I raised my hand. "Here."

"May I have a word with you? Outside?"

I followed him out the door to a buzz of speculation. When the door closed, Marco leaned against the café wall. "I want to hire you to find out what really happened to Son McFee and his mother, Cleo."

"Hire me?"

"Are you deaf?" He wasn't being mean. He really thought I had a hearing problem.

"No, I'm not deaf, but why hire me?"

"You've read Frangelica's book?"

I rolled my eyes. "No. But you can bet it's a pack of lies."

"Exactly. I'm making a movie of what happened based on the book. But I have a hunch there's more to this story. I want to prove what happened to cause the accident, and to find out, beyond a shadow of a doubt, what happened to Son McFee."

"You're really interested in the truth?" I asked.

"Lorraine and I have our suspicions, but we want the truth. And I'm very serious." He brought out his wallet and withdrew a personal check for ten thousand dollars. "This is a retainer," he said. "I'll hire you as a location scout for the movie so that will give you access to everyone and everything." He pulled the check back. "But this could be dangerous."

"Dangerous?" I realized I did sound deaf." I mean this is a cold case. Do you really think there's danger?"

"Someone damaged one of Lorraine's cameras. It was deliberate sabotage."

"Okay."

"For some reason it's very important to Colin and Sister McFee to make Son a villain. My experience as a filmmaker tells me that when someone promotes one and only one version of an unproved truth, there's a reason for it. Colin has a lot to lose and something tells me he isn't the kind of man to go down without a fight. Are you still interested?"

This was a case I wanted. I hadn't been close with Son in college. He was a year or so older than me, but he'd always been pleasant. Where Sister was a total B, Son had been funny and kind. It might be true that Son was drunk or on drugs and lost control of the car. But right at the entrance to the Sunflower River Bridge? It didn't feel right. It never had.

"Let me talk to my partner," I said.

"Yes, we need Mrs. Bellcase on board. Tell her I'll give you both walk-on parts."

"She'd love that." Maybe Marco could cheer up my friend with a chance to be in a movie. It would be the best revenge ever against meanie Sister. "Let me ask her. I'll be right back."

Five minutes later, Delaney Detective Agency was on the payroll of Black Tar Productions. The new year was off to an auspicious start.